Amid Rage

A Mike Jacobs Environmental Legal Thriller

Joel Burcat

Publisher Page
an imprint of Headline Books, Inc.
Terra Alta, WV

Amid Rage

A Mike Jacobs Environmental Legal Thriller

by Joel Burcat

copyright ©2021 Joel Burcat

All rights reserved. This book is a work of fiction. Names, characters, places and incidents, except where noted otherwise, are products of the author's imagination or are used fictitiously. Any other resemblance to actual people, places or events is entirely coincidental. No part of this publication may be reproduced or transmitted in any other form or for any means, electronic or mechanical, including photocopy, recording or any information storage system, without written permission from Publisher Page.

To order additional copies of this book or for book publishing information, or to contact the author:

Headline Books, Inc.
P.O. Box 52
Terra Alta, WV 26764
www.HeadlineBooks.com

Tel: 304-789-3001
Email: mybook@headlinebooks.com

Publisher Page is an imprint of Headline Books

Logo for Rhino Mining Company created especially for Amid Rage by Donovan Thompson, a graphic artist from South Africa.

Back cover photograph of the author by Camera Box, Camp Hill, Pa.

ISBN 13: 9781951556457

Library of Congress Control Number: 2020945454

PRINTED IN THE UNITED STATES OF AMERICA

For Dina, Shira, David, and Lev

*"We don't inherit the earth from our ancestors,
we borrow it from our children."*
—Attributed to Chief Seattle

ALSO BY JOEL BURCAT

Fiction
Drink to Every Beast (Mike Jacobs, Book 1)
(Headline Books, Inc.)

Non-Fiction
Pennsylvania Environmental Law and Practice
(Pennsylvania Bar Institute Press, Co-Editor)

The Law of Oil and Gas in Pennsylvania
(Pennsylvania Bar Institute Press, Co-Editor)

"The energy crisis has not yet overwhelmed us, but it will if we do not act quickly…Our decision about energy will test the character of the American people and the ability of the President and the Congress to govern. This difficult effort will be the "moral equivalent of war"—except that we will be uniting our efforts to build and not destroy…Because we are now running out of gas and oil, we must prepare quickly for a third change, to strict conservation and to the use of coal and permanent renewable energy sources, like solar power.

If we wait, and do not act, then our factories will not be able to keep our people on the job with reduced supplies of fuel. Too few of our utilities will have switched to coal, our most abundant energy source…We can protect ourselves from uncertain supplies by reducing our demand for oil, making the most of our abundant resources such as coal, and developing a strategic petroleum reserve.

These are the goals we set for 1985…Increase our coal production by about two thirds to more than one billion tons a year."

—President Jimmy Carter
Televised speech on April 18, 1977

In the midst of rage—remember to be merciful.
—Habakkuk, ch. III, v. 2

Prologue

October 1

Ernie Rinati loved the smell of sweat, urine, and fear. It signaled weakness, control, opportunity, profit. The living room before him smelled of all of that.

Every stick of furniture, the cheap picture on the wall, the photo of Mom, Dad and the kids, and the lamp lay askew. A single bulb burned in the lamp that leaned against the far wall. Light and shadows were cast at odd angles and garishly lit some portions of the room. The rest was shrouded in darkness.

Phyllis Stevens, had she not been visiting her mother, would have been aghast that her formerly tidy, country-style living room was now in a shambles.

Also, she would have been dead.

"Let's do it," said Ernie.

He nodded at Skel and Wolfie. They worked for Ernie, both on odd jobs like this one and at the strip mine. The men were the coldest killers Ernie knew. No sense of morals to get in the way. Followers. What was really important was they wanted to make him happy. There was never any doubt who was the boss.

Skel's work boots crunched through the shards of broken glass from the sliding door they'd shattered when they broke into the house. He was as skinny as a skeleton, the skin of his face plastered to the bones. A jagged hockey-stick shaped scar caused his face to lift crookedly and made him look like a horror movie ghoul. He retrieved the plastic containers of gasoline they'd brought with them and, with Wolfie, splashed the gas around the living room, on the rug, sofa and furniture.

"Not on the dude," Ernie said.

Marty Stevens, bound with electrical cord, eyes wide, moaned from behind the duct tape that sealed his mouth. The gray hair was disheveled. The face bruised purple. Half of one ear lay on the floor. Blood oozed from the gash on the head. Tears streamed down the face. He strained against the restraints that bound him to the chair. The head shook back and forth like at a ping pong match on fast forward.

"Give me that," Ernie said. He grabbed a jug from Skel.

He poured a trail of gasoline from the living room to the hallway, backed up, looked at Stevens, then tossed the jug back into the living room. The men stood in the hallway.

Ernie surveyed their handiwork. Killing people required finesse. Anyone could shoot or stab somebody, but a connoisseur, like himself, took his time. Used his imagination. Made it last. Did the job with pride and integrity.

Marty Stevens had been no match for them. Lies, though, helped. Ernie was amazed that people thought they could talk their way out of the inevitable. He relied on their capacity to believe the lies, big and small. Just tell them what they want to hear. Comply with us and everything will be okay.

"Do it," Wolfie said. "We need to get the hell out of here." The voice seemed to come out of nowhere, as his nearly black beard enveloped his face, leaving just a narrow space for his eyes and nose. His beard partially covered a large gray sweatshirt that had the Rhino Mining Company logo on it.

Ernie reached into his work pants and found the cigarette lighter. He caressed it in his hand. He loved the lighter. It had been with him since kill one. It was a solid gold Zippo with a dragon engraved on the side. He'd taken it off the dead man. His first kill felt good and the warmth that washed over him when he took that life came back to him every time he felt the lighter. He thumbed the flint wheel and the flame rose three inches.

Inspector Stevens," Ernie said. "Can I call you Marty?"

No reply.

"Oh, right, the tape," Ernie said as he rolled his eyes and smiled at Skel and Wolfie. He flicked the lighter closed and stuffed it back into his pocket.

Ernie ambled to the man and tore the tape from his face. It came off with a loud rip, along with skin, beard and blood.

"Help, help, for the love of God help me," Marty said, looking toward the shattered door.

"Marty, Marty, Marty. Yelling isn't going to help you way out here in the country. Calm down. Now, I asked you nice and friendly to go with my permit. I even offered you a nice cash bonus for you or the DEP" he called it *'dep'* "Christmas fund if you played along. But no. You had to be some kind of Rambo, loner, self-righteous and all."

"I'll do whatever you want. Please don't do this. Please, I'm begging you. Please, please," Marty said. Tears streamed down the face. Snot and blood dripped into the mouth.

"That's a very nice request, Marty, and honestly, if it was just me, I'd help you out. I really would. Unfortunately, we have contracts, unions, all kinds of obligations, so your case has been turned over to the collection bureau. That's us. I really have no choice."

The man in the chair stopped moving and his eyes locked onto the monster who was preparing to kill him.

"This is what happens when you screw with me. You were told to back off, but didn't, so this is on you."

"No. No—"

Ernie pulled the lighter from his pocket, thumbed off the cover, and flicked the flint wheel. Then he bent over and touched the flame to the trail of gasoline. The fire dashed across the room and up the walls.

"Help me. Dear God help me."

The room turned yellow and orange, and the three criminals watched with ghoulish interest.

"Now remember boys, when you do this, you always want to leave an impression," Ernie said. Then he pointed to the door. "Move."

Wolfie and Skel darted for the sliding glass door. Ernie, however, lingered for a moment, looking into the burning living room. The curtains quickly ignited and the flames climbed to the ceiling. The fire seemed to have a life of its own. The man was still seated in his chair, rocking violently back and forth, flames all around him. The face was ghastly, like that crappy painting Ernie had seen on TV. What was it? The Scream? The fire popped and acrid smoke filled the room. The place smelled of gasoline and fire and burning carpet and death. Ernie smiled coldly at Stevens who screamed incomprehensible words. Then he sauntered to the door and his escape.

Ernie drove his red Cadillac Escalade with a bumper sticker that read, "I DIG COAL."

Slow.

Speed limit slow.

In the rear view he could see the flames rising from the house behind him.

"Boys, don't forget what I told you," he said. "Take pride in your work and leave an impression."

They kept driving. Skel opened a bottle of Jack Daniels and he and Wolfie passed it back and forth. Ernie continued giving advice, knowing that neither man cared what he said.

That's okay.

He was a pro.

They were not.

An hour later, Ernie stood on the side of a county road in the browned-out grass. His ancient Carhartt jacket hung open in the chill air.

He'd pulled over so that Skel could puke. The last thing he wanted was vomit inside his Caddy.

Skel got off his hands and knees and washed out his mouth with whiskey. "We turned that DEP sonofabitch into a s'more." He had a hand on Wolfie's shoulder for balance. "Yee-ha."

Skel held the bottle by the neck with his free hand. Steam, smoke, and spit billowed from his mouth as he shouted.

Wolfie shoved Skel hard. "Shut up, you dumb asshole. Hey Ernie, he's had too much to drink."

"Both of you idiots shut up," Ernie said. His saliva spewed into the wind.

Ernie took a deep breath and gazed into the sky. The mountain air was piney and fresh in his face and he could see the Milky Way, but it held no meaning for him.

1

Mike Jacobs white knuckled the overhead hand grip in the DEP Jeep as it bounced across the floor of the strip mine. It felt like they were driving over logs, one after the other. Fast. The mine inspector, Chris Markley, chatted away as if he was cruising down the smoothest, straightest six-lane highway. He swerved to avoid a boulder that easily would have taken out the undercarriage. Mike swallowed hard to keep his breakfast down.

"Hey Chris, maybe if we slow down a bit we can spend a little time enjoying the scenery?" Mike now had his left hand on the dashboard in front of him, in addition to holding onto the overhead grip. He attempted a smile. They drove past a sign with the DEP logo on it:

Mines and Quarries
are not playgrounds—
STAY OUT
STAY ALIVE!

"Where's the fun in that?" Chris took his eyes off the narrow two-rut haul road to look at Mike. The white Jeep with the *Pennsylvania Department of Environmental Protection* logo on the side bounced from rut to rut, kicking up rocks and dirt.

Mike wished Chris would keep his eyes on the trail. The floor of the mine was covered with boulders and loose rock. The haul road wasn't much better, but at least it had the semblance of a trail. He tried to focus on distant points to keep from getting sick.

He often heard people say that a coal strip mine resembled the surface of the moon. Hardly. This mine, Black Diamond Anthracite's Gilberton mine, was part old abandoned mine and part new workings. The abandoned part had a gray and black floor made up of waste coal and rocky overburden. Scrubby little birch trees and other vegetation that tolerated the acidic environment struggled to survive in the hostile landscape.

Water pooled in depressions and turned into acidic mine water where it stood. Any that managed to make it off the mine site was hopelessly contaminated with acid, sulfur, manganese and other metals that poisoned streams and made the water undrinkable. They drove past an abandoned car that had been set on fire. All that was left was a rusted hull.

"I want to make an impression with these guys, so we have to get to the highwall before the boys here have a chance to clean it up too much. We entered the mine ten minutes ago and you just know they're busy tidying up the mess from last night."

The mess was the aftermath of a mishap with explosives. Blasting typically was done when the shift was on break or at the end of the day. Boreholes were drilled into the rock, loaded with a mixture of ammonium nitrate and fuel oil, ANFO, and then blasted. This highwall had a blowout during blasting the afternoon before and sprayed fly-rock about a thousand feet onto the pit floor. Not a huge problem here, since the rock didn't leave the mine and no one was hurt, but a violation nevertheless. In a more populated area an incident like this could have been deadly. Chris would write it up and Mike probably would have to enforce any order he issued.

"I want to impress these guys with the fact that I brought my lawyer with me." Chris forced a wide smile at Mike and raised and lowered his eyebrows, Groucho-style.

Mike liked Chris. He was typical of the new inspectors at DEP. He was young, in his late twenties like Mike, with a degree in environmental science. He was also a fisherman and hunter, and was aggressive about enforcing the law. Mike, an assistant counsel in DEP's litigation and enforcement division, did all he could to support guys like Chris.

"What can you tell me about them?" Mike said as he tried to distract himself from the constant rumbling in his stomach.

"Not too awful. These guys have a couple of strippings. All in Schuylkill County like this one. Nothing underground. Maybe five, ten men at each site. Couple of violations a year. Nothing terrible. The foreman for this mine, Kevin Schultz, is an asshole. Me and Schultzie never see eye to eye. He won't be too happy to see us."

"And you heard about the fly-rock incident, how?" Mike eased his grip on the overhead as the haul road flattened out.

"The only thing better than a disgruntled *former* employee is a disgruntled *current* employee. Got a call on my cell last night and called you right away. I'm glad you were available to come up here first thing this morning."

They drove past a line of derelict mining equipment, standing alongside one another like in some kind of apocalyptic movie parking lot. They had been ravaged for their spare parts, their bodies turned into rust and their guts spilled onto the mine floor. Mike wondered if there were any DEP Jeeps among the junkers.

The Jeep rounded an un-mined outcrop. Right in front of them, no more than fifty feet away, was a D-10 dozer, yellow, covered with dirt and coal dust, billowing diesel smoke from its single stack. Not the biggest dozer on the market, but significantly bigger than the Jeep.

Right in the middle of the haul road.

Huge yellow blade at eye level.

Coming straight at them.

Fast.

Chris stomped on the brake. The outcrop they were driving around prevented him from veering to the left. Huge boulders and the junk trucks prevented him from turning to the right.

The Jeep skidded to a stop, sliding sideways like it was on ice.

The dozer kept coming.

"Hold on." Chris popped the Jeep into reverse and Mike looked over his shoulder.

Directly behind them was a gigantic Deere 944 front-end loader.

17

Bucket at window height.

Bearing down on them.

They were trapped.

"Oh, crap." Chris stomped on the brake and the Jeep skidded backwards as the loader closed in on them from behind and the dozer from in front.

Ambushed. They'd be sandwiched between the two gigantic machines. Crushed. Decapitated by those blades. Death in front and behind.

Mike had to find a way out.

"There," he pointed.

The outcrop had an opening, hard to the left. A few inches wider than the Jeep.

Chris stepped on the gas and they fishtailed into the narrow opening just as the loader flew by. He stomped on the brake again at the end of the narrow pass and the clash of steel on steel crashing together behind them sounded like two locomotives in a head-on collision.

Mike and Chris said nothing for several seconds. Chris's hands still held the wheel, knuckles white from the tension. The Jeep idled in the small hollow of the rock. The exhaust rose into the cold morning air.

"What the hell?" Mike said.

They climbed out and had no more than six inches on either side until they hit rock. Mike squeezed past the sides of the Jeep. His back caught on the rock wall and the front of his jacket slid along the vehicle.

Mike and Chris slowly approached the opening in the rock. The dozer and loader were gunning their engines and the beep-beep-beep of reverse gears pierced through the growling noise. Mike poked his head out from within the outcrop.

In a flash he saw a yellow smudge in the corner of his eye and heard the growl of the engine. His hand flew to Chris and pulled him back as the loader sped by them. Inches away.

Mike was shocked. Instead of a deadly crash, the dozer was backing away as fast as it had approached. The loader made a wide U-turn around the junk trucks and headed back toward them.

Mike and Chris looked at each other.

"What the hell?" said Mike.

The loader regained the trail and pulled up next to them.

"Hey Chris. Morning." said the driver through an open window as though he stopped to chat on his way to the corner convenience store for a bag of chips.

"Yo, Shultzie, you asshole. You almost killed us." Chris shook his fist angrily at the foreman.

Schultzie laughed a hearty laugh. "Hey boys, couldn't see you over the blade in that little Jeep. A mine's a dangerous place. You know what the sign says, *stay out, stay alive*. You come onto a mine anywheres and you have to be careful. This is our turf. Be a little more careful next time. Watch yourselves."

Schultzie laughed heartily and gunned the motor. The loader rumbled down the haul road. The bucket wasn't even dented.

Two hours later, Mike sat in his car scrolling through his emails.

Junk mail.

Circular from the DEP benefits office.

Nothing important.

Email from Roger Alden, his boss—

>>Mike- Are you done playing yet in Gilberton? Don't you have a trial day after tom you should be getting ready for? New case just came in. Ever hear of Rhino Mining? Out west. Somerset County. See me as soon as your trial is done. Thx. Roger<<

2

Ernie Rinati pasted a yellow-toothed smile on his face. The morning was going well. The little problem with the DEP inspector, Marty Stevens, had been resolved. Also, he'd given a couple of Gs, all small bills, to the miner's union steward and that trivial bonus was going to pay huge dividends when the new labor contract was negotiated next month. Just one more task and then lunch. Maybe a bottle of his favorite Chianti.

Ernie stood on the step of the derelict house and knocked. He glanced at the tattered American flag that hung limply by the door and turned his back on it.

Friendly taps.

Like a neighbor. Not the cops. Not a bill collector.

Still smiling.

He heard scraping sounds from inside. Like a cow walking across a barn floor. Slow. No need to knock again.

The door opened and a whale of a man, pasty white face, crew cut, blinked at the late morning light. The TV blared in the living room. Game show. A "Who are you?" look on the homeowner's face.

"Hi, Mr. Post?" Bigger smile. "Can I call you Norman? Norm? I'm Ernesto Rinati. Call me Ernie." He held out his hand.

"Rinati? You own Rhino Minin' right?" said Norman Post. Cautiously. Like he was talking to a rabid dog.

Ernie reached out and took the man's hand, which hung by his side, and shook it. The hand was limp, weak, moist, flabby. He let it fall back to the man's side.

"Do you mind if I come in?" Still smiling. "I mean it's cold and I wanted to discuss a business proposition with you."

Norman didn't move. Ernie stepped over the threshold. Only when the two men were nose to nose did Norman finally move aside and allow Ernie to stroll into the living room. A smell smacked him in the face, dirty feet, something festering, he didn't know what. A giant easy chair, threadbare, ancient. Newspapers on both sides. Crap piled up on the coffee table. Pictures of a woman, children, in the small space not covered with stuff. Piles of clothes and toys on the floor.

The TV blared. Ernie found the remote and turned it off, shrugged and smiled again in the direction of the homeowner. He sat down.

"Have a seat." Ernie pointed at the easy chair.

Norman slowly, cautiously, took his seat.

"Nice place you have here." Ernie looked around at the ramshackle, fetid house and nodded.

"Don't get many visitors. If you'd called ahead, I would've straightened it up. What do youns want? This ain't a social visit, for sure."

"Oh, a businessman. Right to the point. I like that. Let's talk business. You know my company, Rhino Mining, is putting in that new strip mine down the way—"

"You mean across the street." Norman squinted his eyes into slits.

"All according to DEP's regulations." He called it *dep,* like *pep,* "I assure you. No closer than the regs allow."

"Too close in my opinion. How am I supposed to live here when you put a hundred-foot highwall a couple hundred feet from my front door? My daughter'll be scared to death to bring the grandkids. The dust. The trucks. Lived here my entire life and you'll turn this neighborhood into shit."

Ernie nodded like he was concerned. "I hear you Norm. I sympathize, but that's the law. It's going to happen and there's nothing I can do about it."

"Nothing?" Norman ventured a wry smile. "It's your company, Mr. Rinati. Just don't do it."

"Wish I could, I do, but contracts. Obligations. The union. I'm sure a business-minded man like you understands." Ernie nodded like a bobble-head doll.

Norman waited.

"Look, I sympathize with you, I really do. Like I said, I can't stop the mine—contracts, and union like I said—but I can make your life a lot easier."

"I'm listening." Norman narrowed his eyes.

"How much land do you have here?"

Norman eyed him suspiciously. "I don't know, maybe a half-acre."

Ernie smiled broadly. "More like zero-point-four-one acres, to be exact. But for argument's sake, let's round up to half an acre. And this fine house. Built in 1949, right?"

"My pap built it right after the war. 1949 sounds right."

"What do you suppose it's worth?" Ernie leaned forward.

"What? Why?"

"Because I'm going to make you an offer you can't refuse." Ernie chuckled enjoying the little joke.

"Why would I sell it? Why sell it to you?"

"Because you said it yourself. It's not going to be too pleasant around here for at least three, maybe five, six years. With all the dust, blasting. Think of the grandkids." Ernie scratched his chin. "You can move in with your daughter. Maybe an apartment in town. Have some money in the bank. How much?"

Norman put his hand across his mouth and rubbed his lips. "Don't know. Maybe a hundred, hundred fifty thousand?"

Ernie broke out into laughter. A cackle. "Normie, you *are* a businessman. A real Donald Trump. Let's see. Land around here goes for $5,000 an acre and that's top dollar. You have zero point-four-one acres. So that's worth about $2,000. Tops. This house," he looked around, "sorry, but it's not worth fifty-K. But for argument's sake, let's say the total value is $52,000 and that's top dollar. Put it next to an active strip mine and it's not going to be worth ten-K. I'm prepared to give you twenty-five for it."

Norman blinked. "Twenty-five thousand dollars? Are you kidding me? It's not on the market. I'm not interested in moving and I'm not going anywhere."

"You're a tough cookie, Normie. A real hard negotiator. Tell you what, I'll give you the whole fifty-two-K, but you have to work with me to convince your neighbors to sell. Tell them it's in their best interest. I'll pay them top dollar. You sold to me and they should too, that kind of thing. For each one that sells to me, I'll pay you another thou. Cash. You can even stay in this, this palatial estate right up until we begin mining next door. That's quite a good offer." Ernie smiled more broadly. "Do we have a deal?"

He extended his hand.

Norman looked at him silently, not moving. "You want me to sell my parents' house? The one pap built with his own two hands? The house where my wife and me raised our daughter? Sell out my friends and neighbors?"

Ernie sat with his hand extended, the smile glued to his face.

"Get out." Norman struggled to his feet. "Get the hell out of my house. I have no interest in selling my house to you. No way I'm going to help you convince my neighbors to sell to you. Get the hell out."

Ernie let his hand drop as he stood. "Normie, you're making a big mistake. This may be your last chance. Trust me, after today, the price goes down, not up. When the blasting begins and there's a hundred-foot hole next to your house, you won't get ten bucks for this, this, shithole."

Norman pointed to the door. "Out. Get out."

Ernie strolled to the door. "Nice place you have here for a cess pit, Normie. You know, just a little free advice. All that paper, the curtains and shit, they can burn real fast. You should do something about that."

Norman put one hand on the door and motioned with the other. Ernie stood on the step.

"One more thing, Normie. I may send over some associates to continue our discussions. Okay?"

No response. Just heavy breathing. Normie was scared. That was good.

Ernie's three-legged dog Butch hopped on his lap when he returned to the car. He looked at Norman from the front seat of his red Cadillac Escalade.

The morning did not end as a complete success.
The lard-ass, stupid old man stood at his door and watched.
He was scared.
Terrified.
Rinati liked that.
He'd have his way.
He gave Butch a treat and decided he'd have a bottle of Chianti at lunch to celebrate anyhow.

***

Norman dug around in his cluttered closet until he found his pap's revolver in a shoebox on the top shelf. He looked at it and realized it had been a good ten years since he'd last fired the thing at the range. Bullets rolled around in the box. He loaded them into the cylinder. His hands were sweating; sweat beaded on his forehead. His chest felt tight. He would take a nitro pill when he sat down. Norman hid the gun in his nightstand drawer, way in the back behind some old prescription bottles.

He had to remember to move it before his daughter brought the grandkids to visit.

3

"May I continue with my cross-examination, Your Honor?" Mike Jacobs asked the judge.

"Proceed," said Judge Diaz.

"Mr. Burroughs, isn't it true you've been a mine operator for over thirty years?" Mike asked.

"That's right, thirty, maybe thirty-five years." Burroughs said.

"You have three employees?"

"It's just me, my brother, and my son."

Mike stood near the witness and glanced around the Environmental Hearing Board's main Harrisburg courtroom. Rows of empty padded folding chairs lined the back of the room. The floor was covered with orange carpet so faded and worn in places that someone had covered it with duct tape. A scrum of young DEP lawyers sat and whispered to each other. From the repeated taps of his gavel, it was clear Judge Diaz was annoyed with the constant murmur.

The only one in the room whom he did not know was a woman, about his age, maybe a little older, a bit thick around the middle, but with a pretty face, shoulder-length brown hair, who wore a distinctive blue and gold striped dress. She sat in the corner by herself and from time to time pounded the keys of the small laptop computer.

Mike looked back at the witness. "You're familiar with mine permits?"

"Yeah."

"Did you read and understand all of the conditions of your permit?"

"Yeah."

Roy Worley, a DEP mine inspector from Knox, Pennsylvania, sat at the counsel's table in the chair next to Mike's. He handed Mike the next exhibit. At that moment, Sebastian Lewandowski, the Director of DEP's Bureau of Mining and Reclamation, walked in and took a seat in the back row.

Mike nodded at him.

Lewandowski glanced at Mike and nodded tightly, then folded his beefy arms and looked intensely at the witness.

Mike leaned close to Roy and whispered, "Your boss just came in. I guess he wants to keep an eye on us."

Mike turned back toward the witness. "I'm going to show you some papers. I'd like this exhibit marked as Commonwealth's exhibit number eleven." Mike handed the stack of papers to the court reporter, a plain, middle-aged woman with shiny black hair, then handed a copy to the judge and tossed a copy to Burroughs' attorney, D. Wesley Helms, without looking at him.

Mike looked at the judge. "May I approach the witness?"

The judge nodded.

Tommy Bowdoin, his law clerk, sitting to his left, nodded.

Tommy Bowdoin had just graduated from law school and spent all of his time either in hearings with the judge or ghostwriting the opinions and adjudications issued by Judge Diaz. Tommy Bowdoin's title was Assistant Counsel, like Mike's title, but most lawyers, including Mike, tended to think of him simply as Judge Diaz's clerk.

The witness, Kyle Burroughs, was a trim, muscular man in his early sixties and a nearly white military crew cut. Mike pointed at the exhibit and said, "Do you recognize this document?"

"Sure, that's my minin' permit."

"You're familiar with this?"

"Yeah, it's not like I look at it every day but I've seen it."

"Did you *read* it?" Mike asked loudly.

Burroughs ran his hand across his short hair and puffed out a breath. "Yeah."

Mike waited. "You *understood* it?"

Burroughs nodded his head several nods. "Yeah."

"I'd like you to turn to page three, the page marked with the Post-it." Mike flipped the exhibit to the page and pointed. "These are the conditions the Commonwealth asserts you violated. Can you read into the record the paragraphs I've highlighted in yellow?"

Burroughs wore a tight-fitting, frayed white shirt, an outdated suit from Sears and a clip-on necktie that was slightly off kilter. He ran his index finger between the shirt and his Adam's apple. "Condition number twenty-three. All mining operations shall be conducted only within the permitted area."

"And the next?" Mike pointed to the exhibit.

Burroughs looked at his lawyer, then read aloud. "Condition number twenty-four, no blasting shall take place within one thousand feet of an occupied dwelling."

"Do you understand that any earth disturbance activity at a mine site, whether you say you're digging for coal or not, constitutes mining operations under Pennsylvania's Surface Mining Act?" Mike had an average build with wavy, dark brown hair that was just a bit unkempt. He wore an inexpensive navy-blue suit, a white cotton shirt he'd bought online, and a blue-and-red striped necktie—the prosecutor's uniform. He spoke these words loudly and leaned in as he did so.

"Objection, Your Honor," shouted Helms, as he took the short leap to his feet. He knocked over his glass, spilling water across the counsel table.

Helms bragged to Mike that he was the pride of the bar of Indiana County, Pennsylvania. He was a partner in the firm of Helms & Helms, but technically he wasn't a named partner. That honor went to his grandfather and father, who were the original Helmses. Their last names were on the tarnished brass plate on the unpainted door of the run-down office building. It hadn't been updated since 1959. His grandfather at one time represented Jimmy Stewart. Unfortunately, no one of similar fame or fortune had followed. What little remained of Helms & Helms survived on bankruptcy, slip and fall, DUIs, and miscellaneous cases like this one.

"He's asking my client to *state the law*. This objection *rankles* me, I said *rankles* me to the core, Your Honor. As Justice Oliver Wendell Holmes, *Junior*, once said—"

"Save it for your post-hearing brief, Mr. Helms," said Judge Diaz. "He's just asking your client what he understands. No need for yet another speech. Overruled. Proceed, Mr. Jacobs."

Mike looked at the judge, smiled brightly, and said, "Thank you, Your Honor."

The judge shook his head and made a face. Tommy Bowdoin also shook his head. "Mr. Jacobs, don't thank me when I make a ruling. Proceed."

"Mr. Burroughs, do you understand that any earth disturbance activity at a mine site, whether you say you're digging for coal or not, constitutes mining operations?"

Burroughs looked at his lawyer, then said, "Well, that's not my understanding."

Mike returned to his table. Roy handed him a large map mounted on a poster board. Mike took it and nodded at the inspector.

Mike sensed he had the upper hand.

I'm sick and tired of the industry getting all of the breaks. Take the chance. Do it.

He was prepared to take a calculated risk based on his three years of litigation experience.

With his back to the judge, Mike pointed at the door. Roy nodded almost imperceptibly and touched his index finger to the tip of his nose.

"Your Honor, I'd like to have this marked as Commonwealth's exhibit number twelve. Mr. Burroughs, do you recognize this exhibit as your mine permit map?"

"Yeah."

"Now follow along here. Above the northern border of your mine permit, is this where you were clearing brush and grading the land with a Caterpillar D-8 bulldozer?" Mike pointed to an area on the map.

"Like I said, yes I was operating a dozer over there but—"

Mike cut him off and said, "Let the record show that Mr. Burroughs indicated positively he was operating a dozer in an area I'm now marking with a red A, which is north of and outside the permitted area. How far is that from these houses?" Mike pointed to the rectangles on the map.

"Maybe a thousand feet."

Mike picked up a ruler from his desk and held it next to the scale on the map, then put his thumb on the ruler and showed it to the witness. "Mr. Burroughs, isn't it true that the area you were clearing is just two hundred feet from those homes?"

Burroughs looked at him, then nodded. "Okay, two hundred, maybe two-fifty."

Mike continued, "When you began clearing this area, how high was the knob over here before you cleared it?"

"I'd say she was about six, maybe ten feet high."

"You stated during your direct testimony that you knocked down the knob of stone to level it?"

"Right, I just wanted to level the area, maybe park some trucks there."

"When you knocked down the knob, didn't that also involve the use of high explosives?" Mike crossed his arms.

Burroughs paused. "Yeah...maybe that wasn't such a good idea."

"And didn't some fly-rock, that is rock that flew out from the blast, land on the street in front of these homes just two hundred and fifty feet or so from where you were blasting?"

Burroughs rubbed a hand back and forth across his scalp. "Yeah."

"Some of the rocks from the blast were baseball-sized?"

"I think a little smaller."

"Is it true the fly-rock hit the street just a half an hour after a school bus picked up three kids from that neighborhood? Right here? At the bus stop?" Mike pounded the cardboard exhibit with the red marker and drilled a dozen bright red spots onto the map.

Burroughs nodded and said, "Yeah."

The judge leaned forward and said, "Please speak up."

"Yeah," Burroughs said again. Louder.

Mike made a sweeping motion with his hand. "So you admit that your careless blasting caused fly-rock to hit the street where the kids had been standing. Thank God no one was killed as a result of your recklessness and indifference—"

Helms started to stand and cleared his throat. Before he was halfway to his feet, the judge cut Mike off sharply. "I get it, Mr. Jacobs. No speeches please. Move on."

Mike nodded at the judge. "Then you took the rock from the knob and sold it, right?"

"Well, it was good rock, a buddy of mine who's a builder needed some rock for a driveway. I sold the stone, but at cost. I didn't make nothing offa it."

"During your deposition you admitted you received payment of nearly six hundred dollars for the rock from this area about half the size of a football field, right?"

"Well, yes, I guess that's right, but it probably cost me eight hundred dollars to grub it out."

"Digging up and selling rock. That's the very definition of mining, isn't it?"

"Objection." Helms stretched himself to his full five-foot-five and mustered all of the indignity within his being. He wore a cranberry-colored blazer and black polyester slacks which scraped the floor when he walked. When he stood to address the judge his voice reached counter-tenor heights which, combined with its nasal quality, raised a giggle from the young DEP lawyers in the back of the room. "Calls for a legal conclusion."

"Withdrawn," Mike snapped. "After Inspector Worley issued you a cease-and-desist order, did you take any action to restore the area to the north of the mine permit boundary?"

"No, I had a cease-work on me."

"All of this occurred in the area to the north of the mine permit boundary. Outside of the permitted area. Is that right?"

Burroughs looked at the judge. "Judge, he's puttin' words in my mouth. Can't I object?"

"This is cross-examination, that's what he's entitled to do. If your lawyer sees fit to object, I'm sure he will," the judge looked at Helms.

The lawyer was drawing amateurish cartoon characters on his legal pad. Helms shook his head no.

Burroughs slumped in his chair. "I wouldn't put it that way, but yeah, we did all of the work to the north of the permit area."

Mike glanced over his shoulder at the DEP lawyers and winked. He quickly looked at the woman in the striped dress; she had been looking at him. She glanced down at her laptop and continued hammering the keys.

"I have no further questions for this witness."

As Mike took his seat, the judge looked at Burroughs. "Do you need a break? Are you ready to continue?"

"I'm okay."

"Mr. Helms, any redirect?"

Helms did not look up. "No."

The judge looked at some papers, then said, "I have a question for the witness. Any objections?"

Mike was sitting down and began to stand to object, then thought better of it and sat on the edge of his seat.

"Mr. Burroughs, do you have anything else you'd like to say? Anything you want to tell me?"

Burroughs nodded and pinched his lips. "I don't get it. I didn't mine without a permit. All I'm doing is clearing back the brush and flattening out the knob. I made it clear to Roy, Inspector Worley, that I wasn't minin.' It ain't fair that I can be shut down just for clearing some brush and flattening a little ground. I mean, that's not minin'. These guys from DEP, Roy, Mr. Jacobs, the others, they should be helping the little guy, not shuttin' him down. I thought after the election things would change, but no. Back in the old days they used to help you, kinda give you advice. It wasn't as much us versus them. Now they treat me like I'm the Consolidated Coal Company and I ain't big like them. All I am is a workin' man trying to earn a decent living for my family."

The courtroom was silent.

After several seconds the judge said, "Mr. Helms, do you have any other witnesses you'd like to call?"

"No."

"Are you sure?" replied the judge who shook his head in disbelief. "You don't have any other witnesses you'd like to call who could help you verify your client's version of the story, like maybe the mine inspector, who might be able to testify about what he saw and what he understood Mr. Burroughs was doing?" The judge raised his eyebrows.

Helms scribbled a few empty thought bubbles over his cartoon characters' heads. "Maybe I'd like to call Inspector Worley."

The judge looked at the inspector's empty chair. Then he looked at Mike. "Where is Inspector Worley? Is he still here?"

"No, sorry, Your Honor. He left about twenty minutes ago." Mike carefully selected his next words. "He had to get back to Knox for a meeting and left during my cross-examination of Mr. Burroughs."

Helms looked at the judge. "Well, I think I might have some questions for him."

Mike rolled his eyes. "Your Honor, the appellant did not obtain any subpoena for Mr. Worley and it's early enough in the day. I clearly don't need him for my case, so I told Mr. Worley he could head back to his office if he needed to get back to more productive work. If Mr. Helms had gotten a subpoena, I certainly would have told Mr. Worley to wait."

The judge looked at Helms. "You understand, Mr. Helms, if you want a witness to be here, you have to subpoena him? Since you didn't subpoena Mr. Worley, he's no longer available to testify. It's almost," the judge looked at his watch, "noon. We can't wait for you to subpoena him and then come back to the hearing. Unless you have another witness who is here and can testify, then your case is over."

"But I didn't know, I didn't know I needed to subpoena the inspector. I'm not altogether familiar with *your* rules of procedure. The inspector was here in the morning, I just figured he'd be here if I needed to call him as a witness." Helms's voice was nearly soprano-pitched.

The judge looked coldly at the lawyer. "The rules of procedure before this board are quite similar to the rules of any court in the Commonwealth. It's your responsibility to familiarize yourself with our rules before you appear before us. Do you have anything further?"

"I guess not."

The judge looked at the witness. "Mr. Burroughs, you may take your seat at your counsel's table. Do you rest, Mr. Helms?"

Helms looked through his papers and quickly glanced around the courtroom. All eyes were fixed on him. He sighed. "We rest."

"Very well, let's keep it moving. Mr. Jacobs, you may present your case."

Mike stood up. "Your Honor, based on the testimony we heard here today, the Commonwealth does not intend to put any witnesses on the stand. We believe Mr. Burroughs has testified conclusively that he mined without a permit. That is to say, he mined outside of the permitted area. Also, he recklessly blasted in the un-permitted area causing fly-rock to enter a residential neighborhood. He said he was just flattening the knob and selling the stone to a builder, but that's the very definition of surface mining. The inspector was fully justified in issuing the cease-and-desist order that Mr. Burroughs appealed. The exhibits to which Mr. Helms stipulated confirm all of the points of our cease-and-desist order."

Mike heard a furious tapping on the woman's laptop. He concentrated on Burroughs.

"I heard Mr. Burroughs express his concerns. But, just like any mine operator, he is free to engage the services of a mining consultant to assist him with his operations. That's not the responsibility of the department. In its infinite wisdom, the General Assembly has cut our budget again and again and we have scant resources to do our job as it is. The department's job is to *regulate* the industry, not act as its *consultant*. There was no basis for the appeal and it should be dismissed. This is about as open and shut a case as I've ever seen. The board should find in favor of the Commonwealth. Your Honor, the Commonwealth rests its case."

The judge motioned to Tommy Bowdoin. The two whispered to each other and after a minute, the judge straightened a pile of papers in front of him. "I have a slightly unusual request. We don't generally do this, but, honestly counsel, I don't feel as though I'm getting the whole story."

Mike looked over his shoulder at the DEP lawyers in the back of the room and shrugged.

The judge picked up a piece of paper Tommy Bowdoin handed to him and looked at it briefly. "I'm going to call Director Lewandowski to the witness stand."

4

Mike's head snapped toward Sebastian Lewandowski. The director raised his eyebrows and pointed to himself. The judge nodded and smiled.

"Sorry to spring this on you Director, but since you're here and appear to be available to testify I thought you might be able to help us out. Please come up here and take the witness stand. I promise to get you on and off in a couple of minutes."

Mike leapt to his feet. "Objection. Director Lewandowski is not listed on anyone's witness list and as an employee of the Commonwealth, technically he's my witness. I haven't had a chance to go over anything with him. At the very least, I'd like to call a recess to prepare him to testify."

Helms stood too, although he appeared too scared and confused to say anything.

"The director has been on the witness stand in my courtroom at least two dozen times, probably more. I have just a few questions I'd like to clarify with him."

"Well, I object. You can't call random DEP witnesses just because they came in to watch the hearing. Are you going to call the lawyers sitting in the back row, too?" Mike said loudly. He pointed at them.

The young lawyers all shifted uncomfortably in their seats.

"Watch yourself, Mr. Jacobs. Remember, I'm the judge. This is an administrative hearing and I have a lot of latitude."

"In that case, I demand a continuance."

"I wouldn't demand anything if I were you. *Motion* for a continuance denied." The judge scowled at Mike.

"Well, if you're going to ask questions of a witness, then I *request* an offer of proof."

Judge Diaz closed his eyes and appeared to count. "Certainly, Mr. Jacobs. I intend to ask the director questions of a general nature about mining without a permit and mining off of the permitted area. Do you have a problem with that?"

"Yes judge, I feel like I've been ambushed."

"If that's an objection, denied. Anything else? If not, sit down."

Mike's mind raced.

Damnit. I'm the Commonwealth's lawyer. I'm supposed to be asking the questions. I'm about to win this case and shut down this scumbag once and for all. I don't want to let this bastard off. The judge is interfering with my case.

What do I do now?

Mike perched on the edge of his chair.

The judge swore in the director. "Thank you, Director Lewandowski. I only have a couple of simple questions. This shouldn't take more than a few minutes."

"Understood, Judge," Lewandowski answered evenly and crossed his arms. His short sleeves were stretched to capacity.

"How long have you been the Director of the Bureau of Mining and Reclamation?" asked Judge Diaz.

Mike stood. "Objection, Your Honor. I object to this whole line of questioning."

The judge glared at Mike. "Denied."

"About five years. Prior to that, I was the District Mining Manager of the Moshannon District Mining Office. Before that, I was a mine inspector and mine inspector supervisor."

"Let's cut right to the chase. I assume it's unlawful to mine outside of the area for which a mine operator has a permit. Right?"

"Objection, leading the witness. Calls for a legal conclusion." Mike had remained on his feet since his previous objection.

"Mr. Jacobs, you're *really* annoying me now. I understand you don't like me asking questions of Director Lewandowski and you feel you've been ambushed. I'll put a standing objection on the record and you can argue it in your brief. Sit down. I don't want to hear any more objections from you."

Mike sat on the edge of his seat, his legs like coiled springs.

Son of a bitch. Once he testifies, whatever he says will be on the record. If he screws up, my whole case will go to hell.

"That's correct, judge, it's illegal to mine outside of your mining permit. Colloquially we call it mining off of the permitted area, but in reality it's the same as mining without a permit."

"Is there any activity that a mine operator could do in an area outside of his mining permit?" The judge asked.

Lewandowski looked at the ceiling for a moment. "That depends. If he has an erosion and sedimentation control permit, what we call an E and S permit, a dam safety and encroachment permit, or some other approval from the department for that area, he may be permitted to conduct some activities there even though he doesn't have a mining permit."

"Hypothetically, if a mine operator had the proper permits, but not a mining permit, could he conduct reclamation, just reclamation activities?" The judge leaned forward.

Mike was on his feet. "I must object, Your Honor. With all due respect, Director Lewandowski came into this room, I assume, just to watch the proceedings, and now you've asked him hypothetical questions. He hasn't been listed as an expert witness and I haven't called him as an expert witness, but you're asking him for his opinion."

Judge Diaz's eyes drilled holes into Mike. Mike stared back. The courtroom was completely quiet, except for the slightly audible murmur from the court reporter who whispered into a dictation device that looked like an oxygen mask, and the clicks of the woman in the striped dress who feverishly pounded her keyboard. No one moved. "Sit. I won't ask you again."

Lewandowski leaned forward. "You don't need a mining permit to conduct reclamation."

The judge nodded and sat back. "Thank you, Director. That's what I needed to know."

"Any questions, Mr. Helms?" The judge asked.

Helms half stood and his mouth moved, but no words came out. Then he sat down.

"Any cross-examination, Mr. Jacobs?"

Mike stalked forward in two giant steps until he stood between the judge and the witness. He kept his back to the judge. "Director, as you know, I'm Mike Jacobs, the attorney for DEP. Did we talk at all about this case prior to your testimony today?"

"No."

"Have you looked at any files regarding this case?"

"No."

"Are you familiar with the facts of this case?"

"I believe I was briefed on it maybe three months ago by the chief counsel. For maybe five minutes. Other than that, no."

"Why are you here today?"

"Well, I was between meetings and had about fifteen minutes to kill. I thought it might be interesting to catch some of the testimony in this case. I won't be doing that again. Ever."

Everyone in the courtroom—except Mike—laughed loudly.

"A few moments ago, you said a mine operator may not need a mining permit for reclamation, correct?"

"That's right. So long as he's just doing reclamation and he has other necessary permits."

"What if a coal mine operator digs up some stone which he sells to a third party in the area where he's supposedly doing reclamation. Does he need a mining permit then?"

"Absolutely. Whenever a coal operator removes stone from the ground and sells or even uses that stone, that's surface mining."

"So, assuming a coal mine operator had some kind of permission to conduct reclamation activities and then he removed and sold stone, would he need a mining permit?"

"Definitely. We can't tolerate someone claiming to be doing reclamation who, in reality, is conducting a mining operation."

Mike took a few deep breaths and pretended to look at his notes. He was so angry, however, that he couldn't focus. "No further questions, judge. Do you have any redirect? Maybe another witness you'd like to call?"

5

The judge narrowed his eyes and stared Mike back into his chair. "I have no further questions. Do you have any re-cross examination Mr. Helms?"

"No, Your Honor."

"Okay then, we're done here." The judge gave the parties the final briefing schedule and stalked out of the room. Tommy Bowdoin trailed behind him shaking his head.

Helms and the others stood as the judge and his clerk left the courtroom. Mike waited to stand until the last possible moment as the judge exited. He quickly regained his composure, then looked at Burroughs who shrugged on his Steelers jacket.

"Mr. Burroughs? Good luck to you, sir." Mike quickly gripped his hand. "Wes, I guess we'll be talking," Mike shook Helms's hand.

"Not exactly what I expected. A lot more technical than what I thought going into this. And the judge…" Helms did not finish his sentence.

Mike shook hands with the DEP lawyers who had surrounded him at the counsel table and said to one of them, Leticia Rider, "That was interesting."

"I've only second-chaired one trial so far, I assume that doesn't happen very often?" Leticia asked.

"Not too often, like never. It's not unusual for the judge to ask a question or two, but I've never seen anything like this. Sometimes the judges forget they aren't lawyers anymore and want to mix it up with the real litigators. Unfortunately, it's their rules when that happens."

Lewandowski walked past Mike who tapped him lightly on the arm. "Sorry about that, Director. This took me completely by surprise."

"Really? You hid it well." Lewandowski did not smile and left the courtroom quickly.

Mike glanced around the courtroom and looked for the mysterious woman, but she was gone. Mike looked at the DEP lawyers. "Did any of you catch the woman in the striped dress? The one who was sitting in the corner with the laptop?"

"Yea," said Leticia, "Maybe she's your groupie. I've never seen her before, though."

The other lawyers looked around and shrugged.

"My mysterious admirer."

Finally, the young DEP lawyers and Mike filed out of the room. Helms and Burroughs talked quietly as Helms shoved his papers and exhibits into his shabby briefcase.

As the elevator doors closed, Leticia put her hand on Mike's arm and whispered, "Jesus, Mike. That was rough. Well, anyway, that was just great how the inspector had to leave to go back to Knox. He's gotta be, what, thirty miles down the turnpike by now?"

Mike did not respond. When the doors opened they stepped into the grimy lobby of the ancient state office building. Leaning against the wall, chewing on a toothpick, was Roy Worley, the inspector. The DEP lawyers looked from Roy to Mike and broke into big grins.

"Roy! I guess you didn't get out of town just yet." Mike winked at him. "Come on, I owe you lunch." The other lawyers slapped Mike on the back. "I'll see you guys back at the office."

As Mike and Roy proceeded through the door to the fresh air outside the building, Mike caught a glimpse of the woman in the striped dress. She wore a long wool coat and held a large oversized purse, the kind some female lawyers use as an all-purpose briefcase. She stood outside the exit door and adjusted her gloves.

"Hey Roy, give me a minute, will you? I want to see if I can catch her." He pointed toward the exit.

Mike rushed across the long lobby and through the door but couldn't find her. He jogged down the sidewalks near the office building, then returned to his witness.

***

At the candy stand in the lobby, hidden from view by a massive granite column, Tommy Bowdoin paid for the candy bar he intended to eat for lunch while he worked at his desk. He was alone, unappreciated, mocked. Tommy Bowdoin, Assistant Counsel to Judge Alberto Diaz, spied on the lawyers from DEP and saw and overheard everything.

6

Mike returned to the office after lunch and dropped his bags on the floor. He fell into his chair, an ancient leather judge's chair he had bought at the Commonwealth surplus warehouse. It was oversized and the black leather was cracked from age. It smelled like a cross between a wet dog and a fart. Mike loved it. He put his feet up on the desk, his Oxfords resting on a familiar spot on the dented oak trim of his semi-antique, state-issued desk. He stared up at the ceiling.

How many ways did I screw up today?

He thought of every one.

Then he scrolled through his emails. The one that jumped out was the reminder from Roger Alden, his boss, who wanted to see him as soon as the trial was over. He gritted his teeth and headed for the door.

Mike trudged down the dingy hall past his colleagues' small offices to Roger's office, tapped on the door, and was waved in. Roger was the senior litigator in the office and about six months earlier was promoted to Regional Counsel of DEP's Central Regional Office. His predecessor had gone over to the dark side and moved to a job as a partner in the Harrisburg office of a large Pittsburgh law firm. The rumor was he was earning four times what he made as a lawyer for the Commonwealth.

Roger's white hair was puffed up and Mike thought he had put on a few pounds over the years, but he still carried it pretty well on his six-foot-two frame. He had bags under his eyes and white hair stuck out at odd angles from his eyebrows. Roger was known to throw back a few Irish Whiskeys in the evening, and in the twenty-five years he'd lived in Central Pennsylvania, he maintained his distinctive Philly accent. Roger's desk held stacks of paper and files, orderly in a way only Roger would understand.

The senior lawyer listened while Mike told the story of his cross-examination, leaving out how he sent the inspector back to Knox. "I was really steamed at the judge. I'd completely whipped Helms when Diaz jumped in and pulled Lewandowski out of the gallery. Can you believe that?"

Roger said nothing until Mike was done.

"Don't worry about it, Bud. I've had a federal district judge take over the examination of one of my witnesses, right there in open court. It happens. The important thing is not to lose your cool. Make it look like this isn't your first rodeo. You know what I mean?"

Mike blinked, then nodded.

He knew what Roger meant.

He didn't exactly do that.

"Anyway, it sounds like you won and another scumbag has been shut down. Nice work."

Mike smiled and nodded.

Roger's voice turned serious. "I know you're just getting back from a trial, but I have a new case for you, and I need you to jump right into it."

Mike shrugged. "Sure."

"This case is a double appeal from a permit issued to Rhino Mining Company. They've appealed a very generous mining permit we issued to them in Somerset County hoping the Environmental Hearing Board will overturn the permit conditions we imposed. The local neighbors have appealed, too, trying to stop the mining. The proposed mining site is called the Gordon Mine and it's a nice piece of land near the turnpike. The inspector reported that it's kind of boxed in. Neighbors are pretty close on one side, state game lands on the other. Rhino wants to wedge a coal mine on a farm between the houses and the woods, close to the neighbors. The mine inspector was a guy named Marty Stevens, you know, the guy who died in that fire a couple of weeks ago? He was adamantly opposed to mining it. Felt it was too close to the houses and too close to the game lands. Also, he was concerned the mining would screw up the headwaters of some high-quality streams. The district mining manager disagreed, but he did put some heavy-duty conditions on the permit. I personally signed off on it."

"Okay," Mike said, dragging out the word.

"Other than Stevens and the department's engineer, Ben Kemper, our guys saw no good reason they shouldn't be allowed to mine it, but felt any mining ought to be strictly controlled. Rhino is owned by a guy named Ernesto Rinati, who apparently doesn't have a sense of humor about all the conditions our mining guys imposed on them."

Mike wrote *Marty Stevens, Ben Kemper, not issue permit, Rhino Mining* and *Rinati* on his legal pad. He underlined *Rhino Mining*.

"I was told Rinati went nuts at the permit pre-issuance meeting when they told him what they were planning to do. He screamed that the conditions would cost him millions of dollars. He carried on saying we were too tough on him and we were making it impossible for him to get to all of the coal and make a profit. He yelled we were against him because he's Italian, all that crap. Our guys say they didn't want him screwing up the houses, the game lands or the stream. It doesn't matter, the guy's unhinged. He filed his appeal of the conditions a couple of days after we issued the permit."

Mike ran his eyes down one of the papers. "Lots of the jokers we deal with don't have all of their screws tightened down. Does he have any valid gripes, is anyone really out to get him?"

"Not because he's Italian. Maybe because the guy's a scumbag, lower than dog crap, an asshole, phony Mafioso, and he has more violations than any other mine operator who's still in business."

"So, you're telling me you don't care for this guy?"

Roger smiled at him. "Let's put it this way, there are a lot of good mine operators out there. They do their job and maybe from time to time they have an incident. No big deal. All business. Then there's Rinati and a few guys like him. For them it's still the Wild West. They don't want to play by the rules the rest of the industry has to deal with. They try to cheat and bribe their way out of any violation, big or small. Rinati is one of the worst, a real scumbag, the guy makes the whole industry look bad."

Roger appeared to let that settle for a moment, then he continued. "If that's not enough, the neighbors who hate progress call themselves Save Our Somerset, SOS. Get it? They filed an appeal alleging we're not tough enough and never should've issued any mining permit. They say we violated the law by allowing mining near the headwaters and blasting near their homes."

Mike wasn't surprised. "I've never seen a neighbor who wanted mining close to his home. They may be NIMBYs, but if it were my backyard, I'd be a NIMBY, too."

Roger smirked. "For what it's worth, not in my backyard, either."

"What do we know about the neighbors?"

"Roger shrugged and handed him a stack of papers. "They allege that we're in bed with the industry. That's us, always in bed with the bad guys and the tree-huggers at the same time."

"Who's their lawyer?" Mike paged through the documents.

"Someone named Miranda Clymer. I've never heard of her. I called over to the board and the secretary said she's never filed a case with them before. I went online and found out only bare-bones information. She doesn't have a website, no LinkedIn, no Facebook. Other than that, I know nothing about her."

"What about her appeal?" Mike asked.

"I looked at her notice of appeal and it was very detailed. Really, it's pretty good."

Mike looked at the notice of appeal, bound together at the top with a strip of blue paper embossed, *Law Office of Miranda Clymer, Esquire.* "Do you think someone's helping her?"

"It occurred to me," Roger replied. "I wouldn't be surprised if she went to the board's website and copied some notices of appeal from other cases and was able to stitch one together from those examples. There's nothing wrong with that, of course, but she was out of her league the minute she filed her appeal. By the way, her case was assigned to your buddy Judge Diaz and this morning, *sua sponte*, he issued an order consolidating both cases, so we now have one big happy case with Rhino, SOS and us."

Roger stopped talking. Mike was intrigued by the little he knew about this case. "I assume you want me to fight this vigorously. Right?" Mike asked.

Roger nodded thoughtfully. "Hey Bud, what about the thirty or so other cases you're handling right now? Are you giving them the same degree of interest that you're thinking about giving this one? You know, we're seriously understaffed. We have to carefully pick and choose our battles. This office is two lawyers short and we have exactly five lawyers to work all of the cases filed between Philly and Pittsburgh. What about all of those other cases?"

"Well, I think we have to defend the Bureau of Mining from the rapacious mine operator when they issue a conditional permit. It's also our duty to defend the permit they issued from the citizens, too. It sounds like this one requires special attention."

"More attention than the other mining cases you're working on? Than the three landfill cases I gave you in the past three months? How about that hazardous waste case? Not to mention all of those smaller cases."

Mike looked down at the pile of papers in his lap.

"Look, I know you'll want to spend a lot of time on this, but since both Rhino and the citizens have appealed and the judge consolidated the cases, I want you to let them fight it out. All we can afford to do is to make sure the Board upholds the permit and the conditions stay in. Also, keep your ears open during the hearing to defend the integrity of the department. I'm sorry Mike, until we get some more help in this office, this is what you have to do. It makes sense in this case since both sides of the permit are represented."

Mike shook his head slowly. "Will you let me take any depositions at least?"

"Yes, take a deposition of Rinati and his permit engineer. If you can get a dep of his expert witnesses, you can do that too, so you're not surprised by the expert at the hearing. Maybe take one of the ringleaders of the citizen's group. Other than that, I want you to tag along when Clymer takes her deps. Let her do the heavy lifting. At the end of the day, we really don't care if Rinati mines that piece of land, but we do care that the Board doesn't do anything to mess up our mining program any more than it already has."

Mike nodded slowly. "Can you tell me who's handling this for Rinati?"

"About that—it's Sid Feldman and his band of merry bag carriers from Pell, Desrosiers in Philly."

Mike perked up. "Feldman?"

"Yeah, the guy was with me in the second generation of the original DEP Environmental Strike Force. He's still considered a legend around here."

"I know him. He's been with the dark side for years representing the same outfits he once fought. I don't exactly care for a traitor." Mike tapped his finger on Roger's desk, "There was also that time when I'd been here for maybe six months and Feldman went to the judge in one of my first solo cases and accused me of prosecutorial misconduct. I never forgot that. Fortunately, the judge backed me up, but it's not something you forget, ever."

"Well, Sid's a no-holds-barred litigator. He always has been. Doesn't mean it's right, you just have to be ready for it."

Mike nodded. "Do you find it odd that Rinati went to a big Philly firm when there are good law firms in Pittsburgh and some great environmental lawyers here in Harrisburg? I mean, Somerset is a heck of a lot closer to Pittsburgh, or even Harrisburg, than it is to Philly."

"Not that odd. Remember, Sid's the best environmental litigator in the state. He was here for ten years and taught me a lot. He's a fighter, a tenacious litigator and knows environmental law. I get that you don't like him, but don't let your emotions cloud your judgment. He knows his stuff. Do you think you're up to handling Feldman?"

"Are you kidding? I plan to chew him up and spit him out."

Roger smiled at his young colleague. "One more thing, Bud. Can you wait a minute?"

Roger got up and closed the door to his office.

"Do you know, *did* you know, the mine inspector, Marty Stevens?"

Mike thought for a minute, "No, you said he was the inspector for this site, but I never met him. Why?"

"I told you he died in a fire. Suspicious circumstances, a couple of weeks ago. The guy had some serious financial issues—I suppose like all of us—and they're investigating that angle. At the same time, he was a pretty tough inspector and had a reputation for shutting down coal stripping operations. The state police are also looking into some kind of payback scenario, maybe a warning to the rest of us."

"What happened?"

"Awful. The worst kind of crap. I've never heard of anything like this before. Looks like someone broke into his house, tied him up and set the house on fire around him."

Mike blinked. "That's awful…"

"The EMTs actually managed to get him out still alive, but just barely. He died about six hours later," Roger paused. "I can't imagine…"

After a few moments of looking at the desk Mike said, "Did he…did he say anything?"

"Nothing. A state trooper I talked to said he was heavily sedated on morphine and just moaned until he died. They were ready to interview him if he came to, but never had the chance. The poor guy had third and fourth-degree burns all over his body."

Both men sat quietly. "How come this isn't all over the news? I mean, a DEP mine inspector gets hit, it's the worst possible shit you can imagine, and there's nothing in the news about this."

"That's the way the AG's office and fire marshal are playing it. All they've released is that it was a house fire. A tragedy, but that's all. They're withholding details hoping someone comes forward with some info on the attack. Keep in mind they're still not sure if this had to do with some loans he took out from some loan sharks, retaliation for his inspections, or something else. Maybe a real accident for all I know."

Mike looked at the desk. "Any chance there's a connection with Rhino? Rinati?"

"Don't know. It's all speculation. We're not involved in the investigation but the troopers were here to interview me yesterday. Stevens did inspect most of Rinati's operations, in addition to this one, and I heard Rinati hated his guts."

"Well, you said he had financial issues. Maybe he borrowed heavily from the wrong kind of guys, loan sharks, that kind of thing."

"It's possible. Anything's possible. My experience though is that loan sharks, they almost never kill the guys who are behind on their loans. It's bad for future business and the borrower *never* pays up." Roger smiled for the first time in many minutes.

Mike nodded.

Roger ran a hand through his white hair. "So, how long until you can saddle up?"

"Let me throw a few balls back up into the air, then I'll go through the file, get out to the site, talk with whomever the new inspector is, and get up to speed. Also, I'll try to meet with this Miranda Clymer and see if I can talk some sense into her and her clients."

Roger looked at Mike. "That's fine, just remember what I said. Keep your involvement to a minimum. Let Clymer and Feldman duke it out. You have to focus on your other cases."

Mike nodded. He heard what Roger said.

Another strip mine. More coal. More carbon into the air. Just what the world needs.

Another scumbag.

A mafia wanna-be. Big deal.

Rhino Mining—Rinati. Funny.

Sid Feldman. The biggest shark in the ocean.

Mike was twenty-eight years old.

Feldman was a legend.

He'd love to take them down.

7

Mike felt the woman's warmth as she held him in her arms. He slowly awoke and the dark room came into focus. The alarm clock glowed five forty-five a.m. It was still dark outside and the breathing beside him was slow and deep. He didn't move for several moments. Mostly asleep, he put out his hand.

Sherry?

Patty?

Nothing.

No one.

The bed was empty.

He awoke quickly now and sat up. Startled. The dream, so real, evaporated.

Again he heard the breathing. It was just the hissing of the steam radiator in the ancient apartment building.

At five fifty-nine a.m. Mike turned off the alarm and shuffled into the bathroom in the dark, careful not to stub his foot. He flicked on the light and blinded himself for a moment, then gazed into the mirror, careful not to nick his chin as he shaved. He thought about Sherry and Patty.

What a disaster that was.

He still had nightmares.

Jerk.

No, worse.

Not for the first time he shook his head at himself and his unforgivable behavior.

Patty was gone. Mike chased after Sherry after the breakup,

but she made it clear they were through. He didn't blame her. It was a long-shot at best. After that, he entered this self-imposed dry spell. He would have liked to have been in a relationship, but now he just avoided them. Since last year's disaster he hadn't been seriously involved with anyone.

He didn't trust himself. He'd gone on a few dates, but nothing serious. They'd just been company when he went to the movies.

Mike slipped into a pair of jeans and a white dress shirt, then made the bed. He was lonely and needed to be with someone. He wanted to love and receive love in return. He loved the feeling of being in love.

I'm becoming a recluse. I have to shake this. Seriously.

As he finished tidying up his bedroom, he thought, *Rhino.*
Focus.
Rhino.
Sid Feldman.
Rinati.
Miranda Clymer.
Rhino.
Focus.

The one bright spot in his life was Nicky. His friend. The room brightened when she walked in. Her smile. Petite and lovely. No pretensions. She giggled. *Giggled.* He smiled at the thought. He loved her like a friend.

Yeah, right.

Nothing would ever happen between them. He laughed at himself. Nicky's *girlfriend* would kill both of us if something like that ever occurred.

How and why had they connected? He didn't know and didn't care. What a strange friendship.

He went to his favorite restaurant, the Bread Shed, had breakfast, and read his news feed.

8

Mike spent hours bent over his desk going through the Rhino Mining Company mine permit application. Sandy, his secretary, entered without knocking.

She eyed his desk covered with the detritus of yesterday's trial, the Rhino files, week-old mail, and stained cardboard cups of cold coffee. She held up the mail. "Where would you like me to leave this?"

"Sorry, just hand it to me."

She did, but with a frown.

"What?"

"You don't look as cheerful as you usually do after a trial. Everything okay?"

"Yeah, I'm fine, I just have a lot going on right now." Mike shuffled his papers, pretending to ignore her.

Sandy waited for him to say more, since Mike often confided in her. She waited, then shrugged and left the room. Mike glanced at the mail, tossed it onto the growing pile, and continued scrutinizing the reports.

An hour later he picked up the phone and dialed a number from memory. The Cambria District Mining Office. He asked for Ben Kemper, the DEP mining engineer.

"So, I've been going through this file for a couple of hours and I thought I'd talk to someone who can tell me what's going on."

"Well, partner, you came to the right place. The whole thing is screwed up. I mean the permit never should have been issued."

"I heard you're not a fan, but can you give me the department's view of things first?"

"Well, if you insist. A few years back Rhino obtained a piece of land with several seams of coal just outside of Somerset. They were deep, but not too deep to strip mine, about one hundred and fifty feet. His bought-and-paid-for scumbag of a mining engineer claimed the coal could be accessed without harming the neighboring properties or the headwaters to the streams."

"Dude, try to keep the editorial comments to yourself for now. We can talk about his engineer later."

"Okay, you're the lawyer. His high-quality, never-ever-lied-to-me engineer said that following mining, the land would look fairly close to the way it does now, a farm field and woods. He claims that in a few years, any trees that had to be logged would be replaced by new growth. He says it would be hard to tell the area had ever been mined."

"You think otherwise?"

"Shit yeah. Not just me, but Marty Stevens, the inspector that Rinati had killed. You heard about that?"

"Yes," but Mike wasn't sure what he could say and what he had to keep to himself. "And you know this how?"

"It's obvious, don't you think?"

"Well, he may have had a lot of other enemies. The state police say it was an accident."

Ben laughed a phony-sounding laugh, "eh-eh-eh-eh."

"Marty said that mining would have a serious impact on the watershed and on the neighbors. We talked a lot about this and he felt any mining activity would hurt the streams and wetlands. Did you see his pre-mining report? He was against issuing the mining permit."

Mike had the report in front of him.

"He said the headwaters would be irreparably damaged," Ben continued. "Also, the property was boxed in by the Pennsylvania Turnpike to the north, a state route to the south, the homes on the west, and state game lands to the east. The mine would be small—about twenty-five acres—because it was hemmed in. There are hundreds of acres of land to the west of the houses that's all un-mined farmland and woods, but Rhino can't get to it because the homes are in between."

"Well, I looked at the report and Rhino's engineer says it's a nice piece of coal."

"I grant you that, but the property is too small to mine economically."

"So, you agreed with Marty?" Mike asked.

"Shit yeah, but Hicks assigned Lyle Ransom as the new inspector." John Hicks was the district mining manager, Ben's boss. "Just wait until you meet him. He's a piece of work."

"You don't like him?"

"Eh-eh-eh, the feeling is mutual. He's a scumbag, racist, anti-semitic, homophobic asshole."

"Homophobic? He must love you."

"Let's just say if he fell off a highwall, I wouldn't shed a tear." Mike nodded. "Anyway, less than two weeks after he was assigned to the site, he issued his inspector's report and said mining could take place."

"Well, the inspector doesn't issue the permit, Hicks has to sign it." Mike said.

"Like I said, even though a bunch of us, including Marty said not to issue it, Hicks ordered the permit be issued anyway, as long as conditions were attached."

"Okay, I thought the conditions imposed strict requirements for keeping a distance from neighboring homes during the mining, and required Rhino to restore the land and streams after they dug them up. Also, the conditions required that when mining is done, Rhino has to restore the woodland with a new growth of trees."

"If you believe he'll do all of that, I have a bridge I'd like to sell you. Eh-eh-eh." Ben said.

"Well my boss, Roger Alden, says Rinati hates the conditions. He says the setback from the houses alone will cost him, and I quote, millions of dollars since he'll have to leave coal in the ground, plus other extra costs. That must mean something."

"Hey partner, how do you know when Rinati is lying?" Ben didn't wait for Mike to respond. "His mouth is moving. Eh-eh-eh-eh-eh."

9

Mike was studying Rhino's proposed mining maps when his phone rang. He let it ring three times before picking it up without looking.

"Jacobs."

"Hiya Mikey!" said the cheerful female voice, and Mike smiled for the first time that day. Nicky was the only person he allowed to call him 'Mikey.'

"Hi Nicky, how are you doing on this…" Mike looked out the window and saw that it was drizzling, "…rainy day."

"Okay" Nicky said. "I was wondering if we could get together for lunch today. Look, I'll be honest, I'm not really asking you, I'm telling you."

"It looks like I don't have a choice. Is everything all right?"

"We can discuss it when we get together." Nicky said quietly.

"Fine. The Bread Shed?"

"Of course, where else?"

He smiled as he went back to the thick mine permit application.

An hour later Mike squeezed past the crowd of people in line at the Bread Shed's deli counter waiting for takeout. He waved to Frannie, the cute blond owner. She winked at him as she filled brown paper bags with takeout orders. He continued into the cozy, over-heated dining area with its mismatched tables and local artwork on the walls.

Nicky was at their table in the corner. She smiled when she saw him. Mike loved her smile, it defined her. It was as though it went from one side of her face to the other. She kept her light brown hair just below her ears. At five feet tall, Nicky was petite and turned heads when she entered a room. She was the kind of woman people naturally smiled at because, somehow, they knew they would get a friendly smile in return. In the winter she wore sweaters that always seemed to be falling off her shoulder. He was sure he had never met a woman as cute as Nicky.

He'd often thought it would be nice to have more than a platonic relationship with her and sometimes wished she wasn't a lesbian, but it was what it was. He was thankful to have her as his closest friend. Everything was fair game in their discussions. Neither held back. He shook his head and smiled, without realizing he'd done so.

Mike leaned over and kissed her on the cheek. She put a hand on his cheek as she received his kiss.

"So, is there an agenda for this lunch?" He sat at a ninety-degree angle from her, their knees touching.

"Maybe…let's order first." She smiled at him. She always seemed to smile.

She ordered a salad, Mike a tuna on rye, and he talked about the Burroughs trial until after the food was served.

Finally, Mike looked at Nicky. "Well? I don't think you really want to hear all about my exciting trial, do you?"

Nicky leaned her head closer. "It's about Cindy and me. We had a big fight last night and she was icy cold with me this morning." She took a deep breath and looked at him.

"I'm listening."

"It was stupid and horrible. We made dinner last night and instead of doing the dishes right away, I told her I'd like to cuddle with her and watch TV, then do the dishes. We sat for a few minutes and she kept looking toward the kitchen. Then she started berating me, telling me it was my turn to do the dishes, and finally she yelled at me for being a slob. I was so shocked and angry. All I wanted to do was sit next to her on the sofa. I couldn't believe she was yelling at me."

"It doesn't seem to me like you did anything wrong. I mean, you said you were planning on doing the dishes. I don't get why she was so angry."

Nicky bit her lower lip and shook her head.

"It's probably just a lovers' quarrel," Mike said. "Every time I see you two together, you seem pretty good."

Mike patted her hand. Nicky turned it over and squeezed his briefly. They held each other's gaze. Mike could relate but he had no advice because he was afraid to say what he was thinking.

"This is different, it's not the first time. It seems like all we do is bicker any more. I think she waits to come to bed until she thinks I'm asleep." Her eyes had watered, but she didn't cry. "I've been in this situation before. Don't you *just know* when a relationship is having more than a rocky patch?"

"I'm probably not the best one to ask."

They looked into their half-eaten plates.

"We're a great pair," Nicky said as she picked at her food.

"You know, sometimes I wish…" Mike stopped himself and bit his lower lip to prevent himself from saying anything further.

Nicky looked at him and smiled. "Me too."

He'd wonder about that "me too" for weeks.

They were still holding hands.

10

Mike found Roger sitting in his guest chair when he returned to the office at one ten. Roger looked up from his New York Times and indicated with a tight nod that Mike should shut the door.

"Are you here to fire me?" Mike grinned.

"Sit."

Mike sat in his old judge's chair and swiveled to face his boss.

"The thing with the witness and the subpoena yesterday. What exactly did you tell Judge Diaz during the hearing?"

Mike swallowed hard. Time to come clean. "Like I told you, Burroughs's lawyer was doing a lousy job. He'd just about lost the case. His client didn't help him, either. I, uh, might have told the inspector to leave before he was called by the other side to rehabilitate the case, since he hadn't been subpoenaed. So he left the courtroom."

Roger scowled, "And?"

"And I told the judge he'd headed back to his office to go back to work, since he hadn't been subpoenaed." Mike's voice had dropped to a whisper. "Roger, there was no subpoena, he would have only hurt my—the department's—case."

"I got a call from Judge Diaz."

Mike rocked back in his chair. "He called you himself, *ex parte?*"

"He was so mad, he was sputtering. I think he called you an 'effing idiot' in Spanish. He said you violated the ethical rule about candor to the tribunal. He was furious."

"What? How did he know?"

"His clerk, that kid Tommy Bowdoin, was in the lobby and saw the whole thing after the hearing. Apparently, you took the inspector who was supposed to be on the turnpike out to lunch? There was quite a celebration in the lobby, and Bowdoin saw all of it."

That rat.

"The judge was ready to send this over to the Supreme Court Disciplinary Board. That could mean you might be suspended, maybe lose your license."

"My law license? Oh my God. Roger, Helms never subpoenaed the inspector. That shouldn't be on me."

Roger scrubbed a hand down his face. "Don't you get it, Bud? It's not that you sent the guy home, it's that you deceived the judge. You should've told him you sent the guy home without being cute." Roger allowed that to settle in as Mike swallowed back the bile that rose in his throat. "Look, I talked him off the ledge. He wants you to send the lawyer, Helms, a letter apologizing and copy the judge. You'd better be contrite, too. I want to see the letter before it goes out."

"A letter? Sure, I can do that, no problem." Mike exhaled, relieved.

"One other thing," Roger tightly rolled the newspaper, "you lost. He's ruling against us. He's going to rule that the order was improperly issued and find for the coal miner."

Mike froze. "What? But the evidence was clear, he admitted on the stand he mined off the permitted area. There was fly-rock that went into the development. Someone could have been killed. We should appeal—"

"Are you kidding me?" Roger angrily slapped the newspaper on the desk. "Do you really want to be sitting before the goddamn disciplinary board explaining why they shouldn't take away your license? This scumbag is going to get away with it, and we're not going to do a damn thing about it. I have to decide if I'm going to report this to Prince."

"You'd report me to the chief counsel?"

"I haven't decided." Roger stood, indicating the conversation was over.

After he left, Mike closed his door and stared out the grimy window. He watched the railroad hopper cars—full of coal—in the railyard beyond his office as they slowly pulled along the tracks behind the capitol.

11

Hours later, Mike looked up from the file and checked his watch. It was three forty-five. He opened a file folder on his office computer, in which he had typed *Rhino Mining Appeals—Player's List*, looked for a telephone number and dialed it. The phone rang eight times and, just as Mike was about to hang up, a man answered.

"Yeah?"

Mike could hear the television on in the background. He could hear the murmur of talking followed by a laugh track.

"Uh, I'm looking for Mr. Ransom, Lyle Ransom."

"Yeah, that's me."

"Mr. Ransom—"

"Lyle."

"Right, Lyle, this is Mike Jacobs, Assistant Counsel with the Bureau of Litigation. You're the DEP inspector for Rhino Mining in Somerset County, right?"

"Yeah?"

"Look if this isn't a good time, just let me know. I was told you'd be in your home office at three."

"No, this is as good a time as any," Ransom said.

"Didn't Mr. Hicks or anyone from DEP tell you I'd be calling?"

"Yeah. What is it? I'm a little busy right now." The laugh track came in right on cue.

"Like I said, I'm a DEP lawyer and I'm working on that new mine permit case. I'm getting up to speed on the appeal, so I was hoping you could take me to the site."

61

"What did you say your name was?"

"Jacobs, Mike Jacobs."

"What did you want?"

"Rhino. Can you show me the new Gordon Mine site?"

"Sure" Ranson said. "I can take you there. Not much to see, it'll probably take us all of ten minutes to see it. Just a soya bean field, woods, a few houses nearby."

"Since it will take just a few minutes to see the site, maybe you can take me around to some of Rhino's active mine sites in Somerset County? I heard you took them over from Marty, Marty Stevens. That would help me to get a better feel for their operations in your county."

"Well, I get started early, five in the morning. Can you be here that early?"

Mike's idea of a leisurely morning drive to Somerset flew out of his head. It was either get up at two a.m. or stay over in Somerset. "Yes. Also, I'm meeting with the lawyer for the appellants, the citizens, Miranda Clymer, in the late afternoon. Maybe you know her?"

More laugh track from the television in Ransom's office. "I've seen her. A looker, blond hair, big tits, nice ass. You know what I mean?" Ransom laughed coarsely.

"Uh, yeah." Regrouping, he said, "Do you have any *background* information on her?"

Ransom laughed. "Sorry, don't know her. We're in different circles."

"Do you want to come with me to the meeting?"

"Not particularly. Look I work from five a.m. to three-thirty. I come back to my home office and do paperwork until supper. Do you really need me at night? I could drop you at her office."

Must be nice.

Mike routinely put in twelve-hour days.

"I guess not," Mike replied. "How about Wednesday?"

"Let me check my book," Ransom replied. He paused and Mike could hear the television again in the background. "Okay, I can do Wednesday. How about if I meet you at the Somerset Motel parking lot at six a.m.? Got it?"

Mike was jotting a note on his legal pad when Ransom added, "Jacobs. That's Jewish, right? Gotta say, never worked with a Jew lawyer before."

Startled, Mike looked at the receiver. "Yes, I'm Jewish. Do you have a problem with that?"

"No. Never worked with a Jew lawyer is all. Not too many Jews here in this county." Ransom paused, "Cohen, the guy who owns the jewelry store in town. At least his father was. Beats me. Guess they probably have colored lawyers in Harrisburg, too?"

What the hell?

"You have a problem with that, Lyle?"

"Nope. You know this is a lot more like the south than it is the big city. Well, gotta go." Ransom hung up without waiting for a reply.

"Can't wait," Mike muttered. He could almost hear the *Deliverance* banjo warming up.

12

Angela St. Germain, Esq., a senior litigation associate at Pell Desrosiers of Philadelphia, watched her boss, Sid Feldman, angrily pace a dog path on the worn conference room carpet in the offices of Rhino Mining. Angela had flown with Feldman from Philly to Johnstown in a chartered jet for an eleven a.m. meeting with his client, Ernesto Rinati, the president of Rhino. They arrived early for the meeting and now Rinati was twenty minutes late. They could hear Rinati's voice through the thin, wood-paneled walls talking loudly on the phone. His secretary had told Rinati they were there. Feldman fulminated against Rinati to Angela, who listened without response to his ranting. She'd heard it all before.

"You know that prick knows we're here, but he's making a statement." Feldman said, gritting his teeth.

She watched as he shot the sleeves of his navy blue and red pinstriped Armani suit and swiveled his gold cufflinks so they pointed in the same direction. Then he clicked through a dozen emails on his Galaxy in less than five seconds. Angela thought her boss looked like Clark Kent, with chiseled features, jet-black hair, (dyed of course), and glasses. At any moment, she expected him to dash to a phone booth and emerge as Superman.

"Screw him," Feldman said. "I'm charging the bastard full Philadelphia rates so he can make me wait as long as he wants, he's going to pay for it." Angela nodded.

Feldman studied again the pictures on the wall of Rinati with Snooki at a bar, with Donald Trump at a wrestling match, with

David Hasselhoff, and other C-list celebrities and politicians, then looked out the grimy window onto the outskirts of Johnstown. The view overlooked a mini-market and used car lot. Grainy snow whipped across the cars. "Lovely," said Feldman. "What a shit-hole."

Angela wore an Anne Klein dress which had grown tight around her waist. She knew she was paying for spending too many late nights working in the office, eating pizza and Chinese food at her desk, and allowing her gym club membership to lapse. She was only a year, or two, or three, from a partnership and she could lose the weight later. At thirty-two with a new double chin, she knew her once pretty looks were fading. She sat at the conference room table scrutinizing the permit files on her laptop. Early in her career as an associate she learned to make every second count. Since the meeting was delayed, she was glad she'd loaded up with documents. There was no Wi-Fi, of course, but she brought with her the MiFi the firm provided so she could access all of the documents in the firm's document management system. She largely ignored Feldman. She'd seen her boss in this state before.

Finally, the door opened and Rinati strutted into the room wearing dark green work pants and a denim shirt. His brown hair was curly and balding and he walked with his chest puffed out. Feldman had told Angela he thought his client looked like a caricature of Mussolini. Or Trump. His mangy, three-legged mutt hopped in behind him. He pushed the door until it shut with a noisy *thunk*.

"Attorney," said Rinati who looked at Feldman defiantly, and shook his hand. "Sorry to make you wait."

Angela said nothing. Rinati looked at her, smiled and cocked his head. "Angela, the lovely rose of the legal profession."

Angela thrust her hand out as far as she could force it without dislocating her shoulder. Rinati took it, pulled her toward him, then leaned in and kissed her on both cheeks. He squeezed a fleshy arm, too high, and casually brushed a plump breast. Her cheeks warmed, but she held her tongue.

"Ernie, so good to see you. We need to go over some paperwork and discuss our strategy." Feldman settled into the uncomfortable chair at the head of the table and glanced at some of the documents Angela had arranged in front of him. The chairs looked like something King Arthur might have used at the Round Table, if the queen had shopped at Kmart.

Rinati ignored the empty side of the table and sat next to Angela. He made a face and shook his head. "Attorney, do I look like the kind of client who wants to spend hours discussing legal strategy? I'll let you handle that. When you and the lovely Miss St. Germain here develop your legal strategy, call me and we can discuss it. I'm paying you eight hundred bucks an hour and I expect you to come up with a strategy that we can use to crush DEP," he called it *dep,* like *pep,* "and those *goddamned* motherfuckers from Somerset." He put his hand to his high forehead and smiled apologetically at Angela. "Sorry, sweetheart, those *motherfuckers* from Somerset."

A muscle in Feldman's jaw ticked, but Rinati wasn't finished.

"Really, Angela, wouldn't you rather go with me to a nice Italian restaurant and have a good bottle of red wine over lunch?" Under the table, he patted her knee. She shook him off. "Maybe we can ditch your boss and make a day of it." He winked at Feldman. "I'm sure Sid here won't mind if we tell him to fly back to Philly on that expensive private jet he rented and is charging me double for. I promise to get you home tomorrow." Rinati smiled at both of them, rubbing his hand on her thigh under the table, as she pushed it away and maintained her composure above it. She wasn't sure why she bothered. Their client was a lecherous idiot and Feldman only brought her along because he knew Rinati had a thing for her.

She pressed her lips together as tightly as she could so she wouldn't say something she'd regret. She was a *lawyer,* and a damn good one, top of her class at Penn Law and a rising star at the firm. When she got back to the office she planned to tell Feldman, as nicely as she could, that she resented being pimped out. Rinati was a pig of a man and she wasn't going to tolerate his behavior.

Rinati leaned down and patted the dog on his head. "There you go, Butch, that's a good boy." He held out a treat and the mongrel licked it off his hand, leaving a smelly saliva streak on his palm. The dog's hair was both wire straight and curly, as if it couldn't make up its mind, and he was a combination of so many breeds no one could guess his lineage.

"That's some dog," Feldman cracked.

"Yeah? I found him in a dumpster and saved him. Now he won't leave my side." The dog lifted his head and closed his eyes to receive a pat on his neck while saliva dripped from his mouth to the floor.

"Nice story." Feldman rolled his eyes and ran a hand through his jet-black hair. "Now can we get back to this? Look, Ernie, the wine and lunch sound great. But I'm pretty sure you didn't have Angela and me schlep up here just because you want a lunch date."

Angela gritted her teeth and bit her tongue.

"Attorney, Attorney, Attorney, I knew I hired you for a good reason. You handle the legal shit, okay? I wanted you to come up here to talk about the timing. That's the only thing that fuckin' matters to me. That dumb shit engineer of mine said we'd be able to get the permit so we could begin our initial box cut no later than March—that's less than three months from now. He also said DEP would never put any conditions on my permit, so we'd be able to get all of the coal out. I personally talked to the district mining manager before we filed the application, that asswipe Hicks, and he assured me we'd have no trouble. Now those bastards at DEP put conditions on the permit *and* those fuckers in Somerset filed an appeal that could slow me down for another year, maybe more. Whatever we do, I want this case over and done with so we can begin minin' in March."

"I'm not going to argue with you over a quick resolution Ernie. I don't understand why it's so critical, though. If you don't start mining the coal in March, maybe it'll be August or September. What difference does it make?" Feldman said.

"It makes all the goddamn difference," Rinati said. "All of my coal at a dozen mines is currently under contract. I got ten strip mines in Pennsylvania and two in West Virginia, and I've got contracts to sell every ton of coal from those mines. Those are all long-term contracts and I'm locked into whatever shit price I negotiated. Trust me, the price is too low, way too low.

I'm getting killed. Now I've got a brand-new unsigned contract sitting on my desk to ship this fucking coal to Bean Town, beginning in August. I don't have another contract that even comes close on the price. Whatever price I'm making on the other coal, I'm gonna get more than double for this. My option on that land expires on March 4, and I'm not going to renew it unless I know I can mine the coal and get it on the train to Boston on time."

Feldman tented his fingertips and stared at the conference table, an old, converted dining room table. "Maybe you could just break one of those older contracts and let the bastard sue you over that. You could make enough money off the Boston contract to more than justify breaking the other contract."

Just great. Sid is suggesting that Rinati tortiously interfere with a contractual relationship, Angela thought. *And I'm his accomplice.*

"Attorney, I already thought of that. If I did I'd be totally fucked forever. Sure, I'd do the deal with Boston, but who'd want to sign another contract with me if they were worried that the minute I got a better deal I'd drop them? The only one who'd make out on that is you, Attorney. The only way this will work is if I can begin stripping the site by March 4."

"Well, that's only two and a half months away. The Environmental Hearing Board just doesn't work that fast under normal circumstances—"

"Fuck the normal circumstances." Rinati's black eyes penetrated Feldman. "Everyone's told me you're the best fuckin' lawyer in Pennsylvania. If I wanted the normal circumstances, I could've hired some Shylock from Johnstown at a third of the price. I hired you and expect you to make it happen. Get it?"

Feldman stuck out his chin and plumped his necktie. "We'll do everything humanly possible to get you in a position to begin mining on March 4."

"Not good enough, Sid. I don't want *humanly* possible. I want it done. Whatever it takes. Anything."

Anything? Come on, Sid, you're better than that! Push back, man up!

Angela eyed her boss hoping he'd say the right thing.

"Then that's what we'll do," Feldman said. "We'll pull out all the stops."

Oh Sid.
Anything?
Really?

"Is there something you can do with any of your buddies in Harrisburg to put a little pressure on DEP?" Feldman asked.

"Sure. That asshole Mifflin. A dumb shit if ever there was one. Used car dealer and now a state senator. Big fuckin' deal. The only thing that idiot has done right is to get himself appointed to the Senate Environment Committee. I contributed twenty K to his campaign and he owes me big time. I'll talk with him."

Rinati rubbed his chin, "What about that cu—" he looked at Angela and patted her knee, "bitch lawyer from Somerset, Chlamydia Something?"

Feldman smiled and glanced at his associate. "Miranda *Clymer*. We have it all worked out."

Angela pushed Rinati's hand off her leg, again, and clenched her jaw. She'd had it with this little meeting. In her mind she composed a lengthy speech that lashed out at the vitriol, bigotry, and misogyny. She was a feminist, a good and honest person, *damn it*, and they treated her worse than that pitiful dog.

Feldman continued. "She got these clients because she's local, a solo practitioner. She's mostly a business lawyer, general practitioner. The kind of lawyer who will write you a will, incorporate your business, and get you a divorce all in one day. As best I can tell, the locals dropped in on her little office and Clymer saw the opportunity to make a buck off them. Angela has checked all of our sources, and she's never litigated a case that we know of. I had a friend from a firm in Pittsburgh approach her and offer to prepare all of the papers for her. She was skeptical, of course. I told him to tell her a little fib, that the case was being financed by an anonymous donor, a real eco-philanthropist, who wanted to keep his name out of the papers. That was basically true, since you're writing the checks which come from that outfit we created for you, Evergreen Justice Foundation. Now, we do all of the heavy lifting, and she gets all of the credit. I'll see to it that her case falls apart at the right moment. She shouldn't be a problem."

Angela felt sick. She composed her speech to the state disciplinary board. *Members of the disciplinary board, until Mr. Feldman told us about the so-called anonymous donor—who was really our client Mr. Rinati—who paid our opponent's legal fees, I never knew about it. I swear. Mr. Feldman was my boss and I was afraid to come forward because if I did, I might lose my job. I'd never make partner. Please let me keep my license and I'll spend the rest of my days working at North Philadelphia Legal Services.*

"The bigger problem will be young Mr. Jacobs," Feldman said.

"Who?" Rinati asked, leaning over and scratching his dog behind the ears.

"Mike Jacobs, the DEP lawyer. Young stud. I had a case with him in his first year with the department. Nothing to write home about then. Angela watched him throw a few pitches in a hearing a couple of weeks ago, and her scouting report says he's improved a lot in the past three years. He's the one we have to watch. Don't worry, if need be my firm will hire him, make him an offer he can't refuse. We'll do it right before the hearing, and DEP won't be able to get anyone up to speed fast enough to hold their case together."

Oh God, oh God, oh God. Why am I hearing this? I thought we were just updating our database on DEP lawyers. Feldman, you egotistical, arrogant jerk, why are you doing this? Are you that confident in Rinati and me that you don't hesitate to share all of this incriminating stuff with us?

"Even if this goes to trial, he's no match for me. Jacobs may be a smart kid, but I'll annihilate him and overturn the conditions. It'll happen faster than anyone can imagine, and no one will see it coming."

"Pretty big ego, Attorney." Rinati made a face.

"That's not ego, Ernie, that's confidence."

"Well, sounds like a lot of moving parts," Rinati said glumly.

"Ernie, trust me. That's why you're paying me the big bucks…literally," Feldman said through a thin smile. "Look, when we really start getting hot and heavy, I'll send Angela up here for a couple of weeks to work out of your office so we can coordinate all of the moving parts." He smiled at Angela.

Rinati also smiled at her and patted the top of her leg twice. Then he looked at his watch and said, "Well, now it *is* lunchtime. I think we know what we have to do. We've done enough business today. Feldman, you can turn your meter off."

Angela swallowed hard to keep the vomit down.

Rinati looked at Angela. She hadn't uttered a word. "Angela, can you accompany me to lunch? I think I hear a bottle of Chianti Classico calling our names. Il Poggio, born a long time ago in 2005." He smiled at her and squeezed her leg, then Rinati looked at Feldman and said, "And Sid, if you must, you can join us too."

They stood, and Rinati held the door open. Butch hobbled out of the room and into Rinati's office across the hall. He laid down in a doggie bed in the corner and closed his eyes.

"That's a good boy, Butch. Papa will be back in a couple of hours."

As the lawyers found their winter coats, Angela was determined to say something. She was sickened by what she heard and the way Rinati pawed at her. She went to law school to change the world and was president of the Environmental Law Club. Now she was reduced to this. Pimped out by a senior partner. She composed her argument, probably her *closing* argument, and decided it would be pithy and to the point. She wouldn't debase herself by using swear words like Feldman and Rinati. Feldman had taught her how to swear, and she did it to be one of the boys when she was with him—but not today. No, that wasn't her. None of this was. It was time. She was going to be strong, like all of those women who came forward about those bastards—the politicians, the movie guys.

Suddenly, a voice inside her head intruded.

Wait! You're being paid two hundred and fifty thousand dollars a year.

Angela, you are being paid Two Hundred Fifty Thousand Dollars. A. Year. Six times as much as your father. And you expect a bonus of fifty thousand dollars this year.

Think of all the good you can do with that money if you give it away.

Yes, you could donate the money to a cause. You could.

You are Feldman's go-to associate. You are only a year or two away from a partnership…It will never happen if you come forward.

For the love of God, wait.

Wait.

Angela pulled on thick woolen mittens, earmuffs, and a scarf. Feldman slid thin lined, leather gloves, the color of caramel, he'd brought back from Florence onto his manicured hands. Rinati wore no coat against the frigid cold.

As they exited to the street, Rinati took Angela's arm in his, intentionally rubbing his arm against her breast. He chatted about the lovely village in Italy that provided a family name for his father as the three of them strolled down the decrepit street toward the restaurant.

Rinati held the door for Angela and she spoke for the first time that day.

"Thank you, Mr. Rinati."

13

The turnpike near Carlisle was empty. Mike accelerated until the speedometer approached eighty-five. No other cars were headed west, so he sped up until he hit ninety, crossing lanes to maintain a straight line, then he allowed the car to slow itself to seventy-five. That was enough, Mike didn't want another speeding ticket.

After he clicked on the cruise control, his mind fixed on Nicky. He'd never had a friend like her. She'd made it very clear she was *never* going to be more than a friend and Mike didn't want to do anything that would hurt the most cherished relationship he'd ever had. He knew that when he thought he found the right woman he'd compare her to Nicky. Terribly unfair, he knew, but he was being honest with himself.

Mike looked at a large farm as he sped along, with a white barn set back away from the turnpike. Cows stood in a field tinted yellow, brown, and gray, steam puffing from their nostrils. The previous week's light snowfall had melted and the ground was ready for more. The farm appeared serene and trouble-free. For a moment, and not for the first time, he wished his life were less complicated.

His mind drifted to a thought that he pondered regularly—the religion issue. Mike had gone in and out of observance over the years. The high point had been when he applied for, and began attending, the Jewish Theological Seminary after high school. In his sophomore year, however, he transferred to Penn State. *Steve*, he had said to his older brother, a Conservative rabbi and his role model, *I just don't feel it anymore. How would you know what I'm even talking about?* He replied, *Mike it happened to me once, too, then I sat down and learned a page or two of Talmud, and it all came back. Try it, please.* Yeah, that was just not going to work for Mike. He was troubled by this and he couldn't come up with the answer that was right for him.

Eventually, Mike's thoughts returned to the Rhino Mining case. He wanted to represent the department vigorously, to uphold the permit against both the challenge by Rinati and the challenges by the citizens group. Mike felt juiced up that his opponent was Sidney Feldman. Just twenty-eight years old, Mike knew that many of his contemporaries from Vermont Law School were lucky to be writing briefs and attending depositions, while Mike was dueling in court with Pennsylvania's leading environmental litigator.

Roger's words played in Mike's head: *I want you to babysit this case, let Feldman and Clymer fight it out.*

You have to devote more time to the other cases where we don't already have capable lawyers on both sides.

Roger had burst his balloon and made it clear that Mike was to take a secondary role.

Defend the integrity of the department.

Mike hated that. He wanted to be in the middle of the action fighting to protect the watershed and the neighbors. That was why he went to law school.

He wondered about Clymer, who was a complete unknown. Emails and calls to colleagues failed to reveal anything about her. She had no Facebook or LinkedIn presence. The only information he found was a single-line listing in the online Martindale-Hubble Law Directory—Clymer was thirty-nine and a graduate of Chatham College, formerly a woman's college, in Pittsburgh, and Duquesne Law School. Google Maps showed her office was a converted house. Mike knew nothing else about her. He pictured a woman, approaching middle-age, dowdy and plump in a brown dress with sensible shoes like his mother used to wear.

He paid the toll at the Somerset exit, then made two quick turns and found himself in the nearly empty parking lot of the decaying Somerset Inn. The sign was rusty and hung at an angle. It was an old-style drive-up motel with two floors. He could only imagine the state of the rooms. Half of them faced the highway while the other half faced a barren hillside. There was another, nicer hotel in Somerset, a Sheraton, but he had to stay at a hotel that would accept a state voucher or pay for it out of his own pocket. The Sheraton did not accept state vouchers. As he surveyed the dingy motel, Mike wondered which dank hole would be his room.

He pulled open the lobby door, and was hit with a musty odor that someone had attempted to cover up with Clorox bleach. Mike sniffed and walked up to an empty counter where he was greeted by a sign that read *Press Here* with an arrow pointing to a buzzer. He pressed the button and waited. The shabby lobby furniture and the 1950s décor were right out of *Psycho*. Over two minutes passed before a man strolled to the counter gnawing on a bologna sandwich. He had few teeth and chewed with his gums. His rumpled, black wool sweater had a bright red plastic name badge that read, *Hi! My name is Skipper!*

"Yeah?" The man swallowed his bologna.

"Hi, uh, Skipper, my name's Jacobs. I made a reservation last week."

The man looked under the counter and flipped through some papers. "Sure, I got it. Michael Jacobs, state voucher rates."

"Yeah, that's right. Look, would it be possible to put me in a better room? I mean, I know I'm paying with a voucher, but it doesn't look like the hotel will be overbooked tonight."

Skipper reached under the counter and handed Mike a key on a green plastic fob. "Here ya go, it's in front, at the end."

Mike and the clerk exchanged the paperwork, and Mike turned to go back to his car.

"Wait a minute," Skipper called. "You forgot something."

Mike turned, hoping the clerk had a change of heart and was going to give him the key to a better room. Instead, he leaned over and pulled out a towel, washcloth, and sliver of soap with a generic label from a pile under the counter.

"If you need another towel, return this one and I'll give you another."

Mike wasn't altogether surprised to find that his room faced the Turnpike. Lysol fumes enveloped him, mixing with the heavy smell of cigarettes, depression, and twenty-minute quickies. The walls were made out of cement blocks and were painted with a glossy white finish. They looked like cottage cheese and were probably painted that way so they could be hosed off. He sat on the bed and the springs squeaked as he sank almost to the floor. The room had an old color television and remote control. A small desk and a chair completed the spartan furnishings. The heater blew hot air and constantly rattled to a beat. Among the cheap hotel rooms in which he'd spent nights since becoming a lawyer for the Commonwealth three years earlier, this was the worst. Mike was glad he wouldn't spend much time in it.

It was now two thirty. This late in December, Mike knew he had only two hours of sunlight and wanted to make the most of it. He pulled a paper map from the permit application out of his briefcase and returned to the car. Rhino Mining's new Gordon Mine Site was ten minutes outside of town. He found the property easily, as it was on the state route heading out of town.

Pulling his car onto the shoulder, Mike looked across a vast field. A small amount of snow, from a squall which had hit the area several days earlier, remained. Otherwise, it was bare, with just the stumps of soybean plants. According to the map, the field was a good size, thousands of feet wide and long. It seemed to head back toward the turnpike but crested so Mike couldn't see the other side. A dirt road led from the highway back along the fringe of the field, and several houses were just beyond the boundary, some with lights on in the late December afternoon. Christmas lights twinkled between the trees. He could see the woods on the opposite side of the field and knew from the permit application that they were a part of the state game lands.

Mike pulled his car up to the road and saw a sign that read, *Private Driveway, No Entry! No Turn Around!* Next to that was another sign, about the size of a 'for sale' sign, that read, *Save Our Somerset—No Mining Near Our Homes.* Glancing around,

Mike waited until no cars were coming on the highway, then he entered the dirt lane. He crawled past the small group of old and simple houses, modestly decorated for the holidays. The first one was the most modern and was fairly well kept, with a white electric candle in each window. It also had the Save Our Somerset sign in front, as did all of the others. Next was a house trailer, wood smoke pouring from the chimney. A sloppy assortment of lights festooned the doorway, but no more. A man in a sleeveless tee shirt came out onto the stoop carrying a plastic garbage bag and deliberately watched Mike's car as he slowly drove by. Mike waved, trying to appear as though he belonged there. A hundred yards later, he stopped his car and rolled down the window to get a better look at a ramshackle house in the woods, hidden behind hemlock trees.

What little paint remained was peeling off. The roof was deteriorated and covered with leaves, a gutter sagged below the front. Screens were still in some of the windows, and the sills, which looked like they had once been painted white, now were gray. The yard had ancient lawn furniture and a rusting swing set with tall brown grass growing through it.

Mike sat in his car surveying the dilapidated old house, his music turned down, thinking about the people who lived there who would feel the brunt of the mining. The curtains moved. He was being watched. It looked like a man. A very large man. He took his foot off the brake and accelerated until he reached the end of the lane. Mike turned around at the end of the trail and sped back to the main road kicking up dust, rocks and ice.

As he drove away, all he could think about were Roger's words, *"babysit this case...defend the integrity of the department."*

14

Mike's stomach had been growling for the better part of an hour when he found a local bar on the main strip in Somerset. The sign out front read *Gilligan's Bar and Grill.* It reminded him of the bars he'd snuck into as a teenager in Old Hills, near Wilkes-Barre. Expecting to be able to get a good hamburger and a beer, Mike pulled in and parked in the lot among the pickups.

The bar was as predicted, with just a small handful of patrons. A large man with a very full beard watched him walk to his seat. Mike nodded tersely and took a seat in a booth at the rear of the bar, facing the door as he always did, and a moment later a young waitress approached him.

"Whatilitbe, hon?"

"What do you have on draft? What do most people get?"

"You have your Iron City, that's the main one. Of course, you also have your Rolling Rock. A few get Straub's. There's always Bud, Michelob."

Mike smiled and asked the skinny girl who wasn't much more than a teenager, "What do you drink?" He expected her to say "Coca-Cola."

"Depends on whether I want to get wasted or whether I want to hold my own for a while." She put down her pad. "Looking at you, I'd say you're probably a Michelob man, maybe one of those craft beers, but you'd have to go to the bar at the Sheraton for that."

"Okay," Mike said slowly. "Let me try an Iron City, I haven't had one in a while. Also, a hamburger, well done."

As she walked away, Mike glanced at himself: plaid flannel shirt, jeans, and hiking boots. He wasn't sure how the waitress made him for an out-of-towner so easily.

Later, as he was finishing his fairly good hamburger and sipping on his second beer (he had switched to Rolling Rock), the man with the beard got up from his seat at the bar and, with a mug of beer in his hand, sat down across from Mike.

"Can I help you?" Mike asked, wondering what the hell was going on.

"You're not from around here, are you fella?" said the man as he dropped his mug on the table. Beer sloshed onto the wooden top.

Mike figured the guy probably weighed in at Two hundred and eighty, maybe three hundred pounds and had a heavy brown beard. He wore a blue denim work shirt unbuttoned over a Lynyrd Skynyrd tee shirt.

"Nope. I'm just having a beer and a burger. Actually, I'm getting ready to go."

"I'm not making you feel uncomfortable, like, am I?"

You are.

"Depends. Anything I can do for you?"

The man appeared to be lost in thought, then held out his hand. "Name's Wolfie." He smiled and Mike could see the food stuck between his widely spaced teeth. "That ain't what my ma calls me, but it's what ever' one here calls me. What's your'n?"

Mike shook the man's beefy hand, "Mike."

"Okay Mike. We don't get many outsiders here at Gilligan's, unless they get off the turnpike for a quick one. Where're you from?"

Mike knew that bureaucrats from Harrisburg were not the most favored in places like Somerset, so he said, "Old Hills, near Wilkes-Barre." That was true, although he hadn't lived there in years.

"Okay, Ol' Mike. Well, what do you do?"

"You first…Wolfie."

"Fair 'nuff. I drive truck. You name it, I drive it."

"So, you're a real pro?" Mike said smiling. He really wanted to get out of the bar and go hide in his hole of a room. Something about this guy. He felt vaguely threatened.

"Guess so. Well Mike, what do you do? Let me see," Wolfie tapped one of Mike's hands with a beefy finger. Black oil residue was ground into his skin and under his fingernails. "You sure as hell don't work with these. Ain't no calluses, my ol' lady's hands are rougher. I bet you're a college boy. Maybe an insurance salesman, maybe work in an office."

"Well, sort of—"

"Accountant?"

"Not exactly…I'm a lawyer."

Wolfie looked at him and sat back. "Lawyer? Shit, I need a lawyer from time to time. You got a card?"

Mike shook his head. "I'm not that kind of lawyer. I do environmental law for the state. I work for DEP."

"Environmental? Like what?"

"Coal mining, waste disposal, that kind of thing."

Wolfie closed one eye, scrutinizing him. "Okay, Ol' Mike the environmental lawyer. My company's had its run-ins with your kind." He lowered his voice and leaned forward as he talked. Mike could smell the beer and onions on his breath. Mike looked around for the waitress who was on the other side of the bar. He waved at her.

Finally, she returned and said, "Well, do yins want anything else?" She looked at Mike, "I see you've met Wolfie, one of my favorite customers. Wolfie, you're not bothering my customer here, are you?" She rubbed him on both shoulders and Wolfie visibly softened, leaning back in his chair. He seemed to melt at her touch.

"No, I was just chatting with Ol' Mike the environmental lawyer here."

"Well, Mike, here's your check."

Mike quickly paid the girl, in cash, giving her twenty dollars, nearly double the bill, and slid out of the booth. "Well, Wolfie, it's been fun, but I have to get on down the road."

Wolfie looked at him and shrugged. "See you 'round, Ol' Mike."

Mike nodded and winked at the waitress. He got into his car, fumbled with his keys as he started it up, took a circuitous route back to the motel, traveled in a wide circle, then doubled back, and finally parked to the side of the building. When he got into his room, he looked out the window and couldn't see any car or truck that had followed him. Finally, he pulled the ancient, stained bedspread onto the floor, sat on the sheet, and turned on the television. He kept the sound low so he could hear any vehicle that pulled up in front of his room.

Later, Mike fell into an uneasy sleep, waking every time a car pulled into the lot. A little after two a.m., a new noise awakened him. A car, maybe a pickup truck, parked right outside his ground-floor window.

Wolfie?

Mike sat up quickly in the soft bed. He grabbed his cell phone.

Talking.

A man's voice. Laughing.

A key fumbled on the doorknob and it finally found its way into the hole.

The door to the motel room next to his opened and closed. He heard two people enter, a man and a woman judging from the voices seeping through the walls, laughing and talking loudly. Then he heard bed springs squeaking rhythmically as the couple continued carrying on. The bed was exercised vigorously for close to an hour. Loud moaning, sometimes solo and sometimes a duet, accompanied the spring serenade and competed with the sound of the turnpike. Mike put his head under his thin pillow and couldn't fall asleep until after the final, unambiguous coda when the room quieted down.

He slept fitfully.

Dreaming of Nicky.

15

Mike awoke and found himself hogtied in a fetal position. Ransom stood over him, seven feet tall, bald, red eyes bulging, Popeye biceps nearly bursting out of his sleeveless flannel shirt, breathing hard, slobber dripping from his mouth as he poked Mike with a shotgun. *Squeal like a pig!* He laughed.

No! No! No! Noooo!

The alarm on his iPhone buzzed, waking Mike from his nightmare. Ten minutes later, he stood under the portico of the motel waiting for Ransom. At a few minutes before five, the sky was indigo and Mike wondered how much inspecting Ransom could do in the dark. He had stepped into the lobby, which was empty and quiet, but stunk from putrid must and disinfectant, so he waited outside in the December chill. Mostly he smelled the mountain air, but occasionally caught a whiff of diesel exhaust from the turnpike a few dozen yards away. At this hour of the morning, the cars and trucks passed by in short bursts, like trios of jets flying overhead, followed by near silence, which was fractured by the next truck. As he waited, he wished he'd worn Under Armour beneath his jeans. His parka and hiking boots would have to keep him warm.

At ten minutes after five, a white Jeep Grand Cherokee drove up to the motel. Mike saw the reflective DEP logo on the side as it approached, and when it stopped he opened the door and looked inside. The driver, a heavyset man in a camo hunting jacket with a Cabela's logo looked back.

"You Mike?"

"Well, must be, nobody else is out here in the cold and dark."

Mike leaned into the Jeep and caught a strong scent of McDonald's and saw the bag on the floor of the passenger side. They shook hands and he jumped in with his legal pad and a small digital camera. Mike had considered bringing his briefcase, but decided that would be overkill during the site visit. He planned to return to the motel prior to visiting with Miranda Clymer later in the afternoon, when he would change into his lawyer uniform and pick up the tools of his trade.

"What do you say we get breakfast?" asked Ransom.

"That would be great, I'm starving." Mike shoved the McDonald's bag with his feet.

Ransom drove them to a diner on the main road, not far from Gilligan's Bar and Grill, and the men went in. They drank coffee, strong and black, and ate breakfast—Ransom had eggs over easy, sausages, pancakes and grits. Mike had a bowl of oatmeal.

"How long you been with DEP?" Ransom asked.

"Three years. How long have you been with the department?"

"Going on twenty-two years."

Mike estimated that Ransom was in his mid-fifties. He did some quick math and wondered where Ransom had worked for the ten to fifteen years prior to DEP.

"After we see the new Rhino permit area maybe we can go see some of Rhino's active operations in Somerset County so I can see what they look like," Mike said.

"Well, I suppose. I have a shitload of work going on today, and this little tour's kind of on top of that."

"Well, we really need to do this. I should see the site and need to talk to you about Rhino. I'll stay out of the way during your work. Whatever it is you have to do, go ahead and do it. I'll try to be inconspicuous."

Ransom made a face and said, "Hicks told me to show you around today, so looks like I don't have any choice." He belched loudly.

When they were done eating, Mike paid the bill and they returned to the Jeep. Five minutes later, they were sitting on the state route looking across the large field near where Mike had parked a day earlier.

"That's it, over yonder," Ransom said, pointing. "The property is owned by the Gordon family, so they're gonna' call it the Gordon Mine. The proposed strip mine actually includes a fair amount of the woods that you see. There," Ransom indicated with his chin and bull neck, "the state game lands begin a couple of hundred yards past the tree line. The site runs from here right up to the turnpike."

"So what does Rinati plan on doing here exactly?" asked Mike.

"Let's take out the map and have a look-see." The men got out of the Jeep and walked to the edge of the field. Mike's boots crunched the frosty ground. Ransom pulled open the map and handed one end to Mike.

"They're gonna start over there," Ransom pointed to the map and then to the trees, "and then work their way from the back of the property toward the highway. The permit boundary and conditions keeps 'em back three hundred feet from them houses," he pointed at the row of houses along the dirt road Mike had driven on a day earlier, "and the final cut of the highwall is going to be pretty close to the property line, near the houses."

"Well, that explains why the neighbors are opposed to the mining," Mike said.

"I don't know," Ransom said. "But they'll probably mine through the area near those houses pretty quick. The mining's over in about three years, this whole field is supposed to be restored to AOC—approximate original contour—and it'll be a farm field again. You come back here in three years, and this should look pretty much like it does now. Mind you, I suppose I wouldn't want all of this going on next to me either, but Rhino owns the coal, and he has the right to mine it."

Mike bit his tongue and decided not to argue with the inspector.

"Anyways, according to the mine plan, next they mine across the field and over toward the woods. They're gonna take out a piece of the woods, staying back from the property line."

"I thought I read something about a trout stream called Roaring Run," Mike said. "I don't see any stream here, it's just a field."

"The stream's down there," Ransom said pointing toward the woods with his meaty hand. "It's about five hundred feet on the other side of the property line in the state game lands. I walked the entire thing after I took over this site, and there's no way that mining will have any impact on the stream. It's just too far away."

Mike glanced at the seriously overweight inspector and wondered if he was capable of walking to the Dunkin' Donuts from his car in the morning, let alone five hundred feet through the woods and down the embankment to a stream.

"Can we walk the site? I think I'll be better prepared for trial if I've seen the contour of the land. I mean, it's supposed to start snowing any day now and we may not be able to get back into the woods for a couple of months," Mike said, handing the map back to Ransom.

The inspector rolled his eyes. "I got a better idea, let's drive that driveway and cover some ground. We can four-wheel across the back end of the field."

The men got back in the Jeep and started down the dirt road. Mike had the map spread out on his lap in front of him but he was looking away from the field towards the houses along the road. "What do you know about these neighbors?" Mike asked.

"Not much, one or two are city people," Mike assumed he meant Somerset. "I think the rest have lived here for a long while. I've talked to some of them and none are too happy with Rhino or DEP. Or me, I suppose. The ones I talked to really wanted the mining to go somewhere else. Those mining conditions really hurt Rhino though. Mr. Rinati's leaving a big piece of coal in the ground, for no good reason."

Mike looked at the inspector. "So you don't agree with Marty Stevens, the former inspector? He was dead set against mining this property."

"God rest his soul. No, I didn't agree with him. He always gave the miners as little as possible. I know these guys, I know Mr. Rinati. If he says he can mine it safely, I believe him. He owns the coal, he has a right to mine it."

Mike stepped out of the warm Jeep onto the frozen field, his foot landing on top of a stalk of a withered soybean plant, and into the cold morning air. He looked back in and said, "Are you sure you don't want to check out the woods?"

"Man, that's okay. I seen them woods. Like I told you, I have paperwork to do." Ransom pointed to the metal clipboard on the dash.

Mike shrugged and slammed the door. As he started walking away, he glanced over his shoulder. Ransom had already angled his seat back and closed his eyes. Mike shook his head and continued walking. A wintry haze diffused the cold morning light and spread a shadowless grayish-yellow glow. A musty odor rose from the field, like hay, but stronger. As he walked from the edge of the field into the woods, the sounds of the Jeep idling and the highway noise slowly dissipated, overcome by the whistle of the wind blowing through the forest. The sound of the breeze drifted across the frozen field like a snow flurry.

Mike found a slight trail and pushed his way through the thorny brush at the edge of the woods. He stopped about twenty feet into the woods to look around. Everything was quiet except for the trees waving in the wind and the occasional chirping of some winter bird. He pushed on. Several hundred yards later, he finally came across orange plastic ribbons tied to some of the trees near the top of a steep decline. The ribbons marked the edge of the mining permit—it looked like Rhino was permitted to take out a sizable piece of woods. Mike gazed along the line of trees, trying to imagine the mining operation nestled up against the woods.

A couple hundred feet later, he came upon small metal badges nailed to the trees:

PROPERTY LINE
Pennsylvania Game Commission
Managing the Commonwealth's wildlife
resources for all Pennsylvanians

Mike descended a steep bank, his feet crunching through dead leaves and undergrowth as he carefully picked his way down toward the stream. The bank was steep enough in places that he had to hold onto tree branches to steady himself as he stepped down to the watercourse. He smelled the perfume of the musky damp earth rising from the valley below. He continued another two hundred feet until the bank began to level out and he could hear the splash of water from the stream.

The channel of Roaring Run itself was less than six feet wide. He stood at the edge of the brook watching the water undulate as it coursed over the moss-slicked rocks. The aroma was primeval, of earth and decaying plants and water and rotten wood. Mike loved the smell. He took a deep breath and held it in his lungs. He stood quietly for a moment, enjoying the serenity, until he heard a slight noise across the stream. He squinted through the dense trees. A woman, middle-aged, maybe older, sat on a rock with her back to him. She wore a bright orange down jacket and was very thin. Her hair was gray with some black mixed in. He watched her quietly for several seconds, not wanting to disturb or alarm her. He felt as though he had violated her privacy, so he turned and quietly headed back to the Jeep. At the edge of the woods, he looked back toward the stream. He inhaled the lingering aroma, the intoxicating scent of the wild land.

16

Mike and Ransom drove south across Somerset County toward the Mason-Dixon Line. After a half hour of rolling along county lanes and back roads they came to a wide plateau where they passed piles of broken rock littering the middle of a large field. It looked as though the land had been farmed relatively recently as it was not wildly overgrown, and they could still see corn stubble, withered, frozen and brown. Coal seemed to be the principal crop for the upcoming season.

A few hundred feet later, a haul road for heavy vehicles intersected the county road. It was cut across the field. A large sign at the entrance to the haul road read:

Rhino Mining Company
Shoemaker Mine

The sign contained all of the required DEP identification information. Mike snapped a quick picture, then Ransom turned the Jeep onto the haul road. They passed an overlook, and Mike saw the entire operation in one sweep. The pit was about the size of ten football fields and more than a hundred and fifty feet deep in places. They had already begun restoring the far end of the strip mine, and about fifty feet of it had been reclaimed. Parked near them at the top of the pit was an assortment of trucks and mining equipment on what had once been the farm field.

Ransom put the Jeep into low gear and drove down into the pit, keeping to the left side of the haul road. Three years earlier, when he had gone into a coal mine on his first DEP inspection, Mike found it odd that most vehicles drove on the left side in the mines—British style—rather than on the right. An old mine inspector explained to him that this was a custom carried over from the old Welsh miners. He heard from a mine operator, however, that the custom originated with the drivers of the exceptionally large off-the-road vehicles who found it nearly impossible to be able to tell the location of the passenger side wheels on the narrow trail. Rather than risk driving off an embankment, they drove to the left where they would have a better view of the edge. Mike preferred the Welsh story.

As they descended into the pit, a large off-road dump truck, fully loaded with coal, slowly approached them, black diesel exhaust bellowing from its twin stacks. The truck was also driving left and they passed slowly on the narrow road. The huge wheels, large enough to crush the Jeep, were just inches from Mike's door. When they reached the bottom Ransom parked near a collection of pickup trucks, mine vehicles, and miners.

Ransom and Mike got out of the Jeep, and Ransom grabbed a hard hat from the rear seat. It was a heavy-duty blue composite, festooned with stickers proclaiming his mining association affiliations. Mike recalled that these stickers, once common, now were outlawed by MSHA. He couldn't remember why. One caught Mike's eye: a Confederate flag with the words "Redneck Coal Miner" superimposed on it.

Redundant.

The biggest sticker, though, was a cartoon picture of a smiling rhinoceros head, with the oversized phallic rhino horn, plastered to the front of his helmet and the large words, *Rhino Mining Co.*

Ransom opened the trunk, pulled out a filthy white hard hat, and tossed it to Mike. It was a flimsy, plastic helmet, probably more of a gag than a real hard hat. Something they might hand out at a bar mitzvah party while the DJ played "Y.M.C.A.". Mike knocked the caked mud off the cheap hat and adjusted the harness to fit his head. While he was preoccupied, Ransom walked over to a middle-aged miner with short hair wearing a dusty Carhartt jacket. They exchanged a few words and a laugh, and then the miner went to his pickup truck and pulled out his own hard hat as Mike approached.

"Freddie, I'd like you to meet Mike Jacobs, one of DEP's lawyers. Mike, this is Freddie Pascal. He's the foreman for this job."

The men shook hands.

"I was in the neighborhood today, so I'm just tagging along. Don't let me interrupt your work," Mike said.

"Shit no. We have lawyers in here all the time. Hell, I think I have seven or eight of you guys buried right over there." Freddie grinned and pointed toward a pile of rocks near the base of the highwall, the muck pile. He and Ransom laughed. Mike smiled.

"So Lyle, what are you inspecting today?" Freddie asked.

"Well, I'm taking Attorney Jacobs here around to see some mining sites, so not really doing much inspecting today. He wants to see some real strip mines."

"You've come to the right place, young feller," Freddie said, smiling.

Mike looked at Freddie, "What are you guys mining at the moment?"

"Right now, we're mining the C-coal in the second lift. We got a pretty thin seam of B-coal, maybe eighteen inches thick, at the bottom of the first lift. Now we're down to the second lift where we've got maybe twenty-six inches of coal." He pointed to the face of the mine. "You follow?"

"Yeah, I've got that."

"Each lift is fifty feet high and twenty-five feet wide. We blast and retreat the bench as we widen the mine. Understand?"

"Yes," Mike said. He had seen dozens of mining operations and already knew the basics of strip mining, but patiently listened as the foreman described his operation.

"We blast here about twice a week. First, we drill boreholes for the ANFO, that's the explosive we use. Then the blasters fill up the boreholes and we try to blast during the lunch hour while everyone is off the mine in a safety zone, back at the work trailer having lunch."

Mike knew a lot about blasting as he prosecuted quite a few mine operators and blasters for improper blasting techniques. He held his tongue.

"Well, I hope I taught you something about minin' and blastin'." Freddie looked pleased with himself.

Mike could see a huge front-end loader digging the coal out of the base of the highwall and dumping it into a waiting dump truck. He recognized the driver—Wolfie—his uninvited dinner companion from the previous night. Several miners stood near the bucket of the loader, helping with shovels. He noticed the miners, only about half of whom wore hard hats, were working very close to the steep face of the highwall.

"Aren't your guys a little close to the face?" Mike asked pointing to the miners. "It looks like the highwall could come down on them." Mike glanced at Ransom and flicked his eyebrows up once.

Freddie looked at Ransom then said, "Hell no, the stone here is pretty hard, almost no fractures. It takes a shitload of ANFO to dislodge it. It may look close, maybe if the highwall were more crumbly, but this is good hard rock."

"Actually, I don't think so," Mike said. "The regulations require your men to stay clear of the face of the highwall unless they're in protective enclosures and wearing safety equipment. Your men aren't doing either."

Freddie looked annoyed. "Look, I've got a get back to work. Lyle, now you and your lawyer stay back from the working face."

The foreman shook hands with the DEP men and headed toward a front-end loader. He shouted something to the operator, a skinny man with a jagged hockey-stick shaped scar across his face, who reached to the floor of his cab and placed a hard hat on his head.

Mike watched for a few more minutes, then he and Ransom walked back to the Jeep. Mike looked at Ransom and said, "I don't believe a word he just said. It sure as hell looks like he's letting his men and loader operators work too close to the face of the highwall. One small rock falling off the highwall could kill a man. I mean, why take any chances?"

"Well, fact is, it's a safe operation. We've had very few violations and hardly any injuries here. Even Stevens didn't cite

Rhino for many violations here, and he inspected the mine for nearly five years. I've known Freddie for nearly twenty years, and if he says it's safe, then it's safe."

"But it's a clear violation of the safety regulations," Mike said, pressing the issue.

Ransom pursed his lips together and appeared to be holding back.

With that, they both turned to get into the Jeep when they heard a squeal of wheels and the sound of metal scraping stone as rocks fell from the haul road into the pit. It sounded as though a vehicle had nearly driven off the narrow path, but had managed to hang on—just barely. All heads turned to watch it careen down the ramp into the mine. The driver must have been insane; it looked like he was going over the side at any moment. Mike held his breath and waited for the crash.

17

Mike looked at Ransom. "What the hell?"

A spray of rocks rose from the haul road blowing a storm cloud of icy dust across the mine. A red Cadillac Escalade, covered in grime, bounced down the packed-dirt ramp, faster than any sane person would permit. The driver clipped the edge of the road again, then overcorrected and fishtailed into the mine wall to his right. The haul road angled up and the car went airborne, landing hard and spraying rocks and gravel.

Somehow, the driver managed to keep the car on the road, and it bottomed out at the end of the ramp where he took a sharp turn and lurched across the strip mine's rutted floor . The oil pan scraped on the uneven rock-strewn surface before it skidded to a halt next to Ransom's Jeep. The door flew open and a man, medium height, with curly, grayish-brown hair, wearing work clothes, jumped out of the Cadillac and slammed the door.

Ransom tossed Mike a gap-toothed grin. "Looks like you're going to get to meet Mr. Rinati."

"What the hell, Lyle?" Rinati shouted over the Aerosmith CD blasting from the car and drowning out the roar from the mining equipment. Mike recognized the song, from the 1970s, "Big Ten Inch."

"I thought I told you to tell me when DEP"—he still pronounced it *dep*—"was coming onto one of my mines?" Rinati yelled at Freddie and glared at Ransom and Mike.

A mangy three-legged dog stood on the front seat, barking over the loud music.

Amid Rage

Ignoring the driver's outburst, Ransom pointed and replied, "Ernie, I'd like you to meet Mike Jacobs. He's one of DEP's lawyers. Mike here wanted to learn something about minin' so he hooked up with me. I brought him here for a look-see and some on-the-job training."

Rinati walked toward Mike, not in a straight line, but circling like a wolf, beady eyes constantly on him, until he stood directly in front of Mike. "Attorney Jacobs. You know a mine's a dangerous place—a man could get killed here." He smiled and held out a hand.

I've heard that before.

Mike shook Rinati's hand and tried to gauge whether he was merely attempting to get into his head, or serious. "A pleasure, Mr. Rinati," Mike said loudly over the music.

"What the fuck are you doing here?" Rinati said.

"Well, I represent the Commonwealth in this case with the citizens and your permit, and it's important for me to visit the mine site before we have a hearing—"

"Uh-huh. The *proposed* mine site is thirty miles from here. Did you get permission from my lawyer, Feldman, first? Don't you have to do that if we're in litigation? What the fuck are you doin' *here?*"

"Uh, no, I, uh…"

Rinati laughed, "I'm just fuckin' with you. You're welcome here any time. So you wanted to see one of my jobs?"

"Well, Lyle told me I could learn something about mining here."

Rinati winked and smiled at the group of miners that had gathered around. "Look, you want to learn something about minin'? Let me take you up on top of the highwall and I'll give you an eagle's eye view."

Mike looked at Ransom who shrugged, "Sure, I'd be honored to have you show me your operation."

Mike followed Rinati to the Cadillac, where Rinati picked up the three-legged dog from the passenger seat and put him in his lap. Mike slipped into the passenger seat. The interior of the car was clean, except for a coating of fine dust from the mine. A satellite phone sat on the floor in front of his seat.

"This is Butch. He doesn't bite. Much." Rinati popped out the Aerosmith CD and squeezed his legs together to force Butch to stay in place. "So, Attorney Jacobs." He steered with one finger on the wheel as the Cadillac careened through the mine, petting the dog with his free hand. "Is this what you always wanted to do? I mean, some smart guys go to law school so they can make a ton of dough. I suppose some other guys go so they can save the whales. Are you a smart guy or a save-the-whales kind of guy?"

Mike considered his answer as the car bounced over a drainage channel, bottomed out and sent rocks in every direction. They ricocheted over ruts left by the heavy equipment, and Mike grabbed the armrest for support.

"Sure, I want to make money like anyone else." Mike paused as they rocketed toward the top of the back haul road. "I don't represent any whales."

Rinati laughed. "Well, are you against the working man? You against coal? Want to close down strip mines like this one? Put men out of work?" Rinati waved both hands as he talked, steering with his knees and the dog's head. The car veered across the narrow haul road and Mike white-knuckled a ceiling grip. He regretted not putting on his seatbelt.

"I'm not against the working man, Mr. Rinati, but there are laws and my job is to enforce them. In your case, we're not taking sides. I mean, the local citizens' group filed an appeal and you filed an appeal. The department is going to try to be as neutral as possible in this case."

"Neutral? What the fuck does that mean?" Rinati looked at Mike, his eyes bugged out, ignoring the narrow trail. Butch growled. Mike held his tongue. "You guys issued me a fucking permit with all of those conditions. That's not neutral. Now I have to hire a fancy Philadelphia shyster who says if I want DEP's full cooperation, I have to withdraw my appeal. I'll have to leave a shitload of coal in the ground—that'll cost me millions. What the fuck? That's not fair."

Mike was about to explain the need for him to withdraw his appeal to get the full cooperation of the department when Rinati slammed on the brakes and the Cadillac slid to a stop near the top of the highwall. They were fifty feet from the edge of the lift, a narrow shelf of land with the mountain on one side and a shear drop of two hundred feet on the other.

"Here we are Attorney, let's take a look." Rinati put the car into park, but left the engine running. "Whatever you do, don't get too close to the highwall. The rock here is pretty solid, but don't take any chances."

Rinati and Mike got out of the car and the dog stayed behind, barking loudly.

The men stood about twenty feet from the edge of the highwall and Mike glanced into the pit, two hundred feet below. The vertigo hit him: His stomach churned, his head spun, and his legs shook. He widened his stance and stepped away from the cliff.

They stood in a small area with a series of boreholes drilled into the rock, evenly spaced about five feet apart from the edge of the highwall and back about thirty feet. Mike estimated there were one hundred or so drilled openings. Rinati saw Mike looking and said, "Don't worry, that's been drilled for our next blast. The blasters won't be loading them with ANFO until tomorrow morning; they're all empties."

They stood near the edge of the highwall and Rinati placed his hand firmly on Mike's back as he pointed. Mike tensed. If Rinati pushed him, he doubted he'd be able to catch himself before he tumbled over the edge. It was a ludicrous thought, of course. The man was odd, sure, but not *that* odd. Still, Mike knew he wouldn't be the first one pushed over a highwall.

"Over there is where we took our first cut. We started with a box cut and went straight down. Do you have any idea what that cost me? Eighty feet of overburden before we hit a crappy eighteen-inch seam of coal." Rinati glared angrily at Mike, then returned to his more pleasant demeanor. "There is where we store the topsoil. You ask anybody, when my company finishes minin', you can't tell there was a strip mine there. We put back the overburden, the topsoil, plant grass and trees and shit, and it looks beautiful. Maybe later I'll show you one of our reclaimed jobs." Rinati waved his hands excitedly.

Mike noticed a piece of equipment with metal boxes, conveyor belts and gears. It was mostly rusted, although dull red paint showed through the rust. "What's that?"

"That's our old primary crusher. We used to crush stone out here in the mine, but don't use it any more. The boys are going to have to move it before we blast, since the highwall face is starting to get a little close." The crusher was no more than twenty-five feet from the edge of the highwall.

Rinati glanced at his watch. Mike noticed it was a solid-gold Rolex. Then the car started to honk. "Shit, that's my sat-phone. You can't get cell phone reception out here. Let me get it. You're okay here, but stay back from that highwall, okay?"

Rinati jogged to the car, jumped in, picked up the receiver and began shouting. Mike wandered to the rusted crusher, keeping the ancient contraption between himself and the highwall. The old machine had seen better days. As Mike studied it, he noticed again how close it was to the exposed cliff, and he avoided looking over the edge. He glanced at his iPhone and wasn't surprised to see he had no service in the heart of the mine. He slid it back into his pocket.

Suddenly he heard a loud crack and a boom, like an artillery shell exploding. The ground moved violently down, then up, like a trampoline, and then shook. Dust rose around him. Mike looked toward Rinati. A fissure had opened between them, and Mike was on the wrong side of the chasm.

He froze.

Rinati hopped out of the car and just looked at him for a moment.

A moment too long.

Rinati was smiling, a toothy grin, his yellow rat's teeth glinting in the midday light.

Then, after long seconds, he shouted, "Shit! Jacobs! Don't move. For the love of Mary, stand still!"

Another crack shook the ground, like the sound of wood being pried apart. Rocks tumbled into the strip mine. Voices reached them from below, shouting, "get back."

The rock on which Mike stood shook violently and the highwall began peeling away.

Mike's heart raced.

He panted hard.

He fell to his knees, not knowing which way to run or jump.

He grabbed the crusher.

Mike wasn't sure, but he thought he smelled a metallic and diesel odor rising from the floor of the lift along with the rock dust that enveloped him.

18

Ransom sat in his warm Jeep completing paperwork when out of the corner of his eye he saw a rock fall from the top of the highwall into the muck pile below. He looked up and watched in horror as several more rocks dropped into the mine, then he heard a loud crack, like a muffled roar that reverberated around the pit. He tossed the papers onto the passenger seat, grabbed his hard hat and jumped out.

"Jesus, Freddie, get your men back. The highwall…"

Freddie ignored him as he ran toward the cascading rock and screamed into a walkie-talkie as he waved to his men to drive them back from beneath the highwall. In the chaos, a front-end loader driven by Skel roared past Ransom loudly beeping in reverse, missing him by a foot. Several men who had been working near the highwall came running past him at full speed. One miner looked over his shoulder as he ran and collided into Ransom. They both crashed onto the frozen, rocky mine floor.

"Jesus, Wolfie, get the hell offa me," Ransom screamed.

Wolfie's face was white, covered in sweat and dust. He pushed himself up, uttered some unrecognizable words, and continued running.

"Fall back! Fall back! We're losing the highwall," Freddie yelled.

Rocks cascaded from the cliff as the last man who had been working under it—his eyes wide with fear—ran past them. His hard hat fell off and skittered across the mine floor.

Ransom caught up with Freddie as close as they dared to approach the crumbling highwall and he squinted to see the top of the lift on which Rinati and Mike were last seen.

Freddie put his hand on Ransom's shoulder and shoved him back, "Lyle, we're too damn close, get the hell back!" He grabbed Ransom by the wrist and pulled the inspector away from the cascading rocks toward the line of miners' pickups and SUVs.

Suddenly, the rocks stopped falling and the highwall stopped moving.

Calm.

A weird quiet except for the sound of pebbles trickling through the muck pile on the mine floor.

The men stopped retreating and looked toward the top of the highwall, obscured by a cloud of dust. The sun, directly overhead, cast a dim winter light on the scene. Gray and shadowless.

Then Ransom heard a sound that grew slowly at first. It was unlike any he'd ever heard. It came from the highwall and was like someone prying apart a piano with a giant crowbar. It grew louder and louder. Then, in a sight that would never leave him, the entire rocky face peeled away from the solid rock behind it, in a single sheet. Thousands of tons of rock separated from the highwall as a slab. The sight was biblical.

The men turned and ran as fast as their legs would carry them. Ransom glanced over his shoulder in time to see a large red vehicle fall into the pit along with the highwall and thousands of tons of boulders.

"Holy shit! Oh shit!" Ransom yelled.

He protected his face and head with his arms holding his hard hat close to his head and ran behind someone's SUV where he stood watching the spectacle. Then Freddie pushed him to his knees and he bounced on the frozen ground as the rocks crashed just in front of the vehicle. Boulders smashed into the SUV, and rock missiles the size of pumpkins shattered its windows. A cloud of dust washed over them covering everything with a fine white powder. Men screamed behind him, and he heard a voice calling out to God for forgiveness. In the midst of the barrage, while bent over on his knees, Ransom coughed and vomited. He covered his head and waited as the rocks crashed into the pit and all around him.

The noise died down after several long minutes. Ransom waited until he no longer saw or heard any rocks whizzing past, then staggered to his feet. The highwall had receded by at least a dozen feet in a wide arc. Tons of boulders, some the size of buses, lay at the bottom of the face in a new, massive muck pile. The mining equipment—dozers, front-end loaders, dump trucks— at the bottom of the highwall, that had been used by the miners just minutes earlier, was flattened. Loose rocks crashed into the pile and the sound reverberated around the pit.

Ransom was covered with puke, dust and blood. His head felt like it was going to split from the stress. He wiped the vomit residue from his mouth with his sleeve and spit to clear his mouth. The side of the SUV facing the highwall he'd hid behind was destroyed and piles of rock surrounded the vehicle on three sides. The glass was gone. Only the far side of the SUV, where he had cowered, was mostly free of loose rock. The miners' SUVs and trucks parked in a row, which at the beginning of the shift seemed a safe distance from the highwall, were destroyed.

He turned and saw the miners beginning to get up off their knees and bellies, only to stand motionless, covered in dust and dirt, their mouths agape. In his thirty-odd years of mining, he'd never witnessed a rock fall as devastating. Everyone looked at the highwall.

After a few seconds, Freddie tapped Ransom's arm. "Lyle, you okay?"

Ransom drew some saliva into his mouth to wet it then spit bile and vomit onto the ground. "Yeah, shit," he said softly.

Freddie, his face covered in dust with a trickle of blood coming down his forehead, put the walkie-talkie to his mouth, keyed the mic and realized it was dead. He turned to his men and shouted, "Men, let's wait another couple of minutes, then we've got to attack the pile with whatever equipment is left. We've got to see if Mr. Rinati and that lawyer are in the pile."

Freddie waited a full five minutes until the sound of rock falling had mostly ended. Then he picked up his hard hat, grabbed a pry bar he found lying on the ground, and moved forward. Ransom found a pickaxe nearby and joined him. Ransom could hear front-end loaders at the rear of the mine fire back to life and before long the men—the ones who hadn't fled for a tavern and left mining forever—dug through the rock looking for Rinati and Mike.

19

Nicky worked at a mindless task at her computer, checking the papers that had been filed the day before with the Corporation Bureau of the Pennsylvania Department of State. The only good thing about a task as mindless as this one was that it gave her time to think.

I love Cindy, but everything I do seems to make her angry. I suppose I could love her more, but I don't know how. Why is she always mad at me? Why can't she be more like Mike?

Mike's a good guy. A good friend. A good whatever he is to me...

What is he to me?

Nicky looked up at her co-workers, all women at least thirty years older than she was, who processed the tens of thousands of new corporate filings that came through the office every year. They called themselves the Paper Dolls and gabbed as they worked. Years earlier, the Paper Dolls began wearing bedroom slippers and sweat suits in the office. It looked like a middle-aged slumber party. Since this was a state office, no one complained. Dusty Christmas decorations, put up annually by the Paper Dolls, adorned the space. Nicky wondered if she was destined to become one of them some day. Maybe she already was.

Mr. Krieger, her supervisor, a grossly overweight man with a dark, unkempt beard, had evaluated her work and told her to "pay more attention to detail."

Mindless attention to detail, my life as an oxymoron.

She daydreamed and thought about Cindy and Mike as she scanned the computer filings which arrived in email overnight, double-checking to make sure the spaces that had to be signed were signed and the spaces that had to be notarized were notarized. Someday this would all be done by a robot or someone in India. She wondered when her job would be outsourced.

She paid no attention to the details of the documents as she quickly flipped through the electronic papers. She looked, and did not really read. Just looked to make sure the spaces were properly filled in.

Company name. Check.
Incorporator. Check.
Corporate secretary. Check
Notary seal and signature. Check.
Name of incorporator. Ernesto Rinati.
Rinati. Wait a minute.

She backed up to the space. The guy Mike had talked about.

Nicky scanned through it. The document indicated a new company was being incorporated. Ernesto Rinati was the incorporator and sole shareholder.

This is the guy that Mike was talking about.
His new case.
The one he's visiting today in Somerset.
Weird.

She noticed the name of the new company, *Somerset Land Holdings, Inc*. The form announced the new corporation was being formed to undertake "any and all lawful business" in the Commonwealth of Pennsylvania. A law firm in Philadelphia, Pell, Desrosiers, Cox & Drury, prepared and filed the papers. The new company's lawyer was Sidney Feldman. Nothing about this seemed out of the ordinary, it was a rather typical corporate filing. Still, *Rinati.*

What a coincidence.
Mike's new case has just started up.
Rinati's forming a new corporation.

She wondered how many times she'd seen papers filed by Rinati and didn't even pay attention.

She didn't know *why* this might be suspicious, or even if it *was* suspicious. Something about the filing made her scrutinize it.

Nicky cast an eye over the Paper Dolls as they looked at their paper forms and computer filings and chattered endlessly. They were not paying any attention to her.

Maybe...

She thought for a moment. The state's Right-to-Know Law was jokingly referred to as the 'Right-*Not*-to-Know Law.' Getting your hands on a paper like this could be done by anyone; after all, it was a public form filed with the Commonwealth, but that could take weeks or a month before you had your approval. She looked for Mr. Krieger. He was on the phone in his office behind a glass wall.

She hit print and waited while the darn printer warmed up. She watched and could hear it start to work. The old machine whirred and clunked. Finally, papers excreted into a bin. She glanced up and the Paper Dolls were still gabbing to each other. She pulled a blank envelope out of her desk, folded the papers, and jammed them into it. Her backpack was in the well of her desk. She bent over on her hands and knees, jerked it out, and unzipped it. As she shoved the envelope inside and began backing out from under her desk, she bumped into someone.

Mr. Krieger.

He was just inches from her.

His hands nearly touched her butt, and his fat hips were a hairbreadth from her body.

"Nicky! What are you doing?" Krieger's breath was a mixture of stale coffee and onions.

Nicky was stuck in the narrow space between her desk and Krieger. He was so close that Nicky could smell his scent, a mixture of sweat, English Leather and dirty beard. He wore a frayed white shirt and a spotted blue necktie.

"You startled me," she said as she side-stepped away from him. "I was just, just paying my car loan. I didn't take a break this morning so when I had a few minutes I wrote the check." She held up the blank envelope and waved it at him as proof, then jammed it into her backpack and zipped it shut.

He glanced at the envelope in her hands and, not for the first time, gazed down the neck of her blouse. Instinctively, Nicky held her hand across her neck. She could feel the flush rise on her cheeks.

"Okay, get back to work." He smirked at her.

She wasn't sure if anything she had done was improper. After all, these forms were public records. Nevertheless, her heart pounded a mile a minute. She had no idea if the papers meant anything. She had seen people form literally dozens of inter-related corporations in a single day. One of the Paper Dolls told her that this didn't necessarily mean anything improper and in the corporate world, in which taxes and liabilities were minimized as much as legally possible, it was perfectly legal. It was even expected.

Still, *Rinati.*
Mike's Rinati.

20

"Stay back men, let's make sure the highwall is done falling. I don't want anybody killed. Is everybody here?"

Freddie did a quick head count. He counted eight of his ten-man crew, but he'd seen two turn tail and head up the haul road when the wall began to fall. Probably at a bar by now, half drunk.

Skel pointed toward the debris pile, the hockey-stick shaped scar on his cheek reddening with his excitement. "Oh shit, I think that's Mr. Rinati's car."

Sure enough, Freddie glimpsed a small bit of red metal under tons of boulders and stone.

"Let's get some loaders in there, get me them backhoes. We've got to pull those guys from the car."

Wolfie, his beard covered in dirt and dust from the landslide, and another miner jumped into the front-end loaders that weren't crushed in the rockslide and throttled them up, quickly approaching the debris pile. The loaders had a limited ability to dig out large boulders as they were designed to remove smaller stone that had been crushed, set aside, or placed into their buckets.

Several miners climbed on top of the wreckage and started pulling smaller rocks off with their hands, tossing them into the loaders' buckets or off the side of the pile. The loaders dug into the rocks as best they could, and miners steered two backhoe shovels into the pile to pick up and move the bigger pieces. The machines dug into the muck pile, quickly turned, then dumped the stone out of their buckets, turning back to take another bite into the pile. The sound was an angry mix of heavy equipment, back-up beepers, and yelling men.

Freddie raised his voice over the din. "Hard hats, everyone, and stay back from the face. I don't need anyone else hurt."

The men, including Ransom and Freddie, continued working with a mostly silent determination, picking up smaller rocks and throwing them to the side to get to the wreckage. The men groaned under the weight of the rocks and the stones trickling to the ground.

"Freddie, is this a rescue or an extraction?" Ransom said to the foreman. The sweat dripped down his face, even though the temperature was in the thirties. He lifted stones that weighed fifty pounds or more. All of the men hoisted stone after stone, tossing them to the side so they could get to the red Cadillac.

"Shit. If they were in that car, they fell almost two hundred feet and they've got boulders weighing tons on top of them," Freddie said, working as he spoke. The sweat dripped off his mostly bald head, and his collar and shirt were soaked beneath his Carhartt parka. "I suppose we'll find out soon enough."

The roar of the backhoe shovels and front-end loaders was intense and close, accompanied by the constant noise of the backup beepers as the machines dumped their loads. The men focused on getting to the Cadillac while there was still a chance those inside were alive.

"There it is, the roof," Freddie shouted as they cleared the rocks from the vehicle. The men started pulling rock from its sides hoping to uncover the doors or a window.

"There's no way they made it," Ransom muttered to Freddie. The foreman didn't say a word but nodded in agreement.

"What the fuck is going on?" a man shouted from the rear of the work site.

Freddie and Ransom were the first to notice Rinati and Mike standing next to the Cadillac, which idled smoothly behind the excavation. Freddie looked at the wreckage under the rocks and then at the Caddy, covered in mud and dust but otherwise unharmed, next to the wrecked SUVs and trucks. He leaned against the pry bar, put a hand to his mouth, and whistled loudly.

The men slowly stopped working and turned, seeing their boss and the lawyer.

"Jesus, Ernie, where the hell did you come from?" Freddie asked, wiping his forehead with his wrist.

"Well, that little slip wiped out the back haul road so we had to drive on the old logging trail through the woods. We came out the back side of the mine right onto the township road. I tried calling you on the sat phone, but all I got was static. You didn't think I was in that piece of shit crusher over there, did you?" he said, pointing toward the wreckage, buried under the rock that the men had been unearthing. He smiled broadly, his yellow teeth showing.

"Yeah, well, in fact we did."

***

Mike looked from the wreckage to Rinati who laughed and said, "You see Attorney, I told you I'd teach you a thing or two about minin'." He winked at Mike.

Some of the miners sat down on the rocks, exhausted, and some laid back onto the frigid stony ground, the anguish of the previous thirty minutes having drained them fully.

Mike knew he'd learned something that morning. He hadn't yet figured out what.

21

Mike shook hands with Freddie and Rinati. Then he and Ransom got back into Ransom's Jeep and drove out of the mine without saying a word. A fury was building inside Mike.

Finally, Ransom said, "Look, no one was injured, praise the Lord. That was quite a *slip*, and scary as all get out, but no one was hurt."

"I could have been killed. I don't know how I made it to Rinati's car. I'm so angry right now. I can hardly talk. That was no slip. It was a full-blown landslide. Maybe a detonation. He said the boreholes weren't loaded with ANFO. But I smelled something funny. More than rock. Something else. Metallic. Diesel. Sour. Was that ANFO?"

"Well, I checked with Freddie and he said that them boreholes weren't going to be loaded with ANFO until tomorrow. It must have been rock is all. Maybe residue from another detonation."

Mike shook his head angrily. "You're going to write that up, shut down the operation, right? You should call in MSHA. I mean that landslide nearly killed Rinati and me, not to mention you guys on the ground. There must have been a dozen violations of the Surface Mining Act and MSHA safety provisions, I'm sure. I can look it up."

Ransom glanced at him. "That was just an accident, not the kind of thing anyone would write up. We don't really regulate safety, that's more the Feds, MSHA. I say we leave it to them to sort out."

"What?" Mike said loudly. "I was nearly killed and that's the best you can do? Seriously?"

"I just don't see any DEP *mining* violations. It was a *safety* condition, that's possible, but a violation? It was an accident. I just don't see it."

"If you don't write it up, I'll report you myself to the secretary and get you fired so fast it'll make your head spin."

Ransom's face reddened and he looked at the lawyer who glared back at him. "Sure, I'll write it up. Just give me a day or two."

Minutes passed as they drove the back roads of Somerset County. "So, what is it? I can drop you at your hotel or you can continue with me today. It's up to you."

Mike thought for a minute, *if I don't do this now, I may not get a chance to see any other sites out here until spring.*

"I'll need to wash my face and take a leak. But we can continue."

"Okay, then it's supper time. All that work's made me hungry." Ransom looked at Mike and flicked his eyebrows up and down smiling. "Look, up ahead, we're in Normalville. We're close to the county line of Somerset, Fayette and Westmoreland. Three of us inspectors get together here at the Crossroads Bar and Grill every day for lunch when we can. Looks like you made us late."

Ransom grinned.

Mike shook his head.

An assortment of pickup trucks and two white DEP SUVs sat in front of the tavern. Ransom pulled his Jeep alongside the others and the men got out.

The bar was divided into two sections, a typical country bar with wood paneling and mounted deer heads on one side of the door, and a plain looking, linoleum and vinyl clad restaurant on the other. At a few minutes after noon, it was fairly full but Ransom spotted the other two DEP inspectors sitting in a booth and waved. Mike and Ransom approached, and Ransom sat down next to one. He pointed at Mike and said, "This here's Mike Jacobs, one of our lawyers, from Harrisburg. That's Janey Hudson, she inspects in Westmoreland County, and over there is Wes Miller, Fayette County."

Mike reached out his hand. "Hi, I'm Mike."

Janey looked to be in her mid-twenties and was wearing a plaid shirt and a dark red down vest. No makeup. She had a short blond ponytail held back with a band. She shook Mike's hand.

"I heard you boys had a little excitement over at the Shoemaker Mine today," Wes said as they shook hands.

"Just a little," Mike replied. "News travels fast."

"I'm going to find the men's room. I'll be back in a minute," Mike said looking around.

As he washed his face, Mike doubted that Ransom was qualified to be a mine inspector. The man knew mining but seemed to disregard basic safety concepts, not to mention the law. He wondered how someone with so callous a regard for safety and mining regulations could make it as a DEP inspector. He worried that he would have to rely on Ransom in the appeal. Usually, he developed a close relationship with the field men who were his witnesses. He was certain that, at best, he would keep Ransom at arm's length.

By the time Mike returned to the table, the inspectors were laughing heartily. Ransom's face was red from laughter and Wes had tears running down his face. Janey had a slight smile pasted to her face.

"Here's another, here's another," Ransom said, stifling his laughter. "Why does San Francisco have so many faggots and New York so many coloreds?" Ransom paused and looked at them. When he heard no response, he said loudly, "San Francisco had first choice!"

Wes burst out laughing hysterically. "Jesus, Lyle, how do you know so many jokes? I don't think I ever laugh as hard at the TV."

He reached across the table and with his fist smacked Ransom in the shoulder.

Ransom looked up at Mike. "Hey there Mike, it's about time. Were you getting friendly with yourself in there? The waitress's been by twice."

Mike sat down and opened the menu. Nothing appealed to him and when the waitress returned, he ordered a Diet Coke and tuna salad sandwich.

"So Mike, it must be a real hoot traveling all over Somerset County with Lyle, here. I'll bet you he just keeps you in stitches the whole time," Wes said.

"Stitches. Casts. Neck Braces. Whatever." Mike said.

There was an awkward pause, and finally Ransom said, "Well, Mike here is Jewish so I thought, seeing as how he's Jewish and it's Christmas time, I'd tell a story about Christmas time. Did you ever hear about the Jewish Santy Claus?" Ransom asked as he looked at each of them. Wes held his breath getting ready to laugh. Mike glanced at Janey and saw she was not making eye contact with Ransom. Instead, she looked at the table picking at some residue that was stuck to the linoleum. She looked unhappy.

"He came down the chimney and said, 'Hey boys and girls, would you like to *buy* some Christmas presents?'" Ransom said loudly and laughed as he finished.

Wes giggled. "Well shoot, that's just a nice Santy Claus story."

Mike was boiling inside. He looked at Ransom and said, "Lyle, I don't find any of this funny. In fact, I think what I've heard has been pretty offensive to me and a lot of people I know. I'd prefer it if you didn't tell any more of them while I'm around."

The smile fled Ransom's face and Wes quickly looked back and forth between the two men.

Ransom seemed to think for a moment, then smiled again and said, "I know what the problem is, I think we need something that we can all laugh at. Here you go," he said without hesitation. "A Jewish guy, an Indian guy, and an Irish guy were traveling together. As it got dark, they came to a farmhouse and asked if they could have a room for the night. The farmer told them that he only had two beds but he could make the third man comfortable in the barn. So the three guys drew straws and the Jewish guy had to sleep in the barn."

Ransom looked at each of his three listeners. Mike glared and shook his head but said nothing, so Ransom continued. "A few minutes later there was a knock at the door and the farmer opened it and there was the Jewish guy. He said, I'm sorry, I can't sleep in there since there's a pig in the barn and Jews can't sleep in the same room as a pig. Next, the Indian fellah went out to the barn. A few minutes later, there was a knock at the door and the farmer opened it and there stood the Indian fellah. He said that his religion would not allow him to sleep in the same place as a cow so he couldn't stay in the barn either."

The smile on Ransom's face grew wide showing all of his teeth and the large gap between his upper incisors. "Finally, the Irishman was sent out to sleep in the barn. A few minutes later, there was another knock at the door. When the farmer opened it, there was the pig and the cow!"

Ransom and Wes burst out laughing. Wes laughed so hard that he leaned forward on the table, nearly knocking over his water. Mike looked at Janey who, like him, wasn't laughing. After a few moments, Ransom looked at Mike and Janey and said, "Come on Mike, that was an Irish joke. Shit, I'm half Irish, I should be able to tell that joke. You know, like a black guy telling a colored joke. Right?"

Mike's eyes narrowed. "Tell you what Lyle, this has been a rather trying day already and I'm not up for any jokes." At that moment the waitress arrived with their food and they finished their lunch quietly discussing their respective mining responsibilities. Janey did most of the talking.

Mike would have loved to take Janey aside and find out what it was like to be a woman in the mining world. He couldn't imagine.

22

Ransom turned the Jeep onto a small rutted lane. It was now just after two o'clock and they were driving back toward Somerset. Mike noticed a derelict sign by the side of the dirt road, full of bullet holes, covered with dirt and surrounded by weeds. The part of the sign that had not yet collapsed read, *Summit Coal Co.–Mine No. 4.*

"Well, you wanted to see an abandoned job. Here we are," Ransom said as they bounced along the rutted and worn haul road.

"How long has this mine been abandoned?" Mike said.

"About fifteen years. These boys started up during the last coal boom and didn't have the resources to finish the job when the coal ran out. Also, they weren't the best mine operators. Not very experienced running a company, they thought they could just go for the coal and make a pile of money. They're the kind who give the industry a bad name. To make matters worse, the coal turned out to be bad quality—high sulfur—and there wasn't nearly as much of it as they expected. When they quit, they left a good bit of highwall and a really bad acid discharge." Ransom looked at Mike then added, "And if you're wondering, someone else was the inspector, not me."

Ransom and Mike slowly drove along the washed-out trail onto an area that had been scraped flat and parked about fifty feet from the top of the highwall.

"Don't get too close to the highwall here," Ransom said as they got out of the Jeep. "This one ain't stable and I've seen rockslides offa this highwall."

Thinking about the misadventure from earlier in the day, Mike approached only as close as Ransom. He stayed away from the man, thinking that it would only take a second for Ransom to push Mike over the cliff.

From Mike's vantage point, about twenty feet from the lip of the highwall, he could see the cut was over one hundred feet deep and easily five hundred feet long. The entire mine was open and it appeared no reclamation had been undertaken. Inside the open cut, large boulders and piles of mine spoil littered the ground. Water, bright orange from iron sulfate pollution, ponded in about one third of the floor, following a low point to where it exited the mine and entered a small stream. The skeleton of a bulldozer that had been scavenged for parts was partly submerged in the water.

Garbage was piled up in the bottom of the mine. It looked as though someone had dumped truckloads of refuse from the top of the highwall along with an assortment of abandoned appliances and tires. Some vegetation managed to live in the bottom of the cut, but nothing looked healthy or sustainable.

Huge spoil piles littered the area around the top of the strip mine. Here and there were wrecked pieces of equipment and more piles of trash. Nothing looked remotely like it was usable. Mike couldn't see any stockpiled topsoil. The entire area looked like a huge garbage dump.

"Whatever happened to these guys?" Mike asked.

"Well, the department ordered them to do reclamation, but they said they didn't have any money. So our lawyers back then, hit them with a court order and a huge civil penalty too. Then they went bankrupt and that was all she wrote. We forfeited their reclamation bonds but the bonds were so small that the department couldn't pay to do any reclamation. A few years ago, *after* I became the inspector, *I* applied to the state's Abandoned Mine Lands Fund for them to do the reclamation and got this mine on the list to be reclaimed by the state. Unfortunately, there's a pretty long list of abandoned mines, so here it sits."

For many minutes, the men said nothing and gazed into the chasm. Mike pulled out his camera and snapped a few shots.

Ransom ventured a bit closer to the edge of the highwall, as did Mike. While they were looking into the pit, Mike bent down and picked up several pebbles. He took the largest one and tossed it over the edge of the highwall and listened until he heard it hit the pit floor several seconds later.

Mike took another stone and aimed for a pool of orange water. Just as he was tossing the stone into the pit, Ransom turned and walked into its path. He jerked his hands up to cover his face and the rock bounced off his arm. A gold band on his wrist glinted in the pale, late afternoon light and caught Mike's eye.

"Crap." Mike said. "Sorry about that, Lyle. I was just chucking that stone down into the pit. You walked right into it."

As he brushed the dust off his wrist, Ransom could see Mike was looking at his watch. Mike continued looking at it as Ransom straightened his jacket.

"Honest mistake. Don't worry about it." Ransom said smiling uncomfortably.

The two men stood in silence. Both looked at Ransom's watch. After a long pause, Ransom lifted his arm again and displayed his watch for Mike. "How do you like that? A solid gold Rolex watch." The watch glinted in the pale sunlight.

Mike looked at him, trying not to show any expression.

"You knew I worked for Mr. Rinati? Yeah, for ten years until I had the chance to come work for the state as a mine inspector. I thought he'd be mad at me for leaving, but he gave me a real nice retirement party, steak dinner and all. This was the present I got from Rhino Mining at the dinner for all my years of service. Pretty nice, huh?"

Mike looked at the watch and then at Ransom. "Beautiful. Uh, you worked for Rinati?"

"Sure, a lot of the inspectors worked for industry, not just Rinati—Wes Miller, Trevor Buck, Ty Barnes, John Hicks. Some of the younger ones, like Janey, they're college kids and never worked a day in a mine. Most of the older guys though worked for different coal companies."

Ransom spent a moment checking the crystal on his Rolex and brushed off some rock dust that remained on his sleeve.

Then he and Mike walked back to the Jeep and in silence drove back to the motel, arriving as it was getting dark.

"Well Mike, I hope you got what you wanted out of the tour. You let me know when we have to get ready for that trial."

Mike said nothing.

"Don't worry about me Mike, we all work for DEP now. I know who my boss is."

"Sure, thanks. Thanks for the tour," Mike said.

The men shook hands and Mike watched as Ransom drove away.

In a day that was chock full of memorable incidents, all he could think about was Ransom's gold Rolex watch.

23

Mike showered and changed into his blue suit. He had to force himself to shift mental gears. As he drove to Miranda Clymer's office, he thought about the opportunity that she had given him to meet her clients and avoid the necessity for depositions. Since he was not permitted to take depositions, this meeting probably would be his only opportunity to assess the effectiveness of her witnesses on the witness stand.

It would also be his first meeting with Miranda—he avoided thinking of her as his adversary—and they would be able to begin discussions on handling the unusual procedural posture of the case. He wanted to get a read on her, since he was hoping she'd put up a significant fight against Feldman. Roger would like the economy of that arrangement. Mike anticipated the meeting would be a meet and greet, perhaps accompanied by Christmas cookies and punch.

In the early winter darkness, he followed Miranda's directions to downtown Somerset and found the courthouse quickly enough. Then, a few turns later, he made his way to West Church Street driving slowly past a collection of old frame houses, all decorated for Christmas. A number of the houses in the neighborhood had been converted into businesses—a hairdresser, nail salon, insurance office—although it looked as though many were still inhabited by families. He found the one that had been converted into a law office at the corner of Church and Edgewood.

Miranda's office was a plain, wood frame house from the 1920s, but was painted a myriad of gaudy colors, as though it was on Postcard Row in San Francisco. Out front, a small wooden sign, green, red, yellow and blue, with gold lettering, simply said, *Law Office of Miranda Clymer*. A small parking area in front was already full so he parked on the street.

Mike paused at the front door, not sure whether he should knock or just walk in. At that moment, however, the door opened and an attractive young woman with short, jet-black hair and black mascara wearing a black parka looked at him.

"Are you here to see Miranda?" she asked.

"Yes, I'm Mike Jacobs. I think she's expecting me."

Looking at him with dark brown eyes, she eyed him warily, but held the door and said, "Go on in, the others are already here. I'm just leaving."

Mike walked in and without further introduction, the young woman whom he assumed was the secretary, left. He could hear voices coming from what must have once been the living room so he looked in and surveyed the odd collection of furniture on which sat an odd collection of people. They stopped talking when they saw him. Mike saw a woman, middle aged, with curly grey hair and a slacks outfit, whom he assumed was Miranda Clymer.

"I'm Mike… Mike Jacobs. Is Miranda, Ms. Clymer, here?" he said to the woman.

No one said a word as Mike looked at the people in the room wondering which woman was his opponent or colleague, he hadn't yet decided which.

"Mr. Jacobs? I'm Miranda." He jumped slightly and turned around.

"I'm Mike Jacobs, Mike," he said as he turned.

Mike extended his hand toward the woman with long blond hair, wide full lips, and ice blue eyes. She wore a scoop-neck top, which revealed a substantial amount of her ample breasts. Mike was taken aback. She was the kind of woman who turned heads, not a dowdy matron.

Rarely did he think of women who were close to his age as "women." Typically, he thought of his contemporaries as "girls." Without any doubt, Miranda, who was more than ten years his senior, was a *woman,* and in a flash Mike understood the difference between a woman and a girl. Her two-handed handshake was warm, firm and overly long.

Miranda wore a green wool suit, which offset her pale blond hair held back by a wide barrette. He never would have called her hairstyle a ponytail, it was something different, grown up. As they shook hands, Mike realized that she was eye to eye with him. He was average height, about five-foot-ten, and had he dared to lower his eyes and look, he would have noticed that below her narrow waist and attractive hips, she was wearing flats.

Mike immediately found himself both attracted to and intimidated by her.

"Why don't you throw your coat on the rack and I'll introduce you around." She smiled and continued holding his hand.

Miranda waited for him and, as he hung up his coat, she checked him out from top to bottom.

As they walked into the room together, Miranda said, "everyone, I'd like you to meet the Honorable Michael Jacobs, Assistant Counsel with the Pennsylvania Department of Environmental Protection. He's come all the way from Harrisburg to help us overturn that awful permit."

24

Mike gulped. Miranda smiled warmly and swept her hand across the room. "All of these people live on Forest Lane and they've been awaiting their savior from DEP," she said. "You."

"Here are Don and Lily Roberts." She pointed to the couple sitting closest to Mike. "Lily is a bookkeeper at one of our local banks, the Bank of Oxford. Don's retired."

Don Roberts was totally bald with black, caterpillar-like eyebrows. Lily Roberts had grey curly hair. There was something familiar about her, but Mike couldn't put his finger on what it was. Mike guessed that they were in their early sixties and both wore the same hangdog expression of people with troubles bearing down on them. He held out his hand and shook theirs. As Mike shook Mrs. Roberts' hand, it finally occurred to him that she was the woman he had seen sitting on the rock in the woods early that morning. He held his tongue.

"Next are Andrea and Tom McCarthy," Miranda said pointing to the people sitting farthest from Mike. "Andrea McCarthy works for Somerset Memorial Hospital and Tom manages the mini-market at the Somerset turnpike rest stop." Together, the McCarthys may have weighed one hundred pounds. They both wore heavy woolen sweaters and appeared to be the youngest neighbors, probably in their fifties. Rather than lean over the table, though, Mike waved awkwardly in their direction.

"That's Bob and Roberta Willis." He wore a Post Office uniform and she a long-sleeved blouse. Both were older and both looked tired and worn, like their clothes.

"Finally, against the wall, is Norman Post," she said, pointing to a heavy older man sitting in a worn easy chair. Mike shook his soft hand.

So, these are the appellants. They seem pretty nice. This should be an easy meeting.

Mike was still standing as Miranda took a seat across from Norman, leaving Mike the open seat at the head of the table. He wondered which of the people lived in the various houses along the dirt road. He was pretty sure that the fat older guy, Norman Post, was the man who lived in the broken-down house.

There was a long silence. Mike thought he might say something clever but rejected, *I'm from Harrisburg and I'm here to help you.* His chair, like the others around the table, was a wooden Windsor back chair, uncomfortable and creaky. Mike fidgeted the moment he sat down. Finally, Miranda broke the silence.

"Mr. Jacobs, I've explained to the neighbors that after we filed our appeal from the issuance of the permit, Rhino also filed an appeal. I told them the judge consolidated the cases so now we have one big case with Rhino, the neighbors, and DEP. I told them how the Pennsylvania Constitution guarantees them a right to a healthy environment, clean water and all of that stuff. I guess we've all had some confusion, though, about which side you're on. Maybe you can help us out? You're from the Commonwealth of Pennsylvania, so you're on our side, the citizens' and environmental side, right, Mr. Jacobs?"

Miranda was smiling, but her blue eyes were hard. Then she leaned back in her chair and quickly winked at him.

He answered slowly, "Mike, please call me Mike." He paused. "Well, that's right, technically, the department is opposed to Rhino's appeal from the permit conditions. That means if the case were just Rhino versus DEP, we'd fight Rhino as hard as we could to keep in the strong, environmentally-protective permit conditions that Rhino is trying to overturn. We'd do everything we could to ensure the permit was not modified or overturned by the EHB. At the same time, when you filed your appeal, the department found itself on the other side of your clients—I mean you—who are fighting the permit we issued." Mike gestured toward the people in the room. As he moved his hand, his chair creaked, as if emphasizing his point.

"It's not like we're against you. We're really all on the same side, protecting the environment. But when you filed your appeal, we found ourselves on the opposite side from you. That means, and this is ironic I know, that means that since you're trying to overturn the permit, we have to fight to keep the permit in place. So technically, we're opposed to you. We're also opposed to Rhino Mining. It's a bit confusing."

"I don't get it, Mr. Jacobs, I'm having trouble understanding you. Whose side are you on?" said Mr. Post. Post had watery gray eyes surrounded by wrinkled eyelids, a puffy pink face and almost no discernible beard. His hair was short, almost bald. He wheezed asthmatically as he spoke.

"Well," Mike said, clearing his throat, "DEP is kind of in the middle. In a case like this it means that you fight it out, with Rhino and Rhino fights it out with you. The department, not me personally you understand but the department, tries to stay in the middle. Basically, we get out of the way and let you both fight it out. It's not my call, mind you I'd handle this differently, but at the end of the day, you citizens are fighting it out with Rhino and Rhino is fighting it out with you."

"Wait a minute young man, do you mean to say the department with all of its millions of dollars and thousands of employees is going to make a few older folks and retirees fight with a big company like Rhino and all you're going to do is watch?" Lily Roberts said, her permed curls shaking and her voice shrill.

Miranda took over, leaned forward and tapped a perfectly manicured finger on the table. She narrowed her blue eyes and said, "That can't *possibly* be right, *Michael*. After all, you issued the permit and Rhino is fighting it. Why shouldn't you be fighting with Rhino over that? Also, I thought the department was supposed to *protect* the environment. The Pennsylvania Constitution says that. You mean to say that you're going to make *me*, and by that I mean the citizens, do *your* job?"

"No, of course not." Mike was in a turmoil.

He *wanted* to tell the citizens that he would be their champion. In his core that was what he'd do.

Mike wanted to ride up and rescue them, both from Rhino and from their stunning—and probably incompetent—lawyer.

Roger's words kept repeating themselves in his head, *"Hey Bud, you're only defending the integrity of the department."*

"I don't get it," said Tom McCarthy, his voice even. As he spoke, the thin skin on his face was pulled tight, as though his skull might explode through the sinew and muscle at any moment. "We pay our taxes. That Inspector Stevens, he was a good man. I read his report and he was a straight shooter, trying to keep Rhino from minin' near our homes. No one listened to him, but look what they did to the poor man. That new inspector, Lyle Ransom, he's in bed with Rhino—as crooked as they come—and he's the guy who's supposed to be looking out for us now. I talked with him and he's as bad as Rhino. We spent some time investigating him and I don't think there's a mining operation in Somerset County that he didn't think was a good idea. I mean, the man *worked* for Rhino. He's supposed to protect us. What about you, Mr. Jacobs? We can't trust Lyle but I'm wondering if we can trust you? Isn't it your job to protect the environment, the citizens?"

"Well, yes, it is. But our resources are limited, we have to pick and choose our battles…" Mike's voice was barely audible over the growing commotion in the room.

"*Your* resources are limited? What about *us*? Most of us have a limited income," said Lily Roberts. Her legs crossed and re-crossed like a pretzel. "We don't have enough money to fight this. Ms. Clymer told us that we'll need twenty, maybe twenty-five thousand dollars to fight Rhino. Probably more. We have to pay her fees, hire a mining engineer, and there are all those court costs. We really expected DEP to step up and protect us."

Andrea McCarthy, all ninety pounds of her, leaned forward in her chair. Her legs intertwined like a vine running up a trellis. "Mr. Jacobs, there's another thing, coal, it's so dirty. Look at the streams around here. They're running black from coal silt or orange from acid from the mines. My grandpa and daddy both worked in the mines, deep mines, and my grandpa died young from the black lung. I remember my daddy coming home after twelve hours in the mine, coughing up black. It was in his lungs and he died too, suffocated to death from working in the mines. That same coal dust is in the air. What's it doing to us? How's it affecting the air? Coal is a major cause of climate change. Why would we let that go on? We need to stop it and stop it here."

"Nobody gives a shit," growled Norman Post in a voice that sounded like he hadn't cleared his throat in days. As he talked, his thick neck wobbled and he waved a hand in the air. "It's like I told all of yins' months ago, we're gonna get screwed. We all ought to just pack up and move now before there's a giant hole in our front yards and our wells are dry. Like I said earlier, that Rinati wants to give us shit for our houses. Rhino doesn't give a shit. Lyle doesn't give a shit. DEP doesn't give a shit. And it looks like young Mr. Jacobs here doesn't give a shit." When he finished speaking, he sat back in the easy chair which seemed to bend under his weight.

Mike swallowed hard. He was really angry at being ambushed by Miranda and her clients. This was no 'meet and greet.' Another part of him agreed with what they were saying and wanted to help them. "Don't get me wrong," Mike replied. "I didn't say the department would do nothing. I just said we won't be taking the lead. I'm sure Miranda, Ms. Clymer, is fully capable of representing you. I'll be taking depositions and examining witnesses at the trial. You can be sure I'll be helping out."

"Helping out?" Post raised his voice. "You gotta be kidding me. You're a full-time environmental lawyer and Miranda is just a local gal. DEP has, what, three thousand employees and all you can do is help out?"

Forty-five minutes later, they had progressed no further. Mike's shirt stuck to his sweating back, even though the conference room was cool and drafty. Finally, Miranda put an end to the meeting.

"Okay, why don't we call it a night? It's nearly past dinner time. I'll talk with Michael and we'll work something out. I'll give you all a call in a couple of days."

The neighbors got up and several walked out of the room without looking at Mike. Robert Willis, the postman, approached him and said, "Young man, I hope you'll do what's right."

Mike met his gaze and replied, "You have my word, I'll do the best I can."

"I hope so," Robert said and he patted Mike on the shoulder.

As the neighbors left, still loudly talking on the front porch, Miranda shut the door behind them and returned to the conference room. "Welcome to Somerset. You look like you could use a drink."

25

Twenty minutes later, Mike slid into a booth across from Miranda at a steak house on the outskirts of Somerset. The place had red, faux leather seats and wood paneling. A fire smoldered in the fireplace beneath two authentic Pennsylvania long rifles, The walls were covered with color prints of a young George Washington in a British uniform as he might have looked marching through Somerset County in 1754, during the French and Indian War.

Miranda ordered a glass of red wine and Mike a Yuengling Lager. He spent a couple of minutes pretending to look at the menu, when in reality he was trying to quell the anger that welled in him. He was angry with Miranda. He felt like he'd been set up. She should have managed her clients' expectations. The neighbors wanted much more from him than was reasonable to expect. Hell, she wanted much more from him than any opposing counsel ought to expect. He read the list of appetizers over and over. Eventually, the waiter took their orders and they could no longer avoid the issue.

"I have to tell you I felt set up. This was supposed to be a meeting to meet your clients so I could assess them as witnesses, not a chance for them to tell me all of their unreasonable demands about the mining permit and this case. I have to remind you, you're their lawyer, not me." Mike turned his beer bottle as he talked.

"I'm so sorry." Miranda reached out and patted his hand. Hers was warm and she stroked his as she talked. Mike was surprised that she had touched him this way but he didn't pull back. "The meeting got out of hand. I didn't plan for it to go this way, but these people are really passionate about all of this. This is their homes we're talking about." She took her hand away. "I want to make sure we can work together as colleagues, not adversaries."

Mike tried to read her face. Her expression was entirely sincere. She seemed to be serious about what she was saying and Mike *wanted* to believe her.

"I think we need to change the subject a bit, don't you?" Miranda said. When Mike didn't protest she appeared to think for a moment then said, "Are you originally from Harrisburg?"

"No, I'm from Old Hills, near Wilkes-Barre. I moved to Harrisburg three years ago when DEP offered me a job. How about you? Are you from Somerset?"

"Not Somerset, Holbrook. That's a *smaller* town about fifteen miles due south of here, not far from the Mason-Dixon Line. When I grew up, Somerset was the big city. It's hard to believe, I know." She laughed.

Mike was mesmerized. Miranda could be utterly devious one moment, then sincere and warm, even funny, the next. Plus, she had movie actress looks. Scarlett Johansson came to mind. Something about this woman grabbed Mike by the throat.

"So, did you always want to be an environmental lawyer? I mean, I've been practicing for a few years and you're the first one I've ever met…in the flesh," she said. Her eyes held his gaze.

The way she uttered the words *in the flesh* transfixed him.

"No, believe it or not, at one time I thought I wanted to become a rabbi. That's kind of the family business, my brother, he's much older than me, has a pulpit in Chicago."

"A rabbi?" Miranda paused and surveyed his face, "I hope you don't mind me saying this, but now that you mention it, you *do* look Jewish. I don't mean that in a negative way, it's just a fact. You have curly brown hair, intense brown eyes and a dark sultry look," Miranda said as she twisted her head to examine his face.

Mike was certain he was blushing and tried to maintain a straight face as Miranda gave him a hard look over. She was what, German? WASP? He didn't know and at that moment didn't have the guts to ask.

"So, Mr. Jacobs, almost a rabbi, are you married? Engaged?"

Mike wasn't sure if her question flowed from the earlier biographical conversation or if Miranda was determining whether he was available.

"Not married, not engaged." He said. "Unfortunately, not even a girlfriend currently."

"How about you?" Mike asked. His mind raced. He realized that if all she was doing was filling in blanks in his resume, his question would sound like a potential romantic interest.

"Wow, you move fast," Miranda said laughing lightly and sitting back in the booth. Mike tried not to flinch and continued smiling. "Still single. I suppose I've had too good a time looking for Mr. Right."

Mike would spend the rest of the evening trying to figure out the meaning of her words. Fortunately, at that moment, their food arrived.

Miranda took her knife and stabbed at the meat, cutting deeply into her steak. She'd asked for a steak done Pittsburgh rare and the blood and juice dripped onto her plate.

"So Michael, tell me why it is that you and the department aren't going to vigorously defend the little citizens and the environment from the greedy, rapacious mining company?" The blood from her steak coated her teeth.

"I think I detect a bit of sarcasm in that question," he replied.

"Not a sarcastic question as much as a pointed one. You're an environmental lawyer. You may have started life as a rabbinical student, but at some point, protecting the environment meant something to you. Isn't that why you became an environmental lawyer?"

"Well, what about you? Why did you become a lawyer?" Mike hoped he had said enough to turn the conversation away from him.

"Well, I majored in English lit at college and had no desire to go into education and spend my life teaching classics to a bunch of snotty brats. After that, the law seemed like a good idea. I got my law degree at Duquesne and had the opportunity to move to the big city," she said waving her knife around. "Somerset." She laughed as she said it.

"So, being a lawyer is nothing more than a way of earning a living?" Mike said.

"It's a means to an end. I like Somerset well enough. It's comfortable and homey. It seduces you. Being a lawyer is a job, it pays decently, and my commute is up and down a flight of stairs. I'm sure you've checked me out and you know that I don't do any litigation. Most of my practice is transactional, business deals and real estate, so I don't have the ridiculous hours that litigators do. But when a case like this comes in the door, it helps to pay the bills. Plus," she paused and leaned in slightly, her breasts fully on display resting on the table top, and said, "I get to meet some interesting men."

Mike shifted in his seat. "I'll bet you say that to all the guys," Mike parried. "So, is this it for you? I mean Somerset."

"Honestly? I've gotten tired of it. I don't see myself being here for the rest of my life." Miranda shrugged. "I could see myself in the big city, a real city, some day."

She sniffed her wine and appeared to collect her thoughts. "So, really, I have to imagine a guy like you would want to help out the little citizens. Don't disappoint me, Michael. I'm already fantasizing about you leading the charge against Rhino."

"Honestly? I'm really stuck. I have direct orders from my boss to take a backseat to you."

"*Oh Michael*, what will I have to do to convince you of the error of your ways? You don't seem to be buying my oral argument." Miranda leaned forward and smiled at him. As she did, she patted his hand as though she were joking, then stroked it softly with her manicured fingertips, just for a moment, then slid her hand away.

"Really, I can work with you," Mike replied, trying to maintain his composure. His mind was overloaded from the myriad signals he was receiving from this woman.

"Well, maybe you'll teach me what it is I have to do. I'd love to learn new techniques, *litigation* techniques, from you." She talked in a low voice, almost a whisper.

Mike was going nuts trying to decide what was a direct come-on, a double entendre, or just a joke. He had lost track.

Without thinking it through, Mike said, "Don't get me wrong, I'm going to do the most that I can for you and the neighbors. What I can't do myself, I'll teach you to do. I won't leave you on your own."

Miranda smiled at him, leaned back in the booth and said, "You'll teach me new things? Well, thank you Michael. I knew you'd come through. You won't regret it."

Mike wasn't sure to what he'd just agreed.

When dinner was over, Mike paid the check. He didn't know why. This wasn't a date, he was the poor state employee who had travelled to Miranda's town for a business meeting. She'd invited him to dinner. Also, he was certain Roger would never authorize Miranda's dinner as a legitimate Commonwealth travel expense. Somehow, however, it seemed like the right thing to do. Miranda didn't object and she smiled when he reached for the check.

As they walked back to their cars, Mike half hoped she would invite him back to her office for a nightcap and equally prayed that she wouldn't.

"Well, Mr. Jacobs, you're an interesting man. I really enjoyed meeting you. It should be fun working together on this case." Miranda's breath condensed in the cold December air, a puff of steam drifting from her lips as she spoke.

Mike thought about what she just said. It occurred to him that they weren't working on the case together; rather, they really were on opposite sides. Nevertheless, he decided not to respond.

"I'm glad we finally met."

"So, are you heading back to Harrisburg right away?" Miranda raised her perfect eyebrows and Mike wondered if she *would* invite him back to her place.

"Well tomorrow I'm heading up to Ebensburg to meet with the DEP staff and some witnesses. After that, I'm heading back."

"Are you staying at the Sheraton?"

"No, I'm stuck at the Somerset Inn."

"That's a dump. Maybe the next time you come up, I'll fix you up in a better place, something homier, a bed and breakfast you'd like," Miranda said.

Mike held out his hand as they said goodbye and Miranda grasped it with both of hers, then leaned forward almost imperceptibly. As she leaned in, without thinking, Mike leaned forward and kissed her on the cheek.

Miranda lingered to receive the kiss, even leaned forward to prolong it for a moment, but as they pulled back she touched her cheek gently and said, "Wow. *Mr. Jacobs*, I wasn't expecting that. You move fast." She laughed.

Mike felt his face turn completely red in the darkness of the cold December evening. "No, I, yes, didn't, I don't, it's a city thing. Never mind. I'm sorry," Mike stammered.

Miranda laughed and touched his face tenderly, holding his chin with her fingertips for a moment. "You're a sweet man. Michael, I'm looking forward to being together with you."

Mike stammered, "You mean on this case. Right?"

"Of course, Michael. What else could I have meant?"

She turned and walked a couple of steps to her car, a BMW X1. It was probably the only BMW SUV in Somerset. Mike stood and watched as the ignition turned. She looked over her shoulder, threw him a smile, and drove away.

Mike drove back to his motel. For the rest of the night he wondered.

What.

In the hell.

Just happened?

26

Mike sat in a small second-floor conference room in DEP's Cambria District Mining Office with Ben Kemper, the DEP permit review engineer. He reviewed mountains of files relating to Rhino's permit application in the musty office. Mike had known Ben since his first days with DEP and they had become good friends. Ben was single, almost ten years older than Mike and sported an unkempt black beard, which provided no transition from the mounds of black hair that escaped from his open shirt to the unruly hair on his head. He had a habit of straightening and picking at his moustache. His winter outfit was always a heavy flannel shirt and jeans. On the whole, he looked like a mountain man.

Ben sat on a chair with a broken wheel that gouged the already seedy green carpet. Mike's chair had a broken back, which threatened to give out when he leaned back. Word around the office was that they were in line for a new building and furniture, but no one was taking bets. The conference room in which Ben and Mike sat had two windows that looked out onto the low brick buildings of Center Street in Ebensburg. Outside, the sky was gray and overcast, as if snow were on the way. From the second-floor room, they were about eye-level with the dog-eared municipal Christmas decorations that drooped from the light poles.

They'd been reviewing the original documents in the file since Mike arrived earlier that morning. Ben drank coffee from a brown earthenware mug, and from time to time stared over it at Mike as he went through the file.

"What?" Mike said sharply. "What are you looking at?"

Ben shook his head and said, "Did you find it?"

"What?"

"The smoking gun."

"Nothing." Mike sipped his cold coffee, then set down the papers. "So, at the end of the day, given all of the conditions you guys put on the operation, don't you feel the department did the right thing issuing the permit?"

"No. We should have denied the friggin' permit. It's pretty typical of the department to put some meaningless conditions in a permit that should've never been issued in the first place and then leave it to the discretion of the mine inspector to enforce those conditions. This happens all the time. I think this mine is too close to those houses, too close to the state game lands, too close to the headwaters of the trout stream. I'm *not* against mining, you know that. Shit, I have a degree in mining engineering from Penn State. I *am* against mining in the wrong place. I recommended we deny the permit, there's no way Rhino should be mining that property. Most of the office is against it too."

"I'm kind of surprised. I thought the office generally supported issuance of the permit so long as it had strong conditions." Mike sat back and crossed his legs.

"That's what Hicks says. He said we were going to issue the permit even though his engineer and mine inspector were against it. He told us to make sure there were a lot of conditions in the permit, but he made it clear we were issuing the permit."

"Well, maybe there were other factors? Maybe Hicks had more information than you did? Maybe there were other considerations?"

Ben rolled his eyes. "No way. I spent weeks reviewing this application and went out to the site twice. Devon Permian, our geologist, Marty Stevens, the inspector, and I went there together and it's clear just from looking at the site this permit never should've been issued. Tim wrote a report that stuck just to the geology, but if you talk to him, he'd tell you he was against it too. Other guys in the office who had smaller roles in this too. No one really wanted to put their ass on the line. The only one in the office who really pushed for issuance of the permit was Hicks. After Marty died, Lyle took over as inspector and became a cheerleader for issuance, too. It seems friggin' suspicious to me."

Mike got up from the desk and walked to the conference room door, which was slightly ajar. With his finger he pushed it shut until the door clicked. Then he turned and looked at Ben.

"Something else is bugging you about Ransom. I've noticed the way you two interact whenever he's in the office. You barely talk with him. What's going on?"

"I don't mind if I say it, Ransom's on the take. He's crooked, always has been crooked and always will be. He's a racist and a bigot, hates blacks, Jews, gays, you name it. He's lazy. What more can I say about him? They should drum him out of DEP," Ben paused. "One other thing, he's not the only one," he said in a hushed tone of voice.

"That's a pretty tough charge. I agree that Lyle's lazy and he's a racist and a bigot. I hate to say it, but that's probably not enough to get rid of him. Do you really think Lyle's on the take or is he just an incompetent idiot?" Mike asked.

Ben looked around the room and said, "I want to have this conversation, but not here. Let's go down to May's and have a cup of coffee."

The men put on their parkas and went down the steps to the street. It was cold and their breath froze as they talked. The city was quiet and about half the dilapidated storefronts were vacant. At the end of the block, they entered May's Restaurant and found a booth in the back; Mike sat facing the door, as he always did. The diner had rows of booths and gleaming, slick vinyl seats accented with bright aluminum trim. It smelled of coffee, steam, and bacon. The waitress brought them coffee and they continued their conversation in hushed tones.

"You know that Lyle worked for Rinati, don't you?" Ben asked.

"Yeah, I learned that yesterday. Frankly, I was more than a little surprised to find out he used to work for the same company he now regulates. I checked around, though, and learned that many of the inspectors and quite a few of the permit guys worked in the industry before coming to the department. You, Janey Hudson, and others are the new wave."

Ben nodded. "What's that tell you? The department is loaded with corruption."

"Wait a minute. Until fifteen, twenty years ago hardly anyone had a degree. The only guys who had any experience had to come from the industry. Hicks seems like a good man and he ran his own mining company for twenty years before he came to the department. You don't think he's corrupt, do you?"

"There's corrupt and then there's corrupt," Ben said. "I think some guys, like Lyle, are outwardly and completely corrupt. Some just let the system corrupt them, you know, go along and get along, that kind of thing. I know for a fact that Rinati gave Lyle a gold Rolex watch. What's that tell you? I mean every time he looks at that friggin' watch it reminds him who he works for."

"I saw the watch," Mike replied. "According to Lyle, he got that as a going-away present when he retired from Rhino Mining Company."

Ben interrupted with laughter. It was Ben's special laugh, the kind that was forced out too long. "Eh-eh-eh-eh. You don't seriously believe that, do you? You think that was simply a going-away present? A reward for services rendered? I think it was a prepayment for services. No one gets a gold watch after ten years of work, unless he takes a DEP job. I went online and checked it out once. Do you know what they cost?"

Mike shook his head.

"Thirty-four-thousand-dollars. *Thirty-four-thousand-dollars*. It's a solid-gold reminder of who really controls the man wearing it."

Mike looked at his mug and swirled the coffee grounds at the bottom of the cup. "That's a tough case to make out. Claiming a man is on the take and not having something in writing, audio or a witness. If Ransom worked for Rinati and Rinati gave him a nice gift as he left the company, who's to say that it wasn't simply a retirement gift, rather than an advance payment? Rinati and Lyle sure as hell aren't going to admit it was a bribe or an advance payment."

"More like a solid-gold set of handcuffs, eh-eh-eh-eh."

The two men looked at their coffee mugs and didn't say a word. Finally, Ben interrupted the silence. "I need to know you're on my side. I think there's a lot of evidence of corruption and the department needs to root it out. That's good for the department, good for the environment, and good for your clients."

"My *clients*?"

"Yeah, the *people*, you know, your clients," Ben replied.

Mike recalled a former DEP employee who urged him to consider "the people" as his clients. He had been dead for over a year.

"When I started with DEP I was told that my client was the governor. The governor himself signed my commission," Mike said holding Ben's gaze.

Mike noticed that Ben did not move for more than two seconds. Like he was frozen. Then he said, "Yeah, well it's not the governor who pays your paycheck, partner, it's the people of Pennsylvania. You and he both work for the people."

Mike paid the check and they strolled back to the office. A large coal truck trundled by, tiny pieces of the mineral seeped out the tailgate and danced on the street before coming to rest. Mike paused to watch.

As they reached the street entrance for the second-floor office, Mike put his hand on Ben's arm. "Look, you bring me some evidence of corruption. It has to be something tangible, I'm not even sure what that is. But if you do that, then I'll take it to the secretary."

Ben rolled his eyes.

"Seriously, I know the secretary and he's a good man. I know it seems like he's on the side of industry, but one thing's for sure, he won't tolerate any corruption. We have to do this the right way since he's not going to move forward on any investigation without significant evidence. If you get the evidence, just enough for me to get this rolling, I'll do my part."

"That's a deal, partner." Ben smiled as they shook hands.

"One more thing. Do *not* go to the press with whatever it is you find. If we're going to make a case, we've got to do it right, I don't want my case getting screwed up because some reporter is putting news out before we have a chance to investigate it. When I get back to the office, I'm going to clear this with Roger and let him know what we're up to. Okay?"

Ben nodded.

"Okay. Look, I want to get these guys and I trust you. I'll work with you," Ben said. He put his hand on Mike's shoulder and patted it.

The men nervously glanced around like the conspirators they now were.

27

For the second time in a few hours, Mike sat in a booth at May's Restaurant. He was with John Hicks, the district mining manager, and watched him consume a BLT. As he chewed, Hicks's ears wiggled and a vein under his bald scalp grew and shrunk with each bite. Mike poked at his wilted salad.

"Tell me, how did you come to work at DEP of all places? I thought you owned your own mining company?" Mike asked.

Mike wanted to learn what had possessed Hicks to issue the permit when his mining engineer and inspector were against it. He wondered if it was just a bias in favor of mining or if something else was compelling him to issue the permit as Ben had darkly suggested.

"Well, truth be told, I was a pretty good miner, but not such a good businessman," Hicks smiled through a mouthful of sandwich. "I could look at a minin' map and imagine the entire operation, from initial cut to reclamation. That wasn't the problem for me. Runnin' a business? That was my Achilles' heel."

"Yes, but DEP? Why didn't you go work for another mining company?"

"I thought about that and I had plenty of offers. There were several companies that wanted me to come on as a mining manager or foreman." Hicks looked at Mike and winked, "Anything but a business manager. Did you know Wayne Hudson? He was the Director of the Bureau of Mining back in the 1980s and '90s?"

"No, I never met the man. He retired way before I joined. I've heard lots of stories about him, though. Interesting man."

"Well, I knew Wayne for what, maybe fifteen years. When he heard my company was closing up shop, he asked me to come in and run this district. Shoot, he visited me in my office as I was packing boxes and offered me the job before we sat down. I accepted it on the spot." Hicks took another sip of coffee.

"Did you find it hard moving from being a mine operator to district mining manager? I mean, after all, there's a lot of tension between miners in the field and DEP," Mike said as he looked at a grayish-orange tomato on his fork.

"I never had any DEP problems to speak of. I was a pretty good mine operator. Also, I operated my company when things were different between DEP and the regulated world. I never received a cease-and-desist order and there were precious few issued to anyone worth his salt during my years as an operator. Those men who were shut down, they well and truly deserved it. I have to tell you, the transition was fairly easy for me. I operated my company assuming that I'd have to comply with the law. There were no ifs, ands, or buts. Not only was it the right thing to do, but in the end, it was a hell of a lot cheaper to comply with the law. If I had a hired man who wasn't doing the right thing, I'd talk to him and straighten him out. If he couldn't get with the program, I fired the bastard. That was the way I ran my company. I know there were a lot of other guys out there would let things slide, but that's not how I did it. So, I guess when I came over to DEP it was relatively easy for me to put on the sheriff's badge, so to speak."

"You consider yourself the law?"

"In a manner of speaking, yes. Look, I don't agree with all of the laws and regulations. I suspect there are a lot of cops out there who also don't agree with some of the laws. But my job isn't to write the laws, it's to enforce them. If some guy is out there violating the law and we don't enforce the law against him, well that's just unfair to the guy who tries to comply. Isn't it?"

Mike didn't respond since he knew no answer was required.

"Anyway," Hicks continued, "I like the little guy. I'll bend over backwards for him. My inspectors know the difference between enforcing the law the right way and acting like some damn fool who shuts you down for minor infractions. To a large extent, I see my job, our job, as educating these mine operators to do things the right way. The way I run my district, no one gets an unfair advantage and no one gets treated the wrong way by my men."

Mike intentionally popped a large chewy chunk of lettuce in his mouth and chewed so he could take a moment before continuing the conversation. As he chewed, Hicks looked around for the waitress and then held up his coffee mug. She approached the men and filled their cups.

"Anyway, what about this Rhino Mining application?" Mike asked, attempting to talk as innocuously as possible.

"What about it? Rhino applied for a permit, he met all of our criteria and we issued it," Hicks said. "Case closed."

Hicks seemed to scrutinize Mike's face.

"Sure, but what about the proximity of those houses? Then there are the state game lands, that trout stream?"

"I'm aware of all of those. But I know Rhino has to meet all of the setback requirements, and so far as I'm concerned, he's proven he can mine a job without polluting a stream. We put a lot of conditions in the permit just to be sure he doesn't screw up those houses or the stream."

"Were you surprised Rhino appealed the permit conditions?" Mike asked.

"Yes. Rhino can mine that job with our conditions, for sure. There's no doubt that they'd make a little bit more money if they didn't have those conditions, but there's no way they're going broke on that job. They've got a good piece of coal under the ground and it's a question of whether they'll make money or make a lot of money. They'll make money on that deal." Hicks took a long sip of black coffee.

"What about Rinati? I assume you know him."

"Ernie Rinati? Not only do I know him, but we went to high school together. I lived in Windber and he was from Scalp Level, not too far away. We played on the football team together until he dropped out of school. I'm a year or two older than him, but I've known him since we were kids. He's always been a big mouth and a difficult guy, but you have to admit, there's something likable about him," Hicks said smiling.

Mike chose his words carefully and paused to take a sip of coffee before he spoke. "So, you think Rinati can mine that land and that has nothing to do with the fact you've known him for, what, forty plus years?"

Hicks face reddened and showed his disgust. "Really, Mike? You think I'd issue a permit to a man because we played on the high school football team together? You should know better. Like I said, Rinati and his engineer proved his company should get that permit and I think he can mine it without causing pollution. That's the beginning and the end."

"Don't get me wrong Mr. Hicks, John, but it's no secret that Ben Kemper wasn't happy about being overruled when you issued the permit."

"Ben's a…college boy." Mike wondered what Hicks really wanted to say. "He never worked in a mine. He got a good education and certainly understands mining and permit applications and whatnot as good as the rest of them. But he doesn't have minin' in his blood like I do and the other guys who spent years in the industry. That's why I told him to draft up the permit with those conditions. After Ben gets a few more years of experience and is around the industry for a while he'll understand it better."

Mike nodded thoughtfully. "I just need to fully understand the reason the permit was issued."

They sipped their coffees.

"Here's a philosophical question for you," Mike said to the older man. "Do you think the environmental cost of mining the coal, the acid mine drainage, air pollution from burning it, climate change, whatever, is worth it?"

Hicks smiled broadly. "You're making a joke? Of course. It can be done safely. The vast majority of the companies I regulate do it without any serious incidents. They're burning it more cleanly today than ever. We really care about the reclamation, too. I can take you to sites that were reclaimed five years ago and you'd never know there was a two-hundred-foot-deep pit there just a few years earlier. Not only that, do you really trust nuclear? I mean, how exactly are you going to replace coal? Not with nukes. Not with solar. You'd need to cover all of New York state with solar panels just to power New York City. I mean, seriously." Hicks chuckled. "And climate change? I hear plenty from both sides, but I just don't know enough to make an informed decision. I'll leave that to the experts."

Hicks looked around for the waitress and scribbled his hand in the air when he caught her eye. She brought the check. Mike grabbed it, but Hicks took it from him. "You may be my lawyer," Hicks said with a smile, "but I'm still your elder and I've got the check."

Mike smiled. "Thank you. One more thing." He leaned forward and Hicks did the same.

"You ever have any worries about Lyle? I mean, I imagine that he's not exactly the star performer around here."

Hicks laughed, "Lyle has terrific knowledge of the minin' industry. I'd hold him up against anyone in any district mining office on the basis of his minin' knowledge. He doesn't kill himself out there, that's for sure. Of all my inspectors, he's probably the last one to get in all of his mandatory inspections and reports. Also, I'm not crazy about his mouth. He's foul. Frankly, he's a damned fool when he starts with those stupid jokes of his and it would serve him a lot better if he just kept his fat trap shut."

"You have no worries about him inspecting Rinati's jobs? I mean, he did work for Rinati and he lugs around the giant gold watch on his wrist that Rinati gave him."

"Is that what this is all about? Lyle's fake Rolex? I guarantee you Rinati picked that up on Fifth Avenue in New York from one of those boys on the street selling gen-u-ine Rolex watches. It's probably cheaper than this ol' Timex that I'm wearing. Look, if I had to limit my inspectors and not allow them to inspect the minin' companies they used to work for, I'd have no inspectors. Rhino has jobs in five counties. I'll bet half my inspectors worked for him at one time or another when they were still in the industry. The same holds true for other mine operators and the rest of my inspectors. A man grows up in Somerset County or Cambria County, where exactly do you think he's going to work? Even the college boys had summer jobs with the companies they now regulate, and consultants and whatnot. When we get a holt' of him I'm not moving him clear across the state so that he never inspects an operator he used to work for. That ain't happening. Don't worry about Lyle, I keep all my inspectors on a short leash. If I thought for a minute that any of them was doing anything wrong, I'd personally kick him in the ass and show him the door."

Hicks paid the bill and they headed back to the office. When they returned, a secretary handed Hicks a stack of pink slips with the telephone calls that had accumulated over the previous forty-five minutes. Mike thought Hicks might be the last man he knew who still got phone messages that way. Hicks looked at the pile and shook his head.

"Well, looks like I've got at least five emergencies to deal with. If there's anything you need, you know who to ask." Hicks riffled through the slips as he walked back to his office, closing the door behind him.

As Mike returned to the conference room, he saw that Ben was leaning way back in his chair, watching them. When they made eye contact, Ben touched his fingertip to his nose, then went back to the work on his desk.

Jesus, thought Mike. *Now I'm a party to a paranoid conspiracy.*

28

Mike dropped his briefcase on the guest chair and looked at his desk. It was covered with papers where he had left them several days earlier, as well as the pile of papers that others had left for him in his absence. Sandy had stacked his mail on his chair. She'd started doing that a few months earlier, where she knew he couldn't miss it.

He went through his emails and deleted the spam and flagged the more important messages. Then he listened to his voice mail. Several of the calls were from counsel in his other cases. He jotted down the names on a legal pad. Finally, he came across a message from Sid Feldman, Rhino's counsel. He made a note on the pad and drew a large circle around it.

As Mike settled into his chair, he found a large stack of papers held together by a black binder clip with a note on top, "*From the desk of Roger Alden.*" This was a new appeal that had just been filed from an order issued by DEP's Harrisburg Regional Office against a small water company. The note from Roger was scrawled in his handwriting:

Here's a new appeal. Sorry to have to dump this on you now, but you were next on my list. See me when you get in and we can discuss it.

—R

P.S. How was Somerset?

Mike flipped through the notice of appeal and saw it had been filed by a former DEP lawyer that he knew on behalf of a water company in Franklin County. The appeal was fairly bare bones and he expected his former colleague wasn't being paid much to handle the case. He was grateful, however, that someone who knew what she was doing would be on the other side. That always made his life easier.

Mike cleared off the space in front of his desk and picked up the phone. He dialed a number from memory.

"Hi, this is Nicky."

"Hiya, toots," Mike said smiling.

"Mikey, I was wondering when you were going to get back to town. How did it go in Somerset?" she asked.

"Interesting."

"Your favorite ambiguous word," she said laughing. "I want to hear all about Miranda," she pronounced the name, *Meer-ann-duh* in a sing-song voice, "and whatever else you turned up, but I'm busy trying to finish some stuff up before everyone flees the office. Can I talk with you later?" she asked.

"Sure, I'll call you. Maybe we can get a drink or dinner."

After they hung up, Mike picked up the pad with Feldman's number and dialed it.

Feldman picked up on the fourth ring.

"Sid? Mike Jacobs at DEP."

"I'm glad you called me back. Your secretary tells me you were out in Somerset yesterday, meeting with the neighbors and our opponent Ms. Clymer."

Mike's jaw clenched. He made a mental note to have another chat with Sandy about what she told his opposing counsel.

"Yes, well, I'm touching base with all of the parties. Even you."

"Well, what are we going to do about this appeal Ms. Clymer and her clients have filed? I assume we're going to be working together against them. After all, you guys issued the permit, so I'm sure the department will be defending it against the torch and pitchfork-wielding citizens of Somerset."

Mike was taken aback. It hadn't occurred to him that Feldman would seek to enlist him against the citizens, yet, it made perfect sense. DEP issued the permit and the citizens had appealed. If

Rhino hadn't also appealed, there would be no question that DEP would actively defend the permit it had issued *against* the citizens.

"About that," Mike said. "We really ought to talk. I intend to defend the integrity of the department, you know. So far as we're concerned this is your permit to defend."

"Defend the integrity of the department?" Feldman let out a whoop. "I haven't heard those words in a long while. That's kind of like defending the integrity of some floozy on Third Street. Do Harrisburg's whores still hang out there? Well, since I appealed the issuance of the permit, that does make it a bit of a mess. You expect me to defend the same permit I'm appealing?"

"You did complicate things." Mike thought for a moment. "I'll tell you what, drop your appeal of the permit conditions and then you and I can defend the permit from Miranda Clymer and her unhappy clients."

Feldman let out a large laugh. "Very funny Mike, you crack me up. You know those conditions are going to cost Rhino a lot of dough. Hundreds of thousands of dollars, maybe millions. You can't expect him to give that up without a fight."

"Well, if you do give that up, then you get the department fully on your side."

"I'll tell you what, Mike," Feldman said. "Why don't we sit down and talk this through. Do you want to come to Philly or should I schlep to Harrisburg?"

Mike thought for a moment, then said, "Philly, I'd be happy to meet with you in your office."

They made arrangements to meet the Monday after Christmas at Feldman's office.

29

Mike tapped on Roger's door, which was slightly ajar. Roger called out, "Come in."

Mike entered in time to see Roger folding up his *New York Times* and setting it behind him on the credenza. "Come on in. How was Somerset?" Roger asked.

"Interesting," Mike replied.

"Is there anything we need to discuss?" Roger asked.

"A couple of things," Mike replied. He told him about the accident at the mine, then said, "Miranda, Miranda Clymer, she's a piece of work. Seems fairly nice, uh attractive too. Business lawyer, general practice, mostly. Zero litigation experience. Anyway, she's really pushing hard to have us be more involved in the case. Frankly, based on everything I'm hearing from the program and everything I've seen, I think she may have a point. It's a pretty important case."

Roger looked at Mike for a long moment, then frowned. "I thought we discussed this. I told you that there simply weren't enough resources for us to take a lead role in the case. Look, she's a lawyer and she's been practicing for what, ten or fifteen years? She's a big girl and can handle herself. You're just going to have to tell her that," Roger said decisively.

"I think there are special circumstances," Mike replied. "It's sort of the second thing I wanted to talk about. The new inspector is a guy named Ransom, Lyle Ransom. He's a strange dude, a racist, Klan-type, a real piece of work. I was talking with the permit reviewer, Ben Kemper, and he tells me that he thinks

Ransom is dirty, on the take. Based on what I've seen, he may be right."

Roger made a face. "Did he give you any evidence? Anything we could show the secretary?"

"Only one definite thing for now. It turns out Ransom used to work for Rinati. When he retired from working with Rhino, Rinati gave him a solid gold Rolex watch. I saw it. Kemper said it could be worth over thirty thousand dollars. John Hicks thinks it's a fake, but isn't sure. What's that tell you?"

"Maybe a lot, maybe nothing. Do you know if it's really a Rolex? Maybe Hicks is right and it's just a cheap knockoff. Maybe there's a perfectly good explanation. We need more than that."

"I agree," replied Mike. "I've asked Ben to look around and see if there's any other evidence. Something tangible that might show corruption. Something current."

Roger stared at him and frowned. "You asked this engineer to mount an investigation?"

"Not exactly," Mike said slowly. "I just asked him to send me information if he hears of anything. Maybe there'll be nothing, maybe there will be something important."

Roger shook his head. "You should've come to me first, Bud."

"It was a matter of timing. I was with Ben yesterday and I told him I would be meeting with you. Look, I can call him off, if that's what you'd like me to do. I think it's worth it for him to nose around. Maybe he finds something, maybe he doesn't. I told him to be discreet and that if he found anything we would take over."

A muscle in Roger's jaw ticked and his eyes narrowed. "You really should've checked with me before you initiated something like this. Mike, I've always liked you and I think very highly of you and your skills. But this is *my* office. I answer to the chief counsel and secretary. You answer to me. I'll let it slide this time, but don't let it happen again." Roger paused and then asked, "Did you run this by John Hicks? I mean, Cambria is his office, after all."

"Negative, Chief. Hicks thinks Lyle is a knowledgeable mine inspector, basically a harmless good ol' boy. Lazy, yes, but not crooked. I didn't want Hicks undermining this."

"Great. I'll have to talk with Hicks. I don't want him thinking I've initiated an investigation in his office that would undercut him. There are a lot of potential consequences. This is why you can't initiate an investigation on your own." Roger paused again and then said, "I'm almost afraid to ask, but is there anything else?"

Mike thought for a minute and then said, "Hoffa, Jimmy Hoffa."

Roger made a face and gestured with his hand, palm up.

"I think I found his body, Chief. It's down at the bottom of Rhino's pit," Mike smiled broadly. "You mean something like that?"

Roger stifled a smile, "Get the hell out of my office."

Mike smiled as he stood and left the office.

"Thanks Chief," Mike said as he pulled the door shut.

30

Mike's phone rang. He jogged the last few steps to his office, turned the corner and grabbed it. "Jacobs," he said.

"Very formal, Michael, I like it," Miranda said.

"Oh, hi Miranda. I wasn't expecting you." He looked at his Caller ID. All it read was *Somerset, Pa.*

"You know, we never made arrangements for when you would come up here to interview my clients one on one. I assume you're going to want to talk with each of them. Isn't that what you debonair environmental prosecutors do?"

"Yeah, about that. Look, I'm getting some pushback from my chief, Roger Alden. He's really insisting that you take the lead."

There was a long pause. Mike wondered for a moment whether the line had gone dead. Then, Miranda said, "Michael, I'm *very* disappointed. I thought we had an arrangement. I thought you were going to take more of a lead in the case."

"Well, I never said I'd take the lead and haven't said I wouldn't be involved. I'm going to do as much as I can. I just have to…" Mike's voice drifted off.

"Well, Michael, even if I was taking the lead, you probably still would want to come up here and interview my clients, wouldn't you?" Miranda said.

"I don't suppose there's any harm in that," he replied.

"Good, what are your plans for January second?"

Mike wondered what the rush was. He could wait weeks, maybe even a couple of months to interview her witnesses. Mike reached for his At-A-Glance calendar and flipped to the new year. "That looks okay. I mean there's no reason we have to rush this, is there?"

"Well Michael, there *is* a favor you can do for me," Miranda replied sweetly. "I promise it won't be a big hassle and I also promise that it will be well worth your trouble."

"Sure, what else could I possibly do to help you?"

"There's this formal dinner every year sponsored by the Somerset County Bar Association. Technically it's the New Year's dinner, but they always have it after the first. I need an escort. I was hoping you'd take me. It's the evening of January second."

Mike tapped the receiver against his head several times and then said, "Your escort? You want me to be your *date*?"

"Why not? You're an assistant counsel with DEP, a distinguished member of the bar from Harrisburg, my co-counsel and colleague. Plus, you're an attractive man. I'll introduce you around, you'll meet the deans of the local bar, the judges, DA, also the auditor general will be making a guest appearance, all of that is good for your career. I promise you'll have a memorable time."

"Sure," he said, "I'd be honored. Did you say this was formal?"

"Yes. You have a tux, don't you?"

"A tux? Not on my salary. But I'm sure I can rent one."

"Good. Look, it will be late when this is over so you should plan on sleeping over at my place after the dance. I can't invite you up here and expect you to stay in that horrible Somerset Inn. I have a couple of extra bedrooms anyway. Okay?"

"Okay…Sure, of course, that makes sense, thanks," Mike said slowly. "We'll talk next week and finalize things."

After Mike hung up, he walked to the window and looked out across the rail yard. He watched a long line of coal cars pull through the yard before he went back to his work.

That night, Mike had trouble falling asleep as his mind drifted from thought to thought. He reflected on how incredibly easy it was at times to fall into a relationship and how incredibly difficult it was to tear away from one. Falling in love was effortless. The hard part was making it work. He'd expected that by the time he was twenty-eight he would have it all figured out.

He thought about his past lovers, one by one, what was right and wrong about those relationships. His mind drifted to Miranda. She was sexy and he was attracted to her. Nevertheless, he didn't want to be with her in a short-term or long-term relationship. She was wrong on too many levels. The Jewish thing for starters.

Eventually, his mind drifted to Nicky. He heard her say to him, as she had on several occasions with a broad smile on her face, 'you're a good guy Mikey. You'll find the right girl. I know it.'

He fell asleep dreaming, once again, of Nicky.

31

Mike sat at his table at the Bread Shed with Frannie, the owner, when Nicky walked in. It was the day before Christmas and the place was dead. Frannie excused herself and went to the kitchen. Nicky slipped into a chair opposite Mike.

"I wasn't sure you'd be in town today." Mike thought Nicky looked unusually tired, sad.

"Cindy and I decided at the last minute not to visit her family in Williamsport. Maybe I should say she went this morning and asked me not to go. I'm a little pissed, but I get it. Her parents don't accept the whole lesbian thing, so I feel like I'm sitting on pins and needles the whole time I'm there. Cindy said she wanted to visit her family and not have any drama since it was Christmas."

"I thought you were going to say they were uncomfortable having a Jewish girl in the house at Christmas time." Mike smiled at her.

"Actually, they don't seem to mind that. I probably feel more awkward about that than they do. We didn't exactly have Christmas trees and sing carols in our house."

"Me neither," said Mike.

"Actually, things are getting really bad with Cindy. I feel like from the moment we get up until we go to bed at night, there's this tension. Sometimes it boils over, like it did the other night. It's constant. Awful."

Frannie approached with the menus and Mike looked her away with a brief glance. Then he covered Nicky's hand with his own, rubbing her thumb with his.

"What happened? The last time we talked you were going to try and work it out."

"I don't know. It's like there's no way to work it out. I'm trying everything. I love her and this really hurts."

Mike watched Nicky's face. Her eyes were cast down to the table. Her words were forced, not coming easily. He was glad the restaurant was nearly empty.

"Did anything else happen?"

"Maybe. Cindy was in the shower the other night. I was watching TV and her phone was on the coffee table. I just picked it up and keyed in her password. There were a lot of calls. Dozens in a week or two with a friend. A mutual friend—"

"Another…"

"Lesbian? Yes. She was my friend and I introduced them at a bar a couple of weeks ago."

Mike nodded.

"Also, there were texts. A lot of texts. Some of it…sexy, if you know what I mean."

Frannie came up and without a word deposited two steaming bowls of veggie chili on the table. Mike and Nicky looked up and Frannie smiled and silently shrugged at them, then turned and headed to the front counter.

Mike stirred his chili. "What are you going to do about this? Do you think it will blow over? Has she actually been unfaithful? How do you feel about that?"

Nicky made a face. "I feel awful. If it's just chit-chat, I suppose I can deal with that, but if she's been fooling around… it's over."

Nicky reached out and rubbed his hand. Tears began running down her face. She rubbed them from her eyes. "I'm sorry, the whole thing is sad. I really love her."

Mike sat quietly for a while, then said, "There's really nothing I can tell you. Sometimes a relationship has rough spots and sometimes it just ends. Maybe it never should have begun in the first place."

"I thought about that for a long time," Nicky said. "I keep hoping we can work it out. I just don't know."

"Counseling? What about seeing a couple's counsellor?"

"I thought about that too and even mentioned that to Cindy, but she made it clear that wasn't for her."

Both of them picked at their chili.

"Enough about me," Nicky said. "Would you ever consider dating a non-Jewish girl?"

"You mean again?"

"Yes." Nicky smiled at him.

"Maybe. I'm not sure. One thing that surprised me about the whole awful disaster with Patty and Sherry was I really hadn't realized how important the whole religion thing would be. Look, over the years I've had deep relationships with other non-Jewish women. I felt about as close to Patty as anyone ever could. I never let the religion thing enter into my thoughts about her or any other woman for that matter. If anything, it was an interesting difference between us, something new to talk about. It was just unimportant to me."

Nicky nodded.

"I think maybe because I'm older now and when you're in your teens or early twenties there's no real expectation that you're going to get married. It was just for fun. At our age, you date a woman for weeks or months, and friends, even total strangers, ask you, 'is it serious?' I mean, the whole world is expecting you to pop the question. Maybe before, when it was just dating and sex, it really didn't matter that the girl wasn't Jewish. But Patty mattered because…because…"

Mike searched his mind for the right word, when Nicky spoke up. "because you really *loved* Patty."

Mike nodded. "Inside my head I heard my parents' voices and could imagine my brother shaking his head and I knew that for me, this wasn't right. I never talked in detail to my brother about this, but I didn't need to. I could hear his voice in that detached, reproachful, rabbinical way. No matter what words he would've used, he would have said, 'I'm disappointed, your parents would be disappointed, and hundreds of generations of your ancestors would be disappointed.' Does that make sense?"

Nicky's eyes had watered considerably again but no tears had escaped. She nodded. "What about Sherry?"

"Okay, you may not believe this, but it took me months to come to grips with it. I loved her too. She was totally different than Patty, but that was fine. When it ended, I made a decision to go find Sherry, not Patty. As much as I loved Patty, and I really loved her, I loved Sherry more. What she endured for me, gave up for me…no one should do that. That's love. It was why I chased after Sherry when it was over. The problem was it was over. Sherry made that clear. She couldn't forgive my, my… infidelity. Do you know what I mean?"

"How do you think *I* feel?" Nicky held his gaze. "When I first came out, told my parents, and my mom-mom and pop-pop, they actually refused to believe me. One day, months later, my mom-mom took me aside and asked me why I was having trouble finding a date. By date, I know she meant a boy. I know what I am, I've known for years. My parents just refuse to accept it. You're worried about the Jewish thing? Trust me, I could bring home a lesbian thoracic surgeon with a Nobel Prize who also was a rabbi, and no one in my family would be happy. You, at least, have a chance of making your family happy. I'll never have that chance."

They held each other's hands across the table and tears freely ran down Nicky's face.

"I'm sorry Nicky. The whole thing is sad. I'm sorry for you. I'm sorry for Cindy. I'm here for you, I'll always be your friend." His voice drifted off and he looked past her.

"And I'm always there for you," she said.

Mike glanced around the small restaurant. It was empty now except for Frannie standing near the cash register reading the newspaper. He looked at his watch and saw that it was nearly two.

"Shit, it's late. Roger wanted to see me after lunch. Look I have to get back to the office. I don't think either of us can spend the whole afternoon here and I'm sure Frannie wants to close."

Mike stood up and left a ten-dollar tip on the table. As he reached for his coat, Nicky put her arms around him and hugged him long and intensely, making full contact with him. She had never hugged him that way before.

"You're a good friend, Nicky Kane. I love you." Mike said softly as he buried his head in her soft brown hair.

"Me too, Mike. Thank you for listening. You know, the thing with Patty and Sherry, you're not an asshole. Screwed up in the head, yes, but not an asshole."

For the first time that day, he smiled, then gave her a long kiss on her forehead. Nicky slid her hands onto his neck and held him for a long embrace.

32

Christmas had been quiet for Mike and he had spent several hours in the office straightening up the mess. He had been the only one in the office and he enjoyed the quiet. On the day after, Mike looked out the window thinking. One of the things he liked about being a lawyer was that he was paid to think. He sat staring at the railroad yard several hundred feet from his window when the phone rang. He considered ignoring it but picked it up on the fourth ring.

"Jacobs," he said absentmindedly.

"Mike? Mikey?" It was Nicky. "Can I see you? I really need to talk with you."

Mike could hear the tremor in her voice. "What's wrong? Is everything okay?"

"No. Nothing's okay. It's over, Cindy came back from Christmas with her family last night and broke up with me this morning. She's kicking me out," she said, her voice quavering.

Mike looked at his watch. "Do you want to get together for lunch?"

"No, I have a feeling that this is gonna be rough. Besides, I have a meeting at one. I think I can hold it together today, but how about tonight? Can I come over to your apartment?"

They made arrangements to meet at six.

Mike opened the door to his apartment within a few moments of the first gentle tap. Nicky wore her parka, her hair was tangled, and the trails of dried tears streaked her face. He held the door open and closed it behind her.

"Let me take your coat," he said.

Without responding, Nicky threw her arms around him and sobbed pitifully. Mike held her, stroking the back of her head, not knowing what to do. Minutes passed and Nicky finally calmed down enough to take off her coat, which Mike threw on a chair. He led her to the sofa. Mike didn't say anything, he just looked at her face, tears welling up in her gentle eyes, waiting for her to talk. Then, the tears began flowing freely again and black lines from her mascara became etched on the side of her pale cheeks. She kept pushing a clump of hair behind her ear. He held her hands and she vigorously rubbed his with her thumbs.

Finally, she said, "Cindy definitely found someone else. She's been unfaithful and having an affair and I was too stupid to see it. It's been going on for weeks and I feel like an idiot."

"She was seeing," Mike paused for a long moment, "your friend?"

"Former friend. I'm a fool."

"Is there any chance that it's just a fling? Maybe she'll come back to you?" Mike said.

"No, it's over. The apartment was in Cindy's name and she kicked me out. She wouldn't admit it, but I'm pretty sure the other girl is moving in. It's over. Even if she did drop the other girl, I would never trust her again. I don't want to have anything to do with her."

Nicky put her arms around Mike and continued to sob. After several minutes, she had controlled her crying and pulled away. She stood, wiping her nose and face with her sleeves. "Do you have vodka? I need a drink," she said looking toward the kitchen.

"Sure, I've got vodka. Do you want to mix anything in it? Maybe some orange juice?"

"No, just ice."

He put some cubes in a glass and poured about two fingers of vodka. He set the bottle down and Nicky took it and filled the glass almost to the top. Mike wondered whether she would really drink that much.

"Aren't you joining me? You're not going to make a lady drink alone, are you?"

Mike poured a small amount in another glass and they touched glasses. Nicky swallowed several large gulps, and then gasped for air.

"Hey, slow down. I've never slugged back that much vodka and I'm a hell of a lot bigger than you," Mike said.

Nicky took the glass and went back to the sofa. Mike joined her, wondering if she would get sick or just pass out.

Half an hour later, Mike was holding Nicky's head and stroking her hair as she vomited into his toilet. Each heave started out as a violent bark, followed by Nicky spewing prodigious amounts of liquid and bile into the commode. He had seen more than a few of his friends throw up after drinking, in high school and college, but never quite as violently as Nicky did.

When she was done, Mike gently cleaned her face with a washcloth, then helped her to the sofa, where she curled into a ball and quickly passed out. He covered her with a blanket, and dropped into his chair to watch her sleep. He knew he loved her, but had never really come to grips with what kind of love it was. She was attractive in the way Mike dreamed about. She was sweet and innocent. They could talk about anything and she never bored him. He respected that she was on the other team, as she often said, but that didn't stop his feelings.

Eventually, Mike pulled out his briefcase and worked while Nicky slumbered. She awoke a little after eleven, and Mike smiled at her.

"Do you have some place to go tonight? Or do you want to stay here?"

"I suppose I could go to my parents' house, but that's the last place I want to be. Is it okay if I stay here tonight? I'll just sleep on the sofa."

Mike got up and opened the door to the small guest room. He flipped on the light and saw that the bed and floor were piled high with boxes he had never unpacked from law school. There was hardly any room to move.

"Why don't you take my bed. I'll sleep on the sofa," he offered.

"No, I'll sleep on the sofa. I just want to wash up." Looking down at her heavy sweater, she said, "Do you have a tee shirt or something I can wear that doesn't have vomit on it?"

Mike got Nicky an oversized green tee shirt with "Vermont" on it and a towel. He rooted around under the sink until he found a large bottle of Listerine which he left out for her.

"Why don't you wash up, take a shower, and I'll fix the sofa for you."

Nicky pulled the door to the bathroom closed and Mike could hear her sobbing, again, before the shower drowned out her crying.

Well after midnight, Mike was in his bed and Nicky was in the living room on the sofa. Quietly, the door to his room opened. Nicky, wearing the long tee shirt and nothing else, slipped into his room, dragging the blanket he had given her. She appeared half-asleep and silently, she climbed into bed with him, lying on top of the comforter. She pulled the blanket he'd given her over her small body and put her arms around him. She was asleep within moments.

Mike lay awake for a long time, wondering what had just happened.

33

Slowly the room came into focus. Light snuck through the blinds as Mike's senses returned to him. Nicky's sweet, innocent face was just inches from his, lying on the opposite end of Mike's pillow. She breathed slowly through her nose, a peaceful sleep. The green tee shirt had slipped over her shoulder, exposing her pale, bare shoulder. Sometime in the middle of the night, she must have gotten under the sheets and now their legs were intertwined. His hand was on her arm, and hers rested softly on his side.

Oh man.

Mike considered slipping out of bed, to be in the bathroom when she awoke, to disentangle gently, and skulk away. He held back because the feeling of being next to Nicky this way was too peaceful, too warm, too nice. *Too erotic.* He watched for several minutes until her eyes began to flutter, then she lifted her free arm and yawned, stretching like a cat. When her eyes opened, she looked at him and smiled.

"Hi," she whispered. She cuddled with him again.

"Good morning," Mike whispered back.

They said nothing for many long seconds, just looking into each other's eyes. Then Mike said, "How are you feeling today? Headache? Hangover? You put away a *lot* of vodka."

"I seem to remember barfing up a lot of vodka, too. So far, so good. I'll see when I get up."

"Can I ask you a question?" he asked, still whispering.

"Sure."

"What are you doing here, under the covers?"

She took a deep breath, then said, "I was lying under that thin blanket you gave me out in the living room. I was feeling lonely and sad and cold. I wanted to be with you, so I came in here. That was okay, I hope."

"Of course. Any time," he laughed.

"Uh, what about this?" without moving his hand more than a few inches, he patted the side of her hip. Their legs were locked together.

"Oh, that." She laughed. "I got cold. That little blanket wasn't enough, so I crawled under the covers to get warm. I asked you first and you said it was okay."

Mike couldn't remember her asking but had no doubt how he would have answered.

"I hope it was all right. It was just sleeping, right?" She said.

"Right, of course," Mike suddenly realized he had an erection and wondered if she noticed.

Mike backed away and disentangled his legs from hers.

"We should get up. I have a feeling it's going to be a rough day," Mike said, thinking about having to move Nicky out of the apartment she shared with Cindy.

"Yes," she said shutting her eyes. "Do you have a shirt I can wear? That sweater I was wearing last night is going to stink."

"I'll get you one. It'll be a little big, but I'm sure you can do something with it. Let me wash up first and then you can have the bathroom, okay?"

Nicky reached out and put her arms around Mike's neck and pulled him toward her. He didn't resist. She put her mouth next to his ear and whispered, "Thanks Mike. You're such a good friend. The best." She kissed him on the cheek and squeezed his neck. "I love you."

Without hesitating, Mike replied, "I love you too." He paused, "Like a friend, I mean."

"Me too," she said smiling in the dim light.

They disentangled again and Mike sat up, keeping his back to her as he did not want her to see the front of his shorts which now resembled an oversized circus tent.

"Give me a few minutes, I'm going to shave and take a quick shower."

Mike got up and headed straight into the bathroom.

34

A loud banging on Norman Post's front door awoke him from his fitful slumber as he dozed in front of the TV. He looked around his living room—a table littered with bills, framed pictures and a mini-fake Christmas tree, the old sofa covered with a ratty comforter, and the coffee table piled with newspapers going back three months—and decided whoever was at his front door would have to deal with the shabbiness of his home. Norman struggled to lift his massive weight out of his ancient, sagging Barcalounger and decided for the thousandth time that he had to get a new chair. He looked at the clock on the wall. Just after ten a.m. He didn't bother turning down the TV, leaving the volume loud enough to be heard in Pittsburgh.

As Norman approached the door, he looked through the soiled gauze curtains his wife had hung a million years before, through the smudged glass pane and saw two men. The one closest to the door was heavy with a thick brown beard and wore a Caterpillar ball cap. He was vaguely familiar. Norman wasn't sure if he knew him or if he just looked like a lot of men he knew in the country. Behind him was one of the skinniest men he'd ever seen. Skeletal and tall, he had a terrible scar that ran the length of his face beginning next to his right eye and curling around his chin. This created the effect of a Halloween mask. They were both wearing workingmen's clothes and work jackets. Car trouble, probably. He opened the door.

"Can I help you?"

"I suppose," said the man with a beard. "We'd like to talk with you for a few minutes and then we'll be on our way." He smiled the way some men do when they want to ask for something, but won't come right out and say it.

"You boys selling something?" Norman looked behind them and saw a red Ford pickup truck with nothing in the bed except snow and ice.

"You might say that," the man with the beard said, looking at his companion. "This will only take a few minutes. Do you mind if we come in?" Still smiling, he slid a foot over the threshold. "You alone today?"

Something about the man's pushiness put off Norman and he decided that, in fact, he didn't like the look of these men and wished that he had his pap's .45, which was in the top drawer of the nightstand next to his bed. He hesitated a moment too long. The bearded one strong-armed Norman backward and the skinny one followed them inside and shut the door.

"I'll be goddamned. A man lives in the country his whole life and two white boys break into his house to rob him. I'll be goddamned," Norman sputtered. "Look, I don't have much. I might have fifteen dollars in cash and a cigar box full of change. There ain't nothing here worth taking."

"Sit down, you fat pig," said the skinny one. "We ain't here to rob you. We just want to talk."

Norman blinked in disbelief as he stepped back until he was at his BarcaLounger. Then, with a shove, the skinny one pushed him into his chair, which groaned loudly at the sudden weight. The bearded one came out of the bedroom holding pap's .45, which he shoved under his belt behind his back. He looked around in the kitchen, then returned to the living room and the television.

"It's just the three of us and this thing is too loud to have a quiet conversation," he said. He leaned over and flicked it off.

"That's much better, don't you think?" He pulled the telephone cord out of the wall with one quick tug and tossed the phone across the room.

Norman's heart beat rapidly. Between his weight, diabetes, congestive heart failure, and high blood pressure, the docs at the VA constantly reminded him that his health was lousy and he had to do something about it. As he sat in his chair, he tried to control his breathing, which was rapid and shallow, like the therapist had said. He told himself to be cool, not to lose his temper, let these bastards take what they wanted and get the hell out of his place. All he had to do was keep from passing out.

"Now Norman, Normie, we understand that you and some of your neighbors are having a problem and we think that maybe yins are being a bit misguided," the bearded one said, leaning over a little too close.

"How, how did you know my name?" Norman asked.

The two men looked at each other and smiled.

"We know a lot about you Normie," said the bearded one. "We know that you have a daughter and grandchildren living in Cleveland. We know that her husband is in the Marines, currently stationed on a ship in the Pacific. We know your wife, Sally, may she rest in peace, died four years ago."

"Who are you guys?"

"Doesn't matter who we are. Now let's stop with the questions, okay? Like I said, you, your neighbors, this thing yins are doing, enough is enough."

"I, I don't get it. What thing are we doing? What do you want us to stop?"

"This lawsuit you have against Rhino. That suit can put a lot of good working people out of a job. We think you have to shut 'er down. Am I making myself clear?"

"You mean the appeal, the permit appeal? We're trying to protect our homes."

"Not what I'm hearing Normie," said the bearded one. "I'm hearing this has to do with you rascals trying to make a buck offa this."

Norman felt like he could have a heart attack at any moment.

"Look, what matters is that you have a choice to make. You and your neighbors. The lawsuit that you filed, it's fuckin' up a lot of plans, hurting a lot of people. Working people. These plans are bigger than you, shit, they're bigger than us. That's a problem, Normie."

Norman's mouth was dry. His heart raced and he was light-headed. He worried that he would pass out. He willed himself to stay conscious.

"Now Normie, there isn't much you have to do. All you have to do is to back off. Tell your buddies that you thought about it and you've lost interest in this lawsuit. Would you consider that?" asked the bearded one. "That seems reasonable, don't it? Shit, man, if you got one or two of the others to drop the lawsuit, there'd even be a payday in it for you. If all of you dropped the suit, well, you'd get a big bonus. I understand there's an open offer on this fine place. You should take it and move out. It's looking a little tired, huh Norm?"

"But that Rhino, he's gonna put a *strip mine* right in front of my house. That ain't right. This is my home, I raised my family here. I have a legal right to stop that."

"You have a legal right to live, until you eat yourself to death," said the skinny one glaring at him and poking him hard in the chest with a finger.

In an instant, he produced a stiletto knife from the sleeve of his jacket and held the tip of the blade against Norman's face. He pressed it into Norman's cheek, just a millimeter away from cutting him, and said, "Man, I could filet you right now, you fat pig. You'd better shut up and hold your breath, my friend, 'cause if you don't, I'm liable to cut you."

The bearded one looked at the skinny one, "Calm down Skel, back off for now." Skel slid the knife from Norman's cheek to his eyeball. Neither man moved. Neither man breathed. Finally, the bearded one tapped Skel's shoulder.

"Skel," he whispered softly.

Skel closed the knife, returning it to his sleeve. He gave a wicked look to the bearded one.

The bearded one looked back to Norman. "Look Normie, let me make this easy for you. Here is what you have to do. Get out of the lawsuit. Get out today. If you don't, my friend and I will come back and visit you again. Next time it won't be a social visit. Next time it might be at three o'clock in the morning. I guarantee you that we'll be in a real sour mood. As it is, right now, my buddy and I are feeling pretty good. Take that offer and move outta' here." The bearded one patted Norman's shoulder hard, more of a hard punch than a pat.

"I think we've made our point," the bearded one said to Skel, laughing. "I don't think Mr. Post, with a daughter and cute little grandkids in Cleveland, wants to visit with us anymore today or ever again." Then, looking at Norman, he said, "Don't get up Normie, we'll just let ourselves out." He smiled.

When the door shut, Norman heard Skel say, "Wolfie, you asshole, you weren't supposed to use my name."

"Shut up you idiot, what was the deal with the fucking knife? Mr. Rinati said to play it cool. You heard him, you know, *make an impression*. He didn't say we should cut the guy. Mr. Rinati'd be pissed as hell if you left a mark on that guy. Get in the truck, you moron."

"I was playing it cool. For me, that was cool…"

The truck door slammed and Norman couldn't hear any more of their argument.

Norman sat in his chair after the truck doors slammed. Sweat beaded across his brow and ran down his neck. He heard the truck start up. He waited for many minutes after the sound of the truck had faded in the distance.

Waited while his heart tried to slow to a normal beat.

Waited as he tried to will his heart to slow down.

Waited hoping the pounding in his ears would vanish.

As he waited, a pain grew in his chest. The pain he had feared for years. It welled up from his stomach, across his torso to his chest and neck. He wished he could reach his nitro pills, but they were too far away and he couldn't stand up to get them.

The pain grew more and more intense and he looked for the phone, which no longer was within arm's reach next to the chair, but overturned and unplugged, lying on the floor. The cell phone was in the bedroom.

The last thing he saw was the picture of his wife and family as he slumped over in his chair, the pain in his chest so intense that he passed out just a few seconds before his heart stopped beating.

35

Mike double parked his car in the loading zone in front of his apartment house and watched in his rear-view mirror as Nicky parked her Volkswagen behind him. In the early evening darkness, they both turned on their flashers and got out of their cars into the cold night air. Mike pulled two suitcases full of Nicky's clothes out of the trunk, while Nicky hoisted a box from the trunk of her car. Her face was grim.

Mike looked at Nicky and smiled, "Well, that wasn't so bad. As long as you don't mind getting hit in the guts."

"I know you're trying to cheer me up, but maybe later," she said, her voice breaking.

Mike understood and headed to the apartment house. After some maneuvering, they got her things through the front door. They took the elevator up to the third floor and managed to get most of Nicky's stuff into Mike's apartment, when Mrs. Landau, Mike's across-the-hall neighbor, opened her door.

"Hello children." She sang out happily.

"Hello Mrs. L," Mike said.

Crap.

Busted.

"Nice evening, Mrs. Landau, isn't it?" Nicky said, her face transformed into a broad smile.

"Looks like somebody's moving in." Her voice was sing-songy. Happy. She craned her neck, trying to look past them into the apartment.

Neither Mike nor Nicky replied.

"I said, looks like somebody's moving in…"

Nicky looked at Mike for help and Mike said, "My friend, Nicky, had some trouble in her old apartment and I'm letting her use my guest room until she gets situated."

"Oh, your *guest* room," Mrs. Landau said smiling broadly.

"Yes, the *guest* room. Look we're double-parked and we still have some more things to move in, so I'm sorry, but we can't spend time chatting. I'm sure we'll have another opportunity."

"Maybe you two can stop over for cookies and tea sometime soon? Maybe a glass of Manischewitz?"

"Of course," Nicky said brightly, "*we'd* love to."

"I'll be sure to say hello for you to your grandmother, dear, you know she's one of my *best* friends."

Mrs. Landau smiled. Nicky grimaced.

The elevator saved them from further conversation. As they headed back to their cars, Mike took a quick detour to his mailbox. Stuck to the door was a slip from the landlady, indicating that he had a package.

"Can you bring in some more stuff while I see if I can get this?" He said holding up the slip.

Nicky headed outside while Mike tapped on Mrs. Winston's office door. It was almost six p.m. on a Saturday, but he wasn't surprised when she answered. She lived in an apartment next to the office, so she was always around.

Mike had long thought Mrs. Winston was the best-dressed elderly landlady in Harrisburg, and today was no exception. She wore a cream-colored blouse, tucked neatly into a long skirt, and a coy smile.

"Well, Mr. Jacobs," she said. "Happy New Year to you."

"Happy New Year to you, too." He held up the slip. "Do you have a package for me?"

Mrs. Winston went to a counter and examined several packages. "Let's see, Mrs. Stephens, the widow, Mrs. Cheney, the widow, Mr. Booker, the widower. Oh, here it is, Mr. Jacobs, the lady-killer."

She handed him the FedEx envelope with a smile.

Mike tried to maintain a poker face. "Look, Mrs. Winston, my friend, Nicky Kane, lost her lease, so she's going to use my guest room. That's all."

"Oh, that's no problem at all, dear. I've known her grandmother since high school." She gave him a wan smile. "So far as I'm concerned, you can put her name on your mailbox and I'll just make a note in case the mailman asks."

Mike bit back a protest. Every time he opened his mouth he just seemed to dig himself a bigger hole. Instead, he thanked her and got to the door in time to hold it for Nicky who was carrying another box. When the cars were emptied and parked, they returned to the apartment and after sorting some of Nicky's things, Mike opened the FedEx envelope. Before he could peek inside, though, Nicky's heavy sigh pulled his attention back to her.

"I'm not in the mood to clean up the guest room and put my stuff away," Nicky said. "How about if I take you out to dinner and we clean out the guest room over the next couple of days?"

"Sounds good to me," he replied. "Seriously, though, you should take my room, and I'll sleep on the sofa until we clean it out."

"If you offer to sleep on the sofa again," Nicky said as she headed for the bathroom, "I'll tell Mrs. Landau we're sleeping together. I will." And with that she tossed him a cheeky grin over her shoulder, and shut the bathroom door.

Mike stared after her for a long moment, unable to shake the thought that maybe inviting his gay best friend, with whom he may be in love, to move in might not have been his smartest decision. Needing a distraction, he forced himself to focus on the contents of the envelope. Inside were several papers and a handwritten note. The note read:

Dear Mike,

Here are the papers we discussed.

Your friend.

B

Mike knew immediately that the letter was from Ben Kemper, even though it was not signed. He turned to the handful of papers.

The first one was from the First National Bank of Meyersdale. It was a photocopy of a statement for Lyle Ransom. The account had been opened on November 19 with five thousand dollars. A few days later there was a four thousand dollar withdrawal. In the subsequent two weeks, thousands were deposited and thousands withdrawn every other day. Mike did the math quickly in his head. In the month of November, Ransom had deposited a total of thirty thousand dollars into his account.

Mike turned the paper over and frowned. As he began going through the remaining papers, Nicky came into the living room pulling on her parka.

"Are you ready?"

"Sure," Mike replied unconvincingly. He wondered how Ben got these papers and got them so quickly.

"If you don't want to go, we don't have to," Nicky said smiling. "I can make some dinner if you have anything in the fridge."

"No, this can wait."

As he shoved the papers back into the envelope, he decided not to ask too many questions about the source of the documents.

Not yet, anyway.

After dinner Mike sat on the sofa in the living room going through the papers. He was surprised Ben had been able to obtain incriminating documents so quickly as it had only been a week since they'd decided to look into Ransom's activities.

Mike analyzed the papers. Ransom made a lump sum deposit of five thousand dollars, apparently in cash, to open the account and was making cash deposits every few days of thousands of dollars, for a total of thirty thousand dollars. He made a number of large withdrawals of cash. The was no other activity on the account. If this was money from Rinati, that was incriminating enough for Mike.

Should I take this to Roger now?

Do I wait until I have more incriminating evidence?

He could hear Nicky in his bedroom, changing her clothes. They decided that they would switch rooms depending upon what they were doing until the guest room was ready. Nicky told

Mike she wanted to shower and get ready for bed. That was fine with Mike, who wanted to go through Ben's papers.

The door to Mike's bedroom opened and Nicky walked into the room wearing a long flannel granny nightgown and heavy socks. Her hair, still damp from the shower, was wrapped in a towel.

"So is this what hot lesbians wear to bed?" he asked.

"You think I'm hot?" Nicky said. She giggled.

Nicky looked at Mike's ratty stuffed chair and then sat on the sofa next to Mike. She wiggled next to him until he put his arm around her. Mike looked at her and made a face.

"You go back to work," she said. "I'm cold and remember, I'm also a big cuddler. Pretend I'm not here."

Yeah right. Nicky, wearing her flannel nightgown, tucked in under my arm is not here.

Mike picked up the papers and began examining them again, however, his thoughts were all about Nicky.

Later, through his bedroom door as he tried to fall asleep, Mike could hear Nicky as she moved around on his sofa. He heard her get up and walk around the living room. His old apartment had one bathroom, and the only way to reach it was through his room. Nicky lightly tapped on his door and entered without Mike having to reply. She went into the bathroom without a word, closed the door and the light went on. Mike heard the tinkle of a girl peeing, and the toilet flushed. A few moments later, the sink ran and then Nicky returned to the living room.

Mike closed his eyes and tried to go back to sleep. No more than five minutes later, he heard his door open again and looked up as Nicky came into his room in her granny nightgown, pulled down the covers and climbed in next to him.

"What's going on?" Mike asked.

"I'm cold and your sofa is lumpy," Nicky replied.

She got into bed, turned on her side to face him and whispered, "Go to sleep."

"Seriously?"

"Seriously," she said sternly as she took his hand and cuddled next to him.

Mike, wide awake, his hand holding Nicky's, tried to go back to sleep. A few moments later, he turned and his legs were next to Nicky's side. Immediately, she backed away from him and sat up on her elbow.

"What was that?"

"What do you mean, 'what was that?'"

"Your…thing dug into my leg. Don't even think about it," she whispered. "It's never going to happen."

"Look, I don't want it to happen either, but a good-looking woman I really like climbs into bed with me in the middle of the night and some things happen spontaneously. I can't help it. I mean it's not controllable. This wouldn't be happening right now if you weren't here."

Nicky looked at him, still on her elbow, "Do you want me to go? I can sleep on the sofa."

Mike paused for a long moment and rolled over on his back and said, "No, I happen to like your company."

Nicky backed away from him a couple of inches, patted him on the shoulder and said, "Good, me too. Now go to sleep, sweetie."

A few moments later Nicky's breathing became rhythmic as she fell asleep.

Mike laid on his back and looked at the dark ceiling.

This is never going to work.

Eventually, he fell asleep too. A couple of hours later, he barely noticed when Nicky worked her arms around his neck and they slept peacefully with their faces inches apart.

36

The Amtrak locomotive rumbled past the last, slow curve in the rail-yard as it entered Philadelphia's 30th Street Station. Passengers waited for the train, the Pennsylvanian, arriving from Harrisburg on track seven, to take them to New York City. The engine shuddered as it inched along the platform and stopped with a clank, sleet and rainwater dripping off the sides of the cars.

Mike detrained, thinking that although he loved to drive, he hated driving into Philly. You were almost always guaranteed a parking spot on the Schuylkill Expressway, no matter what time of day it was. The two hour drive could easily stretch into three.

On the train he could work quietly without any interruption and he cherished the quiet time. Also, the small boy in him liked looking out the window as the Pennsylvania countryside rushed by. Near Lancaster, he often saw Amish people in their buggies or working in the fields. Their lives seemed uncomplicated and simple. The men looked sturdy and strong. So did the women. Today, he had seen no one working in the fields, but there had been several buggies, steam venting from the horses' nostrils, the passengers hidden inside black canvas-enclosed carriages, as they waited patiently in the cold, winter drizzle for the train to pass a crossing. The scene had a nineteenth century feel to it. Mike wondered if the Amish were hiring.

He took his briefcase and walked up the steps to the main concourse. Thirtieth Street Station was an art-deco marvel with an endless ceiling. There was always excitement in the air and people from all walks of life filled the place. An Amish family had exited the train ahead of him and he wondered where on earth they were going in Philly. They passed a Chassidic man who was moving toward the line for New York City. Businessmen in their suits and long coats, students in Levi's, and Main Line women shoppers in Ralph Lauren jeans and Prada boots crisscrossed in front of him. Mike loved the commotion. He walked through the station until he arrived at the SEPTA regional train platform. An added benefit of taking Amtrak was that your ticket included a free hop onto any SEPTA light-rail train heading downtown.

Ten minutes later he was on Market Street, in front of the building housing Feldman's office. A large, well-maintained, but oddly antiquated, brass sign proclaimed the Law Firm of Pell, Desrosiers, Cox & Drury. As he sat in the ornate lobby on the thirty-eighth floor, he looked around and appreciated the dark woodwork, parquet floors, leather chairs and oriental carpets. The building was fairly new, but the decorations looked like they were out of a nineteenth century barrister's office or perhaps a gentlemen's supper club. Somehow, the firm had found an attractive British receptionist who greeted everyone as though they were in London, which added to the overall ambience of money, influence, and power. Mike stood in the reception area looking out a large plate-glass window across from Philadelphia's City Hall and toward the Delaware River.

"Mr. Jacobs?"

Mike turned and eyed the young woman. She would have fit comfortably on the pages of a fashion magazine or a high-end men's magazine. She was in her mid-twenties, attractive face, drop-dead body, and wearing a short dress that no secretary who worked for the Commonwealth could afford to buy.

"Hi, I'm Chrissy, Mr. Feldman's assistant. Won't you follow me?" she asked with a warm smile as she extended her hand, which Mike happily shook.

I'd follow you anywhere. Mike smiled to himself as much as he did for Feldman's assistant.

Mike wondered how such a comely woman fit into this austere, buttoned-down environment. Then he realized that she was exactly the type of woman that Feldman wanted on display as his assistant.

Chrissy walked them into Feldman's gigantic corner office—he wasn't there—and motioned to a seat in a sitting area in the corner, overlooking City Hall.

"Would you like some coffee? A toasted bagel? Perhaps a warm croissant?" she asked with a smile that looked like it could turn into a giggle without much prodding.

"Coffee, black, would be nice."

She turned and Mike watched her as she disappeared. Then he looked around at Feldman's lair. His desk chair was leather, of course, with a high back. Surprisingly, his desk was spindly, almost feminine. He could see that it was old and he suspected it was some kind of antique, maybe French. The other furniture in the office looked as though it was made out of cherry wood and had recently been cleaned and oiled. Modern oil paintings hung on the wall near the sitting area. He didn't really appreciate the art, but he could see that they were signed originals, the real deal, not prints.

On one wall, Mike saw pictures of Feldman: Feldman and Joel Embid, both wearing suits, Embid towering over Feldman; a much younger Feldman and Mike Schmidt on the field at a game, Feldman in casual clothes and Schmidt wearing a soiled uniform as though the game had just ended; Feldman and Senator Bob Casey; Feldman and Benjamin Netanyahu at a formal dinner. Mike thought of something he had once heard: you aren't important when you have pictures of yourself and famous people on *your* wall, you are important when famous people have pictures of *you* on *their* walls.

On the wall next to the door was a single framed document over a photograph. Mike got close to read it and saw that it was on old pushcart license issued by the City of Philadelphia. The license allowed the holder to operate the pushcart in Philadelphia to sell fruits and vegetables. It was issued to one Moses Feldman and was dated 1939. Below that was a picture of Sidney Feldman shaking hands with a smiling George W. Bush, both wearing tuxedoes and posing at what looked like a formal state dinner.

It was inscribed, "To Sid Feldman—my trusted friend and advisor," and signed *George Bush*.

As he looked at the picture, Feldman came in carrying Mike's coffee in a ceramic mug.

"Here you go, Mike, service with a smile." Feldman held out his hand. "Pretty nice digs for a kid from South Philly, don't you think?"

"Thanks, Sid. Moses Feldman was your—"

"—*is* my father." Feldman pointed to the pushcart license. "From the old country to a pushcart in South Philly, to a grocery store on the Zibbiter—South Seventh Street—to a chain of supermarkets. Only in America."

"His kid didn't do too badly either," Mike smiled. "It's funny, when I looked at these, something popped into my mind, 'Know from where you come, and where you are going—"

Feldman interrupted him and added, "and before whom you will have to give an account."

"You know it? The Talmud?" Mike asked, surprised.

"Let's just say, I dabble. Besides, that's *Pirkei Avot*, hardly one of the difficult books."

They took seats at the sitting area and chatted about the Eagles and Mike's trip to Philly. Feldman and his family had just gotten back from a ski trip to Vail, something they did every Christmas season.

"It's either that or dinner at a Chinese restaurant." Feldman enjoyed a good laugh.

Mike looked around, curious about the intimate and even royal treatment he was getting. He had heard of many other lawyers getting no further than a small conference room next to the lobby, yet here he was sitting in the great man's *sanctum seclorum*. He wondered if he should be honored or worried.

Feldman interrupted the small talk and said, "Look, I think the department is in an odd position in this case. You guys issued a permit which Ernie—Mr. Rinati—isn't thrilled with. I mean, if he mines the way the permit allows him to mine, he'll never be able to get at all of the coal. His mining engineer estimates that he'll have to leave at least half a million dollars' worth of coal in the ground that he could otherwise access without the conditions. That's a shitload of coal. I hope you can understand why we filed an appeal."

"I suppose, but the fact of the matter is that he wants to mine too close to those homes and the road. The houses, the road, could be undermined. Also, my people are concerned about fly-rock and other potential damage from blasting. I know the regulations say you can do it, but our permitting people feel this location is just too dangerous. We're not going to let that happen. Also, he's proposing to mine very close to the watershed of that trout stream. That's why they added an additional setback there. There's also a question regarding the overburden. Our geologists feel that when he mines the coal, the waste rock he leaves in the ground may cause an acid discharge. They added those conditions requiring him to segregate the overburden and take care to prevent an acid mine discharge after mining is over. I know that's more expensive, but in the end, it protects both the environment *and* your client."

"We appreciate your concern, but frankly, our engineers think you, I mean the department, are just wrong. We know we can safely mine it and we know how to handle overburden. Rinati has about a dozen active operations and maybe twice that many completed jobs. He's never had an acid discharge problem and at most a handful of nuisance violations. Maybe there's a compromise we can work out so that Rinati can get seventy-five or at least fifty percent more of that remaining coal? As I see it, we're really on the same side against those citizens with the pitchforks. We ought to be working together against them."

"Sid, those citizens think that *we*, I mean the citizens and the department, ought to be working against *you*," Mike said.

"I'm not surprised. You couldn't possibly agree with them, though, do you? A smart kid like you? I mean DEP issued the permit and I expect that you'll stand by it. After all, if we dropped our appeal then it would be the irate citizens of Somerset versus the department. I don't see how in good conscience the department could possibly consider supporting them. If the department didn't want the mining in the first place, then you never would have issued the permit. But you did. I think it makes the most sense for you to work with us against these misguided neighbors."

Mike nodded without responding.

"You know Mike, I want you to know my real feelings about this coal mining thing. I'd be interested in yours, too. You're too young to remember President Carter, right? Generally, he was a disaster, but in 1977 he went on television and gave that speech and said the energy crisis was the moral equivalent of war. A lot of people didn't take him seriously. I was in law school and although I had a lot of doubts about our former president, I did agree with him about that. He said we had to, what, double our output of coal? Something like that. We simply couldn't be beholden to foreigners, the Arabs and others in the oil cartel, for our energy needs. He was right about all of that. Where I think he went off the rails was in saying we ought to rely more on solar."

Mike held his gaze without nodding.

"I mean, come on, if you had to rely on solar can you imagine how many acres it would take to power one city, one steel mill? You'd have to cover the whole state. The next thing you know, we'll be building windmills." He laughed. "No, seriously, we need coal, nukes, oil and gas, that kind of thing for base generation. I don't ever want to see us having to depend on other countries for our energy needs. I mean it. They would just have our balls in a vise and who wants that? How about you?"

Mike wasn't sure whether he wanted to share his views with Feldman. "Well, I agree that we don't want to be beholden to a foreign government for our energy. You're leaving out the messy issue of climate change. Personally, I'd like to see more use of solar, conservation, and wind if we can do it. I guess we need to continue using coal, oil and gas, at least for now until we phase them out. Quickly, I hope. I'm not too crazy about nuclear, though, Sid. Keep in mind I live ten miles from Three Mile Island. Its one good point is that nukes don't emit carbon dioxide."

"So, you do support the expanded use of coal for now, just like Carter said?"

"Not exactly. I'd like to see it phased out as soon as possible. In the meantime, I'd like to see it burned without emitting carbon and other pollutants and mined without harming the environment," Mike said slowly. "Continuing to mine it at all leaves me uncomfortable, though. I've seen thousands of acres of devastated land, acid mine drainage, air pollution from power plants, you name it."

"The crap, I understand, you're uncomfortable about the crap. But that's from old, abandoned and unregulated mining. Climate change, if it really is man-made, is just an engineering challenge, that's all. You know *technology* can solve all of those problems," Feldman said, as though he had just switched on the light bulb for Mike. "I've read that existing technology can cut carbon emissions by ninety percent. Did you know that?"

"And so long as industry abides by its permits, regulation and enforcement, everything will be fine." Mike said smiling back at him.

Mike noticed Feldman had leaned forward as he was talking and he couldn't help but notice that Feldman's shirt was the kind that probably cost more than all of the clothes Mike was wearing. Feldman's necktie was a beautiful heavy silk weave and he wore large gold cufflinks. Feldman's hair was black and combed over in a way that Mike thought made Feldman look a bit like Clark Kent.

"You know, in cases like this, I'll be present to defend the integrity of the department," Mike said. "You're a capable litigator and no doubt Miranda is also capable." As Mike said this, he wondered if she really was capable.

"I don't see any reason why the two of you don't just duke it out and I'll just sit there watching the Sid and Miranda show and making sure nobody says anything bad about the department." Mike smiled at his adversary. "Better yet, why don't *you* work it out before any hearing?"

Feldman sat back in his chair, re-crossed his legs and said, "You're too damn good a young lawyer to be satisfied babysitting a case like this. C'mon, who are you kidding? I was hoping you'd think about taking a more active role. DEP *issued* the permit and at the least you ought to be *defending* it. I'll tell you what, let's leave the door open a crack, okay? You know our position."

Feldman stood up and looked out the window toward City Hall, its gray stone set against the coffin sky, then he turned and looked at Mike, "I'm going to give you a little heads up because I like you. Ernie is a big believer in using those political connections he's nurtured for oh-so-long. Keep your eyes open for something from one or more of his legislator buddies. I've advised him not to do it, but Rinati is his own man. When he gets something in his mind, he's going to do it. Whatever it is, don't take it personally and keep in mind that it's not coming from me."

Mike nodded without responding.

"Another thing," Feldman continued. "This is free advice from an old bull to a young stud. When it comes, play it cool. I don't know if you've ever been the recipient of a legislative inquiry, but when I was with DEP, it happened to me. More than once, too. There's nothing quite like having the CEOs of all the major steel companies in Pennsylvania writing to the governor and demanding your balls in a jar. Listen to me, Mike, think of it as a high inside fastball. In a way, it's kind of a compliment. Step back from the plate, give the pitcher a hard stare, and get ready for the next pitch; don't overreact." Feldman looked at Mike and with a smile added, "Normally I charge eight hundred dollars an hour for that advice. For you, nothing."

"Thanks, I think."

Feldman smiled again and looked at his watch. "Come on, I'll take you to the Union League for lunch."

Feldman went to his desk and flipped through his emails. While he studied his monitor he said, "By the way, have you ever considered leaving DEP? Maybe going into private practice?"

Mike was surprised at the question. "Uh, sure. I've been with DEP for over three years and I've first-chaired over a dozen trials now and done two or three oral arguments in Commonwealth Court. I may be ready for a new challenge."

"You ever think of moving to Philly?" Now, Feldman was giving him a hard look.

Mike tried to picture himself working for Feldman and was wondering where this conversation was going, whether it was even appropriate as they were in active litigation. "Not currently, but I like the town. I could see myself here."

Mike expected another question, but Feldman, his point made, let it drop.

As they exited Feldman's office, they walked past a small room, with a window overlooking South Philly. It held a desk loaded with two monitors, piles of paper and open law books. Mike looked in and saw a woman, pleasant face, somewhat plump, bent over her laptop, an empty cup of yogurt and a paper wrapper from a deli on her desk. Feldman walked in without knocking.

"Angela, I'd like you to meet Mike Jacobs. Mike, this is Angela St. Germain. She's my go-to associate." Angela stood and they shook hands. Mike noticed crumbs fall from her chest, which she swept away the moment before she shook his hand. As she looked up, Mike remembered her.

"Angela? The hearing. Burroughs Mining Company. That was you in the corner, wasn't it? You sat through the hearing and when I went to introduce myself, you disappeared."

She smiled at him. "Well, it's a public proceeding. Nothing wrong with me getting a few practice pointers from you, is there?"

"Practice pointers? You came all the way from Philly to Harrisburg for some tips from me? Seriously?"

"Hey kids, let's call it what it was, that was a scouting trip," Feldman interjected. "No different than when a baseball scout sits behind home plate with a radar gun when the rookie starter you're going to face someday is pitching a big game against another team," Feldman said with a smile.

Mike looked at him, "So what was the report? The scouting report?"

Feldman looked at Angela and he nodded. "Self-assured, talented, knows the rules, that kind of thing," she said.

Mike looked at Feldman, "Uh-huh."

"Well, shit Angela, why don't you tell him exactly what you told me. *Cocky, arrogant, mouthy, smart-as-hell, clever, like when he had a potential witness who was not subpoenaed by the poor schlemiel from Hooterville hit the Turnpike until the trial was over.* Wasn't that it?"

Angela smiled at Mike, "Like I said, self-assured and talented."

Mike smiled weakly trying not to think about the letter he had sent several days earlier to Helms apologizing for his lapse in judgment.

"If I were to follow the baseball analogy," Feldman continued, showing a row of artificially whitened teeth, "the scouting report would say, a young phenom, showing good power, if he can keep his mouth under control. He's considered the best prospect in all of environmental litigation, currently playing in Triple-A, ready for the major leagues."

Mike listened and nodded, "I thought I *was* in the major league."

Feldman smiled.

Mike turned to Angela. "So, are you working on anything interesting these days?"

Angela looked momentarily at Feldman who nodded at her. "Yes, in fact I'm working on the Rhino Mining case. Ever hear of it?"

"Rhino? Rhino? Yes, I've heard about that one," Mike replied. "Let me know how that turns out, would you?" He winked at Angela and shook her hand as he left. Angela watched him until he disappeared down the hall.

Mike and Feldman continued to another, even smaller office, stacked high with bankers' boxes and file folders. Inside was a young man, about twenty-five, hunched over a pile of papers. Feldman, without entering the office, called, "Jimmy."

The young man jumped to his feet and Mike wondered if he had purchased his outfit from the kid's department of whichever high-end store Feldman shopped. He wore a shirt that looked a lot like Feldman's, with French cuffs and cufflinks made out of old coins, a bow tie and suspenders. "I'd like you to meet Jimmy Podwall, a first-year associate out of Yale. Jimmy, this is Mike Jacobs from DEP." The men shook hands.

"Jimmy's been with us since September. Quite an education, eh?" Feldman asked.

Jimmy nodded, looked over his shoulder at the papers, and muttered something under his breath, almost gibberish, that Mike couldn't understand. Feldman was already striding down the hall and Mike waved at Jimmy, then did his best to keep up. As Mike and Feldman hurtled toward the elevator, Feldman's trophy secretary trotted after them and said something in Feldman's ear.

"That's okay, Chrissy, tell him I'll call him back after lunch," Feldman said, not breaking his long stride. "No, on second thought, tell him *I'm having lunch with Mike Jacobs of DEP* and I'll call him back after lunch." Feldman lightly punched Mike's shoulder and they continued to the Union League.

37

Roger tossed a brown manila envelope onto Mike's desk. "Merry Christmas."

Mike looked up and shrugged. "What's up?"

Roger's face was grim. "Have a look."

The envelope was marked, *Roger Alden, Regional Counsel, PERSONAL AND CONFIDENTIAL.* He looked into the envelope, which had already been torn apart, and pulled out the contents. Inside was a letter with a note stapled to the front with a short hand-written message on cheap notepaper, *From the Desk of Anthony Capozzi, Secretary of Environmental Protection.* All it said was, "Call me."

The attached letter was on fancy embossed stationery, from Senator Gary Mifflin, a state senator from somewhere in west-central Pennsylvania. It was addressed to The Honorable Anthony Capozzi.

> Dear Secretary Capozzi:
>
> I am writing to support the issuance of a coal mining permit in my District to Rhino Mining Company. Rhino is owned by my longtime friend and constituent, Ernesto Rinati.
>
> Mr. Rinati's business is being hampered by an appeal that has been filed by a misguided group of people, whom I have been advised are trying to fleece him for money. They are delaying his efforts to mine property for which he has a permit. I would not write merely to

complain about the ill-advised citizens. Rather, I am writing to complain about the conduct of one of your lawyers, Michael Jacobs.

Mr. Rinati expects the Department will vigorously seek to uphold the permit that it issued. Instead, it appears that the Department, under the direction of Mr. Jacobs, is not supporting Rhino Mining and may be improperly favoring the neighbors over the Department's permitting decision.

I would never ask you to make a decision or take any action that would inappropriately favor a constituent, however, I believe it is proper to call your attention to what I believe to be the misguided efforts of Mr. Jacobs. I only ask that you scrutinize his actions and that you make certain he acts evenhandedly.

I look forward to your presentation to the Budget Committee which will be meeting shortly to discuss the Department's budget.

With best regards, I remain,
Very truly yours,
Honorable Gary Mifflin
State Senator

Mike looked up from the letter and cleared his throat. "Other than that, how was Dallas, Mrs. Kennedy?"

Roger took the letter out of Mike's hands. He glanced at it as he spoke. "I wouldn't worry about this. It's nothing more than a shot across the bow."

Mike shook his head indicating that he didn't understand.

"What I mean is, the good senator is not directly threatening you, he's only telling the secretary that you're in his sights," Roger advised.

"*I*? *I'm* in his sights? I haven't done anything yet. What happened to 'sit back and defend the integrity of the program?' I thought I was doing what I'd been told to do?"

"Don't worry," replied Roger. "This is a shot across the *department's* bow, not yours. I spoke to Capozzi a few minutes ago after I received this from him and he assured me that we were to continue with our litigation strategy. I think you can see why I said that we're not to take sides in this dispute. Trust me, the citizens also have their champions and the next letter we receive could be from their favorite state senator."

Mike made a face and looked at his desk. After a moment he looked up and said, "so, what exactly am I supposed to do with this? I mean, if I'm supposed to be even-handed, how can I do that and still satisfy the gentleman from Johnstown?"

"Don't worry about it," replied Roger. "The secretary asked me to draft a response for his signature which I'll do this morning. It will thank the good senator for his thoughtful comments and then will tell him, in the politest way imaginable, to go screw himself. For now, just continue as we discussed. I'll let you know if there's any response to the secretary's letter."

"I could save you a lot of effort and draft an appropriate two-word response to the senator," Mike offered.

Roger smiled and said, "Thanks, Bud, this is why I'm paid the big bucks."

38

Not for the first time in his career Mike found himself sitting in Secretary Capozzi's office. He and Roger had been summoned in response to Roger's request that the department initiate an investigation into the allegation that Rinati had bribed Lyle Ransom. Also on the agenda was the legislative inquiry from Senator Mifflin. After quick handshakes, the secretary sat and looked through the short memo Mike had prepared and Roger had signed.

"Roger, first of all, your memo is four pages long. You know I've told you on more than one occasion to say what you need to say in two pages if you must, one page is best. That aside, the allegations and this information from the bank here are serious."

Capozzi studied the bank statement attached to the memo. He wore a grey flannel suit, white shirt and bright red necktie. The suit and whatever hair he had were the same color.

"That's right, Secretary, we obtained a copy of this bank statement and it looks as though he's on the take," Roger said. "Also, he admits to having received a gold Rolex watch from Rinati, although, in fairness, he says it was his retirement gift. But those two things, along with the allegations that he's on the take suggest we should be investigating him at the very least. My preference would be to start small and discretely so we don't tip him off or unnecessarily offend anyone working in the district office."

"I think that's a good idea," the secretary replied. "What you have isn't decisive. If he did receive a retirement gift, that was before he started working with the department, and this thing with the bank statement doesn't prove he's on the take. We don't know where the money is coming from. For all we know, he works weekends at a Walmart and is depositing his paycheck."

Without realizing it, Mike rolled his eyes.

"Mr. Jacobs, I would appreciate it if you would reserve your comments, both verbal and nonverbal. I'm the secretary and if you have any comments, speak up."

"With all due respect Mr. Secretary," Mike replied trying not to look at Roger, "I apologize, but this guy is different. He's lazy, I think he does a lousy job out in the field, and he's a bigot. I mean he's an out and out racist. This guy's a disgrace to the department. On top of that we now have serious allegations he's being bribed. I think we have significant and mounting evidence he's on the take. What makes it worse is that he's inspecting Rhino's operations."

"Okay Mike, if you were secretary, what would you do?" the secretary asked, not smiling.

Roger gave Mike a hard look.

Mike cleared his throat. "Well, I agree we don't have adequate evidence at this point. I think we need to scrutinize the Rhino mine sites Ransom's been inspecting to see whether he's doing what he ought to be doing or if he has a pattern of ignoring violations. I would bring in a team of inspectors from outside and have them re-inspect every one of Rinati's jobs. At the same time, I'd have the attorney general subpoena his records from that bank and identify the source of those deposits. Finally, I'd call him in before a grand jury and ask him a lot of hard questions."

Secretary Capozzi sat back and looked at the young man. Without realizing it, Roger had placed his hand over his mouth, suggesting to Mike he should shut up.

"Okay Mike, I like some of your ideas. But we're not going to bring in a big team of inspectors. I think one inspector, somebody who's trustworthy from another region should do. Let's see what that turns up. Maybe the guy is the best inspector we have out in the field. Maybe he's completely corrupt. Let's find out. Depending upon the results of that re-inspection, we'll take it to the next level. What do you think, Roger?"

"I think you're right, Mr. Secretary. It would be a mistake to go overboard with this inspection, not to mention it would undermine the activities of our other inspectors across the state. I'm happy to go with the step-by-step approach."

Mike started to say something until he caught the death look in Roger's eyes.

"One more thing," Capozzi said. "This inquiry from Mifflin. He's an idiot, but he's powerful and has seniority. I'll handle him, but you watch what you say, since I'm the one who will be testifying before the Senate budget committee."

When Roger and Mike were back on the street, heading to their office, Roger stopped on the street corner and looked at his young colleague. "You have a pair of stones, son. Don't ever show me up again. Sometimes you forget who are your friends and who are your enemies."

Mike was about to reply. He thought better of it.

39

Mike picked up the office phone, glanced at his iPhone, and dialed. "Ben, it's Mike. Is it too early to say happy New Year?"

"Well, you might as well, I think I'm the only one in the office today."

"Yeah, me too. Anyway, I'll be coming up your way on Thursday, right after New Year's Day. I'm meeting with Miranda's clients in the morning and then going to some kind of bar association dinner on Thursday night in Somerset. I'll drive up to your office on Friday and we can start preparing for this case. Also, when we're together I want to talk with you about some interesting developments regarding Ransom."

"Really? Tell me you got his ass fired."

"Do me a favor, will you?" Mike asked. "Anything I tell you about Ransom you have to keep to yourself. I don't even want to talk about this over the phone, so it'll have to wait until I get up to Ebensburg."

"Sure, sure." Ben paused. "By the way, have you heard the news about Miranda's client?"

"What? Who?"

"Norman Post, didn't you meet him? A big guy. Heavy, I mean. Anyway, he's dead. One of the neighbors found him yesterday. It's been in the news here."

"Jesus. What happened?"

"Well, if you believe the papers, he was seriously overweight, had diabetes, heart disease, high blood pressure, you name it.

The newspaper said it was a heart attack and he'd been dead for a couple of days. That's what they said, anyway."

"And you don't believe it?"

"It's just too coincidental. I mean one of the neighbors standing in the way of Rhino dies of a heart attack? Seems very convenient."

As Mike hung up, he wondered if Ben had any side of him that wasn't paranoid.

Mike touched the hook and dialed Miranda.

"I heard Mr. Post died. Any word on if it was foul play?" Mike said into the phone.

"Nothing Michael," Miranda said convincingly. "If something happened, I'd be one of the first to hear about it."

"Was there anything out of the ordinary?"

"Nothing. I spoke to a state police trooper, good looking man in a uniform."

"And…?"

"Oh, and he said Norman's phone was pulled from the wall, but that was it. They said it may have just been him yanking at the phone when he was having the heart attack. Trying to call 911. Nothing was disturbed or stolen, it seems. They said he owned a gun, but they couldn't find it. There was no evidence of a break-in or robbery. He seems to have died in his chair taking a nap."

"What do you think? That telephone thing. Seems suspicious." Mike wondered aloud.

"I think he was seriously overweight and sickly. I'm surprised he didn't die sooner."

Neither said anything for a moment, then Miranda brightened and said, "Well Michael, I'm so glad you called. I hope you're confirming our date for Thursday night."

For the second time that day, Mike rolled his eyes, but this time he was the only one in the room. "Miranda, I am looking forward to the attorney's ball—"

"I'm looking forward to the ball too," Miranda said laughing.

Mike shook his head, "I want to be as productive as possible. Maybe you could line up all of your clients so I can interview them every hour on the hour starting at ten a.m. on Wednesday. Then, we'll go to the...dinner and that will be a full day. I have a meeting in Ebensburg on Friday so if your offer of a room for the night still stands, I'd appreciate that."

"Don't worry, Michael, I have a bed for you."

40

Mike toweled off after his shower and looked at himself in the full-length mirror on the bathroom door. He was putting on a little weight and decided his New Year's resolution would be to get to the gym more often, and try to get back to the running that he had done regularly in college and law school. He hung up his towel and opened the door. Much to his surprise, Nicky was in his bed reading a book.

"Whoops," he said turning back to the bathroom. "I didn't know you were in here."

"Don't worry, I didn't look," Nicky said. "By the way, you have a nice butt."

Mike wrapped his towel around his waist and retrieved his shorts and tee shirt from the bedroom, then returned to the bathroom where he dressed for bed. Nicky continued to giggle.

"So, I guess this is how we're going to live together, is that it?" Mike asked.

"You're so old-fashioned," she said. "I think this is nice. Just two friends sharing an apartment."

"Seriously? Come on. You don't think this is just a little strange?"

"Meh," Nicky shrugged.

Mike lifted the covers and made sure she was wearing a nightgown that reached down to her feet. "Okay Nicky, this is a little weird. No, this is *a lot* weird. I mean I'm a guy and you're a girl and we're sleeping in the same bed."

"Not exactly. You're a hetero guy and I'm a lesbian girl. We're best friends, that's it. Nothing's going to come of this. I mean, really, isn't it nice having company in bed?"

Mike thought for a moment. "Well, what's going to happen if I ever find a girlfriend? How exactly am I going to explain this?"

Without hesitating Nicky replied, "Well, Mike, what's going to happen if *I* ever find a girlfriend? How exactly am *I* going to explain this? Look, you're a gentleman and I expect that this will be one of those things you and I just have to keep to ourselves. Other people might think it's weird, but I've never had a friend like you. Somehow, this feels right."

They looked at each other. Nicky's smile turned devious.

"I got you a gift. A New Year's gift."

Mike sat up.

"Oh, is that a thing? I didn't get you anything."

Nicky leaned over and took a small gift-wrapped package from her drawer. She handed it to Mike and said, "I hope you find some use for this."

Her grin was from ear to ear.

Mike looked at the size of the box and weighed it in his hand. He wondered if it might be a watch. He pulled off the ribbon and paper.

He smiled as he recognized the box. "Trojans? You got me a dozen Trojans?"

"Read the note."

"Take these with you to Somerset. I hope you get lucky. You really need it. Love, Nicky"

Mike shook his head as he turned the box over. "Wait, these are Magnums, extra large…"

"Well, aren't you? From what little I've seen you look pretty big to me. What do I know?"

Mike shook his head as Nicky turned off her light.

Mike reached over and turned out his light. He could see her facing him in the darkness.

"This is so weird," he said. "You're so weird."

"Not really. I think what we need to do is find us a couple of girls." They both laughed. "Don't you think it's a little sad it's New Year's Eve and neither one of us has a date? I mean it's not even midnight and we're in bed already."

"Normally, I'd say I need some female companionship, but I think I'm getting my share of it."

"Oh Mike, you can be honest with me. What you *really* need is some good old-fashioned sex. The wild, back-board banging, screaming out loud kind. I really appreciate your effort to keep our relationship platonic, but I've been noticing this problem you've been having. I keep bumping into it in bed in the middle of the night and you nearly fall over running into the bathroom in the morning," Nicky said, giggling.

"Well, I…"

"And another thing, you keep taking longer and longer showers."

"Jesus, Nicky. I'm really doing my best to be a gentleman here."

"That's okay, honey, I know you are." She said as she patted his head. "I've got my eyes open for a nice girl for you. We need to take care of your problem and find you a nice Jewish girl you can fall in love with."

She leaned over and whispered in his ear, "You really do have a nice butt, by the way."

In the dark, Nicky reached and found his hand which she held as they fell asleep.

Half asleep, Nicky said, "I really love you Mike Jacobs."

"I love you too, Nicky Kane."

He realized he'd never meant that as much as he did at that moment. As Mike drifted off to sleep he wondered if Nicky might be a little more fluid than she proclaimed. He hoped. *Maybe. Probably not...*

41

Miranda double locked the front door to the office. She flipped the switch, extinguishing the front light.

"Well, that was a long day," Mike said, making conversation as he unbuttoned his coat. "First I spent the whole day interviewing your clients and then the Somerset County Bar Association New Year's Ball."

Miranda ignored his nervous chattering. "I'll bet you'd like a drink, Michael, I know I would." She said as she gracefully unbuttoned her wool coat.

Mike watched her manicured fingers. Something about the way they handled and turned the buttons was incredibly sensual. He was fairly sure how this evening would end, but he was uncertain how things would begin. Mike was never the kind of man to shy away from kissing a woman, but he knew there was an art to picking the right moment. If he didn't wait long enough, then his date would think he was a creep, only interested in sex. Conversely, if he waited too long, he would send the wrong message. He sensed he wasn't quite yet at the point where he could put his arms around Miranda and plant one.

The two walked past the office to the first-floor kitchen.

"You do want a drink, don't you Michael?" she asked.

"Sure. how about a lager?" he replied.

"A beer? I'm sorry, Michael, but a beer just won't do. I was thinking whisky, single malt."

Miranda turned and opened a cabinet. Mike admired her from the back noticing her shapely ass and unbelievable legs.

The stockings she wore had a seam that ran up the back of her legs that Mike found very sexy. The seam disappeared under her black dress which was tight and short, but not too short. He wanted to reach out and touch her, but held back.

When Miranda turned back she had a bottle of Glenlivet and one glass. She poured a significant amount of the brown liquid into the cup, no ice cubes and no water. Then she held it up and approached Mike, studying his face. When she was inches from him, she put the glass to her lips and sipped some into her mouth. Then, she wrapped her arms around him and placed her lips on his. A moment later, Mike felt her tongue press into his mouth and, with it, the whisky.

This is different.

Mike accepted the kiss, long, and burning from the whisky. He had done something like this before, with another woman, but that was not a first kiss.

Miranda pressed her hips against Mike's and repeated the process several times until they had both consumed about half of the drink.

"Let's go, Michael, why don't we finish this in your bedroom?" Miranda asked.

"Should we get another glass? That might be easier," Mike said shrugging.

Miranda narrowed her eyes and let go of Mike. She turned back to the counter and took the bottle, but not another glass.

"Come on, upstairs."

Mike led the way and when he reached the top of the stairs Miranda took his hand and led him into his bedroom toward the four-poster bed. As they entered, she touched two switches. A solitary light over the bed came on, bathing it in a soft glow. Then, she turned him as they stood in the middle of the bedroom, and kissed him again, another whisky kiss.

By now, Mike was wondering if he would have to drink the entire bottle this way. Not that it wasn't pleasurable, it was, but Mike found it a bit odd.

Miranda set the tumbler on the bureau and Mike put his arms around her, turning his head to initiate a kiss. Miranda placed her hand to his lips, gently pushing his face back.

"Don't. I have a surprise for you," she whispered. Miranda let her hand drift down to his bow tie and she untied it, placing it on the back of the chair. Then she placed her hands on his shoulders and removed his jacket. Again, she carefully placed it on the seat back. Mike reached toward Miranda to touch her and she firmly took his hand and moved it away.

"Not yet, don't touch me." Her words were sharp, but she spoke softly.

Miranda unbuttoned each stud of his tux shirt. As she did, Mike began to help her and started to unbutton one of his buttons. Miranda grabbed his hand hard and shook her head *no*. When his shirt was unbuttoned, she took it and laid it on top of his jacket. At this point, Miranda bent down on her knees and untied Mike's shoes. She removed his shoes and socks. By now, Mike was complying with her game. He had placed his hands on her shoulders and she didn't resist.

Finally, Miranda unbuckled his belt and slid the zipper down. A moment later, Mike was standing in front of Miranda, wearing nothing but his boxers, his erection the size of the Washington Monument, her head just inches from his waist. The two of them paused and Mike lightly caressed Miranda's hair. Miranda pushed his hand out of the way.

"I said don't touch me," she hissed.

Miranda stood. In her bare feet, she would be slightly taller than Mike, but she was still in her heels. She towered over him. Mike had always felt awkward when he was with a woman and one of them was naked, or nearly so, and the other was entirely dressed. He felt awkward now.

"Michael, do you trust me?" Miranda whispered in his ear as she ran her hands through his hair.

At this moment, Mike wasn't sure whether he trusted her or not, but he very much desired her.

"Yes, of course I do," Mike said quietly if not sincerely.

Mike was ready to burst.

"And I trust you," she said quickly. "Before we go further, I just have one question for you, Michael."

Miranda looked down at him, her eyes seeming to enjoy every contour of his body. As she looked, she ran her hands up and down his sides, and Mike, nearly naked, looked with unimaginable desire at the sexy, exquisitely dressed woman. He was a little drunk and delirious with anticipation and the pleasure he was experiencing at the hands of this unbelievably provocative and skilled woman. Mike wanted her right now more than he'd ever wanted anyone.

Miranda slid a hand to his stomach, the other was on his back just above his butt. Her fingers gently pried at the elastic of his shorts. She placed her mouth on his ear. Hot breath tickled his ear for a moment before she spoke.

She breathed, "Do you promise you'll take the lead in the Rhino case?"

Up until that moment, Mike had never felt there was a direct connection between his cooperation and Miranda's flirtations. Maybe it had been implied, but now he knew if he was to have this woman, there were strings attached. The Washington Monument was reduced to a pile of rubble.

Miranda noticed his momentary indecision and gently rubbed his chest, nipples and stomach, studiously avoiding his waist. As she caressed, she breathed onto his neck and in his ear. Finally, after a small eternity, Miranda stopped and placed her warm palm over his navel. Fingertips just inching under the elastic of his underwear.

"Well?" she breathed into his ear.

Mike couldn't believe the words that escaped from his mouth, "Of course. I hope you never doubted me."

"Good boy," she purred.

***

Mike's wrists and ankles were free of Miranda's handcuffs and were a little sore, but not overly so. It was now past two a.m., and he realized that the experience with Miranda had lasted over two hours. When they were done, completely done, Miranda released him from the restraints and got out of the bed.

Mike was utterly spent and still panting. Miranda gently ran her hand through his hair, leaned over and kissed his forehead, then said, "I prefer to sleep alone. See you in the morning, seven a.m. We'll have coffee."

He watched her naked back and ass as she turned out the dim light, holding her high heels and toys as she left his room and closed the door. He'd made a commitment, and in exchange Miranda had given him something indescribable.

I'm an idiot.

What did I just do?

He had just sealed a pact with the devil.

42

Mike watched Ben smell the three-hour-old coffee sitting in the pot on the burner in the district mining office conference room, make a face, then pour some of it into Mike's mug.

"You look like shit, today," Ben said.

Mike looked up from his papers, through the slits of his eyes, and said, "That's the nicest thing you've ever said to me."

"Seriously, are you okay?"

"Well, last night, too much Scotch, too much partying, not enough sleep, too much…" he didn't finish the sentence, closed his eyes and thought *Miranda*.

"You young guys," Ben said, smiling at him.

"You don't know the half of it." Ben's face was ashen. "How about you? Are you okay?"

Ben put the coffeepot back on the burner and sat down. "Yeah, fine. Headaches, that's all." He looked at the desk, then said, "So, tell me about the investigation Capozzi authorized." He coughed and pulled a red bandana from his rear pocket and wiped his mouth.

Mike sat back in the chair and took a long sip of the rancid coffee. "This tastes like shit."

"Finish it, it's good for you."

Mike took another sip, grimaced, then said, "I told Capozzi there ought to be a full-bore investigation of Ransom, but he turned down the idea." Ben made a face. "He did authorize we bring in an inspector from another region who will work with Ransom and will shadow him. The operative story is the other inspector is with Ransom so he can be trained. The reality is the inspector will be reviewing all of Ransom's inspections and preparing a report. Look, it may turn out Ransom is doing a decent job." Ben rolled his eyes. "I doubt it, but that's a possibility. If the other inspector finds a pattern of abuse, then we get to go after Ransom with both barrels blazing."

"I liked your idea better than Capozzi's. Any idea who the outside inspector is going to be?"

"Yes. A guy named Pat Murphy, from Pittsburgh. I never met him, but we talked and he sounds like a straight shooter. He inspected hazardous waste facilities until a month ago and then was transferred to mining. The guy has a geology degree from Pitt and is finishing a master's degree in engineering at Carnegie Mellon. He understands exactly what he's supposed to be doing. I have to pretend not to know him, at this point we've only talked on the phone. He'll be meeting with Hicks when he gets here."

There was a tap at the door and, without waiting for a response, the receptionist opened it and looked in. "Ben, there's someone here to see John. He says he's with the department but, well, see for yourself."

Mike and Ben looked at each other, then got up and went into the small lobby. A man looked out the window with his back to them. He wore a leather cap.

"Hi, I'm Ben Kemper, a permit engineer, can I help you until Mr. Hicks is available?" The man turned around and they saw a muscular black man, maybe six feet tall, with short hair and a goatee, wearing an army desert camouflage cold-weather parka. The parka had the name "Murphy" stenciled on it above the pocket.

"I'm Murphy, Patrick." He held out a large hand which first Ben, then Mike shook. Mike felt the steel in his grip.

Hicks came into the lobby from his office. "Is there something I can do for you?" he said to Murphy eyeing him suspiciously.

"Patrick Murphy, reporting for duty, sir," Murphy said without smiling.

"*You're* Murphy?" Hicks said, his ears wiggling as he clenched his jaw.

Amid Rage

"Yes sir, I'm here to train with Lyle Ransom." The men and the receptionist all looked at each other.

Finally, Hicks broke the silence. "Well, Lyle won't be here until after lunch, maybe one o'clock. Why don't we meet in my office and chat for a few minutes? I'll give you the lay of the land. Then we can go to lunch."

Mike had been eyeing Murphy as he spoke with Hicks. "I'm Mike Jacobs, a DEP lawyer. So, are you new with the department?"

"No, Counselor, I've been working out of the Southwest Regional Office, Pittsburgh, for the past four years doing inspections in hazardous waste. I transferred over to mining about a month ago. My manager told me to come to Cambria for a couple of weeks so that I could learn something about mine inspections from Lyle."

"What did you do before DEP, if you don't mind my asking," Mike asked.

"U.S. Army Rangers, Afghanistan. Then college, Pitt, bachelor of science in geology, and some graduate work in civil engineering at Carnegie Melon. Hazardous waste inspections at DEP for the last six years. Any more nosy questions, Counselor?" Murphy said without smiling.

Mike shook his head no.

"Well, this ought to be interesting," Hicks said mostly to himself as he led the way to his office.

Ben and Mike returned to their conference room. "Did you know? Did you know he was African-American?" Ben asked, smiling and coughing several times.

"No, I talked with him on the phone for about an hour yesterday morning, but it didn't dawn on me that he was black. No one back in Harrisburg mentioned it either."

"I can't wait to see Ransom's face when he meets his new student," Ben said, not bothering to suppress his smile. "I'm glad he has a geology degree and engineering, but he only has one-month experience with mining. Won't that be a drawback? I mean how's he going to know whether Ransom is bullshitting him?"

"We talked about that in Harrisburg and decided we really didn't have a choice. Ransom likely would know any of the mine inspectors who'd been around for a while, and it wouldn't make any sense to have a mine inspector with years of experience supposedly training with him. Murphy has the educational background and solid inspection experience. He has enough mining experience he'll know if something's right or wrong."

Ben looked at the dregs of coffee in his cup and swirled them around. "You know Murphy is going to be out in the middle of nowhere with Ransom. If Ransom figures out what's going on here, I wouldn't put it past him to have Mr. Murphy stand just a tad too close to the edge of a highwall. He wouldn't be the first inspector to fall two hundred feet into a muck pile."

"Did you take a good look at Murphy?" Mike asked. "I think he can handle himself."

"Well, he's a long way from Pittsburgh. I hope you're right."

43

Mike was in that twilight state of consciousness, more asleep than awake. Nicky, in her granny nightgown, had her back to him and Mike was coiled around her, holding her warm body tenderly. Over the weeks they had been together, the invisible boundary line in the bed had disappeared. First their legs touched. Then they fell asleep holding hands. Now this. His face was in her hair and he let her scent fill his lungs. If she was awake, she hadn't protested.

His cell phone rang. The ringing didn't register in Mike's mind at first until Nicky jabbed him in the side with her elbow. Mike sat up, rubbed his eyes and looked first at the digital clock next to his bed—seven thirty—then reached for the phone.

"Hello?" he said, forcing the gravel from his throat.

"Michael? This is Miranda. We have a situation."

"What? It's Saturday morning. What's going on?" Mike said sitting up in bed, still groggy but awakening quickly.

"Rhino, they're doing work in the field at the mine site in Somerset. They showed up at five a.m. with a fleet of bulldozers and I don't know what. He has another team in the woods chopping down trees. I got a frantic call from Lily Roberts about an hour ago. What the hell is going on? I didn't think they could mine until the appeals were done."

Nicky slid out of bed and headed to the bathroom. Her nightgown had folded under itself and Mike watched her attractive and naked butt until she disappeared behind the bathroom door. Mike wondered momentarily when she stopped wearing underwear to bed.

"No, the appeal doesn't stay the permit," Mike said, rubbing the sleep from his eyes. "The permit is valid and Rinati can do anything under the permit he wants until the board stops him."

"What can *we* do? Can't we get an injunction or something?"

Mike noticed Miranda's use of "we."

"Well, *you* can apply for a supersedeas. That's like an injunction. It will take a week or two just to have the hearing. The board rules pretty quickly on those though, within a day or so."

"Two weeks? They'll dig one hundred feet deep by then. *We* have to stop them sooner than that."

"There's also this thing called a temporary supersedeas that's like a temporary restraining order. You have to file a petition for a supersedeas and apply for a temporary supersedeas. You would need affidavits from the neighbors and the like. The board will schedule a conference call hearing, sometimes on the same day you apply and generally no later than the next day. I've seen them issue a temporary supersedeas at the end of the conference call. The temporary supersedeas would stay in place only until the supersedeas hearing."

"Well, let's do it. That's what we have to do," Miranda said, her voice rising, anxious.

Mike was annoyed that Miranda called him and that she sounded so helpless. This was not the typical Miranda. Her usual speaking voice was feminine, yet authoritative. He had never heard her appear uneasy or worried. When she was angry, or annoyed, her voice became sharp. Not now. Still Mike was wondering how far his deal with Miranda would go. Ordinarily, in a case such as this, he might call the attorney for the mining company and warn him that if the permit were overturned, then the department would file an action to require the operator to restore and reclaim the land. Now Miranda was pleading for more.

"I can make a few calls, but remember you have to take the lead. Can you contact your friend, the one who's helping you, and see if he'll prepare the paperwork for the petition for supersedeas? We issued the permit and I'm defending the permit from you and your clients so I'm pretty sure Roger won't let me take your side."

The line was silent for a moment. "I learned yesterday that my benefactor withdrew his support. I got a call yesterday morning from Pittsburgh and was told he'd run out of funds and that was that. It didn't occur to me they would begin mining operations the next day, which seems suspicious. I figured we were months away from a hearing and with your help, Michael, things would turn out okay. Look, I'm really counting on you."

Nicky climbed back into the bed and laid on her side with her hand holding up her head, watching him. Mike was sitting up in bed, wearing his forest green Vermont Law School tee shirt and gym shorts. He looked at her and mouthed *Miranda*. Nicky made a face and nodded.

"Well, no matter what, I have to make some phone calls. I'll get back to you later this morning."

"Call me back no later than eleven a.m.," Miranda demanded, then hung up without waiting for a reply.

"Trouble?" Nicky asked.

Mike slid down and pulled the covers up to his neck, closing his eyes momentarily. "Remember how I told you I was looking forward to a quiet Saturday? Maybe I would catch up on some of those *other* cases that Roger wants me to work on? That'll have to be another Saturday."

Mike pulled the covers off and his feet touched the cold floor. As he shuffled to the bathroom he glanced back longingly at the bed, suspecting it might be a long time until he climbed back in.

44

"Sorry to call you so early on a Saturday," Mike said.

"No problem, partner. Been up for hours. I've had this headache. Tylenol doesn't seem to touch it."

"You sound great," Mike said.

"Yeah, shitty. This headache just won't quit. I'm seeing the doc on Monday. To what do I owe the honor of this early morning call?"

"Have you heard anything? About Rhino?"

"No," Ben said, coughing lightly.

"I got a call a few minutes ago from Miranda. Rhino's guys showed up in force this morning. She said there's a crew there with dozers leveling the property and another crew in the woods chopping down trees. She was pretty upset."

"This is the first I'm hearing about it. I don't live anywhere near there, maybe seventy-five miles from the mine. The weather here is pretty rough, snow and sleet, but I could be down there in about two hours."

"Let me call Ransom. He's the inspector and he ought to know what's going on."

"You're giving him a lot of credit. Of course, he may have known about this all along. There's a standard mining permit condition that requires the operator to give forty-eight hours' notice to the mine inspector before commencing operations," Ben said. "Almost always, the inspector calls the district office when they get that notice. We heard nothing at the office, though."

213

"So either Rhino's violating the terms of its permit or Rinati's been in touch with Ransom and he didn't think to let the district office or me know?"

"Neither of those options would surprise me," Ben replied. "You know, Rinati could take the position that he doesn't need the department's permission simply to do some logging and leveling that field. If his activities are under five acres, then they're not regulated. All he needs is an erosion and sedimentation control plan and he's got that."

"Except that he has a mining permit with the department," Mike said tapping his finger on his lips. "It's a long shot, but I could make the argument that once he obtained a mining permit, he had to comply with it, regardless of the kind of activities he was undertaking."

"Any chance that will work?"

"Don't know. If he's smart—and I think he is—then he's going to keep this land-clearing operation small and see if Miranda or I file for a supersedeas."

"Well, I don't trust Rhino and I don't trust Ransom. I'm going to head down there in about ten minutes. As long as I don't hit any really bad patches, I should be there around ten. I'll take pictures and text them to you."

Mike hung up and finished tying his shoes, he was wearing jeans and a flannel shirt. The door to the bathroom opened and Nicky came out, also wearing jeans and a flannel shirt. Mike looked at her.

"At least we're wearing different color shirts," he said chuckling.

"I feel like pancakes," Nicky said. "It looks like you're going to have a busy day and it's crappy outside. I'll make the pancakes and some eggs and coffee. I have a feeling I won't see much of you today." She put her arms around his shoulders and kissed him on the cheek.

Mike watched as she walked toward the kitchen and heard the sound of her loading the coffee maker. As he held the telephone getting ready to dial, he thought for a moment again how perfect his relationship with her was in every regard except one.

He found Ransom in his contacts, then tapped his number. He let the phone ring ten times before he hung up. There was no machine, so there was no opportunity to leave a message.

He hung up and dialed Roger. On the sixth ring, Mike heard the phone being picked up and dropped. Noises in the background indicated that someone was trying to get to the phone.

"Hello?" Roger said with a thick voice.

"Roger? It's me, Mike. Sorry to call you so early on a Saturday morning." Mike glanced at the clock and saw that it was now eight thirty. "Is it too early?"

"Sarah and I had some people over last night. I'm pretty sure we opened and finished a bottle of Jameson's. I need some water, aspirins, and then some coffee and I'll be fine. What's up, Bud? This had better be good."

"Rhino. Rinati showed up at that mine site in Somerset at five a.m. this morning and started doing some site work. I got a frantic call from Miranda Clymer at seven thirty asking me what the department was going to do. I wanted to give you a heads up and touch base with you."

"Is he violating his permit? Did the department restrict his hours of operation or days on which he could operate? What exactly are they doing out there?"

"I put in a call to Ransom, but didn't get a response. According to Miranda—uh, Clymer—they're cutting down trees and starting to level the site."

"I didn't think we regulated lumberjacks. If his site preparation is less than five acres, we don't regulate that either. Do you know if he gave proper notice to the inspector?"

"No, I haven't talked to Ransom in a few days," Mike said. "At the same time, he never called to tell me Rhino gave notice of their intent to begin operations."

"So, for all you know Rhino gave the proper notice and he's entirely permitted to be doing what he's doing."

"That's possible..."

"Also, didn't we talk a couple of weeks ago about you staying out of this case as much as possible? I think my exact words to you were to let the citizens and the mining company fight it out themselves."

Mike looked out his bedroom window at the sleet falling from the sky. His view of the Susquehanna River was mostly obscured by the precipitation. It looked like an Impressionist painting. He could hear cars moving on Front Street, but he could tell from the sound that they were moving slowly.

"Yes, that's right, Chief."

"Just leave it alone, Bud. Let it play out a few days. If Clymer and her clients really have their underwear in a bunch, they can file a petition for a supersedeas. You stay out of this."

45

Mike hung up and sat on the edge of the bed. He could hear Nicky in the kitchen and took a few minutes to collect his thoughts.

Roger wants me to stay out of this.

If I listen to him, Rhino's going to begin mining before we ever litigate this case.

If I don't listen to him, I'll probably lose my job.

If I help Miranda, she'll assume this is payback for...that night.

I want to do the right thing for the right reasons.

Crap.

He wandered into the kitchen. Nicky had set two places. She was flipping pancakes and already had a stack of about half a dozen on a plate.

"You're the best," Mike said, taking the coffee pot off the warmer and pouring two cups.

As they ate, Mike explained what happened.

"What are you going to do?" Nicky asked.

"I guess it depends on what Ben reports. I should be hearing from him in an hour or so. Maybe nothing. Maybe I'll be ghostwriting a petition for a supersedeas."

"Won't you get in trouble with Roger if you help out Miranda? Is it worth it?"

"He doesn't have to find out about it. I *want* to do this. Something inside is telling me this is the right thing to do. That mine really is too close to the houses and the stream. The whole permit stinks and Ransom is the least trustworthy person I've met in a long time. I don't trust Rinati, and I don't really trust Miranda. I never should've slept with her because no one would ever believe I'd be helping her for the right reasons."

Nicky winced, then made a tightly drawn smile and raised her narrow eyebrows. As soon as he returned from Somerset, he told Nicky, in vague generalities, that he'd slept with Miranda. As much as he enjoyed himself, he felt it was too embarrassing and humiliating to tell Nicky about what he'd submitted to and had left out all of the details. Nicky claimed she was happy for him.

Nicky's response barely registered with Mike who helped himself to more pancakes.

At eleven thirty, Mike's iPhone rang and he spoke with Ben for ten minutes. He hung up and immediately began putting on his winter coat.

"I'm heading down to the office. I could do a lot of the drafting on my laptop. But I have all of my research materials there. I guess I'll be gone the rest of the day."

Nicky hurried over to him as he put his hand on the doorknob. In her stocking feet, she barely came up to his chin. She put her arms around him and hugged him for several long moments. Mike thought she might kiss him, but they parted and he pulled on a wool ski cap. Outside, Mike looked up at his apartment and saw Nicky watching him as he trudged through the sleet to his car. He waved and could see her wave back.

***

**Before the
Commonwealth of Pennsylvania
Environmental Hearing Board**

Save Our Somerset, et al, Appellants,

v.

Commonwealth of Pennsylvania, Department of Environmental Protection, Appellee,

And

Rhino Mining Company, Permittee

No. 2325-AD
and
No. 2327-AD

Consolidated Docket No. 2325-AD

PETITION FOR SUPERSEDEAS

NOW COME Appellants, Save Our Somerset (an unincorporated Association), Andrea McCarthy, Thomas McCarthy, Donald Roberts, Lily Roberts, Robert Willis and Roberta Willis, by and through their attorney, Miranda Clymer, Esq., and aver as follows:

Introductory Statement: The Appellants all reside in Somerset, Pennsylvania and are neighbors of a proposed coal strip mining operation in Somerset County ("Gordon Mine" or "Site") that was proposed by Permittee, Rhino Mining Company ("Rhino") and permitted by the Department of Environmental Protection ("DEP"). The Site is a tranquil farm field and woodland that abuts both the residences of Appellants and a State Game Lands. The area is inappropriate for mining as it is too close to Appellants' properties and is in an area that forms the headwaters of Roaring Run, Special Protection Waters of the Commonwealth. DEP issued a mining permit to Rhino on November 18, and the above-designated appeals ensued.

Heretofore, no mining was taking place on the Site. On Saturday, January 11, at approximately 5:00 a.m. under cover of darkness, Rhino began mining operations at the Site. Despite the existence of these appeals, Appellants were not given notice of the commencement of operations and it is believed that the Department did not receive notice of the mining operation either.

The issuance of the mining permit by the Department was in clear violation of the requirements of The Clean Streams Law and the Surface Mining Conservation and Reclamation Act and the Constitution of the Commonwealth.

Because they will be irreparably harmed by Rhino's activities, Appellants are seeking a Supersedeas and Temporary Supersedeas to preserve the status quo and prevent any further mining activity, pending a full hearing on the merits of this case.

***

At eleven thirty p.m., Mike emailed the complete petition for supersedeas, an application for temporary supersedeas, draft affidavits for the appellants to sign, and detailed instructions to Miranda. He scrubbed the meta-data from the documents then sent them from his personal Gmail account. He hoped his electronic fingerprints weren't embedded in the guts of the documents somewhere. He was confident that Feldman would have one of his little assistants checking to see who was helping Miranda.

46

On Tuesday morning Mike sat in his office with the speaker on his telephone turned up to maximum. He had spread around his desk a volume of the coal mining regulations and all of the relevant papers that might come in handy during the temporary supersedeas telephone conference call. On his computer screen, he had the computerized version of the regulations as well. Feldman, Miranda and he were on the call waiting for Judge Diaz, who would come on last. No pleasantries had been exchanged by the lawyers other than terse hellos.

In addition, Mike had an email chain with Miranda open. All either one of them had to do if either had a concern was to type a few words and hit send. The other would get the message immediately. Despite the script he had sent to Miranda, Mike worried she would screw it up somehow.

There was a click on the line and a voice said, "Good morning counsellors, this is Judge Diaz. With me is Mr. Bowdoin my assistant counsel. Also with us is Ms. Jean Smith, the court reporter who will be taking down the argument. I have you on speakerphone so please speak up so Ms. Smith can get down your arguments. We're here today to hear oral argument on the application for a temporary supersedeas filed by Ms. Clymer on behalf of her clients, Save Our Somerset, and her individual clients, all of whom are appellants in this case. This is consolidated docket number 2325-AD. I have reviewed the affidavits filed by Ms. Clymer. They all appear to be in order. So there will be no testimony taken during this temporary supersedeas hearing, only oral argument. Ms. Clymer, you filed the petition and application for a temporary supersedeas, so the floor is yours."

There was a lengthy pause and Mike could hear papers being shuffled. After at least thirty seconds had elapsed, the judge said, "Ms. Clymer, perhaps you didn't hear me but you may begin your argument."

"I'm sorry Mr. Diaz. I'm new to this…"

"Excuse me Ms. Clymer, but refer to me either as Judge Diaz or Your Honor. Please proceed."

Mike shook his head. He'd seen experienced lawyers choke when they stood before a judge. Unless you'd done that you really had no clue how nerve-wracking that could be. Miranda may have had experience as a lawyer, but not in front of a judge.

Miranda cleared her throat, "yes sir, Mr. Judge, I mean *Judge Diaz*." She paused again and finally said, "I represent Save Our Somerset and several residents of Somerset, Pennsylvania. They oppose the permit that has been issued by DEP. They request the court overturn the permit since DEP should not have issued it."

Miranda paused again. Finally, the judge said, "Ms. Clymer, I understand your clients oppose the permit. You have filed a petition for supersedeas and an application for a temporary supersedeas. We're here today on the application for temporary supersedeas. It's up to you to present a legal argument and convince me that I should issue an order temporarily suspending the permit and stopping the mining activity from going forward. Can you tell me why I should temporarily stay the mining permit?"

Mike held his breath. So far, this was the worst oral argument he'd ever heard. He sent a quick email:

>>Jump right into your main argument. Skip the prelims. OK?<<

"Yes judge, yes, I was getting to that…" Again, she paused for many long seconds.

"Ms. Clymer, can you proceed now?" asked the judge.

Miranda cleared her throat again. "The area where Rhino, the permittee, wants to mine is a beautiful farm field. Well, it used to be a beautiful farm field, but now it looks like a construction site. Also, there are these beautiful woods that lead into the state game lands. They're also very pretty. There are also these drainage areas on the farm that lead into the woods. I was told they are headwaters to streams that are considered high-quality streams. DEP and the board shouldn't let them mine that, okay?"

Mike quickly emailed:

\>>DEP's approval was illegal.

Rhino didn't give proper 48 hours notice.<<

After another long pause, Judge Diaz said, "Is that it, Ms. Clymer? I mean, is that your argument? Don't you want to tell me about the illegality of what the department did? Rhino's violation of its permit? The irreparable harm to your clients or the environment? The likelihood of success on the merits? Maybe you can discuss the likelihood of injury to the public?" the judge asked.

Mike shook his head. He had spoken with Miranda several times on Monday and over the phone he had outlined an oral argument. She claimed to have it under control and seemed to understand the various points she had to make. This morning, however, she'd lost all of her composure. He'd seen that happen many times with experienced lawyers who otherwise seemed competent. Now the judge was trying to help her. Big time. He'd seen that, too.

"Yes, that's right, Mr. Diaz, what the Department did was illegal. It never should have issued a mining permit for an area that is a headwaters to high-quality waters of the Commonwealth of Pennsylvania."

"Why?" asked the judge. Why shouldn't the Commonwealth have issued a permit for the headwaters?"

There was dead silence from Miranda. Ten, twenty seconds went by with no response.

Mike quickly typed:

\>>Irreparable injury to the stream. Hold status quo till full hearing<<

Finally, Judge Diaz said, "Is that because the chapter ninety-three regulations prohibit degradation to high-quality waters?

Perhaps impacting the headwaters area will pollute and degrade the high-quality streams down below in the valley. Is that it?"

"Yes, yes judge. That's it," Miranda said in a child-like voice. "Also, irreparable injury to the stream. Hold status quo till full hearing."

Jeez, thought Mike, the least she could do was change up his words a little.

"Well, don't the conditions placed on the permit by DEP limit the activity in the headwaters area? Also, didn't the department put requirements and restrictions on sediment and other contaminants from entering the stream channel?" Judge Diaz asked.

"I don't know judge," Miranda replied. "Honestly, I just don't know. I just know that on Saturday morning, before sunrise, Rhino's crew showed up and started conducting activities and they are destroying the farm field and the woodlands. They shouldn't be allowed to do that. Once those areas are destroyed, then they will never be the same. The stream will be irreparably injured and may never come back. I beg you to issue an injunction and stop this activity from proceeding. I have nothing further to say at this time."

The judge sighed loudly. "Mr. Feldman, do you have any response to the appellants' argument?"

"Well, Your Honor, I'm tempted to say nothing, but as you and the other counsel know, that's nearly impossible for me."

Everyone on the phone was relieved to laugh at Feldman's candid admission.

"Your Honor, the burden for obtaining a temporary supersedeas is heavy. The appellants must show not only that the Commonwealth acted unlawfully or unconstitutionally, but also that they have a likelihood of prevailing on the merits. They have to show that preserving the status quo is necessary and it will not place an undue burden on the permittee. They must show irreparable harm. Ms. Clymer and her clients have shown none of these things."

Feldman continued, "My client, Rhino Mining Company, of course, will change the landscape. That's a part of the surface mining process. But the permit, with its many conditions, I would say *excessive* conditions, requires my client to restore the land to its pre-mining condition and to protect the headwaters. They have acted lawfully at all times and gave more than forty-eight hours' notice directly to the mine inspector, Mr. Ransom, in advance of mining."

Mike knew this by now and was still pissed off at Ransom for not alerting him.

"Rhino's posted a substantial bond with the Commonwealth and has an exemplary record in conducting restoration activities. The department issued to my client a permit and my client is acting pursuant to its permit. The mere filing of the appeal does not act as a supersedeas of that permit, as this honorable board has ruled on numerous occasions. My client is fully within its rights to begin mining activities, and neither Ms. Clymer nor her clients have presented any viable justification for preventing my client from undertaking its lawful activities. We request that the board deny the application for temporary supersedeas."

Mike could hear papers rustling and assumed that either the judge or Tommy Bowdoin were shuffling the papers filed by the parties. At two o'clock on Monday afternoon, Miranda filed the paperwork Mike had prepared for her along with the affidavits signed by her clients. Somewhat miraculously, Feldman and his crew filed a twenty-page response by eight a.m. on Tuesday morning. It was chock-full of references to appropriate cases and well-written. Mike was certain that Angela St. Germain, Jimmy Podwall and a regiment of Pell, Desrosiers associates had been up all night drafting and refining the response.

"Thank you, Mr. Feldman. Does the Commonwealth have a response?" asked the judge.

Mike had thought long and hard about how he could both oppose the application and support it in some way. He knew a transcript was being made, and he did not want to appear to be overtly supporting the neighbors, contrary to the interests of his client and Roger's direct order.

Mike chose his words carefully. "Your Honor, the Commonwealth of course opposes the application for temporary supersedeas. We issued a permit that stands on its own merits and which the board ultimately will uphold. Likewise, we believe the board will endorse the commonsense permit conditions we added to the permit, contrary to the desire of Rhino Mining. At the same time, we want to be sure Rhino conducts its operation in accordance with its permit. While we oppose the application for temporary supersedeas, we certainly would have no problem with the board imposing an additional condition that would mandate strict compliance with all of the permit conditions. Alternatively, I suppose we could endorse a temporary stay maintaining the status quo until the hearing. We request the board deny the application for a temporary supersedeas."

"Wait a minute, just to be clear, Mr. Jacobs," said the judge, "you oppose the application for temporary supersedeas?"

"Absolutely, Your Honor."

"At the same time, you'd like the board to further condition the permit the department has issued or issue a stay to maintain the status quo, is that correct?"

An email from Miranda popped up on the screen:

\>\>You're opposing my temp. supersedeas?<<

As Mike took a breath he quickly wrote back:

\>\>No alt for me. Sorry. Trying to argue for a stay<<

Mike paused and thought hard. "Not exactly, Your Honor. All I'm saying is we agree the application ought to be denied. We also want to be sure Rhino mines in accordance with its permit. If the board decides the best way to do that is to put another condition or a temporary hold on the mining activity, we could endorse that. Temporarily of course, until the hearing."

"Won't the department oversee Rhino through the usual inspection process, rather than requiring something additional from the board?"

"Yes, of course, judge. I should have been clearer during my argument."

"Anything else counsel?" asked the judge, sounding perturbed.

Feldman spoke. "Just one thing, Your Honor, if I may address Mr. Jacobs. The department is opposing the temporary supersedeas request. Right?"

"Of course," said Mike.

"And you're also saying you'd accept a stay on the mining activity?"

"Yes," said Mike.

"Your Honor, it sounds like the department is trying to have it both ways." Feldman spoke loudly and Mike could hear clicking in the background. He imagined Angela pounding on her laptop.

"It does at that," said the judge. "Okay, I'll get an order out by the end of today. Regardless of how we rule, we'll set a time for the hearing on the petition for supersedeas within the next two weeks. I'm inclined to hold the hearing in Somerset, in the courthouse, since it looks as though virtually all of the witnesses are located there. I'm sure you don't have a problem with that, Ms. Clymer. Correct?"

Miranda cleared her throat, "No, no, Your Honor, that's fine."

"And Mr. Feldman, you would have to travel whether or not we held the hearing in Harrisburg or Somerset, so I'm sure you won't mind either. Plus, your witnesses are all located in or around Somerset, right?"

"Of course, Your Honor. My client and I have absolutely no objection to holding the hearing in the courthouse in Somerset. Do you know if there are any good restaurants in Somerset?"

The judge ignored the comment, then asked, "How about the Commonwealth? Mr. Jacobs, any problem if we hold the hearing in Somerset?"

Mike realized he probably would be inconvenienced the most by having a hearing in Somerset. The state would never pay for the Sheraton Hotel and he couldn't risk staying at Miranda's office, not if he wanted to be awake and sober for the hearing. That meant he'd be lodging at the El Crappo Motel, next to the turnpike. Also, unlike any of the others, he'd have no help. He didn't have a squadron of associates or helpful neighbors to assist him. He wouldn't trust Ransom to help, and hoped that he'd be able to handle the hearing on his own.

"Of course, Your Honor. Somerset would be fine," Mike said.

Amid Rage

Less than an hour later, an email from the board appeared on Mike's screen. It read:

>>AND NOW, Appellants' application for a temporary supersedeas is DENIED. The hearing on the petition for supersedeas shall be held on January 27, in the Somerset County Courthouse, Somerset, Pennsylvania, courtroom No. 2 at 10 a.m.<<

47

Mike sat at the small desk in the corner of his guest bedroom. The big black brief bag he had picked up secondhand was stuffed with papers. The only light was from the gooseneck task lamp. The rest of the room was in shadows. Outside, the trees shivered loudly in the January wind.

His mug sat on top of some of the papers he'd read earlier. He lost track of how much coffee he drank that evening. As he sifted through the thick permit file again, he underlined or circled passages with a red felt-tip pen. He took notes for his examinations and cross-examinations on the cheap and ratty legal pads provided by his employer. He had already burned through four of them and was working on his fifth.

Two hands leaned on his shoulders and pressed down gently. Mike was startled, but he immediately recognized them as Nicky's. She rubbed his shoulders and his neck.

"Oh, that feels good," Mike said, bowing his head.

"You're very tight. How late are you planning on staying up?" She asked.

"Until I'm done, no later than one a.m."

"I hate to tell you this, honey, but it's almost one thirty. Why don't you come to bed? You're exhausted and I'm cold."

Mike looked at his watch and shook his head. The apartment *was* cold, but he knew that Nicky was just looking out for him. "There's so much to do. The judge gave us two weeks to prepare for the hearing and I'm down to my last six days of prep. This is not like a regular trial where we have months to get ready, take depositions, and hear from the other side who they're calling so we can prepare. I'm trying to memorize the entire permit file. I have to guess who the other side is going to call as its witnesses and prepare my cross-examinations. In this case, there are two other sides, so more witnesses than usual. Also, I have to figure out who I'm going to call and prepare their direct examinations. I know I've got to call Ransom, but I'm afraid of what he'll say on the stand. I'll call Ben. He should do fine. If I need an expert, he's got a degree in mining engineering. He's pretty strongly against this operation. I may call one or two others from the district office. I still have to decide which exhibits I'm going to use and make sure I have enough copies for the trial. There's just so much to do."

"Can you get any help?" Nicky asked, resting her head on his shoulder and putting her arms across his chest. "Isn't there another attorney in the office who can work with you?"

"Everyone else is booked solid. I checked with Roger and he told me since we're down two lawyers, no one's available to help. He reminded me that with nearly four years of experience under my belt, I'm pretty senior, so I have to do this all on my own. I suppose Ben could help, but he has responsibilities getting out mining permits in the district office. I'm not sure I can count on him, even if he's willing. He's been sick lately and the docs can't seem to figure it out." Mike took a deep breath. "It's not a problem, really, I'll just power through it."

Nicky pushed herself between Mike and his desk, reclining against the desk. She wore her granny flannel nightgown and thick woolen socks. "What about accommodations? Are you going to stay at that disgusting motel by the turnpike you were telling me about?"

"Maybe. I can use a state voucher there. It's just an awful place, though. It's depressing as hell, noisy, smelly, really dreadful."

"What about Miranda?" she asked lightly.

"She offered. She has a really nice place but it would be more than a bit awkward staying in her house or office or whatever, when I'm litigating on the other side of her. Plus, I'm pretty sure there will be strings attached—"

"So to speak—"

Nicky put a hand on his shoulder and rubbed it gently. "Why don't you come to bed, honey?"

"I'll be there in a minute."

Mike heard Nicky as she returned to the bedroom. A minute later, he heard the toilet flush. As he was shoving some papers into his briefcase, Nicky came back into the guest room, her smile lighting the way.

"I have an idea. How about if I help you? I could be your paralegal. I have a huge backlog of vacation days and I could take a week off and go up with you. I mean, I don't know anything at all about being a paralegal, but I'm sure I could help keep your papers organized and, if nothing else, get coffee. I'll even call you Mr. Jacobs if you like. It would be fun."

Nicky was smiling that big smile, the one that made her eyebrows go up. Mike smiled back.

"I have to tell you, hon, as you began talking, my initial reaction was 'no,' but the more I think about it, the more I like it. There's so much to do at the trial and I'm sure you'd be able to help."

Mike looked for a moment at the stack of papers in front of him, then said, "I suppose I'll have to tell Roger and get his approval. I may make up a bit of the story, like you have some paralegal training and you're looking to do an internship or whatever. He'll never pay for anything for you. Thanks to the legislature, the department is broke, plus he's really cheap. I'll take care of any expenses you have."

"Well, you know me, I don't eat much. We can share a room, I mean, we do now, so why not?"

Mike looked at her and bounced his forefinger off his lips. "Usually when I'm in a hearing I'll work with witnesses late into the night. If I'm in the office, that's one thing. If it's an away game though we generally work in my hotel room until we crash. How's that going to look to the department's witnesses if they think I'm sleeping with my paralegal?"

"They don't have to know. I'll keep my stuff in a drawer and I'll be working with the rest of you until the last witness leaves. Problem solved." She grinned at him.

Mike smiled. "You're the best. I've never had a friend like you."

Nicky threw her arms around him as he sat at the small desk. "That goes both ways, honey."

Mike had a nearly overwhelming desire to pick her up and carry her into the bedroom. Instead, he put his arms around her and they clung to each other swaying back and forth.

48

Mike loaded the luggage cart with eight banker's boxes jammed full of papers, his suitcase, Nicky's suitcase and two hanging garment bags. He struggled to push it through the automatic door of the Sheraton in Somerset. Nicky held his briefcase and Mike's large black brief bag and shook her head. "You know, you don't have to do this all in one trip. It would probably be a lot easier to come back for some of the stuff in a few minutes."

Mike looked over his shoulder as he continued shoving the luggage cart and said, "Where's the fun in that?"

The lobby was large and open. It had sofas arranged in front of a working gas fireplace and two couples were sitting and talking near the fire. They looked normal. Mike sniffed, but could not detect any odor of disinfectant or pesticide. The entrance to the hotel restaurant and lounge were off to the side of the lobby. A hockey game was playing on the television in the lounge. Whatever it was going to cost, this was much better than the alternative.

The woman behind the counter had short brown hair, gold ball pierced earrings, and was wearing a pressed gray jacket and colorful silk scarf with a small Sheraton logo nameplate that read, *Betty*. She looked at the giant stack of stuff Mike had with him. "Good afternoon sir. Are you planning to stay for a while?" she smiled.

"Hi, I'm Mike Jacobs. I have a trial coming up. Believe it or not, it should only last a day or two."

"All the lawyers from out of town who come in for a trial at the courthouse stay here. There's no other decent place to stay in Somerset so we often have the attorneys for the plaintiffs and defendants staying here. I try to put them on separate floors." She smiled again. "Anyone I should be looking out for?"

"As a matter of fact, is Sid Feldman, from Philadelphia, registered here?"

Betty looked at the monitor, then said, "Yes, his firm reserved a king suite—our largest room—and three other standard rooms, also a conference room. They should be arriving today. I'll make a note and keep them on another floor."

Mike thought to himself, *four rooms, he's bringing a frickin' army*.

"If you have a standard room with a big desk or extra space, I'd like it. I'll need to spread out."

"Well, a standard room is not all that large. If you really want the desk and extra space, though, I can put you in what we call a junior suite, but that's two hundred and forty-nine dollars a night. Is that okay?"

Mike had planned on spending one hundred and twenty-nine dollars a night for the room at the Sheraton. Since Roger had vetoed the idea of paying for the nicer hotel in Somerset, the cost was coming out of his pocket. Three nights in the hotel would cost almost as much as one month's rent. "I'll take it."

"King-size bed? I do have one with twin beds," she said staring into a computer monitor.

Mike resisted the urge to look or even glance at Nicky. "King will be fine."

In hospitality school or hotel school or whatever school it is that people who go to work for hotels attend, there must be a class on keeping a straight face. Whether you're going to a hotel by yourself, with a group of coworkers, your spouse and kids, girlfriend, boyfriend, mistress, secretary, or whatever the match-up, there comes a moment when the clerk behind the counter asks a seemingly innocuous question. *All* of them *always* ask the same question. They *have to* ask the question. It's really a logistical issue, not a judgment, and they're doing the guest a favor by asking the question, rather than making the guest ask the clerk. Generally, the answer comes quickly. Sometimes there is a pregnant pause. Sometimes, however, the guest's answer conveys to the clerk much more information than a stranger ought to know.

Betty looked at Mike and her eyes may have flickered for a moment to Nicky, who was standing beside him. With a blank expression she must have acquired from many years in the hotel business she asked, "One key or two?"

Mike resisted looking around the lobby to see if anyone had come in behind him. He also resisted lowering his voice, which would imply some salacious intent. "Two," he croaked.

Betty concluded the transaction quickly from that point, and as Mike and Nicky prepared to head up to their room she called after them, "Good luck, Mr. Jacobs."

Mike wondered whether she was referring to the trial or Nicky.

49

The room was spacious, clean, and quiet. It had a small seating area with a table and two chairs, a sofa and a desk, larger than the one he had at home. The desk was covered with hotel announcements and menus from the restaurant. Opposite the bed was a large entertainment center with a television behind double doors and a small fridge. The suite had a large and decently appointed bathroom. It also had a king-size bed.

Mike's apartment had a full-size mattress. The small guest room had a twin-size bed that was always covered with the stuff that Mike never put away. To Mike, the gigantic bed looked like it could hold a family of six and several pets.

"Wow," Nicky said surveying the room. "That bed is so much bigger than ours at home."

Mike thought, *ours at home*. Nicky's comment said so much with so few words.

Mike organized the boxes next to the wall. He decided to use the table and the desk so he cleared them of all of the hotel flyers. Nicky began putting her underwear, stockings, and clothes into a drawer. She had brought two dresses for the trial which she hung in the closet. "You don't think any of your witnesses will need to look in here, do you?" she said closing the louvered closet door.

Mike shook his head.

"I'll keep my toiletries in the bureau. Nothing says 'girlfriend' like two toothbrushes sitting next to the sink."

Mike thought about the fact that in his apartment their toothbrushes occupied the same glass.

Nicky sat on the edge of the bed and kicked off her shoes. Then, she dropped back on it and bounced slightly. "This is pretty firm, do you mind if I take the bathroom side?"

Mike shrugged. For some reason he found it hard to find his words. Something about being in a hotel room with Nicky. They'd been living together for a month and sleeping together—just sleeping—for as long. He couldn't put his finger on it, but he just didn't know quite how to handle being in the hotel room with her.

"You want to take this baby for a spin?" She said patting the cover on the bed next to her.

"What?"

Nicky's smile broke into peals of laughter and she giggled, "You should see your face, honey. I love you."

Suddenly, there was a knock at the door. Nicky jumped up and smoothed the covers. Mike quickly looked around and Nicky went to one of the boxes, popped it open, and pretended to organize the papers.

"Yes? Who's there."

"Ben. Are you going to make me stand in the hall?"

Mike opened the door for Ben Kemper and they shook hands. Ben was pale and he stared right through Mike for a moment.

Then he was back and said, "Nice room." He surveyed the suite and his eyes settled on Nicky.

"I'd like you to meet my..." Mike paused, "Nicky Kane. My *paralegal*, Nicky Kane. She's going to help us during the trial."

Ben and Nicky shook hands. "I didn't know the department had paralegals. Is this something new?"

Without a pause, Nicky said, "I know Mike from the Pennsylvania Bar Association. I'm working on my paralegal certificate at the community college and need to do an internship to graduate. Mike's doing me a huge favor allowing me to help out on this trial since I get credit for it. I'm not getting paid, but the experience should be great."

Ben nodded as she talked. Then he looked at Mike and brushed his forefinger across the tip of his nose.

50

On Monday, Mike and Nicky met with their witnesses during breakfast, then straight through until two p.m. The DEP witnesses arrived in Mike's room, boots dripping, and complaining about the snow storm and their lack of enthusiasm for being forced to take the witness stand.

Mike was a little anxious about Ben's testimony, which would have to be carefully worded at times to avoid the appearance that he was taking sides. He was sure he could ask Ben the right questions and get the right answers from him. He didn't worry at all about Miranda's cross-examination. He was deeply concerned, however, about Feldman's cross-examination and spent hours going over a mock cross with Ben.

Ransom was another story. Since he was the inspector, he would have to testify about the site conditions, including the impact of the current activity at the site, as well as his recommendations. Mike didn't trust him during the direct examination, let alone the cross-examination. He decided to put Ransom on for as short a period as he could afford and hoped he could quickly march him through his recommendation to allow mining at the site. He hoped Ransom would not blurt out anything damaging.

As two o'clock approached, he had to break off the preparation with his witnesses, owing to the arrangements he'd made with Miranda to meet with her. Mike and Nicky slowly drove to Miranda's office through snow that was falling at nearly an inch an hour.

Mike thought about not having told Nicky everything about his night with Miranda. With little embellishment, he'd told her he'd had sex with Miranda and that was it. She claimed she was happy for him, but Mike sensed a bit of jealousy when they talked about it. There was nothing exclusive about his relationship with Nicky. They were just friends of course. Roommates. They were rigorous about not having sex together and she encouraged him to date women. In the past, they'd often talked about their dates and partners, sometimes whispering steamy details, but he was embarrassed and more than a little ashamed to admit the lurid and twisted particulars of that night with Miranda. The more he thought about it, the more he felt it was best if the specifics of his fling with Miranda remained a private matter.

At the same time, Mike had a certain fascination with Miranda and was of two minds about her. On the one hand, he wanted to believe she had a sincere interest in him. On the other, he was fairly certain he was being used and this was nothing more than a brief fling. It might already be over. When he called her, she rarely returned his calls unless she needed something. Nicky was observant and a good listener and told him *she* suspected Miranda was using him. At first, Mike didn't want to believe that, but as the weeks wore on and Miranda never suggested or agreed to a follow-up date, he had to agree. Mike really didn't feel there was anything reciprocal. Still, she was beautiful, smart and intriguing. She was wrong on so many levels, but he was drawn to her, like a child to a red hot burner on a stove.

Mike and Nicky carefully navigated the four inches of snow that had already fallen on Somerset. From Betty at the Sheraton's front desk, he learned that Judge Diaz and Feldman's group had arrived ahead of the snow. Miranda's dour secretary answered the door, as aloof and unfriendly as ever. Mike unpacked his briefcase, while Nicky, who had familiarized herself with the papers, was laying out the exhibits on the conference room table as Miranda walked in.

Miranda wore a clingy, white, cowl neck sweater and stretch pants. She had pulled her blond hair back into a tight ponytail. As she walked into the room, she looked Nicky up and down

Amid Rage

and then put her arms around Mike, who had stood to greet her. "Michael, I'm so glad you've come to Somerset to bail me out," she said, hugging him warmly and planting a long, overly wet kiss on his lips.

Nicky watched with an amused smile. Miranda stared at Nicky as she hugged Mike.

"Who's your little friend?" Miranda asked.

"Miranda Clymer, I'd like you to meet my paralegal, Nicky Kane." Nicky stood and offered her hand. Miranda, a good six inches taller, clasped it in both of hers, and stroked it more than shook it.

"So nice to meet you, Nicky, Nicole. I hope we'll become good friends." She angled her head, "like Michael and me."

"Me too." Nicky smiled.

Mike winced.

"How old are you, child?" Miranda asked sweetly.

"Twenty-six."

"Twenty-six? I would have guessed eighteen."

"I'll take that as a compliment." Nicky smiled again.

"My, you are a sweet little thing." Miranda finally let go of Nicky's hand and smiled back at her.

Mike watched the exchange, not sure what angle Miranda was playing. Finally, he took a stack of documents that Nicky prepared and handed them to Miranda. "I thought we might go over these exhibits. I'll outline for you my examinations and we can go through what you plan to do at the hearing."

Nicky looked around the room and said to Miranda, "Before we really get started, I have to make a quick call to the office and use the ladies' room. Can you direct me?"

As soon as Nicky left the conference room. Miranda slid her chair close to Mike and said in a loud whisper, "Your *paralegal*? Come on Michael, I wasn't born yesterday. She's cute, tender, young. Very innocent. Quite a piece."

"No. We're just really good friends."

"So, there's nothing going on between the two of you?"

"No."

"Really? Did you know one of my *most intimate* girlfriends is Betty at the Sheraton? So tell me, is the DEP so frugal that they're forcing you to share both a room *and* a bed with your paralegal?"

A denial sprang to Mike's lips, but he swallowed it back. What he did or didn't do in his hotel room was none of her damn business. "Why do you care?"

She smiled, a glint of mischief in her eyes. "Because I have an idea. I'm busy tonight, but how about tomorrow night you, me, and your *really good friend* go upstairs and engage in some *really good* adult entertainment?"

Mike stared at her.

"Leave her out of this," Mike growled. "Just leave her alone. I don't want you to bother her."

"That's a little grouchy, Michael. Maybe later you can check with her and see what she says."

Mike shook his head. "We're not up here to do a three-way, we're here to try this case. Nicky's not my girlfriend. We don't have sex. It's not going to happen."

"I get it Michael. After a night with me she might not find you that interesting." Miranda squinted and smirked. "Let me think. You share a bed with her, but say you don't screw her? That delicious girl? Let me process that." She tapped a manicured fingernail on her lip. "Hmm, this is so confusing. You share a hotel room and sleep in the same bed. It's clear you care for her and she must love you or else why..." She rolled her eyes, "Okay, I get it. Assuming you're not lying to me, there's only one reason you two wouldn't do it. Which one of you is it? Her? *You*? Are *both* of you gay? Well, if she isn't sure what she is, I'll convince her."

Mike shook his head.

Miranda continued staring at Mike, then narrowed her eyes and changed her tone. "Okay, Michael, this is most interesting. We can plan the fun later, but what about our deal? We had a deal, if you recall. You certainly seemed enthusiastic about accepting it the last time you were here."

Mike swallowed hard and broke the stare with Miranda. "I guess I didn't realize how adamant Roger, my boss, was going to be about me not helping you. I don't want to get in trouble with him or the secretary. It could cost me my job. You can understand that, can't you? Look, I actually think you filed a good notice of appeal. I'm not sure how you pulled it off, but the comments you've made in the appeal were really good. Everything you need is in there. I'll do what I can to help you."

"It sounds like you're throwing me a bone, Michael. I did much more for you than that."

"I've already helped you. I drafted all the papers for your supersedeas and I outlined your oral argument. Also, I'm here right now, aren't I? So it's not like I'm welching. I just can't handle your case for you. If I do it'll get me into trouble."

"You don't want to get into trouble? You're leaving me in the lurch the day before the hearing. I was counting on you. Maybe you need to be reminded about what we did? What you agreed to? What do you think would happen if Roger Alden and Secretary Capozzi found out about our deal? What if they got a video of your performance just three weeks ago? It has a date stamp on it and everything. One of my favorite parts is where you're mostly naked with a cute little boner under your shorts, agreeing to help me with this case in exchange for sex. You looked straight into the camera for me. You were so sweet and you wanted it so much."

Mike said nothing. His face turned white and his expression was blank. "The camera?"

"Oh yes, of course. It's very good quality and requires very little light to get a high-resolution picture. You know, in addition to your boss and your boss's boss, maybe your little…paralegal, friend, whatever…would like to see it too? What would she think? Actually, I've watched it a few times and you performed admirably well for an amateur. You make very funny faces."

Mike blinked and pushed his chair back.

If she had a video and sent that to Roger and the secretary, he'd be summarily expelled from DEP.

The trial might be delayed and she'd have to deal with a new attorney—one who wouldn't be trapped by her.

She didn't gain any advantage.

He wondered.

She wouldn't do that.
She might just be crazy enough to do it.

Without hesitating, Miranda picked up a remote control from the credenza behind her chair and pointed it at the television. The screen lit up with an image of Miranda's four-poster guest room bed in shadows. A light came on brightening the scene. Mike heard Miranda's voice off-camera, *I have a surprise for you.*

Just at that moment, Nicky returned to the room.

Miranda pressed a button and the screen froze.

Pause.

"Did I miss anything?" Nicky asked brightly.

"That depends, Nicole, I was just going to show Michael a video that I think you'll find interesting too. Come here dear and sit with us for a few minutes."

"Uh, Miranda, we really don't have time for that right now," Mike said quietly.

"Oh, really? It's no trouble." She pointed the remote and the image sprang to life again. Mike could see himself coming into view in front of the camera in his tux. Miranda's hand guided him into position, dead center on the screen.

Nicky watched the two of them. Miranda looked at Mike.

"That thing we agreed to a couple weeks ago?" Mike said. "We're still good," Mike said looking at the table.

"Really? I was so hoping you'd see it my way. Wonderful," Miranda said happily, turning off the TV and putting down the remote. "Let's get started, shall we? Which witness do you recommend I call first? Maybe you can give me an outline of the questions I ought to ask?"

"Mike?" asked Nicky. "Don't we have some other witnesses to meet with starting at three?"

"Tell you what, get out my player's list and call all of the rest of them at home. Apologize and tell them I'll call them tonight when we get back to the hotel."

"That's a good boy, Michael." Miranda smiled at both of them then took out a legal pad and a gold Cross pen to take notes.

At 5:45, Miranda abruptly ended the session and sent them into the snowstorm.

"That was awkward," Nicky said as they trudged through the snow to the car. "What was that Michael this and Nicole that business?"

Mike didn't respond other than to shake his head as he pushed through the deepening snow.

51

Ordinarily, the courtroom in the Somerset County Court of Common Pleas was set with two tables for counsel—plaintiff and defendant or prosecution and defense—located in front of the public gallery seating area separated by the bar. Since there were three parties an extra table had been brought into the courtroom and all three were arranged in a tight row.

Mike was located at the middle table with Sid Feldman and his hoard of assistants to his left and Miranda to his right. This meant anyone walking from the gallery to the front of the courtroom had to squeeze between the tables. This also meant that anyone at one table could easily overhear a conversation at the next table.

Mike watched Miranda and Feldman as they set their tables. He always noticed this as he looked for some glimmer of insight into their thinking. How they organized their minds. The message they wanted to send to the judge. He noticed the clothes they wore to court and even the cars they drove. He wondered what others thought of him.

Miranda's table was very neat. Laptop in the middle. Legal pads in a tidy pile. Her notes. Post-its in a squared mound. Pens and colored highlighters in a cup. The opposite of Mike's table. Miranda wore a dark blue, low cut business suit with a tight skirt that hit well above the knee. Her suit was sharply tailored and a distraction to most everyone in the courtroom. She also wore a white silk scoop-necked blouse with a bra that appeared to be more sling than brassiere, so that whenever she leaned over she gave Judge Diaz—and Tommy Bowdoin—an impressive show. Mike thought she looked more like a high-priced call girl than a lawyer.

Sitting with Miranda was Lily Roberts. Lily Roberts was wearing a thick, hand-made sweater and black slacks. On her feet were ladies' boots, not the kind you would see on Fifth Avenue in New York, but the kind you might see on Main Street in Somerset in the dead of winter. All of the neighbors and many of their friends sat directly behind Miranda's table. None wore suits, but in their flannel and wool they all looked like earnest country people.

Feldman was resplendent in a worsted wool dark blue, red pinstripe suit from Italy. He also wore a vest of similar material, which made him look every bit the successful Philadelphia lawyer that he was. He and Miranda could have been featured together on the cover of some high-end fashion magazine. As the clock approached ten a.m., he sat in his seat primping and joking with Rinati. Feldman was the epitome of invincibility and arrogance.

Angela St. Germain sat next to Feldman. She was wearing a heavyweight winter dress with vertical stripes and sensible pumps. She had bags under her eyes and Mike guessed she hadn't slept in days while she readied Feldman for the hearing. Rinati sat next to Angela, wearing green work pants and a blue work shirt. He also wore a blue blazer, two sizes too small, that was not buttoned. He looked like the simple coal miner that he wanted the judge—the only member of the audience who mattered—to believe he was.

In front of Feldman was a single legal pad. Angela had arrayed in front of her numerous files and her laptop. In front of Rinati was a single yellow Post-it pad and a pencil. Jimmy Podwall sat on a bench behind Angela, just in front of the gallery surrounded by banker's boxes full of papers, files and law books. His laptop sat across his knees. From time to time, as they waited for the judge, Angela would lean back and whisper ferociously into his ear. He would then either paw through the stacks of papers piled on the bench to either side of him or he would lean over and talk to another young Pell, Desrosiers lawyer, Claude Montgomery, whom Mike had met for the first time that morning.

Behind them was an array of Rhino employees. Mike overheard one talking when they were standing in the hallway and heard they had been given the day off to make sure the gallery was full of coal miners. Considering the weather outside, none complained. They wore jeans and work pants, insulated vests over a variety of tee shirts with slogans like, *I Dig Coal, American Miner*, and *The Deeper I Go, the More She likes It.*

Mike wore his best blue suit, a white button-down shirt from L.L. Bean, and red-and-blue striped tie. He liked his prosecutor's uniform and felt it was appropriate considering his role in the litigation. He hoped he sent the right message to the judge. The message was: *I represent the Commonwealth. The whole Commonwealth. I've got nothing in this fight except the real interests of the people.* Nevertheless, he might have been featured in a small picture in the back of *Prosecutor Today* magazine, certainly not *GQ*. Next to him was Nicky. She wore a bright floral print dress she'd purchased at Dress Barn and she'd pulled her hair back into a neat ponytail. In addition, she wore brown horn-rimmed glasses. Having her next to him made him feel he had to do especially well. Rarely did he have an audience about whom he cared so deeply.

"You look like the sexy librarian in the before picture," Mike whispered to her without cracking a smile.

"Mr. Jacobs, I'm a professional. Please control yourself," she said under her breath the corners of her lips almost turning into a smile.

Outside, the snow had finished falling, leaving nearly a foot of new powder on the ground, and the world was mostly silent. Only one lane was open on the turnpike, and the sound of the jake brakes from the trucks that moved slowly on the highway occasionally reached into the town, but the silence from the snow enveloped the town. At about nine fifty-five a.m., Tommy Bowdoin took his place in the courtroom at a table below the judge's bench and the courtroom quieted.

There is that moment in the few minutes before a trial begins when the clients and witnesses understand they can no longer talk freely with their attorneys. Like a pitcher about to start a big game, whom none of the other players would dare bother, the people in the courtroom intuitively know to stay away from the lead lawyers. This is a unique moment of precise clarity. The attorney focuses all of his or her intellect on the things he or she must do in the opening minutes of the trial. She shuts out the rest of her life. He concentrates on the initial motions he will argue or the initial examination that he will make. Perhaps she considers the objections that she knows she will have to offer the minute the judge takes his seat. The world slows down for the litigator and, as if in a tunnel, all he sees is the case ahead of him. Nothing else in the world matters. No one should dare to talk to a lawyer in those last few minutes as he gathers his wits at the gates of the arena.

Mike looked at Feldman and saw his expression had changed. Ten minutes earlier, he had been confident, jovial, and laughing with Rinati. Now he stared straight ahead, his brow furrowed, and he appeared lost in thought. Angela looked worried. Creases had formed across her brow and emanated from the corners of her eyes. She had rings of sweat under her arms that had bled through her heavy winter dress. Miranda looked surprisingly confident. He had never seen her like this. In the days leading up to the trial, she'd repeatedly expressed her doubts about her ability to handle this, her first trial. Now, as the judge prepared to enter the courtroom, she seemed poised and ready. Mike looked at Nicky, who just looked like Nicky in a dress. A broad smile was on her face. She surveyed the courtroom with curious eyes.

At exactly ten o'clock, Judge Diaz entered the courtroom. He did not have a tipstaff, but everyone automatically stood as he entered the courtroom and did not sit until he settled himself in the high-backed judge's chair.

"Call your first witness, Ms. Clymer." Judge Diaz sat behind the judge's bench in the ornate, century-old courtroom. A mere administrative law judge, he looked smug and satisfied as he sat on an elevated judge's bench in a real courtroom in a genuine courthouse. This was a far cry from the multipurpose room in which he typically conducted his administrative trials. Despite this noticeable satisfaction, Mike studied his face and noticed the bags under his eyes and that he looked exceptionally tired and drawn. He sipped from an extra-large cardboard coffee cup.

All eyes were on Miranda. Mike had spent hours with her going over her examinations and cross-examination questions and getting her ready for the hearing. He outlined for Miranda the questions she would need to ask. They'd settled on a brief and pithy examination of several of her clients. In addition, he agreed to allow her to call Ben Kemper. Mike called Feldman in his hotel room late on Monday afternoon and offered Ben as a witness to Feldman as well, just so it wouldn't look like he was playing favorites.

She had before her the same legal pad on which she'd written the outline of her examinations. Mike hoped she followed it. He'd talked with Miranda about her demeanor in the courtroom and went so far as to tell Miranda to err on the side of standing and to ask the judge's permission to sit. He didn't think that reminding Judge Diaz this was her first trial would help her.

Miranda looked at the judge. Mike was almost certain he saw her wink at Judge Diaz—Mike shook his head—then she slowly rose from her seat.

52

Miranda stood. She appeared to enjoy the fact that everyone's eyes were on her. She turned toward her clients in the gallery and beamed with a new-found confidence as she boldly and loudly said, "The citizens call Lily Roberts."

Mrs. Roberts rose and awkwardly walked to the witness stand. She glanced over her shoulder. Everyone in the courtroom was watching her. Judge Diaz swore her in and she sat her ninety-pound frame lightly onto the witness chair. Miranda continued standing to ask her questions.

"Judge Diaz, do you mind if I stand or sit?"

"Whatever you prefer, Ms. Clymer," the judge said, barely concealing his smile.

Mike was impressed, Miranda appeared self-assured, poised. Mike glanced over his shoulder and noticed all of the eyes on her, or was it her shapely ass and long legs?

"Is your name Lily Roberts?"

Mike thought *leading question*, but okay this early in the testimony.

"Yes."

"Do you live at 105 Forest Lane, Somerset?"

Another leading question.

"Yes."

"You work for the Bank of Oxford as a bookkeeper?"

Another. Compound question.

"Yes."

"Are you familiar with the land owned by Fred Gordon?"

Her fourth leading question, but this one's okay.

"Yes, that's the farm across the road from us."

"I assume you're familiar with the woods on the other side of the Gordon Farm?"

"Yes."

Another leading question, again okay, but get on with it.

Mike glanced at Feldman who sat on the edge of his chair. He had his elbow on the table and he rested his chin in his left hand. He looked like he could leap across the room on a moment's notice. He was studying Miranda's face.

"Are you familiar with Rhino Mining Company?" Miranda asked, her sixth or seventh leading question in a row.

"Not personally. I know that's the mining company that has the permit across the way from us."

"Have you seen the mine permit application and the mining permit?"

"Yes."

Again, a leading question. She should have asked some foundation questions, but basically okay. She really has to get into the direct testimony.

By now, Mike was watching Feldman and Angela more than he was watching anyone else in the courtroom. Feldman looked at Mike and made a face nodding toward Miranda. Mike briefly motioned his palms up, but did not otherwise reply.

"Would you say you were shocked when you saw that DEP had issued a mining permit to Rhino?"

Oh shit, one too many leading questions.

"I object Your Honor, leading question." Feldman said, jumping to his feet, pulling his glasses off and pointing them at Miranda. "In fact, all of Ms. Clymer's questions so far have been leading questions. I can tolerate leading questions when they are establishing a foundation on direct, but not when she starts asking questions about substance."

Miranda didn't seem to know what to do next.

"Ms. Clymer, how do you respond?" Judge Diaz asked pleasantly.

"I don't think they were all leading questions, maybe just one or two," she said in a perky, girlish voice. Laughter rippled through the courtroom.

The judge picked up the gavel and tapped it twice, lightly. "Please observe decorum in my courtroom. The objection is sustained. Ms. Clymer, please do not ask leading questions on direct. Rephrase the question. You may proceed."

Miranda stood, looked at her papers, less sure of herself than before.

"When DEP issued the permit to Rhino, would you say you were shocked?" she asked.

Feldman leapt to his feet. "Same objection, Your Honor. All she did was restate the same question as a different leading question."

From his vantage, Mike saw Miranda's knees shaking slightly, although from the waist up she appeared still.

Mike half stood and said, "Uh, Your Honor, to move this along, I think Ms. Clymer just wanted to ask the witness how she felt when the permit was issued."

Miranda looked at him and mouthed, "Thank you."

"Well, very nice of the Commonwealth to help our mutual opponents, especially since the witness now knows the answer," Feldman said standing and pointing his glasses at Mike.

"Is there an objection, Mr. Feldman?" Mike asked.

"Mr. Jacobs, why don't you allow *me* to control *my* courtroom," the judge said. "You may recall from our last meeting that I'm the judge here, not you. If there was an objection, it's overruled. The witness may answer the question."

"Well, frankly, I was shocked," Mrs. Roberts replied.

Again, there was laughter in the courtroom. The judge looked annoyed and picked up his gavel, but did not bang it. He glared at the crowd of neighbors and coal miners in the courtroom.

"Were you shocked because you didn't feel it was appropriate for DEP to issue a permit to mine the Gordon property?" Miranda asked.

Feldman shot to his feet. "Your Honor!"

"I'm so sorry Your Honor, I withdraw the question. Let me rephrase that," Miranda said. "Why did you feel it was not appropriate for DEP to issue the permit?"

"Well, my husband and I have lived on Forest Lane for thirty years. We've raised our family there. We know that farm and we know those woods. It's a beautiful farm and the headwaters to Roaring Run start up in that field. I take a walk almost every day down to the state game lands. My husband and boys have hunted in there for as long as we've lived here. It doesn't seem appropriate that someone should be able to mine in that area."

"When you looked at the permit application, Lily, did it say anything about protecting the headwaters?" Miranda asked.

"Objection. Now she's failed to lay a foundation." Feldman said loudly pointing his glasses at Miranda. "We don't know anything about how Ms. Roberts came to look at the application, where she saw it, why she was looking at it, or if she's qualified to talk about it. Until Ms. Clymer lays a proper foundation, we should not hear any testimony from this witness about the application."

Judge Diaz looked at Miranda, waiting for a response.

"I thought I did lay a foundation," she said weakly.

"Sustained. Ms. Clymer, you have to lay a foundation before your witness can discuss any of this. You know, ask some questions to establish she's familiar with the application, any expertise, that kind of thing."

The judge leaned forward as he issued his ruling, nodding his head as he tried to help her. Mike looked at Feldman who made a *what the hell?* face at him, as the judge assisted Miranda.

"Your Honor!" Feldman said sharply jumping back to his feet.

Judge Diaz glared at Feldman, "I want to move this trial along, Mr. Feldman. I'd do the same thing for you."

The lawyers other than Feldman all broke into grins, but managed to hold back any laughter.

Miranda was still standing and Mike could see her knees shaking badly and her legs wobbling on her four-inch heels. After a few moments, she sat down and began paging through her notes. Then she looked through the pile of exhibits that Mike had given her the day before.

Abandoning the line of questioning, Miranda asked, "Mrs. Roberts, Lily, are you shocked and unhappy that Rhino is mining across the street from you?"

As Feldman began to rise, Mrs. Roberts said, "yes."

"Move to strike, leading question," Feldman said.

Miranda continued paging through the papers as if she were looking for an answer hidden in her notes. Mike knew her client had spent days looking through the application. While she had no technical training, she did have an associate's degree in accounting and worked for the Bank of Oxford. He had discussed with Miranda the importance of having a leadoff witness who would set the stage. Lily Roberts was supposed to be that witness. Now, all that the judge heard and all that the record showed was a series of leading questions and discombobulated testimony.

"I have no further questions for this witness at this time," Miranda said, dropping about half of the direct examination that she and Mike had planned.

"Mr. Feldman, your witness," the judge said.

Feldman stood up sharply. With a smile he said, "Good morning Ms. Roberts, my name is Sidney Feldman. I am the attorney for Rhino Mining Company. I have just a couple of questions for you. Do you have any training that would specifically provide you with expertise to review the permit application?"

"A degree in accounting. Otherwise, no."

Feldman nodded and continued smiling.

"You're a bookkeeper? You look at books and financial records at the bank, that kind of thing?" He nodded.

"Yes."

"Are you a CPA?"

"No."

"You don't look at mine permit applications in your job, do you?" he said with a big grin.

"No. My job sounds pretty boring to most people, but I like it. All day long all I do is look at financial forms, bonds, applications for mortgages, that kind of thing. I'm the one who makes sure they're complete and the numbers add up."

"You live on Forest Lane?"

"Yes."

"Do you have a sewer or septic tank?"

"Septic."

"The effluent, that is to say the waste water, from the septic tank flows downhill, of course, doesn't it?"

"I don't know, it's underground."

"Your house is on a hillside above the headwaters area?" Feldman asked.

"Yes," she answered slowly.

"So your waste water from your septic tank flows by gravity toward those headwaters, right?"

"I guess so," Mrs. Roberts said, looking at Miranda and then toward her husband.

Mike could see Feldman was trying to show the Roberts' septic tank could be contaminating the headwaters, but he didn't think the point would register through this witness.

"You're not a geologist, are you?"

"No."

"You're not a mining engineer, are you?"

"No."

"You're not a hydrologist?"

Miranda started to rise and Mrs. Roberts stopped herself from answering.

"Your Honor, he's asking leading questions..." she started to say.

"Judge, this is cross-examination," Feldman cut her off, looking annoyed. "*Of course* I'm asking leading questions, Ms. Clymer. That's what we lawyers do on cross-examination. As an experienced, *senior* member of the local bar, she should well know that lawyers ask leading questions on cross."

The judge leaned forward. "Mr. Feldman, please leave out any personal references. That aside, you're right. Ms. Clymer, if Mr. Feldman or Mr. Jacobs choose to ask leading questions on cross-examination, they may do so. You may do so too, on cross-examination. Overruled."

Miranda looked down at her counsel table, but it was apparent that her face was bright red. This was not just a rookie mistake, it was a first-day-of-law-school mistake.

"So, you're not a hydrologist, are you?"

"No, but I know what's right. I know that it just isn't right for Rhino to come in here to our town, our beautiful community, and destroy it. Come and destroy the farm, the woods, the headwaters of Roaring Run," she answered staring straight at Feldman.

"Judge, I move to strike everything after 'no.' None of the rest of that was responsive."

The judge looked at Miranda who shook her head.

"The reporter will strike everything after Ms. Roberts' initial 'no' answer."

Feldman continued, "I understand that you looked at the application, but really, Ms. Roberts, you have no expertise as a geologist, mining engineer, or any other expertise in the mining process, do you?"

"I guess not," she said in a small voice.

"I have no further questions for this witness."

Feldman sat and Rinati leaned over and slapped him on the back three times. He whispered a few words in Feldman's ear, and they both laughed quietly. Angela looked stoic.

"I guess the Commonwealth is trying to be neutral in this proceeding, Mr. Jacobs. I don't suppose you have any cross-examination for this witness, do you?" asked the judge.

Mike thought for a long moment. He had just seen one of the worst direct examinations ever by Miranda followed by an effective cross-examination by Feldman. Not only had Miranda not scored any points, but she had lost ground on her lead-off witness and she was just getting started. He knew if he asked any questions, he could not appear to be favoring either side and had to be careful.

"In fact, Your Honor, I do have just two or three questions for clarification purposes."

Feldman glared at Mike, who ignored him. Mike picked up an exhibit and handed it to the witness. He also handed copies to the judge, Feldman, Miranda and Tommy Bowdoin.

"Ms. Roberts, I'm handing you a document that has been marked as Commonwealth's exhibit number one, the permit application. Have you ever seen this before?"

"Yes."

"Where did you see this?"

"When I did my file review at the Cambria District Office. I requested the mine permit application and they gave me this."

"You reviewed this application?"

"Yes, very thoroughly. I probably spent more time looking at this than any other document. Maybe five or six hours in total."

Mike glanced at Miranda who almost imperceptibly nodded. Then he looked at Feldman who looked fiercely at him and shook his head.

"Now, you're not a geologist or mining engineer, are you?" he asked looking at Feldman and nodding.

"No, just a bookkeeper. I review financial documents for the Bank of Oxford and its subsidiaries."

"When you looked at this, you weren't able to reach any understanding regarding the geology, hydrology, engineering, mining engineering, anything like that?"

"No, not really. Some of the things I read in here scared me, but I don't have any book learning about what I was reading."

Mike heard a chair being pushed back and turned to see that Feldman was standing. "Your Honor, there were no questions about this exhibit or Ms. Roberts' review of it. I'm not quite sure why the Commonwealth would press this issue, but Mr. Jacobs has gone way beyond the scope of both Ms. Clymer's direct examination and my cross-examination of the witness. He has no basis for proceeding any further. Frankly, he ought to just sit down." Feldman glowered at Mike.

"Judge, Mr. Feldman's cross asked numerous questions about the witness's review of the application. I think you'll see with my next question that my questions bear directly on Ms. Clymer's direct examination *and* Mr. Feldman's cross examination. Also, the Commonwealth is here today to see to it that the integrity of the application process is maintained and the truth comes out. Really, I have just one or two more questions for the witness."

"Mr. Jacobs, I think you told us you only had two or three questions to begin with," the judge said smiling thinly. There was muffled laughter from the back of the courtroom. "My patience is wearing thin. I'll give you one or two questions but that's it. Overruled."

"Ms. Roberts, during your direct *and* cross-examinations, you testified you were a bookkeeper for a bank?"

"Yes."

"And you testified that all day long you review financial documents, mortgages, loans, forms, signatures and the like?"

"Yes, I do it eight hours a day, every day, and I've done it for thirty years. Nothing gets final approval by the bank unless I've initially approved it."

"Do you review signature pages, notary seals, too?"

"All day long."

"You spent five or six hours studying this application?" Mike asked.

"Yes."

"Would you please take a look at the very last page of the application? The page that says *certification*."

There was a general rustling in the courtroom as the lawyers, judge and witness all turned to the last page. Out of the corner of his eye, he could see Angela madly turning pages and pushing them in front of Feldman.

"Did you look at this page when you were reviewing the application at the DEP office?"

Lily smiled broadly. "Why, yes I did. I studied this very hard."

"As a bookkeeper with thirty years of experience reviewing financial documents, signatures and the like, what can you tell us about this page?"

"Objection! Objection, Your Honor, this is so far beyond the scope of direct and cross-examination—" Feldman began. He had picked up the exhibit and moved in front of his counsel's table, just feet from where Mike stood.

"I see where he's going Mr. Feldman," the judge said. "Overruled. Please sit down. You may answer the question."

"If you look at the signature. It's signed Ernesto Rinati. The date on the application is July 1 of last year. The signature is notarized. But if you take a look at the notary's stamp it indicates that her commission expired over a month earlier on May 31. This document is supposed to be notarized, but the notary was not authorized to notarize this or any other document since her commission had expired."

"And what does that mean, Mrs. Roberts?"

"Objection!" Feldman was back on his feet as he spit out the word.

"Overruled, sit down, Mr. Feldman," the judge said sharply without awaiting a response from Mike.

"It's as though the document was never notarized or even signed. It says right here on the DEP form that the signature has to be notarized. This is a faulty document. If this were submitted to my bank as a loan application, we would reject it even if everything else was in place and proper."

"So the document was never properly notarized?" Mike asked for emphasis.

"That's right. When the notary's seal is bad, the whole document is faulty. This means you can't trust the signature on the document as being Mr. Rinati's. No responsible institution would ever accept this."

"What the fuck?" Rinati said loudly. "What the hell, Feldman, you told me that DEP would be on our side. That little prick just tore me a new one." He was pointing at Mike.

The courtroom erupted in noise and commotion and Judge Diaz banged the gavel until it quieted down. "Quiet, quiet in the courtroom. Keep your comments to yourself, sir." He pointed the gavel at Rinati.

Mike looked at Nicky who grinned back at him. Miranda caught his eye and slightly nodded. He was afraid to look at Feldman.

"No further questions, Your Honor," Mike said as he sat down.

"No shit. You already crapped all over my application," Rinati said loudly staring at Mike.

"Any other questions for this witness. Ms. Clymer? Mr. Feldman?" The judge asked.

Miranda shook her head.

Feldman stood and said, "No, Your Honor." He continued to stand and said, "Judge, there's a notary public down the hall in the courthouse. During the break, we'll have Mr. Rinati re-sign the application in front of the notary. We're not conceding that the original signature was improper, but to allay any unwarranted fears, and since this is a *de novo* proceeding, you can consider new evidence, even evidence up until the time of your ruling. If you like, you can ignore the older signature and just consider the new signature, notarized here in the courthouse."

"I'll take that under advisement, Mr. Feldman. We'll take a fifteen-minute recess."

As the lawyers and observers stood and the judge slipped out the back door, Rinati positioned himself close to Mike. He didn't say a word. He just stared at him, with his eyes narrowed into slits. Nostrils flaring.

53

Mike exited the men's room and walked directly into Feldman who tapped him on the shoulder and motioned toward the corner of the spacious and ornate hallway.

"Hey buddy boy, what was the deal in there? I thought you were only here to protect the integrity of the Commonwealth. What happened?"

Mike refused to step back under the weight of Feldman's glare. "The department screwed up by failing to notice the out-of-date notary seal. I wanted to get out in front of that before Clymer made an issue of it. So far as I'm concerned, that *is* protecting the integrity of the Commonwealth. Besides, we want a complete record, don't we? We have to get to the truth."

"Really? You've been practicing law for what, three, four years? A trial has nothing to do with that. It has to do with winning. Last I checked, Clymer and those holier-than-thou clients of hers were trying to overturn the permit your client issued and my client needs to operate. What we want to do here is *win*, we don't want to get at the *truth*," Feldman said, moving his head closer to Mike's ear.

"Sid, I'm just doing my job."

"Yeah? I spoke with Roger Alden and he assured me that all the Commonwealth would be doing is babysitting this case. He told me if either Clymer or I said anything bad about the department we should expect you to jump in. That was it. I didn't expect to see you bail her ass out."

"You spoke to Roger?"

"Of course. I've known Roger for nearly thirty years. Why wouldn't I talk to him?"

Mike was surprised, but not shocked. Roger hadn't mentioned any conversations with Feldman and maybe that was a good thing. He was concerned, though, that Feldman apparently had an open line to his boss.

Before Mike could respond, he glimpsed Nicky over Feldman's shoulder. She was at the other end of the hall, talking with Angela. They glanced his way as if they felt his attention. Nicky grinned and waved at him, but Angela looked away. Strange. He wondered what they were talking about that had caused the slight flush to Angela's cheeks. Knowing Nicky, it could be anything. The crowd in the hall began to filter back into the courtroom. Mike watched Nicky and Angela disappear into the courtroom and then dragged his attention back to Feldman who was still yammering on, something about how often he played golf with the governor.

"I think we have to go back in," Mike said.

"This is all very interesting," Feldman said with an odd smile, then he turned and wandered off.

Mike sat next to Nicky who piled more papers on their desk. Tommy Bowdoin entered the courtroom and took his place.

"You seemed to be having a pretty intense conversation with Mr. Feldman," she whispered in his ear.

"Just lawyer stuff. Nothing to worry about. What about you? You seemed to be having quite a conversation with Angela."

She looked at him and smiled. "It was just girl stuff. Also, she asked me how long I'd been a paralegal."

Mike narrowed his eyes.

"Don't worry, I told her the company line that I was interning for the department and getting college credit for this." Nicky paused for a long moment. "She did ask me one unusual question. She wanted to know if you were my boyfriend. I told her we were very close friends, but not seeing each other."

Mike was taken aback. He turned and looked at Angela who was hammering the keys of her laptop. Next to her, though, Rinati stared at him. He didn't smile or nod, just glared, his beady eyes boring a hole through Mike. At that moment, the judge returned and everyone in the courtroom stood.

"Ms. Clymer, call your next witness."

Miranda stood. "The citizens call Mr. Don Roberts."

Miranda did somewhat better with this witness. She seemed to remember the difference between a leading question and an open-ended one. Following the outline that Mike gave her, she got through the testimony with few objections.

Feldman's cross-examination was perfunctory, establishing again that Roberts had no credentials to review a mining application, and Mike declined to cross-examine him, which earned him a tight nod from Feldman. They broke for lunch after the next witness, after which Miranda would call her final witness: Ben.

After the courtroom emptied, Nicky broke out peanut butter sandwiches, warm Cokes from the hotel, and a package of cookies. Mike, Nicky and Ben put their heads close together like conspirators. "Ben, I need you to be careful in your testimony. Remember to avoid offering your personal opinion. We can't have the department looking as though it's favoring the citizens over Rhino since we issued the permit to Rhino. Everyone in the courthouse is beginning to think we're on the citizens' side. Ultimately, that's not going to be helpful." Mike was thinking about himself.

Ben stared at Mike for a long moment, then said, "Got it, partner. You don't have to worry about me." An hour later he was on the witness stand.

54

The public gallery was less full after lunch. The lawyers had settled into their routines and the remaining audience appeared to be waiting for something to happen.

Miranda called Ben to the stand where he was sworn in by the judge. He wore jeans and a flannel shirt. One might have thought this was in deference to the foot of snow outside the courtroom, but he wore the same outfit most of the time from September to April. Mike had tried to talk him into wearing a jacket and tie, but Ben's response had been his typical "eh-eh-eh-eh."

"State your name." Miranda stood as she asked the question.

"Ben Kemper."

"What's your job?"

"I'm a mining engineer for DEP."

"What is your degree?"

"Mining Engineering, Penn State."

"How many years have you worked as a mining engineer?"

"Ten."

Mike was reasonably impressed that Miranda appeared to have found her stride. For the most part she was handling his examination decently and with authority.

"So, Mr. Kemper, you were the permit reviewer for the Rhino application?" she asked.

Feldman objected. "Judge, can Ms. Clymer please, please ask open-ended questions on direct? This business with the leading questions on direct has got to end."

Mike thought that Feldman's objection was unnecessary, since Miranda was still establishing the foundation with this witness.

"Overruled. Ms. Clymer was just establishing foundation," the judge said, still leaning backwards.

Miranda didn't break stride. "Mr. Kemper, what was your role in the application process?"

Mike looked at Feldman, who made a face and allowed one side of his lip to curl up.

"I'm a mining engineer with the department. I review mine permit applications and this is one of the applications I reviewed."

"Are you the only one who reviewed this application?"

"No, the inspector has input, we have an engineer in training who reviews it, our geologist spends some quality time with it. A few others have a hand on it like our licensed blaster, then the permit manager reviews it and nothing goes out of the office until John Hicks, the district mining manager, reviews it and approves it."

"So that's a total of seven separate reviews?"

"At least. There are others who review any given permit application. There are specialists in Harrisburg, like a hydrologist, who may look at it, a forester, and I'm sure I'm leaving out one or two."

Miranda had gone off script and Mike was wondering why she was taking him through this. It seemed this testimony was bolstering the thoroughness of DEP's review.

"So, there were maybe eight, nine different reviews?"

"Yes, that's very possible, maybe more. There's a paper somewhere in the file where everyone who's involved in the application process signs off. That would tell you for sure."

"Does everyone involved in the review process have to agree the permit should be issued?" Miranda asked.

Mike heard Feldman's chair scraping the floor as he pushed back. Feldman was half standing, then sat back down.

"No. Sometimes one or two of the reviewers will recommend against issuing the permit. Ultimately, the decision is the district mining manager's to make."

"Did everyone on the review team agree that the Rhino permit application should be issued?"

"Objection. Failure to lay a foundation. Calls for hearsay," Feldman said sharply, pointing with his glasses.

"Ms. Clymer?" asked the judge.

"I thought I did lay a foundation. He said he reviewed it, discussed the others who reviewed it, and all of that."

"What about Mr. Feldman's hearsay objection?"

Miranda paused.

Business records exception to hearsay, Mike thought. He quickly wrote BUSINESS RECORDS EXCEPTION on a clean legal pad and passed it to Nicky. She glanced at it and without moving her head took the tablet and held it against a large redweld file at the end of the desk. The file blocked Feldman's team from seeing what she was doing and the only one who could see it was Miranda, if she looked.

Mike waited a moment, then faked an epic cough that was as loud as he could make it. "Sorry, Your Honor, I just need a drink." He poured some water from the pitcher on his desk into a small paper cup, then held it up as though it were evidence of him losing a lung.

"Your honor, there's the business records exception to hearsay," Miranda said a moment later. "I could have Mr. Kemper page through the file to find that page he was discussing, but this is an administrative proceeding and there is that exception to hearsay."

The judge nodded, then said, "Very well then. Overruled, the witness may answer the question." He leaned his chair back.

Mike gently bumped his shoulder against Nicky's while looking straight ahead. A moment later, she bumped him back.

"As a matter of fact, several of us opposed issuance of the permit. I was against it and so was Marty Stevens, the original inspector. He died in a fire in early October and Lyle Ransom took over about a week later. Lyle filed his recommendation supporting the issuance of the permit on October 14. I know that the geologist, Devon Permian, didn't want it issued either."

"How is it that the permit was issued if three of you—Inspector Stevens, the geologist and yourself— were against the issuance of the permit?"

"Mr. Hicks issued it on behalf of the department. He can overrule us and that's his prerogative. He did insist on adding several permit conditions which he felt would protect the headwaters and the neighbors."

"You don't seem so sure of that. Do you have an opinion on whether the mining will have an adverse impact on the neighbors on Forest Lane?"

Mike jumped up. "Objection. Calls for an opinion. We haven't offered Mr. Kemper as an expert witness yet."

"Mr. Jacobs, you're saying the department's mining engineer is not qualified to testify as an expert witness on the mine permit application he reviewed?" asked the judge sitting up in his chair and not bothering to stifle back a grin.

"No, not that, just that we haven't offered him as an expert witness. Of course, he's eminently qualified to testify as an expert witness."

"Overruled."

As Mike was sitting he heard Feldman's chair being pushed back. "In that case, Your Honor, the permittee objects. Not only does this call for an opinion, but Ms. Clymer did not advise us she was going to seek opinion testimony from this witness. I mean, we knew she was going to call him as a fact witness, but we didn't know he would be called as an expert witness. We have no expert report from him, nor did we have any notice."

"Ms. Clymer?"

"Judge, this is a supersedeas hearing. No one has filed expert reports. Michael, I mean Mr. Jacobs, offered Mr. Kemper as a witness to both myself and Rhino Mining yesterday. Mr. Jacobs agrees, as he should, that Mr. Kemper is qualified to testify and give his opinion on this question."

Trying to regain some control over this, Mike rose to his feet. "That's not exactly what I said."

"Okay, everyone, sit down. I'm going to let him answer and give his opinion. This is a supersedeas hearing and it's an administrative proceeding. We may be in a courtroom of the Court of Common Pleas, however, our rules are more lenient than the court's rules. I'm curious anyway. Go ahead, Mr. Kemper."

"Like I said, I was against issuing the permit. I don't think it should've been issued. Even with the conditions, my opinion is that mining cannot take place without damaging those homes."

Without pausing, Miranda asked, "What about the headwaters of Roaring Run?"

Mike and Feldman were both on their feet.

"Your honor!" spit out Feldman.

"Same objection," Mike said.

The judge looked at the two lawyers. "Same ruling. He may answer."

"My opinion is that the mining will destroy the headwaters of Roaring Run."

Miranda held up her chin and looked triumphantly at Feldman, then flashed a brilliant smile at Mike. "Nothing further for this witness."

Feldman's cross-examination was methodical and detailed. As he strutted around the courtroom, he dissected Ben's education, limited to a bachelor's degree, his training, and showed the limitations of his technical background. Then he took Ben through each component of the application. As Ben described each step, Feldman would stop him and ask whether he agreed on the basis of that part of the application that the permit should have been issued. At each stage, Ben answered, "Yes."

"So, to be clear, Mr. Kemper, you believe that on the basis of the mining plan, the permit can be issued?"

"Yes. But I have other concerns unrelated to the mining plan—"

"Just limit your answer to my question. Ms. Clymer can redirect, if she cares to do so."

Step after step, Feldman showed that Ben's concerns related to geology and hydrology, not mining engineering.

"Mr. Kemper, is it fair to say that your gut tells you that mining may have an impact on the homes and stream?" Feldman asked.

"Yes."

"No further questions." Feldman sat down and looked at Mike.

Judge Diaz looked at the clock. It was almost five. "Mr. Jacobs, do you want to begin now or tomorrow morning?"

Mike looked at his notes and slowly stood. "I have a couple of foundation questions and then one ultimate question, Your Honor. I think I can get through this in five minutes."

"Go ahead."

"In what is your degree, Mr. Kemper?"

"I have a bachelor's of mining engineering from Penn State."

"Any graduate work?"

"No."

"Are you a licensed professional engineer?"

"Yes."

"What is your job with the department?"

"I'm a mining engineer."

"You said you worked for DEP for ten years. How many mine permit applications have you reviewed for the department?"

"Full reviews, about ten to twelve a year, or something north of one hundred by now. I've reviewed bits and pieces of maybe another two hundred applications."

"You reviewed the entire Rhino mine permit application for the site?"

"Yes, I was the primary reviewer."

"How many times have you visited the proposed Gordon Mine?"

"Twice. I walked the entire site when I began my review and again in September. Oh, and I was there the Saturday they began mining operations at the site two weeks ago."

"Based on all of that, what is your opinion on whether the department should have issued this mine permit application?"

"Objection!" Feldman said loudly as he jumped out of his chair. "Failure to lay a foundation. The witness is not qualified to answer. No expert report. No business records exception."

"Overruled. You may answer."

"Honestly, my opinion is that this permit should *not* have been issued. It will not protect the headwaters of Roaring Run, and it will not protect those homes. I've been doing this for a long time and I just don't think we should've issued it."

"This is based solely on your gut reaction to the application?"

"No. This is based on my training and years of experience." Ben looked directly at Feldman as he answered.

"Judge, I have no further questions for this witness on Ms. Clymer's direct examination. We may wish to recall Mr. Kemper when we put on our case."

"So noted. We are in recess and will resume at nine a.m. tomorrow. I'm going to remind counsel that this is a supersedeas hearing, not a full-blown trial. So, I hope we can finish this up tomorrow. There will be time at the full hearing to get into all of the details. Let's keep this hearing limited to the issues on the supersedeas petition."

Judge Diaz stood, as did everyone in the courtroom, and he exited through the judge's back door.

Mike and Nicky gathered up all of their papers. While they did this, Miranda's clients gathered around her in animated discussion. Feldman and Rinati watched Mike as he packed his brief bag.

As the courtroom emptied, Mike noticed two men he hadn't seen before in the hearing. He recognized the first one: Wolfie, who was at Gilligan's bar the first time he came up to Somerset and also at the Shoemaker Mine when the landslide occurred. With him was a skinny man with an ugly hooked scar on his face. Mike vaguely remembered also seeing him at Rhino's mine site. They studied Mike carefully, as if they were sizing him up.

A chill ran down Mike's back.

55

Angela St. Germain, Esquire, glanced at her two Philadelphia colleagues who, like her, were frozen to their seats. Feldman's face was fixed in an awkward smile and his right eye twitched. Sweat trickled from Angela's armpits and down her plump arms, ruining her silk Chanel blouse. A reeking bubble of gas worked its way through Jimmy Podwall's colon, past yesterday's digested burrito, escaped through his anal sphincter, and seeped out of his Canali trousers. It was a silent neutron bomb of a fart that Angela struggled not to notice. Rinati's black eyes drilled holes through the three lawyers who sat opposite him.

"I don't wanna' kill Jacobs, I just wanna' hurt him bad. Real bad." Ernesto Rinati's raspy voice was just above a whisper.

Rinati leaned over and scratched the ears of his smelly, three-legged mutt, Butch, who lifted his head and closed his eyes. Saliva dripped from his muzzle onto the hotel conference room carpet.

"My boys'll jump that little DEP prick, take a baseball bat to his kneecaps. I wanna' hear them crack a mile away. I wanna' hear him scream. I want him in agony like he's done to me. Beat the shit out of him, break some ribs." Spittle flecked Rinati's chin as his voice rose and he punctuated his words with jabs to the air.

"Knock out his teeth, bash in his pretty face. When he's flat on the ground like the piece of dog shit he is, I'll bend down and say 'Hello Mikey', so when he looks in the mirror at his messed-up face, he knows it's me done that to him. Then I'm gonna' lift my foot and stomp his balls." Rinati slammed his fist on the table. "And when he's puking up his guts, I'll say 'Mikey, you fucked with me so I'm fuckin' you back. Then I'll give him one last kick to remember me by, right between his legs."

Rinati paused, ran a calloused hand through his curly hair, then looked across the table directly at Jimmy Podwall, the youngest one in the room.

"Jimmy, you know what the perineum is?"

Jimmy shuddered. He smacked his lips together but no words came out, then he finally shook his head 'no.'

Rinati slyly angled his head toward Angela. "It's the real estate between your balls and your asshole." One side of his lip curled up into a half-smile. "Angela, sweetheart, you know why you kick him in the gooch?"

"No," Angela croaked.

"Because a kick to the balls ain't no big deal, a man will get over it in a few days, but a good shot behind his balls gonna' hurt him for months, every time he moves, turns, walks, sits, stands."

Rinati let out a contented sigh. His pock-marked face melted into a docile grin.

Feldman tented his fingertips and he smiled placidly at Rinati. "Ernie, Ernesto, can we please get back to preparing you for this trial? You're fighting these permit conditions and we want to get them overturned so Rhino Mining can mine that Gordon Mine without them. We have to finish getting ready."

Rinati pushed his chair back and stood up. "Attorney, fuck the trial, fuck Jacobs, fuck DEP."

"Come on Ernie, we have a lot more ground to cover, a lot more to prepare." He ran a hand through his jet-black hair.

"Fuck you too. I'm done. I've done this shit before. I'm *prepared*. I'm going home and *preparing* a bottle of Chianti. I'll see younz and that fuckin' excuse for a lawyer tomorrow."

Rinati rounded the table as he wrestled himself into a tight blue blazer over his work clothes, his one concession to Feldman's request that he dress for the trial. He smiled broadly as he swaggered toward his legal team and held out his hand.

"Angela," he leaned forward and kissed her on both cheeks. "You should smile more. Ummm, you smell nice, honey." His hand stroked her side, gravitated to her hips and would have continued downward until Angela angrily pushed it off with her elbow.

To Jimmy, he said, "You look a little uncomfortable kid. Lighten up." He patted Jimmy's face. "You smell nicer than Angela."

Next, he extended his hand to Feldman and peered into the man's eyes. "Attorney. You know me, I'll do okay. Jacobs won't get to me."

"Ernie, don't play any games with him. Jacobs is young, but smart. Quick. And watch your language. There'll be a judge, DEP, and a court reporter, maybe even the press."

"Don't worry, Attorney, I'll be like a little choir boy, a little fuckin' choir boy." He cackled and strutted out of the room. Butch hopped along after his master and Feldman jogged to keep up.

The blood had drained from Jimmy's face. Despite the room's chilly temperature, beads of sweat dotted his forehead. "Do you think he'd really do what he said? Maybe we should ask Mr. Feldman if we have to call the cops or something."

"I don't know, I don't know." Angela, eight years senior to Jimmy, shook her head. "Let me do the talking when he comes back. Sid always seems to know the right thing to do. I've never heard anything like this before."

Angela poured herself a glass of water and wished it was vodka. She sipped slowly and gazed out the conference room window into the night and snow outside.

Feldman returned, wearing what Angela recognized as his game face. He gathered his papers and barely glanced at his two young associates.

"Mr. Feldman—Sid," Angela said. "About Mr. Rinati—is there something we ought to do?"

"Yes, start working on those motions *in limine* that we'll file tomorrow morning."

"Of course, but that stuff he said about Jacobs. Shouldn't we report that? I mean to the police or someone?"

Feldman fixed her with a glare. "Seriously? Didn't they teach you legal ethics at Penn? You can't talk with anyone about what your client said to you in confidence. That would be a breach of the attorney-client privilege."

Feldman wheeled to Jimmy. "What do you think? What did they teach you at Yale? Do you think we should report Ernie to the cops?"

Jimmy's eyes shifted from Angela to Feldman, Philly's preeminent litigator. "Well, maybe not, you know, attorney-client privilege and what you said before."

Feldman chortled. "Well children, you're both wrong. The only thing that trumps the attorney-client privilege or client confidentiality is that a lawyer may rat out his client if he *reasonably believes* his client is going to cause certain death or substantial bodily harm. I'm pretty sure that's an exact quote of Rule 1.6; you can look it up. There's no *reasonable* expectation that Ernie will do anything except go home and guzzle some Chianti." His eyes hardened. "But if either of you violates the attorney-client privilege, I'll bring you up to the Disciplinary Board myself."

"But," Angela said, "suppose he really means it?"

"And suppose he doesn't? Look, I've represented the Rhino for five years. He's gone on rants before about kicking the shit out of other lawyers, judges, state senators, the governor. Hell, I've heard him threaten the president. They're fantasies. Do I think he's really going to hurt anyone? No. He's just blowing off steam."

"But what if you're wrong?" Angela asked.

Feldman closed his eyes and shook his head. "In that case I guess there would be a continuance and we'd have to deal with a different DEP lawyer."

Angela flinched as if he'd slapped her.

"Look, if you disagree with me, call Mr. Drury." Feldman invoked the name of the surviving senior partner of the law firm of Pell, Desrosiers, Coxe & Drury, the name on the hefty brass plaque bolted to the Italian granite at the front of their commanding office building on Market Street. "Tell him. Why not go to the Supreme Court Disciplinary Board and tell them I ordered you not to go to the cops. You want to do that?"

Jimmy and Angela blinked. Feldman laughed and picked up his leather folder and gold fountain pen.

"Get to work on those motions—I want them in final and printed out by eight a.m. tomorrow." Feldman strode through the door and left it open behind him.

Angela picked up her laptop. "Nice, Jimmy—you worm. You set me up with all that boo hoo hoo, what are we going to do? Then you side with Feldman." She stomped out of the room.

***

Jimmy watched her go, then closed his eyes for a long moment. Finally, he hefted the six huge red-weld file folders that he had lugged from the courthouse, along with his laptop. As he left the room he muttered loudly, "I should've gone to medical school when I had the chance."

56

Mike, Nicky and Ben spent a long evening in the hotel room getting ready for the next day of the hearing. Miranda was going to rest her case first thing in the morning and then Feldman would begin his case. Mike felt that Miranda had made a minimally persuasive case. He hoped she would present more testimony that showed irreparable harm, but that wasn't likely to happen. What *was* likely to happen was that Feldman would seriously damage her case. There was a small possibility that the judge would agree with Miranda and issue the supersedeas, but Mike was betting against that.

There was one other alternative. If Mike could help her, seriously help her, it would increase the chances that the judge would issue an order halting the mining. He knew he could help both by an effective cross-examination of Feldman's witnesses, and by putting on his own case.

The problem was, putting on a strong case probably meant the end of his career as a DEP lawyer. Even if Roger didn't get a blow-by-blow description from Feldman, there would be a transcript and Mike wouldn't be able to talk his way out of his own words. Mike wrestled with the potential consequences.

"We know Feldman is going to call Rinati," Mike looked from Nicky to Ben. "He has to. First of all, I can't imagine Rinati wouldn't want to testify. The man's a narcissist, he's not going to be a spectator at a trial where millions of dollars are at stake. Also, while Rinati can rely on some of his employees to testify regarding the planned mining operation, the best one to testify, the one who can put it all together, is Rinati himself. He's got to testify tomorrow."

"So how long do you think Feldman will have him on the stand?" Ben asked. Mike thought he looked exceptionally tired and drawn. Gray. Mike had caught him staring into space on several occasions that night, but assumed Ben, like the rest of them, was just exhausted from the trial.

"If it were me, as short as possible. Rinati's just too unpredictable and uncontrollable. I think Feldman will have him on the stand for under an hour. On and off, if possible."

"What about your cross-examination?" he asked.

"That depends. He has such a temper, I'd like to get under his skin and ignite the fireworks. If I can do that, then Rinati will self-destruct and we may not have to put on any case at all."

"Do you think Feldman will call an expert witness?" Ben asked.

"Yes, that's been troubling me. Miranda and I turned you into an expert witness. She asked for your opinion and then I did too. After she opened the door, I felt it was important to do that, and we got some serious testimony out about the dispute within the department on whether the permit should've been issued at all. Feldman has to call an expert."

"So, has Feldman told you yet who will be his expert?"

"No. If this were a regular hearing he would've told me months ago and he would've sent me an expert report. Because this is a supersedeas hearing, we'll find out tomorrow. I'm hoping it's some kind of rent-an-expert, a real schlockmeister. One of the guys who testifies about whatever you pay him to say. I should be able to handle that."

There was a tap at Mike's door and Mike looked at his watch, it was nine fifteen. "He's fifteen minutes late," Mike said to Ben.

Nicky opened the door and Ransom stood in the hallway, snow melting from his Red Wing boots onto the carpet.

"Helluva thing to drag a man out this late in shitty weather," Ransom said.

"Sorry, we just have so much to do and we still need to prepare you for your examination and cross-examinations tomorrow. I appreciate this," Mike said.

Close to two hours later, Mike paced the hotel room while Ransom sat in a cushioned chair. The temperature in the room was cool and outside the wind howled and the snow drifted, but Ransom still had a thin bead of sweat across his forehead and upper lip.

"Feldman will be calling you as a witness tomorrow. I'm not designating you as an expert, so he won't be able to ask you any opinions, just the facts relating to the permit. Be sure to answer only the questions that you're asked. Don't be too helpful and don't offer anything other than what he asks."

Ransom nodded.

"Since you work for the department, when I get to cross-examine you, it won't be the traditional cross-examination questions, it will be more like direct examination. Feldman is not calling John Hicks, so at this point I'll need you to testify regarding the department's position on this mine site. Remember, I'm not going to ask you for your personal opinion, I'm just going to ask you for the official company line," Mike said.

Ransom looked angry. "Whatever you say." Mike glanced at Ben and Nicky and just slightly shook his head.

"Can I count on you?" Mike asked.

"You know how I feel about all of this. I see no reason for all of these conditions. I've walked all over that site and I think Rhino can mine the site just fine without them. I'm sure those headwaters, them houses, won't be impacted one bit. He don't need them conditions."

"Well, that's not what the department says. That's also not what John Hicks said. The department's official position is that mining can take place, but only with the conditions. Look, John's not against coal mining. He's a big supporter, in fact. If he said the conditions are necessary to protect the stream and those houses, well, they must be necessary. The department isn't against mining, as long as it's done right." Mike watched the mine inspector as he looked away. "I need to know I can count on you to answer the questions exactly as I ask them."

"Whatever you say," Ransom said flatly.

A half hour later, as soon as Ransom left the room, Ben looked at Mike and said, "Do you have to call him?"

"Feldman subpoenaed him. That's his right. I don't really have a choice."

"Well, what about his testimony for the department?"

"Yeah, I've thought about that. He's promised to stick with the company line, so I think it's really unlikely he'll go off the rails."

"You really think that?"

Mike looked at Ben and shook his head no.

"If we need to, I can call Hicks to testify," Mike said. "The judge is really limiting the time we have for this hearing, so hopefully we won't have to do that."

No one responded. Finally, Mike said, "Anyone want a beer? The bar downstairs closes at one."

Mike and Ben looked at Nicky who had pushed off her shoes and slumped into the corner of the sofa. A pile of folders covered her lap and her eyes were closed. Ben threw a smile at Mike.

Ben put his hand to his head for a moment, pressing his eyebrows, then finally said, "Well, it's getting late and I have to drive home."

"If you want, I can get you a room here. That would be easier than making the round trip tonight and tomorrow morning."

"That's a great idea, but I know it would be coming out of your pocket. The department doesn't have money for that. Besides, I want to work on those calculations I told you about earlier tonight."

"Do you think that will pan out?"

"I'm pretty sure it will make one hell of an exhibit when you're cross-examining Rinati."

"You could do that here, tonight."

"Thanks, but I'd like to sleep in my own bed. Also, I have some migraine pills at home, so I'm going to head back."

Mike angled his head. "Is everything all right? I mean you've been out of sorts for weeks and you look like shit."

"Thanks for making me feel better. Just exhaustion. When this trial is over, I'm going to take a few days off and stay in bed until I snap out of it, but that's it."

The jingling of Ben's keys awakened Nicky. She stretched like a cat and said, "I'm sorry guys, the days have been pretty long and stressful."

She hugged Ben and kissed him on the cheek. "Drive carefully."

"You two kids get some rest." Ben shook Mike's hand and winked.

After Ben left, Mike turned to Nicky. "Does everyone here suspect we're sleeping together?"

"No, everyone *knows* we're sleeping together."

57

Mike wore a clean shirt and a fresh necktie under his blue suit. Nicky wore a different dress. They'd been up since five a.m., getting ready for the trial. Despite getting very little sleep, Mike felt refreshed. The adreniline and caffeine that pulsed through his veins helped. He was anxious to get started.

Not surprisingly, Miranda started out by resting her case. The next twenty minutes were spent arguing over Feldman's lengthy motions to dismiss with accompanying briefs that were between twenty and thirty pages long each. The judge glanced at the briefs and let the three lawyers argue: first Feldman, then Miranda, then finally Mike.

Mike was amazed by the ability of Feldman and his team to produce quality documents out of their hotel rooms. His three associates looked exhausted. He imagined that Angela, Jimmy Podwall, and Montgomery had been up most of the night researching and writing. Angela had confided to Nicky that Feldman had arranged with a local law firm to have secretaries and a law office available around the clock. Mike only had his wits and his memory at his disposal to respond to Feldman's motions. Less than half an hour after the motions were handed to the judge, he denied them.

"Mr. Feldman, call your first witness."

Feldman stood and struck a pose. "The permittee calls George Peterson to the witness stand."

Mike looked around, as did most everyone else in the courtroom. Miranda, resplendent in a bright red suit that clung to the curves of her hips, watched nervously. The rear door opened and a distinguished looking man in a three-piece heavy wool suit entered the courtroom. He squeezed by Mike's desk and, as soon as he had passed, Ben put his mouth near Mike's ear and said, "Shit, that's the dean of the School of Mining at Penn State."

Mike felt a weight, like a sack of coal, press down on his shoulders. This was no schlockmeister rent-an-expert.

As soon as Peterson was sworn by Judge Diaz, Feldman asked him to state his name.

"George Peterson," he said in a melodious voice.

"What's your position?" Feldman asked.

"Dean of the College of Earth and Mineral Sciences at the Pennsylvania State University." Peterson looked directly at Judge Diaz as he spoke evenly. That alone told Mike he was an experienced expert witness.

"Tell us about your degrees."

"I received my Bachelor's in Mining Engineering from Penn State. Then, I received a Master's in Geology from the Colorado School of Mines. Finally, I received my PhD in Mining Engineering from West Virginia University."

"Did you have to write a dissertation to get your doctorate?"

"Of course. The title of my dissertation was, *Reclamation of Coal Surface Mines so as to Cause Minimal Disruption to Surface Water and Groundwater*. My dissertation was turned into a textbook that is used at universities around the US, including Penn State, and in twenty other countries."

It was clear that the witness was unimpeachable and Mike decided that the last thing he wanted was for the dean to put all of his credentials on display. With this, Mike stood, interrupting the testimony, and said loudly, "Judge, there's really no need to go through all of this, the Commonwealth is willing to stipulate that Dean Peterson is an expert in the field of mining engineering." Mike looked at Miranda who also stood.

"We'll also stipulate," Miranda said.

"Now judge, I appreciate that, but I'd like to get all of Dean Peterson's qualifications onto the record," Feldman said, smiling at Mike.

"Go ahead, you're entitled." Judge Diaz looked at Ben as he spoke.

"Do you have any professional certifications?" Feldman asked.

"Yes, I'm a professional engineer in Pennsylvania and twelve other states," he paused, "also a professional geologist in six states. Do you want to know in which states?"

"No, I think that's more than adequate. What is your involvement with the mining engineering program at Penn State?"

"I started out as an Assistant Professor of Mining Engineering, first at the Colorado School of Mines and three years later I moved back to Pennsylvania when I was appointed an associate professor here at Penn State. Eight years after that, I became a full professor in the Department of Mining Engineering and two years later, the chairman of the department. Mining engineering is a division of the College of Earth and Mineral Sciences, and, five years ago, I became the dean of the college. So, I've been a Professor of Mining Engineering, Chairman of the Mining Engineering Department and now dean of the college under which the mining engineering program falls."

Ben whispered, "Shit."

The weight on Mike's shoulders grew heavier.

"Dean, or is it Dr. Peterson, have you ever worked in the mining industry in some capacity other than as an academic?"

"Yes, my family had a small mining company and I worked summers in a coal mine in Pennsylvania as a teenager and while I was attending college."

Nicky looked at Mike who looked back and nodded slightly.

"Did you ever work for the Department of Environmental Protection in Pennsylvania?" Feldman asked.

"Not DEP, its predecessor, the Department of Mines."

"When did you do that?"

"I worked for the Department of Mines from the time I graduated from Penn State as a mining engineer, until I began at the Colorado School of Mines two years later. So, two years."

"Doing what?"

"A little bit of everything at first. Then I spent about a year and a half reviewing surface mine applications and reclamation plans."

"Judge, we're going to offer Dean Peterson as an expert in mining engineering, geology, and reclamation. I'm alerting you to this now, in case the Commonwealth and Ms. Clymer want to take a chance and *voir dire* the witness."

Miranda stood and looked at Mike who quickly shook his head 'no.' After a moment she said, "No, we have no *voir dire* of this witness."

"Mr. Jacobs? Do you want to *voir dire* the witness?" asked the judge who smiled broadly.

Mike stood and thought for a moment. "Yes, Your Honor, I have just a couple of questions for him."

Mike understood how dangerous it was to ask any questions of a witness when he did not know the answer. It was either foolhardy or desperate. Mike suspected he was both.

"Dean Peterson, when was the last time you reviewed a mine permit application as an employee of a regulatory agency?"

"Let's see, I started my master's program thirty years ago, so thirty years. Of course, I'm regularly asked to review mine permit applications for mining operations all around the world. I probably review ten or so a year on behalf of both mining companies and government agencies. DEP asks me to review two or three problematic applications every year so the last time might have been two or three months ago."

Mike didn't want to look around the room. He had just asked the proverbial question to which he did not know the answer. He hesitated to go forward but decided to plow on.

"Have you ever been to the site of the proposed Gordon Mine?"

"Not exactly. I've been all over Somerset County and I'm guessing I've driven by the site a dozen times, but not recently."

Mike perked up. "So, you did not walk the site, correct?"

"That's right. I've driven by the site, but I've never walked on it."

"I think the speed limit near the site is forty-five miles per hour, were you driving by the site at the speed limit or were you crawling by it so you could see the site?"

Peterson laughed. "Probably more like fifty-five or sixty miles per hour."

"You reviewed the United States Geological Service map for the site?"

"Yes, I reviewed the USGS map. I also looked at aerial photography over the last twenty years, LiDAR, false color, wetlands and several other maps of the site."

"Is the topography shown in twenty-foot increments on those maps?"

"Yes, let me say something about that..."

"Dean Peterson, please just answer my question."

Peterson looked at the judge who nodded affirmatively.

"So, you would not be able to distinguish a feature where there was a change in elevation if the change was nineteen feet or less, is that right?"

"You can extrapolate a bit, but if what you're getting at is whether it's better to see the site in person or to review a map, I agree that it's better to see the site in person."

Having received a concession, Mike allowed himself to breathe.

Mike smiled, then said, "As you were zooming by the site at sixty miles an hour, did you happen to see Roaring Run?"

"No. It's on the maps, but I have not physically laid eyes on it."

Mike looked at his papers, then looked at the judge and said, "No further questions for this witness on *voir dire*."

"Do you object to the permittee's use of Dean Peterson as an expert in this case?" The judge asked.

"No, Your Honor."

As Mike sat, Feldman stood up quickly. He took Peterson through the permit application step-by-step. For the most part, Peterson expressed no concerns regarding the application or the review statements, contained in DEP's file.

"Dean Peterson, yesterday Ben Kemper, a mining engineer with DEP testified and gave his opinions regarding the mine permit application. Are you familiar at all with Mr. Kemper?"

"Why yes, he's a graduate of the Department of Mining Engineering. Every year I teach a course in mining engineering. I do that to this day, so that I stay close to the students. Mr. Kemper was in my class eleven years ago."

"Do you remember him?"

"Regrettably, only vaguely. Your Ms. St. Germain pointed him out to me this morning and I see him sitting behind the Commonwealth's attorney. He looks familiar, although he's put on a few pounds. I did look up my old records last night and I see that he got a C+ in my class which is why I don't really remember him all that well. It's a very hard class, though."

The courtroom erupted in laughter. Tommy Bowdoin broadly smiled. Judge Diaz put his hand over his mouth and barely concealed a smile. He gently tapped his gavel twice. Mike forced himself not to look at Ben.

Behind him, Mike heard Ben say in a loud whisper, "I'm never giving another penny to Penn State."

"Dean Peterson, Mr. Kemper testified that he felt the houses were too close to the mining operation and that the mining operation would damage them. What's your opinion regarding that?"

"They're not too close at all. The department has setback requirements. For example, the bonded area has to be more than three hundred feet from an occupied dwelling. Rhino will be well outside the setback mandated by the regulations."

"In general, what's your opinion of this mining operation?"

"It will be a relatively small mining operation, but not too small to be profitable. There are some challenges, but all of these can be dealt with during the mining process. Of course, it will be important for the mine operator to protect the homes and protect the headwaters of Roaring Run. But that's very doable."

"Are you familiar at all with Rhino Mining Company?"

"Oh yes, Professor Knight is evaluating one of their mining operations in Clearfield County. I'm supervising his work."

"Can Rhino deal with the challenges you described a few minutes ago?"

"Yes, it's done all the time."

"Dean Peterson, do you have an opinion regarding whether DEP should have issued the mine permit to Rhino Mining Company?"

Miranda stood to object. On Monday, Mike had given her general instructions and told her to object whenever an opinion was about to touch on the ultimate issue in the case. It hadn't occurred to Mike that if the world's leading authority is the expert, you don't bother.

"Objection, failure to lay a foundation and outside of the scope of the expert's expertise."

Feldman turned to face the judge and was about to respond when Judge Diaz said, "Don't bother, Mr. Feldman, overruled."

Miranda, her face visibly reddened, sat down.

"DEP did the right thing issuing this mining permit. There was no reason *not* to issue it, especially with the conditions the department imposed. Those conditions more than adequately protect the residents, their homes and the headwaters of Roaring Run."

"I have no further questions for this witness, judge." Feldman looked smug and sat down.

The judge looked at the clock at the back of the room, then said, "We'll pick up the cross-examinations after lunch. We're in recess, be back here at one."

During the lunch break, Mike, Nicky, Ben, and Miranda all sat in the district attorney's conference room.

"I feel like we just lost the case," Miranda said. "I don't have a clue on how to cross-examine the dean."

Everyone looked at Mike. "Look, this guy is a litigator's nightmare. We have no expert report or deposition. Every question is a potential landmine. He's just waiting to sucker punch me. I can maybe put a few chinks in his armor, but that's about it. He did criticize Ben, so I have some justification for going after him. But I just don't know."

Amid Rage

"Did I tell you I'm not going to any more football games at Penn State?" Ben said.

Mike punched Ben's shoulder and looked at his watch.

***

"Dean Peterson, you're being paid for your testimony today, aren't you?" Mike asked.

Peterson, looking relaxed, sat back in his chair and smiled. "Not exactly. Rhino Mining Company is making a five thousand dollar contribution to the college's scholarship fund. The condition of my testimony was that he would have to give to the scholarship regardless of what I said and regardless of the outcome. So Rhino is paying five thousand dollars, but it's not going to me. Rather, it's going to some needy student who would be too poor to attend college."

Again? Mike knew better and took a deep breath.

"During my *voir dire* you stated that you had never been on the site, correct?"

"That's right."

"Have you ever driven on Forest Lane?"

"No, by it, but not on it."

"Then you're not familiar with the houses on Forest Lane, right?"

"I've seen some pictures, but I've not seen the actual houses."

"Are you familiar with the Roberts' house?"

"No, I can't say that I am."

"So you don't know whether the foundation is made out of stone, poured concrete, logs, or bales of straw?"

"Well, I doubt straw, but that's correct, I don't know."

"It's true that no one has done a pre-mining evaluation of the houses or the foundations?"

"I did not see any during my review of the files."

"You really have no way of knowing whether a foundation or walls could withstand the rigors of mining or blasting?"

"That's technically correct, but as I testified during my direct examination, the houses are outside of the setback."

"Isn't it true they are only twenty to thirty feet outside of the setback area?"

"That's correct, they *are* close."

"Dean Peterson, if Rhino violated its permit, say by blasting improperly or inadvertently mining too close to those houses, could that damage the houses?"

Mike heard Feldman's chair scrape the wooden floor before he heard him speak. "Objection, calls for speculation, hypothetical question, asking facts not in evidence."

"Overruled," said the judge sitting forward in his chair.

"Assuming Rhino violated its permit, could that damage the houses?

"Hypothetically, yes."

"So, if I understand your testimony correctly, you believe that, hypothetically speaking, it's possible for Rhino to damage the houses by blasting or mining too close to them?"

"That's what I said."

"You acknowledge, don't you, that mining will take place in the area that currently is the headwaters area to Roaring Run?"

"I acknowledge that mining will take place in an area that is a *small part* of the headwaters to Roaring Run. That stream drains quite a large area. The mine makes up only a small portion of the headwaters, a rather insignificant portion, in fact. Maybe less than one percent."

"But, at least insofar as those headwater streams, as small or insignificant as they may be, will those streams be impacted by mining?"

"During mining, yes, of course. Assuming that mining and reclamation are conducted in accordance with the application and the permit, there should be no long-term effect on headwaters."

Mike looked at the papers in front of him and then at his side of the courtroom. The eyes of the neighbors and DEP personnel were all on him. Miranda looked at him in a way that he had never seen, kindly, imploring him. He had never seen anything like that before and doubted he would see it again. Nicky looked at him and smiled slightly, as if to encourage him. Mike focused all of his attention on his next question.

"If Rhino fails to reclaim properly or fails to mine in accordance with the mining plan, could the company cause an acid discharge that would impact all of Roaring Run?"

"It's possible, but only slightly."

"So, it *is* possible that there could be an impact to Roaring Run from the mining operation?"

"Yes, but only a very slight possibility."

"Referring only to the portions of the headwaters that would be impacted, Dean, if Rhino caused an acid mine discharge, would the acid discharge kill any fish in those streams?"

"I'm not admitting there would be an acid discharge, but if somehow there was an acid mine discharge, that *could* kill the fish in those streams."

"And, if there was an acid discharge, how long would that last?"

"How long?"

"Yes, in months, years."

"Well, decades at a minimum, probably forever until someone came along and reclaimed those streams."

"No further questions," Mike said sitting down.

"Redirect." Feldman jumped up without waiting to be asked.

"Dean, if Rhino mines as planned, will they hurt those houses on Forest Lane?"

"That's not likely."

"If they mine as planned and reclaim as planned will there be any impact to Roaring Run?"

"Again, not likely, as long as they mine in accordance with the mining plan and conduct the reclamation as described in the application."

"No further questions, Your Honor."

The judge gathered his papers, then said, "Dean Peterson, I have a question. Is there anything underground, like a fault or fracture that could change your opinion? By that I mean if Rhino mined through an unexpected fault or fracture, could that result in damage to either the homes or Roaring Run?"

"I suppose that's possible. Geology being what it is, we do not have perfect insight into the conditions underground. Not until we dig it up, anyway."

The judge paused, then asked, "Any re-cross on my question?"

Feldman, Mike and Miranda all stood and said no.

"Then we'll take a break and return in fifteen minutes."

58

Feldman called Ransom and took him through his testimony, laying out some basic facts about DEP's review of the permit application and mine site and nothing more. Mike didn't have to object to any of his questions.

Miranda, on the other hand, tried to do too much with Ransom's testimony and Mike objected twice when she asked him for his opinions. After stumbling through her examination, she gave up and turned it over to Mike.

Judge Diaz leaned so far back in his chair he was almost horizontal. From Mike's angle, he couldn't tell whether the judge was staring at the ceiling or sleeping. He'd been groggy all day with big bags under his eyes and Mike hoped he was awake.

For the most part, no one in the courtroom expected any drama from Ransom's testimony, just routine but necessary information to complete the record. Spectators quietly chatted in the back as Mike took Ransom through his initial inspection report.

Toward the end of Ransom's testimony, Mike asked, "Mr. Ransom, did the department reach a conclusion regarding mining at the site?"

"Yeah, it did. So did I."

"I'm interested in *the department's* formal findings and conclusions," Mike said sharply. "*Just DEP's*. Did the department reach any conclusion regarding mining in the vicinity of the houses on Forest Lane?"

"Yeah, *my* opinion was that mining could take place and no conditions were necessary," Ransom slouched in his chair as he answered.

Mike looked at Ransom, wishing he could slap him in the face. "Maybe you didn't hear my question. I didn't ask you for *your* opinion, I asked you for the *department's* perspective on this only."

"I told you, I felt that the conditions were not necessary."

"Just a minute, Your Honor," Mike said as Judge Diaz came to life and snapped his chair forward. "I'd like a minute."

Mike glanced at Feldman who smiled broadly. He sat down next to Nicky and pawed through the exhibits, both whispering to her and muttering under his breath. "Ransom's gone rogue," Mike said into her ear. "Not only that, he's answering the questions based on his opinion, which means he's offering expert testimony. The last thing I want is for Ransom to be designated as an expert witness and have Feldman go after his opinions regarding mining at the site. Shit, I need to get him under control."

"Mr. Jacobs?" the judge said, leaning forward.

Mike walked to the middle of the courtroom and said, "Mr. Ransom, I want you to think long and hard about your answer to the following question. What was *the department's* view, not yours, as stated in the mining permit regarding mining in the vicinity of those homes?"

"You're not listening to me. There's no good reason why it couldn't be done *without* the conditions." Ransom sat forward in his chair with his elbows on the wooden rail in front of the witness box.

Mike looked around the courtroom and saw that Feldman watched him closely and grinned. Miranda scribbled notes on her pad, and the judge looked at Mike intently.

"Permission for counsel to approach the bench, Your Honor," Mike said and the judge immediately waved the lawyers forward. Feldman stood on one side of Mike and Miranda on the other.

"I'd like permission to treat Mr. Ransom as a hostile witness," Mike whispered loudly. "I've asked him a simple question regarding *the department's* position, three times, and he insists on giving *his* personal opinion, which is not what I've asked for. He's the department's employee and our witness regarding the facts of the permit and I need the correct testimony from him. He's gone off the reservation and the only way I can maybe drag him back is by treating him as a hostile witness."

"His testimony seems perfectly reasonable to me," Feldman said with a huge smile. "I object to treating this man as a hostile witness. He's *DEP's* employee and Mike's stuck with his testimony."

"Well, *Sid*, you know full well that when one of your own witnesses refuses to answer a question, then it's proper to treat him as a hostile witness," Mike said.

The judge waved them all back from his bench then announced, "Permission granted. You may treat Mr. Ransom as a hostile witness."

Ransom looked confused.

"Mr. Ransom, I'm going to ask you very specific questions. Please answer only the question that you've been asked. Did the department issue a permit to Rhino Mining Company?"

"Yes—"

"Did that permit contain conditions imposed by the department?"

"Yes, but I didn't—"

"Just answer my question, Mr. Ransom." Mike snapped. "I'm not asking you for your opinion and you've not been qualified as an expert witness to give one. Was the reason for the condition regarding mining in the vicinity of those homes because Mr. Hicks, the district mining manager, felt it was the best way to protect those homes?"

"Well, that was Mr. Hicks' opinion."

"Doesn't Mr. Hicks have the final say on permits in your office?"

"Yes, but—"

Mike held up his hand, then turned and walked back to Ben. Very quietly, he whispered, "Time for Plan B. Get me those papers."

Ben reached under his chair and handed him a stack of papers. As he did, Ben whispered, "If this doesn't work we're screwed."

We may be screwed either way, Mike thought as he pulled out the top group of papers, held together by a paperclip, and handed a copy to the attorneys and the judge.

"I'm handing you a document that has been marked as Commonwealth's exhibit number twenty. I direct your attention to the signature at the bottom of the page. Is that your signature?" Mike asked, pointing at the document.

Ransom quickly looked at the document and held it inches from his face. "Well, it looks like my signature, but I've never seen this document before."

"Mr. Ransom, I ask you again, is that your signature?" Mike asked, tapping the page.

"It could be," Ransom said slowly.

"Let the record show that Mr. Ransom has identified his signature on a certified copy of a new account application with the First National Bank of Meyersdale. The date on the card is November 1, over two months ago," Mike said holding up the exhibit.

Mike pulled out the second stack of papers and flipped copies to the other attorneys, placing one in front of the judge and holding another in front of Ransom. "I'm showing you now Commonwealth's exhibit number twenty-one. This is a certified copy of the account printout for Lyle Ransom from the First National Bank of Meyersdale. Mr. Ransom, does this show deposits of thousands of dollars every week into your account?"

"Well, that's what it says, but I don't have an account at the Meyersdale Bank," Ransom said, holding up the sheet.

"Mr. Ransom, you took over from the previous inspector, Marty Stevens, on October 7, is that correct?"

"Yes."

"You filed your recommendation to issue the permit on October 14. Correct?"

"That sounds about right."

"The permit was issued on October 28?"

"Yeah."

"According to this exhibit, you made a five thousand dollar deposit to your account at the Bank of Meyersdale on November 1, correct?"

He squinted at the papers and said, "That's what it says, but I didn't—"

"Do you have another bank account? Where do you deposit your DEP paycheck?"

"PNC."

"Do you have another source of income, maybe a job as a store clerk? Maybe putting in a few hours at UPS during the holidays?" Mike asked sarcastically.

"No, just my state job."

"Do you have any relatives who are giving you any money as a gift, inheritance?"

"No, I'm not getting any additional money from anywhere, anyone. This is not my money, this is not my account. I have no idea where this five thousand dollars came from."

"Well, Mr. Ransom, it's actually fifty thousand dollars when you add it all up over the course of the next few weeks after your first deposit through December 31."

"Well, this ain't mine, I have nothing to do with this, I'm being set up."

Mike glared at Ransom, then ignored his comment and addressed the judge. "Your Honor, we're prepared to call the vice president for the First National Bank of Meyersdale who will certify the documents and verify that the Lyle Ransom who owns this account is the same one who is sitting before us today. We also intend to call the vice president to present all of the confidential, personal information contained in Mr. Ransom's application for an interest-bearing checking account, stuff like his Social Security number, PIN, automobile registration information, mortgage information from PNC that he used to open this account and other identifying information."

"So noted," said the judge, watching Ransom.

"No further questions for this…witness." Mike did a sharp about-face and stalked back to his table. As he sat down, he glared at Ransom.

"Wait a minute, don't I get to say something?" Ransom said, rising.

"We're done cross-examining this witness, no further questions," Mike said loudly.

"Well, I'm not done. I'm being set up. That's not my account and not my money—"

"You can step down for now, Mr. Ransom," the judge said.

The courtroom buzzed and Judge Diaz tapped the gavel several times to restore order. "We'll take a fifteen-minute break and come back with any cross-examination, I guess you'd call it, from the other lawyers."

Mike, Ben and Nicky retreated to a corner of the hallway. "Who's up after Ransom?" Nicky asked.

"Just Rinati. Feldman told me that his next and last witness would be Rinati."

"Well, nothing could go wrong with that, could it?" Ben said.

59

"Please state your name for the record," Feldman said.

"Ernesto Rinati, but my friends call me Ernie." Rinati relaxed in the witness stand and smiled broadly. He looked around the room, grinning at his many employees in the gallery.

"Do you own a mining company?"

"Yes, do you want to buy it?" Rinati mugged for the crowd.

Feldman shot him a sharp look, which Rinati ignored.

"What's the name of your company?"

"Well, I own several companies, but the mining company is Rhino Mining Company."

"Did you file a mine permit application for the proposed Gordon Mine with the Pennsylvania Department of Environmental Protection last year?"

"Yes," Rinati said, sitting back in the witness chair and placing his hands behind his head.

"Who prepared the application for you?"

"We do that kind of stuff in-house. I have a mining engineer, geologist, blasting engineer, all of that shit in my office in Johnstown."

Judge Diaz sat up in his chair and leaned forward so that he caught Rinati's eye. "Mr. Rinati, you're in court, please watch your language."

Rinati looked up at the judge and grinned. "No problem, judge, it was just a little slip." A group of men in the gallery, all Rhino employees, laughed.

"So, your mine permit application was prepared just by your own employees?"

"Yes and no. I sometimes use consulting engineers and whatnot, but I find it's cheaper to use my own in-house team. They're all top-notch guys though, former DEP guys."

"There has been some testimony that the area of the mine is on the small side. Do you agree with that?" Feldman asked.

"Shit yeah…sorry judge, yeah. It's small, but not too small."

"Did you talk to the neighbors when you were planning the mine?"

"Yeah, I met with many of them and offered all of them a buyout. I offered to pay fair market value for their houses and they could live in it for as long as they wanted, unless we needed the property for mining. That's a pretty good deal, I pay them for their house today and they can live in it rent free."

"Did anyone take you up on your offer?"

"No, one gentleman's family did reach out to me after he passed. The family of Norman Post contacted me a few weeks ago and I made a good-sized payment and bought his property."

"If some of the homeowners stay in their houses, will your company respect the setback?"

"Yeah, of course, that's what the permit says I have to do and that's what I'll do. We've placed markers on the ground and I've instructed my men to stay away from the setback markers. Also, we're going to be installing a fence between the mine and those houses as soon as weather permits."

"If somehow you did damage one of the houses, what then?"

"Well, that ain't going to happen, but if it did, we'd fix it for free or pay to fix it."

Feldman walked over to a large map of the site that leaned against an easel. He pointed to a portion of the map. "I assume you're familiar with Roaring Run?"

"Yeah, I've seen it, tiny little nothing of a stream, and I know some of the headwaters supposedly are located in the area we plan to mine."

"Are you aware of the mandatory provisions in the permit that protects the headwaters?"

"Am I aware of it? Those conditions are going to cost me a load of dough. You bet your ass I'm aware of it."

Feldman held up his hand. "Mr. Rinati, please."

Rinati put his hand on his mouth and nodded. "Sorry, I get carried away."

"One of the conditions requires you to segregate any acid-forming rock high above the groundwater table. Is your company planning on doing that?"

"Yeah," Rinati said, looking at the floor.

"Another condition requires you to segregate topsoil, subsoil, and any non-acid forming shale and that you place that back in the pit in such a way as to approximate the original contour of the land as a part of your reclamation. Will Rhino be complying with that requirement?"

"Yeah, that's gonna cost me a mint, but I'm willing to do that."

"Finally, Mr. Rinati, what can you tell us about the compliance record of Rhino?"

"We have a lot of regulations we have to deal with. I don't know of any other industry that has as many regulations and laws. We've had some violations and I've paid some civil penalties. But I think we have a pretty good record."

Mike glanced at Ben who rolled his eyes.

Feldman looked at his watch, as did Mike. Rinati had been on the witness stand for thirty-five minutes. "No further questions, Your Honor."

Judge Diaz looked at Miranda, "Your witness, Ms. Clymer."

Miranda picked up her legal pad and walked about halfway between her table and Rinati.

"Mr. Rinati, my name is Miranda Clymer and I represent the citizens who filed the appeal from your permit."

Rinati slowly and obviously surveyed her up and down and said, "Umm, my my, honey, what'll it cost me to get you to switch sides and represent me?"

The group of men in the back of the courtroom guffawed and Judge Diaz tapped his gavel hard three times. "Mr. Rinati, this isn't entertainment. Please limit your comments to the questions."

"I'm sorry, Your Honor, it's just that I hadn't realized how good looking she was until she was standing in front of me.

There's nothing wrong with me complimenting someone, is there?" He shook his head.

Mike and Nicky exchanged raised eyebrows.

Miranda didn't wilt. "Has your company conducted any pre-mining tests of my clients' homes?"

"No. Then again none of your clients would let my engineers into their houses to do those tests. It's kind of hard to test somebody's home when they've slammed the door in your face."

Miranda leaned to one side as she fumbled with her legal pad. Rinati crooked his head and followed the angle of her body as she leaned.

"Has your company, Rhino, ever violated a setback requirement?"

"Not that I recall."

"Wait a minute, hasn't your company had several violations of its mining permits at other sites for violating the setback requirements?"

"Not to my knowledge."

Miranda turned and walked to her table. As she did, Rinati angled his head back and forth, clearly enjoying the movement of her butt. She fumbled through the papers on her desk, finally giving up. As she was about to turn, Nicky handed her a paper. Miranda looked at it, smiled at Nicky, and turned back.

"Isn't it true, Mr. Rinati, that last year at the Flickinger Mine your company mined into the setback area?"

Rinati shook his head. "Not that I recall."

"Look at this, Mr. Rinati, do you know what this paper is?" Miranda said holding it in front of him.

"No, I've never seen it before."

Miranda approached Rinati and handed him the paper, then pointed at the title. "Doesn't it say 'DEP violations docket, Rhino Mining Company, Flickinger Mine'?"

Rinati put his hand over Miranda's hand and she quickly withdrew it. "It says those words, but I have no idea where this paper came from or who made it up. It doesn't mean anything to me."

"So, you've never had any violations of your setback requirements?"

"I don't think I said that. I don't *recall* any violations."

Miranda grabbed the paper and stomped back to her table where she slapped it down.

"Do you have any mines, where your company has violated its reclamation plan?"

"No."

"Are you sure?"

"I'm pretty sure, but I have a lot of ongoing and completed operations. You never know."

"You sit here today and say that you've never violated your reclamation plan? I remind you that you're under oath."

"Objection," barked Feldman as he rose to his full height. "Asked and answered. Argumentative. Ms. Clymer is having a rough afternoon, however, that does not give her the right to badger the witness."

"Sustained," Judge Diaz said without moving from his reclined position in his judge's chair.

"Did you offer my clients money prior to the hearing today?" Miranda asked.

"Of course, I offered to buy their houses from them and that offer still stands. I'm a man of my word and if they want to sell me their houses I'll buy them. Of course, those houses may not be worth as much with a coal mine in the front yard."

"You didn't offer them money to withdraw from this litigation?"

"No, I offered them money for their houses."

"How can anyone trust you?" Miranda stammered.

Feldman was on his feet. "Objection, argumentative question. Ms. Clymer can ask my client legitimate questions, but she has no right to insult my client."

"I withdraw the question."

Miranda flipped through her legal pad, shook her head and slowly returned to her chair. After she sat down, she looked at the judge and said, "No further questions."

Judge Diaz sat up and said, "We'll take a fifteen-minute break and then the Commonwealth may cross-examine Mr. Rinati."

***

Mike and Nicky huddled in the district attorney's conference room, alone. Sunlight, enhanced by the glare of yesterday's snow, spilled in through the ancient windows. Feldman had scored numerous points on Rinati's direct. Mike thought it was a textbook example of how to examine a problematic witness. Miranda's cross had been fruitless. His cross-examination was going to be crucial, and by far the most challenging of the twenty-eight-year-old lawyer's short career. He had draped his jacket on a chair and he stared at the blank legal pad on the table in front of him. He rolled his head, loosened his necktie, crossed his arms, and leaned back, eyes closed.

After a few moments of silence, Nicky stood up and began to rub the stiff muscles in his shoulders with her petite hands.

"Thanks, Nicky, I really need that."

"You're welcome. It's the only thing I can think of to help you right now."

"That makes two of us. I'm not sure what I can do to help me either. Rinati…he's very cagey. He knows a lot more about the legal process than he lets on. He knows he can deny random questions and it would be almost impossible to cross-examine him about that on short notice. He says pretty much whatever he wants to say and is careful to say he doesn't recall, rather than an outright no. If he gets caught in a lie, all he has to do is say he just didn't recall when he was first asked."

"So…"

"I'm going to keep it tight. I'll focus on two or three areas. Keep those papers I gave you close at hand. Ben's also ready with the other papers we discussed. Everyone says Rinati can get unhinged. I'd love to make him explode, destroy his credibility. Of course, if I can do that I'll have to enter the witness protection program I guess."

Nicky's fingers had reached Mike's neck and into his longish brown hair as the door swung open. Ben walked in. "Uh, I didn't know we were getting neck rubs. Can I get in line?" Ben wiggled his eyebrows.

Nicky smoothed Mike's hair and shrugged.

"The judge's clerk just came back so I thought I'd better fetch you. Are you ready for this?" Ben asked.

"No. Yes. As ready as I'll ever be."

Mike stood up and put on his suit jacket. Ben held the door and all three of them marched to the courtroom together, Mike, the tallest, leading the way.

60

"Mr. Rinati, my name is Mike Jacobs. I'm an assistant counsel with the Pennsylvania Department of Environmental Protection. Good afternoon."

"Let's cut the crap, Attorney. I mean, let's get to the chase. You're not here to make friends with me." Rinati leaned back in the witness chair and lifted his chin.

Mike picked up his legal pad, strode to the center of the courtroom, and stood directly in front of Judge Diaz.

"Okay then, you're familiar with Roaring Run?" He pointed to the map on the easel and traced the blue line of the stream with a finger.

"Yeah."

"You testified earlier that you'd seen Roaring Run?"

"Seen it, walked it, your inspector, Lyle Ransom, slipped into it and splashed some water from it onto me. Everything but taste it."

At this, Mike's head swiveled in surprise toward the obese mine inspector, who sat in the gallery surrounded by a crowd of DEP personnel. Ransom shrugged, then looked away.

"You and Mr. Ransom were at Roaring Run together?"

"Yeah, during his first site inspection at the beginning of October. He wanted to see the whole site. He's a little…large and we had to drive almost everywhere, but we couldn't drive down to the stream. He was pretty spent by the time we walked down there. He was huffin' and puffin.' He slipped on one of those wet rocks and did one hell of a breakdance trying to keep from falling in."

Laughter filled the back of the courtroom and the judge lightly tapped his gavel.

Mike glanced at Ransom, whose round face radiated red like a neon sign.

"You testified earlier that Rhino Mining Company would have no difficulty reclaiming the headwaters area to Roaring Run?"

"Yeah, we do it all the time."

Before Mike turned around, Nicky pushed forward a pile of permit files. Mike held up the top folder. "Mr. Rinati, I have here the permit file for your Anderson mine. You're familiar with the operation?"

Rinati hesitated and looked upwards. Then he said, "Yeah, that's a reclaimed operation."

"There were no headwaters anywhere near that operation, right?"

"Yeah. We did a beautiful job of reclamation. You couldn't tell that there usta' be a strip mine there."

Mike picked up a second file and held it up. "I have the permit file here for the Butoski Mine; this one has also been reclaimed. Any headwaters near it?"

"None, nada. Jim Butoski, the farmer who owns that site, is farming that land today. It's beautiful. We mined out a nice piece of coal that was under it and that site is better for farming today than it was before we started minin'."

"I have twenty more permit files here, both reclaimed and currently in operation. Let's cut through this, Mr. Rinati. None of these sites have headwaters on or near them, right?"

Rinati sat back in the chair and rubbed his chin. "I don't know, maybe *you* can tell me?"

"I'm happy to go through each and every one of these files with you, Mr. Rinati. But I'll tell you that none of these permits have headwaters on or near them."

"So?"

"I'm not going to argue with you regarding how good or bad a reclamation job you say you've done on those sites, but the fact remains that neither you nor your company have ever had to deal with headwaters at *any* of your mining sites, isn't that right?"

"I wouldn't say that."

Mike picked up the stack of permit files which stood nearly two feet high. "Okay, Mr. Rinati, here are all of your permit files, active and inactive. Pick out one permit where your company had to deal with headwaters. We can take all day, but I'll tell you right now there isn't a single one."

"Okay, maybe you're right…But I have foremen who've worked at a lot of other mines before they came to me and I'm sure some of them have worked at those kinds of sites."

"The foreman does what?"

"He's the main man at the site. Everything that happens, the mining, everything, he's in charge of it. He reports directly to me."

"He makes sure the mining plan and reclamation plan are implemented?"

"Yeah."

"So, if you had headwaters, he'd be the man to make sure they're not impacted?"

"Right."

"Your foreman for the proposed Gordon mine in Somerset County, the one on appeal today, you identified him earlier as Freddie Pascal?"

"Yeah, he's my most experienced foreman."

Mike went back to the bar that separated the gallery from the lawyers and Ben handed him a hefty stack of mine permit files. "Okay, Mr. Rinati, I pulled every permit file for the past twenty-five years where Mr. Pascal was the foreman. He never worked at a site where there were headwaters. Did you know that?"

Rinati thought for a moment. "So? What the hell difference does it make? I've got experts out the wazoo. Geologists, mining engineers, shit, I've got the Dean of Mining at Penn State. All of them could be brought in as consultants."

"Yes or no, does Mr. Pascal, your main man at the mine, the one who implements the mining plan and reclamation plan, have any experience mining in headwaters areas?"

"Not that I know of," Rinati shook his head.

Mike returned the stack of files to Ben while Rinati glared at Feldman, who shrugged. Next to him, Angela fixed her eyes on her laptop screen. Jimmy furiously pawed through a stack of Rhino's permit files.

"Mr. Rinati, when you testified this morning, and when Dean Peterson testified, you both said that this mine was small, twenty-five acres, correct?"

"Yeah?"

"Dean Peterson also testified that the coal could be mined and the site would be marginally profitable, even with the permit conditions. Did you hear him say that?"

"Yeah."

"This is not going to be one of your more profitable mines, is it?"

"It'll do okay."

"Based on the information in Rhino's application, I had Mr. Kemper, the department's mining engineer, calculate the amount of coal you could mine and then calculate the value of that coal based upon the highest spot price on the market today. He then calculated the cost of extracting that coal based on the amount of overburden." Ben handed him a large poster board, which he placed on the easel.

"Mr. Rinati, this exhibit shows that you'll make a profit of about one hundred and fifty thousand dollars, given the best price on the market today for that coal. This is assuming there were *no* special conditions imposed by the department that would limit the area you could mine. Do you disagree with Mr. Kemper's calculations?"

"Objection." Feldman stood. "Facts not in evidence, failure to lay a foundation, speculative."

The judge looked at Mike.

"We'll put all of this testimony in during our case in chief, if we need to. Mr. Kemper is here and is happy to go through all of his calculations. This is cross-examination."

"Overruled." The judge sat back.

"Where'd he get this?" Rinati asked.

"He learned how to do this in Dean Peterson's class."

Mike looked over his shoulder and saw Ben grin. Dean Peterson, who sat behind Feldman, nodded affirmatively, and beamed. Laughter rippled through the gallery.

Rinati said, "I'd say that's not right. Our calculations show that we can mine a little more cheaply and that'll help us make more, maybe two-fifty K in profit."

Ben handed Mike another exhibit and placed it on the easel. "Mr. Rinati, I said a moment ago that the calculations were based on *no* special conditions. I also asked Mr. Kemper to run the profit/loss calculations with *all* of the conditions that the department has imposed. This results in an increased cost to mine the coal and less coal that you can mine. If you mine in accordance with the conditions, the calculations show that the added cost of the mining operation will result in a net loss of a half million dollars. Do you agree with the calculations?"

"Objection, beyond the scope of direct."

"Overruled."

"Do you agree that you will lose a half-million dollars if you comply with all of the conditions?" Mike asked.

Rinati sat forward in his chair. "Maybe, not that much. We, the dean, think we can make some money offa' this. Like I said before, those conditions will cost me a shitload of money. I have other considerations, like contracts, that I take into consideration when I decide whether to mine a site."

"So you're saying you would start up a new mine if you knew in advance you'd lose money?"

"Shit no."

"But you agree that you *could* lose a half-million dollars if you mine *with* conditions, but that you might make just two hundred and fifty thousand dollars if you mine *without* the conditions?" Mike pointed at the exhibit.

"Roughly, like I said, I think I can do it more cheaply and make more money. Maybe break even with the conditions. Maybe a little more. I mean, you don't know much about minin' but there are other considerations, other things you can do to make the operation more profitable. Perfectly legal things." Rinati smiled at the judge and sat back.

"I'm guessing that as a savvy businessman you want to make money no matter what?"

"You guessed right."

Mike glanced at Nicky. "You said there were other things you could do to make the operation more profitable. Would you make more money if you had a larger mine site?"

"Yeah, a bigger mine would be more profitable. That's just the economics of it."

Mike pulled the map of the site from behind the other exhibits and placed it in front of the other poster boards. He pointed to the area to the west of Forest Lane. "If your company could mine all of the land on both sides of these houses on Forest Lane, and take out those houses, wouldn't you make more profit?"

Rinati's black eyes narrowed to slits. "Yeah, but Rhino Mining Company doesn't own that land."

Mike stared at Rinati. He paused to let the witness's last statement settle in. Finally, he said, "Rhino Mining Company doesn't own that land. Have you ever heard of a company called Somerset Land Holdings, Inc.?"

Rinati looked at the ceiling. "Not that I recall."

"So, you say that you have no involvement with Somerset Land Holdings?"

Rinati shrugged. "I have an interest in lots of companies."

Mike turned to retrieve a stack of papers from Nicky. The corners of her mouth turned up slightly. These were the papers she had found a few weeks earlier, when she stumbled on them at the Corporation Bureau.

"Mr. Rinati, this is an exhibit that's marked as Commonwealth's exhibit number twenty-four. Have you ever seen it?"

Rinati glanced at it. "How do you expect me to know anything about your papers?"

"Have you seen this?"

"No."

"You incorporated a company called Somerset Land Holdings, Inc. just two months ago and you don't recall it?"

"It's not ringing any bells."

"Is this your signature on page two, where it says 'President'?" Mike flipped the page and pointed. As he did, Nicky handed a copy to Feldman. Mike handed a copy to the judge and Tommy Bowdoin. "Take your time, Mr. Rinati, I want to be sure you recognize your own signature on the articles of incorporation." He stood close enough to Rinati that he could smell the onions on his breath from lunch.

"Yeah, that's my signature, I signed this. But I sign a shitload of documents every day. You don't expect me to recognize everything I sign, do you?" Rinati sat forward and closed the space between him and Mike to inches.

"I expect you to tell the truth!" Mike bellowed as Rinati jumped back in his seat. "Yesterday, during the snowstorm, the courthouse was nearly empty. One of the few offices that was open was the Recorder of Deeds. I had Mr. Kemper go down to the Recorder's office and he obtained a certified copy of a deed."

Mike grabbed another paper that Nicky was already holding out for him. He handed one to the judge and tossed copies at Feldman and Rinati. "Mr. Rinati, this is a certified copy of a deed from Mr. and Mrs. Bernard Voigt to Somerset Land Holdings, Inc. On page one of the deed it shows that Somerset Land Holdings became the owner of the three hundred-acre tract on the other side of Forest Lane on December 31, just one month ago. Do you remember that *your company*, Somerset Land Holdings, just bought three hundred acres of land or have you forgotten that too?"

Rinati glared. "Yeah, I guess."

"Just so it's clear, Rhino Mining has the right to mine twenty-five acres on the east side of Forest Lane and your other company, Somerset Land Holdings, owns three hundred acres on the west side of Forest Lane. The only thing that stops you from mining all three hundred and twenty-five acres at one time in one gigantic mine are all of those inconvenient houses on Forest Lane right in the middle. Am I right?"

"So what?"

"Answer the question. Is that right, Mr. Rinati? You could profitably mine the area where you currently have the permit, plus the new land in one huge mine, but only if you forced out the homeowners on Forest Lane and mined through their homes?"

"So what? It's a free country, if I want to buy land and mine it, that's my right."

"IS THAT RIGHT?"

"Yeah, that's right," Rinati answered shrilly. He sat on the edge of his chair, as if he was prepared to leap out of the witness box.

"So, you agree that the profitability of your mine depends on purchasing the properties on Forest Lane and doing away with the conditions that protect Roaring Run?"

"No, I said I could mine it economically and save money." Rinati's face flushed with anger. His eyes bugged out of his head.

Feldman rose halfway in his chair, poised to spring to his full six-foot height. Angela whispered angrily to Jimmy who banged on his laptop's keyboard as she berated him.

"Actually, Mr. Rinati, you said you could mine it without the conditions and make money. You also said that if you mined it with the conditions you could lose money, just not as much as the department's calculations show."

"I might've said that."

"If I understand this correctly, to make money at this mine requires you to overturn the conditions or force out the residents on Forest Lane, then mine through their houses. Is that right?"

"So what?" he spat back, his face bright red.

"Or, you could just ignore the conditions and try to get away with it. Even your own expert said the only way to protect Roaring Run was with the department's conditions, right?"

"Objection." Feldman leaped into the air. "That's not what Dean Peterson said."

Rinati stood. His black eyes locked on Mike's and his nostrils flared with each heavy, labored breath. "Shut up, Feldman. I'm gonna' answer this. You know what, Attorney? My company mines coal. We mine coal for your lights, your heat. If we didn't do what we do, you and your granola-eating friends would sit in a cold, dark house in front of a blank TV wondering 'what the hell?' That president, Carter, back in the seventies, told us to mine more coal and fuckin' A, we're doing it. A third of our electricity comes from coal. We're doing it despite the shitload of regulations you and those assholes in Washington heaped on us. You think they worry about all these goddamn regulations in Russia, China? Shit no. Wasn't that long ago that everyone had to line up every day just to get gas. I remember that. Those A-rab's had us by the balls. Energy independence, the president says. Well, we won't pull out of that shit unless people like me mine the coal. You may not like it, you may not like the way it looks while we're doing it, but this is how it's done. You talk about climate change? The climate will be just perfect for you when everything's shut down if there's no coal. Maybe you'd prefer nuclear? Oh wait, you live in Harrisburg, near that Three Mile Island. You probably ain't a fan. Maybe some windmills, solar? You'd have to cover the whole damn state to have enough of that shit to power one small town. So yeah, that's how it's done. My men work outside in every kind of shitty weather, one hundred degrees, today when there's a foot of fucking snow on the ground. I'll do whatever I can to produce the coal and mine it. If I make a buck, well, I'm the one risking everything, not you and your government job."

"You'd do whatever you could to save some money and make a profit, right?" Mike shot back.

"Damn straight."

"Even destroy those headwaters, right?"

"Fuck those headwaters, fuck your conditions, fuck you DEP bastards."

"Objection, objection." Feldman rushed toward the judge waving his arms. Miranda stood but said nothing.

"Mr. Jacobs," said the judge pounding his gavel.

Mike ignored them.

"You'd do whatever blasting was required just to get as much coal no matter what, right?"

"Whatever it takes," Rinati yelled.

"Objection." Feldman's face was bright red and veins throbbed in his neck.

The judge hammered his gavel, repeatedly and loudly. "Mr. Jacobs…"

Mike glanced at the court reporter to make sure she was still taking down the testimony. "You don't care about those headwaters, you don't care about those people, do you?"

"Objection." Feldman waved his arms as he stood directly in front of the judge. He yelled over the rising commotion in the courtroom.

"Mr. Jacobs…" The judge thumped his gavel.

"Fuck them! Fuck the goddamn headwaters! Fuck the conditions! Fuck you, Jacobs! Fuck you, Feldman! Fuck you too, judge!"

With that, Rinati jumped up, and pushed the large collection of exhibits that sat on the rail onto the floor. He bolted past Mike and shoved him into the easel which clattered to the floor. The charts and maps spilled across the courtroom. He thrust himself between the counsel's tables and knocked a pitcher of water onto Angela. Her neat stack of papers fluttered onto the floor. Then he ran out the courtroom doors.

Judge Diaz beat his gavel fruitlessly as the courtroom erupted into chaos. In the gallery, Miranda's clients stood and yelled at the miners who pointed at them and bellowed back.

"Order, order in the courtroom," roared the judge.

Mike stood quietly in the center of the room, head bowed. He clasped his hands as if in prayer as the exhibits floated to the floor. When he looked up at Nicky he had the slightest smile. Then, almost imperceptibly, he winked at her.

61

Mike was scheduled to introduce his case the next day and, despite Rinati's meltdown on the witness stand, he wasn't going to leave the case to chance. Feldman was too egotistical a lawyer to allow his client to screw up his case, so Mike expected that Feldman would figure out a way to fix things. He worked with his main witness, Ben, until after ten o'clock, then sent him home to get some rest. Mike caught him staring into space and once saw him hold out his hand as though he was grasping thin air. Ben looked like shit, but he told him he was just dog-tired. Also, the headaches.

Nicky nodded off from exhaustion and Mike hoped for a good night's sleep but still had notes to review. As soon as Ben left, she went into the bathroom and took a quick shower. Mike sat in the easy chair reading over his notes when Nicky came into the bedroom, dropped her towel on the floor, and bent over to pull her flannel granny nightgown out of the drawer.

Mike looked up and Nicky stood facing him completely naked, her eyes half-shut, until the nightgown slid over her head and down her nude body. The sight of her body burned into his memory. This was the first time he'd seen her completely naked. He knew the vision of her slim frame, generous pink breasts, and surprisingly straight brown tuft of hair at the junction of her legs, would remain with him for a long time. Then she kissed him on the forehead and wordlessly got into their bed. She turned out her light and seconds later was asleep.

Exhausted, Mike needed some sleep too. A half hour later, just after eleven, he was in bed with Nicky curled up next to him.

One of her hands was across his chest, resting on his shoulder, and she had pressed up against him for warmth in the cool hotel room. Her legs curled around his. He inhaled her clean, shower-soap smell. For a moment he allowed himself to enjoy her peaceful company and the feeling that he was holding his own against Feldman and Rinati. This had been a good day.

On his back, one arm around Nicky, he mulled over the fact that they'd seen each other naked in bits and pieces over the previous weeks, but never all at once. One or the other had walked into the bedroom as the other was going into or coming out of the bathroom or getting dressed. This was like a strange long-term relationship, maybe a marriage, he didn't know. It wasn't love-less, he had no doubt that he and Nicky were in love in their own unique way. He'd never loved a woman as deeply as he loved Nicky. It was a sensual relationship, but they never kissed or made love.

He was so exhausted.

As he drifted to sleep, one thing was certain: They were going to have to resolve what it was that they had as soon as the trial was over.

Mike wondered if there was some way he and Nicky could work things out. Maybe go somewhere else. He fully understood and respected what she was, but couldn't imagine life without her. He'd never loved anyone like this.

Maybe have children together.
An arrangement of some sort.
We can make it work.
Because we love each other.
Stay together.
Forever…

62

Mike's cell phone chirped and he searched for it in the darkness. He knocked it off the nightstand, leaned over and picked it up on the fourth ring.

"Mike? It's me, Pat Murphy." Mike thought about the black inspector from Pittsburgh who had been shadowing Ransom for the past several weeks. As per their plan, he had sat in the back of the courtroom watching Ransom's testimony and barely acknowledged Mike. Mike fumbled for the lamp next to the bed and Nicky rolled over, pulling the covers around her neck.

"Sorry to call you so late, Counselor. Look, I've got some information on Lyle and you need to see it tonight before the trial is over. I'm in the lobby. Can I come up to your room and show it to you?"

Mike looked at Nicky, who had fallen back asleep.

"Uh, my room's a mess, I'd rather not. How about if I meet you in the lobby and we'll find an empty corner and talk there. Just give me five minutes."

He stripped off his gym shorts and tee shirt in front of Nicky, not caring if she saw him, then dressed quickly in his jeans, flannel shirt, and boots. He leaned over and whispered into Nicky's ear, "Hey babe, I'm going downstairs to meet Pat Murphy. I'll be back in a half hour."

She mumbled something incomprehensible and smiled, but didn't open her eyes.

Two minutes later, Mike shook hands with the tall inspector who wore an insulated Army desert camo jacket and black woolen cap. His boots were still wet from walking through the snow. There were several hotel guests in the lobby and a hockey game played loudly in the bar. Murphy said, "Let's find someplace where no one will overhear us."

Mike saw Betty behind the hotel counter and she offered Mike a key to a small function room down the hall. It was windowless, but quiet and away from any potential eavesdroppers or busybodies.

"Sorry to get you up, Counselor, but this seemed important. I didn't want to let it wait until tomorrow." Murphy took a pile of paper out of a leather satchel and laid it on the table.

"This better be good," Mike said yawning.

"I've been with Lyle for the past couple of weeks and I've come to a couple of conclusions about him. He's a racist and an asshole—there's no doubt about that. And lazy. Also, he *knows* mining. I mean, the guy can just look at a mining map and figure it all out, from initial cut through reclamation, in his head in seconds. It's like he's got a mining computer in his brain. He was showing me things I never would've noticed on my own and I didn't see a single thing out in the field that Lyle missed. Like anyone else, he'll look the other way when he sees a minor infraction as long as the operator agrees to clean it up by the next time he's back. If he sees a major problem, though, he'll cite the guy."

"No one's ever said Ransom doesn't know his stuff," Mike said resting his head on his hand. "I think the information we've got shows he's on the take, not that he's incompetent."

"About that. Where did you get that information?"

"An anonymous source," he lied, refusing to betray Ben. "It showed up in my office in Harrisburg a couple of weeks ago with a Pittsburgh postmark. A plain manila envelope containing the application for an account with the Bank of Meyersdale, the account ledger, other related information from the bank, his mortgage with PNC, all of that. I was skeptical, of course, but I personally called the vice president of the bank and scanned the documents to her and she confirmed they were genuine documents from the bank. She was royally pissed we had them, but was willing to work with us. We got the updated information directly from the bank last week."

"Did you wonder where they came from originally?"

"Of course, but this case has been in the news so any one of dozens of people could have sent them. It's not that unusual for us to get papers in the mail sent anonymously. Besides, they were always my Plan B, if Lyle lied on the witness stand or went rogue, so I was hoping not to have to use them."

"Well, I got a call from Lyle after he testified today. I was surprised since we're not exactly buddies. He was angry and said some…unkind things about you. He kept denying he had anything to do with those documents or that account. He said he's never had an account at that bank and has no idea how it was opened in his name."

Mike looked at the inspector for a long moment, "You don't expect him to admit to accepting a bribe, do you?"

"Of course not." Murphy narrowed his eyes. "I can't imagine why the guy would have reached out to me if all he wanted was to rant about you. Maybe I'm so far outside of his circle of friends that he trusts me, maybe he suspects I'm working with you and this will find its way back to you. I don't know. So I went back and looked at all of the exhibits you had regarding Lyle."

He pointed at the application. "I noticed the application was typed out, not filled in by hand. The only handwriting was his signature. Someone could have forged that."

Murphy handed Mike the application form. Mike looked at it and shrugged. "I'm sure a lot of applications are typed."

"What if someone had access to all of this information, typed it in, and forged his signature?" Murphy asked. "It's not that difficult to forge someone's signature if you can do it in the quiet of your room and take several tries to get it right."

"Yeah, but that would require access to a lot of personal information. Where do you get information regarding someone's Social Security number, bank accounts, mortgages, all that stuff in the application unless it's yours? I mean even hackers might only get one or two bits of information, not all of it." Mike pointed to the entries on the forms.

"I've been thinking about that. How about if you got it from your doctor, your mailman, and a bank employee who all have access to that information?"

Mike made a face. "What are you talking about?"

"Let's start with the Social Security number," Murphy said, holding his wide thumb under the entry. "Every doctor's office in America has that number on file if you're a patient. Not only the Social Security number, but they also have a lot of other personal, identifying information. Did you know that Andrea McCarthy works for Somerset Memorial Hospital in the records office? If Ransom was ever a patient, she'd have access to a lot of his personal information. It would be easy enough to find out if Lyle went to the hospital as a patient or sees a doctor there, don't you think?"

"So, you're saying that Andrea McCarthy, one of the little old lady appellants in this case, took confidential information from Ransom's files at the hospital and all on her own set him up?" Mike asked. "There's no way she could do that. Even if she did, there was a lot of other financial information on the bank forms, not just personal information you could get in a doctor's office. Why would she do it, anyway?"

"Well, maybe because Ransom is an easy target. Not only that, but he was one of the strongest supporters of Rhino's mine in the department. Discredit him and the permit starts to fall apart."

Mike held up the account application and held it to the light.

Murphy continued. "Also, I agree she couldn't do this on her own, but how about this? Bob Willis? Another appellant, he's a mailman. How difficult would it be for him to know or find out which bank is Lyle's? Assuming he never opened an envelope which probably would be a federal felony, he'd still be able to tell what bank mails Lyle a monthly statement and what bank or banks he has loans with. Those envelopes are pretty obvious. Hell, my own mortgage bill has the word 'invoice' written all over the outside of the envelope so I don't chuck it out with the other junk mail. Think of all the shit we find out at the department that has nothing to do with any case we're in on.

Also, he could intercept any mail coming from the Meyersdale Bank before Ransom ever got it."

"Okay...You still haven't explained how the two of them got the financial information or how those two were able to open an account and deposit fifty thousand dollars into it. I've seen their houses and that might be the life savings for all of them combined."

"I'll get to the fifty thousand dollars in a minute. Do you remember where Lily Roberts works?" Murphy asked.

"Not the Bank of Meyersdale, she works at the Bank of Oxford."

"Well, Counselor, you have one guess about what bank is the parent of the Bank of Meyersdale," McCarthy said without smiling.

"*Shit*. The Bank of Oxford?"

"You're pretty smart for a lawyer." Murphy almost smiled. "She's a bookkeeper. That means that if you're opening a basic checking account, like Ransom's, the papers go through her. The credit bureau report has lots of basic information in it and she'd have access to that. As a bookkeeper, she does the initial review of the application, before it goes to the vice president for approval. It's possible Ransom never set foot in that bank."

Mike looked at the papers. "Well, I don't believe it. What about the fifty thousand dollars? That's a lot of money and from what I've seen, I doubt that those people could scrape together more than a few thousand dollars."

"All they needed was five thousand, not fifty thousand, to make it look like a big payoff. You could leverage a five-thousand dollar investment to make it look like fifty-thousand dollars or even a hundred-thousand dollars in payoffs over a few months. Look at this," Murphy said, pulling out the account statement. On November 1, there was an initial deposit of five thousand dollars. Then, two days later there was a withdrawal of four thousand dollars in cash and one day after that, a deposit of three thousand dollars, again in cash. Then, another withdrawal of three thousand dollars, followed by a deposit of four thousand dollars. If you add up just those deposits it looks like Lyle deposited a total of twelve thousand dollars in ten days and that would be a substantial down payment for his services. But if someone, like Lily Roberts, was taking money out of the account and then depositing the exact same dollar bills back into the account a couple of days later, all you'd need was a bankroll of five-thousand dollars to do that. It's the *same money* coming in and going out. When you introduced this as evidence this morning, the current statement showed total of deposits of fifty-thousand dollars, but if you do the math, all you needed was five-thousand dollars going out and coming back in to leverage this and make it look like fifty-thousand dollars."

"Shit," said Mike as he scrutinized the paper.

"What did you think he was doing with all the money that was coming out of his account?" Murphy asked.

"I didn't think too much about it. I figured gambling, whores, cocaine, a condo in Florida. Whatever. It never occurred to me that someone could be churning the money through that account to make it look like he received a lot when it's possible that the same dollars that came out of the account went back in a day or two later."

Mike leaned his elbow on the table and ran his hand through his hair. Murphy watched him as he paged through the documents, then Mike said, "Oh shit. What if they were looking for an angle to overturn the permit? They don't really trust their lawyer to come through for them. I wouldn't trust Miranda, either. They despise Lyle. I'm guessing everyone knows he's a racist-scumbag-asshole. Maybe they thought he deserved to be sacrificed. These people are fighting for their homes and I bet they're willing to do anything to protect them. If I had to guess, I'd say the neighbors decided Lyle was the biggest problem they were facing and had to take him out. That probably would result in the department suspending the permit at the very least. Also, get rid of him and the next inspector could be another Marty Stevens, totally opposed to the mining. Based on what you're saying, they had the capability of doing it."

"Well, that's my theory, but it looks more and more feasible."

Mike slapped his head. "Crap. When I met the neighbors at Miranda's office back in December, Tom McCarthy, the manager of the turnpike mini-market actually told me the neighbors were investigating Ransom. Maybe…"

Mike felt vomit push its way into his mouth and he swallowed hard. "That's cold. Ruining a man like this, even a scumbag like Lyle, is ruthless. I'm not sure what to do with this. If you're right, I played right into their hands and crucified Ransom on the witness stand this morning. Everyone in the room, and I mean everyone, thinks he's a dirty inspector who's on the take. Based on the testimony and exhibits, the DA and attorney general's office should be investigating him. He'll lose more than just his job."

"Well, here you go," Murphy said, pushing the papers across the table. "This is above my pay grade, Counselor. I'll stick around for another day or two if you need my help."

Mike's head spun as he and Murphy walked out to the lobby. They shook hands and agreed to meet up in the morning at the courthouse.

Betty was gone and Mike handed the conference room key to a black woman wearing a similar Sheraton uniform who had taken her place behind the counter.

Mike took the elevator, which slowly climbed to his floor as he looked at the papers. Murphy's theory whirled around in his brain. It was more than a theory. Mike was afraid it was fact.

Mike walked back to his room trying to figure out what to do next. He wondered if the neighbors were playing him or if Murphy and he were just imagining the whole thing. Part of him was saying that there was no way the neighbors could have organized this. Another part of him believed it was entirely possible. He immediately wondered if Miranda was in on the scheme, or whether she was being played, too. Miranda was the ultimate player, but Mike wasn't sure she was in on this plot. If it was true, the neighbors probably cooked this up at a potluck supper on Forest Lane. The more he thought about it, though, the more likely it seemed to be true and the angrier he got. If Murphy was right, then the citizens were more corrupt than Rinati. He began formulating a plan to talk with the DA early in the morning to see if he could have one of his detectives pay a visit to the bank and ask questions. Mike would have precious little time, however, to set things right before Judge Diaz. His stomach churned.

Mike fumbled for his key and played with the door to his room. It was jammed tight. He looked again at the number to make sure he was at the right room. He wedged the papers firmly under his armpit, put his shoulder to the door, and finally was able to push it open. A suitcase had fallen over and blocked the door. Mike shoved the suitcase with his foot. Light beamed up from the floor where the lamp had fallen, casting the room in oddly angled shadows. Some chairs had been knocked over and Mike's papers were scattered across the room. The blankets on the bed were twisted and pulled to the floor.

Nicky was gone.

63

Mike frantically searched the room trying to figure out what happened to Nicky. He speed-dialed her cell phone and a couple of seconds later heard it ring from under the bed. He pulled it out and slid it into his pocket. He yanked open the dresser drawer. Her jeans were still in it, neatly folded. He opened the closet and pawed through her dresses until he was sure all of her clothes and shoes were still there. Nothing in the bathroom seemed out of place. The only thing missing was Nicky.

Mike paused and took several deep breaths.

Where is she? Maybe she's down the hall. Maybe she went looking for me at the bar.

Barefoot and in her nightgown.

Right. Not likely.

Maybe she's sick, wandering the halls?

Maybe she was kidnapped?

Mike threw open the door and looked down the long hallway. Everything seemed quiet and ordinary. He jogged to the elevator and saw nothing. Then he turned and ran to the stairway at the opposite end of the hall, ripped open the door and took the steps two and three at a time. The door at the bottom opened to the parking lot.

The pile of snow on either side of the door was a foot and a half deep. It had been shoveled and the sidewalk salted near the door, but farther away there were piles of snow and large patches of ice where it had melted and refrozen in the cold night air. Several dozen cars were parked near the door. There was one empty space close to the exit and he slipped across the ice as he hurried to it. He searched the ground in the dark and slush with no luck. But then saw it: Nicky's barrette. She often wore it to bed. He picked up the piece of plastic and metal from the ice, and held it up to the street lights. It was closed, a clump of hair stuck between its clamps. He looked around the parking lot, but saw no movement of people or cars.

Mike sprinted to the lobby. The bar was closed, the room dark, chairs turned up on top of tables. He found the hotel clerk who had taken his key after his meeting with Murphy. "Have you seen Nicky? Nicky Kane?" he asked breathlessly.

"Who?"

"My, uh, girlfriend. The one who's staying with me in room 215."

"Sorry, I came on at midnight and haven't seen her. Hardly anyone's been through here tonight."

Mike thought for a second, "What about Betty? She was here when I came downstairs at eleven thirty."

"She left a little early tonight. Around a quarter till."

"Did she say where she was going? Anything at all?"

"No, she seemed in a hurry, but I didn't ask."

Mike thanked her and jogged to the elevator, jabbing the button repeatedly until the doors opened. The climb to the second floor seemed to take forever. Mike ran back to his room hoping to find some further evidence of Nicky. Maybe a note. There was nothing.

At a loss for what to do, he called Miranda. After eight rings, he hung up and dialed again. This time, she answered.

"Miranda, it's me, Mike. Nicky, is she there? Is she with you?"

"Michael, it's awfully late to be calling. Sorry, but your little friend isn't here. I wish she was. That would be fun."

"I don't have time for this tonight, Miranda. What about Betty? Is she there?"

"My my, you're quite the busybody. Sorry, Michael but she's not here either. Look, I'm…entertaining a colleague. Got to go." She hung up.

Mike held his cell phone in his hand and it rang almost immediately. He didn't recognize the number, but he quickly answered. "Miranda?"

There was a pause, and then a man said, "What? Jacobs? We've got your girlfriend." The man on the other end of the line didn't identify himself, but his voice sounded familiar.

"You have Nicky?"

He heard Nicky near the phone, "Mike! Mike, help me!"

Mike swallowed hard.

"Does that answer your question?"

"Who is this?"

"You like asking questions, don't you, you dumb shit? Ask another question and she's dead."

"What do you want me to…I'm sorry, please…tell me what you want to tell me."

"The Shoemaker Mine, you've been there before, meet us at the Shoemaker Mine and you can see your girl."

"It's a big place, anywhere in particular?"

"Another question?"

"Sorry, sorry I just don't know where."

"The lift at the top of the highwall. Where you were with Mr. Rinati. You got one hour." Mike looked at his watch: twelve forty-five. "If you take too long, well, let's just say our pants are getting itchy. That's when the fun begins with that fine piece of ass. I'm not sure we can wait that long. Come alone or she's dead. If you take too long, she's dead. Call the cops, she's dead. Yins' got that? Any more stupid questions?"

Mike nodded. "No, no, I get it."

The line went dead. Mike looked at the phone for a moment. Then he opened his contacts and dialed a number.

"Ben, they have her. Nicky, they took her."

"Who has her? Mike, what are you talking about?"

"I'm not sure, I think it's Rinati's goons. They're going to rape her, kill her. They've threatened her. Rinati's getting back at me and they're doing it through Nicky. I don't know how, but I'm going to, going to…save her."

"Wait a minute partner, where do they have her?"

"The Shoemaker Mine. They told me to come to the highwall in an hour. If I'm not there in an hour, they're going to hurt her. If I bring anyone, they're going to kill her. I don't know what to do."

"Hold on, let's figure this out. Let's call the cops."

"No, don't call the cops, they said they'd kill her if I did. There isn't time to figure this out if I'm going to get there before they hurt her. Offer myself in exchange if they let her go. They want me anyway. Thanks for everything. I have to go."

Mike clicked off the phone, grabbed his parka, wool ski hat, and gloves and headed out. He had no plan, no weapon, no idea what he would do to save Nicky other than offer himself as a sacrifice.

Call the cops, call the cops, call the cops.

Call.

The.

Cops.

Mike ignored the voice within him and ran to his car, sliding on the ice. He slammed it into gear, spun his wheels on the ice and snow and hated his lightweight car. He fishtailed out of the icy hotel parking lot as he drove into the dark, snowy night.

64

It took Mike fifty-five long minutes to reach the Shoemaker Mine. The drive, through the snow and ice, was infuriatingly slow and dangerous. He moved quickly enough on the state routes, but navigating the narrow, snow-packed county roads took time. His Prius was too light for the snow and ice.

About a half hour after he left the hotel, he got behind a plow truck that was traveling twenty miles an hour. In a fit of courage, or perhaps desperation and madness, he passed the truck on a two-lane road, completely blinded by the ice, snow and a spray of salt kicked up by the wide vehicle.

He kept the music off and concentrated on developing a plan to free Nicky, but was unable to formulate anything that made sense or resulted in the two of them leaving together alive. They wanted him, not Nicky. The best play he had was to trade himself for Nicky.

Mike drove onto the mine property along the darkened haul road in the wide tracks laid down earlier that day by the mining trucks. He stopped when he approached the overlook, looking down into the pit. He was where he'd driven with Ransom, on the opposite side of the mine from the highwall.

Mike got out of his car and crept onto the ice and snow-covered overlook. The stiff wind cut right through his parka. The temperature must have been in the single digits. The night sky was spectacular; he looked up and clearly saw the Milky Way. He wished he had time to enjoy it. Within a few seconds of leaving his car, he began to freeze and pulled his ski hat low on his head. He wondered where they were keeping Nicky.

Searching across the expanse of the mine, Mike noticed that, in the darkness, the pit was as black as the coal being unearthed. Other than a few pieces of oversized mining equipment parked near his car, he saw no sign of life. He scanned the darkened highwall, five hundred or so feet away, and then he saw it—a light, very dim, opposite from where he stood. It glowed slightly brighter, then dimmed like a distant star.

Mike calculated a route to the light and recalled the narrow haul road down which he had driven with Ransom several weeks earlier. The road was narrow and steep. It was dangerous enough in the daylight let alone at night, covered with ice. He knew that driving across the floor of the mine could be treacherous since he didn't know, nor could he readily see, any excavations that may have been dug. A fall of even one foot could derail his efforts to save Nicky and a longer drop could kill him. He also thought about the crazed drive in Rinati's Cadillac up the side of the highwall and figured that at best he had a fifty–fifty chance of getting to Nicky in one piece by driving through the mine.

Mike thought about the landslide. He wasn't even sure if the haul road on the other side of the mine was still there.

Then he remembered that after the landslide, Rinati was able to go from the highwall to the mine entrance, traveling through a small patch of woods and a labyrinth of township roads to get there. That seemed slightly safer and quicker. He got back into his car and just before he turned it around, he flashed his lights several times in the direction of the light on the other side of the mine. He hoped Rinati's men who were holding Nicky would see the light and realize he was there and not harm her. He also hoped Nicky might see the flash and would know he was coming to save her.

He hoped.

The narrow township roads had been barely plowed. As he drove, trying hard to remember the route in the deep snow, he wondered if it was possible that some of the back roads hadn't been plowed or driven on since the blizzard. He was afraid he would miss the turnoff. After several long minutes, he came to a patch of woods that seemed familiar. He spotted a trail. It looked as though heavy vehicles had traveled on it recently. He put his

Prius into low and slowly made his way along the wooded path. After several minutes of anxious second guessing, he saw a small sign that said simply, "SHOEMAKER MINE – KEEP OUT."

Twenty-five feet later Mike could drive no farther as the trail descended steeply and only a heavy vehicle with four-wheel drive or tracks would be able to proceed. Before he turned out his headlights, he saw the light he had seen was coming from the dome light of an ancient car, a Cadillac the size of a battleship, parked precariously on the edge of the highwall.

He pulled his car into a small clearing.

He looked at his phone.

No service.

Then he got out and sank into twelve inches of fresh snow. It found its way to his legs, so cold it burned his skin. He trudged along until he was in the car tracks then followed them to the top of the upper lift of the highwall. He was two hundred feet above the floor of the mine. All was black except for the stars and the dim light in the car perched on the edge of the lift, not more than fifty feet away. He thought to use the flashlight in his phone, but decided that made him too easy a target for Rinati's henchmen.

The wind howled steadily, about thirty miles an hour, and his footsteps quickly blurred in the drifting snow. Snow and ice crystals stung his face as he labored toward the dim, pulsating light. Mike looked around, wondering if Nicky was in the car and where Rinati's men were hiding. He shivered and couldn't decide if it was due to the circumstances or the cold.

"Nicky?" he called out in a loud whisper as he approached the car. His voice was drowned out by the wind.

There was no answer. Mike wondered whether he should approach the car or if he should go back, drive away, and get help.

Get help, get help, a voice inside him repeated over and over. He ignored the voice.

"Nicky!" he called more loudly.

Mike thought he saw movement inside the car. Keeping low, he slowly approached the vehicle noticing that it was parked on the very edge of the highwall. He felt the same dread and panic he did the first time he was here with Rinati. Someone or something was moving inside. He edged out to the derelict sedan. When he got to the rear window, he looked in and saw Nicky. She was prone on the wide back seat, struggling to move.

Mike yanked open the door and in the glow from the dying dome light could see someone had put duct tape across her mouth. Her hands were taped together behind her. Her head was bloodied and all she wore was her granny nightgown, dirty and torn, her pale white skin exposed through the rips. Her head, shoulders and chest were covered with greasy black smudges. Nicky's breasts were exposed through a large rip across the top of the nightgown—they were bruised and black smudges, greasy fingerprints, insulted her skin. Her feet were bare. A tattered old woolen blanket had been thrown across her, but otherwise she had no protection from the cold.

Mike pushed his way into the creaking car, pulled Nicky to a sitting position, and slowly freed the tape from her mouth. Blood had congealed on her forehead and her hair was matted down. As soon as her mouth was free, she uttered a loud sob and words that Mike could not understand. Tears ran down her face. Holding her in his arms, he reached around her body, cold as a stone, and pulled the tape from her wrists. When her hands were free, she threw her arms around him and clung to him tightly, sobbing in great heaves.

"Oh Mike…those men…were awful…Somehow…they got into our room…I awoke long enough to see them for an instant… One had a beard…the other was skinny and so ugly. Those men in the back of the courtroom. They hit me on the head and the next thing I knew, I was in the back of their car, all taped up."

"Don't worry, honey, I'm here. You're going to be okay." He held her tightly wondering what they had done to her while she was unconscious and how the hell he would get her out of here.

"They did things to me…I came to and the one with the beard was on top of me…in me," she wailed, "and then the skinny one, he laughed as I was crying…he got on top of me too…they hurt me…It was awful…Oh, Mike," she continued to sob.

Mike gritted his teeth, the anger rising in him. He would

kill Wolfie and Skel if he had the chance. He hugged her more tightly and her tears freely dripped onto his parka.

"Honey, honey, I know." Instinctively Mike knew he could never truly understand. "We have to move, honey, get out of here, while we can. Before they come back." He stroked her hair, noticing the clotted blood on her scalp.

Suddenly, a bank of high-intensity work lights flared to life, less than one hundred feet away, bathing the wrecked car in a blaze of blue–white light. Nearly blinded, Mike threw his arms across his eyes.

65

The lights remained on for thirty seconds as Mike tried to see if anyone was standing near them. After what seemed like an eternity, a shape passed in front of the lights.

"Attorney, I hate to interrupt your little reunion, but what the hell, I guess I'm going to interrupt it."

Mike could only see that someone stood in front of the lights. The bright lights obscured any features of the person standing before them. The voice, however, was unmistakable.

Rinati.

"Ernie, Mr. Rinati, what do you want?" The window wouldn't open, so Mike opened the door an inch and shouted. "Let Nicky go, she has nothing to do with this. Let her go and we can work this out, man-to-man."

"Hey did you hear that? Attorney Jacobs wants to work this out man-to-man," he laughed. Others were laughing with him. Mike heard two other men's voices, one deep, the other more of a cackle. "We're about to work this out, Attorney. We're not gonna' work this out in that fuckin' courtroom of yours but out here, in the mine, my turf. We're gonna' work it out my way."

A dog barked and Mike could see Rinati lean over and pick up something. He assumed it was his smelly, three-legged dog.

"There you go Butch, that's a good doggie. Calm down now and I'll get you a treat, Papa's got some business." Rinati placed the dog back in the clearing. It continued barking.

"Ernie, do you really think you can get away with this? I…I called the cops. I called the state police and they're on their way."

"I know guys like you, Attorney. You're a pussy. Wolfie here told you not to call the cops and I'm willing to bet you didn't do that. If you did, then we'd see their lights coming ten minutes before they got here. When they do get here, I'll just tell them it looks like it was some kind of suicide pact. A real fucking tragedy. You and the girl threw yourselves off the highwall. We don't know how you got here, but we did everything we could to save you. That's what the boys and I will tell them. What do you think of that?"

Mike got angrier but felt the bile rising up in his throat as he realized Rinati was toying with him. He was going to have to do something, or he and Nicky were dead. Mike pushed the creaky door open, stepped out of the car, and held out his hands.

"You want me, you asshole? Come and get me."

A gunshot and a muzzle flash fractured the winter night.

Nicky screamed and pressed herself into the car seat, her arms hugging her legs. The bullet missed them and embedded itself in the front door of the car. Mike ducked and hid behind the open door. The sound of the shot echoed around the mine for several seconds. Rocks slid loose from somewhere, clicking on the highwall, until they found the muck pile below.

Mike hoped again they weren't too close to the edge.

"Skel, you dumb fuck! Put that piece away! Someone's gonna find the bodies and we don't want any lead in them. Christ, don't be an idiot," Rinati screamed.

"Sorry boss, I got carried away." Skel's voice came from behind the lights.

The dog barked furiously as the sound of the gunshot reverberated across the mine. Mike could see better now. The dog hopped in a circle in front of Rinati. Mike gathered up his courage and stepped out from behind the door.

"Looks like we have us a Mexican standoff, Ernie. You don't want to shoot us and the only way you're going to get us is to come out here to the edge of the highwall and take us. I guarantee you, you and your men are going over the highwall." Mike crouched in a wrestler's stance.

"Attorney, Attorney, Attorney, you watch too many movies," Rinati said laughing. "First of all, it's three against one, three against two if you count the girl. We'll kick the shit out of you if we have to and trust me, I'd love to do that. But we're not going to have to do that. You see those wires? They're a little buried in the snow, but you can see them in the light."

For the first time Mike noticed a pair of wires that stretched from behind the work lights to under the car.

"In a few minutes, were gonna make this highwall go boom and you and dolly over there are gonna be a couple of hundred feet south at the bottom of the pit."

Mike stood with the snow up to his calves and the wind whistling through him, looking at the wires. His mind raced, but he just knew Rinati was toying with him. Without hesitating, he picked up the wires and held them in his hands.

"Go ahead, Attorney, pull them. They're set so the charge will detonate, the car will blow first and then the whole lift," laughed Rinati.

Mike noticed Rinati didn't move from his position in front of the lights and he didn't pick up his dog either, perhaps fifty feet from Mike and Nicky.

"Don't do it Mike," shouted Nicky.

Butch barked furiously.

Mike looked at Nicky and then at Rinati who still hadn't moved. He took a deep breath, shut his eyes and pulled the wires as hard as he could.

66

The wires came out from under the car in one easy tug. Mike waited for seconds, but nothing happened. From behind the lights Mike could hear peals of laughter.

"You got a pair of stones, Attorney, I give you that. I was just fucking with you."

"You're full of shit, Rinati."

"I wouldn't say that. The whole lift was drilled four days ago. We have to take it down according to our DEP-approved reclamation plan. It was loaded with waterproof ANFO and wired up just before the storm. It's all set to go. All Wolfie has to do is finish wiring the blasting machine and push the plunger."

Butch barked furiously at Mike. The dog charged toward him, then turned around and hopped back to Rinati, wagging his stub of a tail.

Mike tried to formulate a plan—anything—that might make Rinati back off.

Nothing.

He felt like there was nothing he could do to make Rinati reconsider whatever torment he had in store for them.

There was one thing he was sure of, though: Nicky had to survive.

Whatever the cost.

"Mr. Rinati, wait. I have information. You're going to want to hear this."

"What?"

"Trust me, you want this information. It's about the landowners and Ransom. Nicky, you have to let her go and I'll tell you. I don't care what you do with me then."

"No, Mike," Nicky said from inside the car.

"Yeah, I know, Ransom's not on my payroll." Rinati laughed under his breath. "Those fuckin' neighbors framed him. He should've taken the dough I offered him years ago. He's a redneck Boy Scout. So, no deal, Attorney."

Rinati looked over his shoulder and smiled. "Wolfie, wire up the blasting machine."

"You got it, boss."

Rinati's dog was going nuts. He charged closer and closer to Mike, then turned and hopped back toward his master, over and over.

A plan began to emerge in Mike's mind.

Nicky has to get out of here.
She has to live.
I don't care what happens to me.
That's all that matters.

He waited until Butch charged again and held out his hand like he had a piece of food in it. This time, Butch charged at Mike and leapt at him. Mike grabbed the dog as he sunk his teeth into his glove. He held him tightly by his neck, the dog's snapping jaws pointed away from Mike's body. He immediately backed into the car and shut the door. Nicky recoiled from the awful dog.

"Nicky, take off my shoes and socks."

"What? Why?"

"I want you to put them on. Don't argue with me, just do it, please, this is our only chance." He stuck out his feet and, Nicky untied the laces.

"Faster."

The dog snapped at Mike and he held him over the front seat. The mutt gasped as Mike clutched his collar and neck.

"Jacobs! Jacobs, you asshole, give me back my fuckin' dog." Rinati ran back and forth trying to see what was going on in the car. "I swear to Christ that if you hurt him, I'll mess you up and make you watch while I mess up the girl."

"Hurry up, get my shoes and socks on as fast as you can."

Mike cracked open the door with his free hand and suffered a blast of frozen air. "The dog goes over the highwall if you come any closer. Stay the hell back or I *will* throw him into the pit."

Nicky had on Mike's socks and boots. "I want you to come with me. I don't want to leave you back here with them." Tears streamed down her face.

"Sorry, sweetheart. I think I can do this. Hold them off while you get away. It's the only way. I want you to get in my car and drive to…Miranda's. Odd, but I think I can trust her. Then call the state police."

"No." Tears ran down her face.

"Nicky, I love you more than anything. Do this. You need to live. Have a life. I don't care what happens to me. Just listen to me. Please."

Holding the dog with one hand over the front seat, Mike said, "Help me with this," he started shaking his arm out of his parka.

"You'll freeze."

"That's the least of my worries."

She pulled the parka off his arms and slid hers into the warmth of the coat. It smelled like the bed they shared.

"When you get to my car," Mike wondered if she would get to the car, "get out of here as fast as you can. My keys are in the front pocket. Honk three times when you get out of the woods and onto the road so I know you made it, then don't slow down for anything. If any of Rinati's goons get in the car with you or chase after you, honk four times."

"I can't leave you Mike—" she was sobbing.

"You have to. Swear to me. This is the only way. Just go."

"I love you, Mike. More than you'll ever know."

"I love you too."

She threw her arms around him and kissed him tenderly on the lips, then Mike opened the door, holding Butch in front of him like a shield as he stepped into the calf-deep snow in his bare feet. The cold snow stabbed his soles like daggers. A moment later they were numb.

"Rinati, Nicky's coming out. I want you to let her go."

Mike held Butch in front of him. The dog squirmed and gasped for air, its eyes bugged out from Mike's grip.

"You bastard, you son of a bitch, let my dog go."

"I'm going to walk Butch to the edge of the highwall. I want you, Wolfie, and Skel to step in front of the lights so I can see all of you. After Nicky leaves, then I'll give your dog back to you. You have to stay with me in front of the lights until she goes or Butch gets a flying lesson. Nicky has a code that she's going to honk with the car horn after she's gone. If you have someone else out there who's going to try to carjack her, then she'll honk a different code and this dog is dead. After Nicky's safely gone, I'll give you back your mutt and you can do anything you want to me."

Mike wondered if his plan would really work. He was freezing and stiff in the icy wind.

Nicky got out of the derelict car and reluctantly walked away from it. After two steps, she turned around and ducked back into the car. She grabbed the old blanket. "Mike, I'm putting this over your shoulders, you need something to keep you warm."

"Get out of here. Don't look back," were his last words to her as she tucked the blanket around his neck and arms, like a *tallis*, a Jewish prayer shawl.

Mike gripped the squirming dog by the neck over the edge of the highwall. "Rinati, I'm not kidding. If one of your goons touches Nicky, this dog is gone. Stay the hell away from her."

"I'll kill you with my own two hands if you hurt that dog, you bastard," Rinati shrieked, running from side to side in front of the lights. "You're a dead man, Jacobs."

I know.

That's the deal.

Mike watched as Nicky struggled through the snow in his boots. He stood as close to the precipice as he dared, fighting the effects of the cold and his fear of the chasm. The icy wind howling from the pit was like the breath of Hell itself. He was so cold he was afraid he would drop the mutt before Nicky got away. It seemed like forever, but finally Mike heard the sound of the car plowing through the snow. Finally, after many long minutes, he heard the horn honk—once, twice and after a pause, a third time. He waited. No fourth honk. In the distance, he heard the car gather speed on the road until it was gone.

Frozen, Mike stood on the cliff's edge not sure what to do. He heard the sound of feet moving in the snow and in the glare of the work lights three ghostly shapes slowly approached him.

"Attorney, we had a deal. I want you to give me my dog and then…"

"And then what?" Mike surprised himself. He was sorely tempted to toss the dog over the edge but held himself back.

The men stopped walking three feet from Mike, near the old car. Mike shuddered, differently than the shivers he'd experienced from the moment he took off his shoes and stepped into the snow.

"We have a deal. The broad is gone, now give me my dog."

Rinati held out his hands. Standing next to him, Mike recognized Wolfie with his heavy beard and Skel with the hockey stick scar across his face, half grinning and half sneering.

Mike's arms were tired and numb. He figured he was only a minute or two from full-blown hypothermia.

A deal's a deal.

Nicky is safe.

Soon it will all be over.

He held out the squirming dog as Rinati slipped on the ice and started to go over the edge. Wolfie's big hand shot out and grabbed him by the collar. He saved Rinati from falling over the highwall.

Slowly, Rinati reached for his dog. For a moment, both men had their hands on Butch, Mike's were nearly frozen as he clenched Butch's collar, hair and skin. Rinati tugged on the dog and Mike thought with a small amount of effort he might be able to pull Rinati with him into the abyss.

If I wrap my arm around him and hold on, all I have to do is lean over the edge.

Gravity will do the rest.

Mike held the dog out with his frozen hand.

67

Mike let go, his hand frozen in an icy, arthritic grip from the cold and the tension of holding the dog. He stood on the edge of the highwall in his bare feet, frozen stiff, ready to die. The wind and snow whipped through him.

Rinati gingerly held his dog, "There there, Butchie. Papa is here. Papa loves you." He hugged the dog in his arms and rocked him back and forth as the dog looked up groggily, drool coating Rinati's jacket, still gasping for air. Then he stepped back from the highwall. The other men did not move.

"Grab him. Beat the shit out of him. Then throw him over the highwall," Rinati said loudly enough to be heard over the shrieking wind as he walked toward the lights cradling his dog.

Four hands reached out and took Mike roughly. He was so frozen he couldn't resist. They pulled him away from the edge of the highwall, dragging his stiff body through the snow.

When the group was about ten feet from the highwall, Rinati, holding Butch, looked at Mike and said, "Attorney, what did I tell you? You fuck with me and I'll fuck you back."

"Boss, what about the broad?"

"I'll call on my sat phone and have Freddie pick her up and bring her back," Rinati stroked Butch's neck. The words reached Mike as if in a dream, a nightmare.

He paused for a moment then looked at Wolfie and said, "What are you waiting for? Do it."

Skel wheeled around and grabbed Mike by the shoulders. Wolfie landed several hard blows with his fists to Mike's solar plexus causing him to gasp for air and double over. Wolfie then reared back and hit him with a fist to the back of his head. Mike's head snapped down then up. Skel's elbow hammered Mike squarely in his face. Then Wolfie cocked his leg to plant a knee in Mike's balls.

Above the howling wind, a voice yelled, "Stop it! Stop! Just stop it!"

The three criminals looked around as Mike crumpled into the snow. Blood streaming from Mike's head as he gasped for air.

"Don't move, let go of him."

Through the haze of the hypothermia and pain from the beating, Mike heard Nicky's voice from behind the lights.

Nicky.

A crepuscular beam of sunlight broke like a spotlight from the heavens to the ground.

A warm summer breeze.

Nicky floated before him, just out of reach.

She wore a gossamer nightgown through which he glimpsed her beautiful nude body.

She held out her hands to him, beckoning, and smiled.

Her smile.

Angelic.

Mike struggled to keep his brain from shutting down. He held out his arms to take hold of her.

Skel yanked Mike to his feet and Wolfie turned to look toward the voice.

"What the fuck?" yelled Rinati. "It's the chick. She's back. Throw Jacobs over the fucking highwall. then grab her. You boys have some more fun with her. Hurt her. Ya hear that Jacobs? Then she can join him down there."

Mike felt like his head was about to burst, "Nicky, I told you not to come back," he said groggily through the pain.

Wolfie started to move toward the lights when Nicky yelled, "I'm holding the detonator thingie. It's all wired up. All I have to do is push this little plunger. I'll do it you bastards, I swear to God I will."

Mike looked up at the men. They all stopped moving and glanced nervously at one another.

"Did you wire that fucker up?" Rinati asked Wolfie over the wind.

"Yeah boss, you told me to do it. It's set to blow. All she has to do is push down the plunger on the blasting machine."

"Damnit. Look here, girly, you won't do it," Rinati said in a friendly voice looking at Mike. "Your boyfriend is here and if we go, he goes."

Spitting blood out of his mouth, Mike yelled, "Do it, do it Nicky, blow it up! It's okay, I swear. Do it."

The men looked at Mike.

"Let him go," she yelled.

"Sorry, sweet cheeks, he's the only thing keeping us alive," Rinati said.

"Do you really trust me you bastard?" Nicky spoke harshly. "After what those two assholes did to me? After they raped me? Do you think I'm such a girl that I won't do this thing? I don't have the balls to do it? Are you really that confident you, you dumb idiot fuck? The ugly asshole with the gun. The one with the screwed-up face. Give it to Mike. Also your boots. Now."

The men looked at Rinati. He shrugged. "Do it."

Mike and Skel sat in the snow and Mike put on Skel's boots.

"The fat one's coat too," Nicky said. "Then Mike and the ugly one come here."

Mike tugged Wolfie's parka over his shoulders. Then he waved the gun groggily and pointed it at Skel who looked at Rinati. Rinati nodded and he walked in the direction of Nicky's voice. Mike staggered behind him nearly tripping on his untied shoelaces in the snow.

When they rounded the bank of lights, Mike saw Nicky. She wore his boots and parka, the tattered remains of her nightgown flapped in the wind. She stood in the snow with the blasting machine in her left hand and her right-hand over the plunger.

Mike saw Rinati and Wolfie edging off the lift, "Don't move, or the plunger will go down," he shouted.

Skel looked from Nicky to Mike, only two feet away from them, and said, "Unless you want to kill me in cold blood, with me here and the boss and Wolfie out there, I'd say we have us a situation." He half grinned, half grimaced and added, "Hey Mike, we have a little titty and pussy in common, why don't you talk some sense into that girl?"

Nicky looked at Mike and, with black eyes as cold as the wind from the pit, quietly said, "Mike. Kill him. Shoot him now. Do it."

68

"What?" Mike and Skel said simultaneously.

"You heard me," Nicky said over the howling wind. "What he did to me? Raped me. Violated me. Enjoyed it. Laughed while I cried. Kill him. If you won't do it, give me the gun and I will."

Mike looked at Skel and stood back from him pointing the gun, considering what to do next.

"Nicky, I know you don't mean that." Mike kept his eyes on Skel who watched him warily. "Let's take a few breaths and calm down."

Rinati and Wolfie had edged further away from the highwall. Mike caught the movement with his peripheral vision and ventured a quick glance their way.

Keeping his eyes on Skel, he said, "Rinati, on three I'm going to shoot you and Wolfie if you don't move back closer to the highwall. Three!"

He swiftly pointed the gun toward where the men stood, aimed at a spot, and fired two rounds. The shots hit on the ledge near the men and ricocheted into the frozen night. The sound echoed around the mine for several seconds. They hurried closer to the highwall. Mike pointed the gun back at Skel. Less than a second had elapsed.

"Skel, how about if you turn around and go back to the highwall? Nicky and I will come up with a better solution and we'll tell you and the other guys what it is."

Skel, in his bare feet, turned toward the highwall. He was shivering with spasm-like jerks. Mike felt a surprising momentary pang of empathy for the man. Skel's hands slipped down to his sides and Mike said, "Keep your hands in the air."

Skel raised his hands. In the light Mike saw they were bare, but covered with black grease. The same grease that coated Nicky's breasts and body. His anger returned.

One false move and I will kill you.

Skel's right hand disappeared again for a moment in front of him. Suddenly he turned back toward Mike. With a quick, practiced motion, he slashed at Mike with his stiletto. The blade glinted in the light. His eyes were focused on Mike's face and his knife hand moved at lightning speed.

The razor-sharp blade caught Mike. It slashed him across his chest, cutting his parka open from one side to the other. Mike looked at his chest, not sure yet if he'd been cut. The blade had missed his skin by millimeters.

Mike jumped back and yelled, "Nicky, watch out."

Nicky screamed.

She fell backwards into the snow and dropped the blasting machine. It fell plunger up in the soft powder.

Before Mike had a chance to level the gun and fire, Skel lunged again. His knife and hand narrowly missed Mike and went under his arm. Mike clamped his arm down before Skel could pull it back. Skel's feet were nearly frozen. He fell forward on top of Mike and, with his free hand, pummeled him into the snow.

And he lost his grip on the knife.

The knife plunged, blade down, into the snow under Mike.

Skel wrapped his arms around Mike battling with him. Skel slapped a hand on Mike's wrist, holding his gun arm above his head. The gun was in Mike's hand, behind his head, useless. They both searched in the snow for the knife as they rolled in the snow and fought.

Skel pounded Mike's hand onto a rock and was able to dislodge the gun from his nearly frozen hand. The gun sunk into the powder near Nicky.

Skel and Mike locked bodies as they fought in the snow and lunged for the knife and gun. Mike pushed his hand into Skel's face with all of the force he could command. Skel shrugged his way around Mike's hand and slugged Mike with his forearm across his head. Mike saw stars. Skel leaned forward, jaws snapping, trying to bite off Mike's nose as Mike pushed on his jaw.

Skel's face maintained a ghastly grin. He rolled away from Mike and plunged his hand into the snow and came up with the knife. With his free hand he grabbed Mike by the neck as Mike desperately tried to push back. Skel's grimy fingernails lacerated Mike's neck. It was like being grabbed by the devil himself. He pushed Mike's head into the snow and pulled the knife back over his head for the killing thrust.

Nicky hunted for the gun, repeatedly plunging her hand into the snow. Finally, she grabbed the gun by its grip. She pulled it out and looked up in time to see Skel pull back his arm, the blade catching the light.

She pointed the gun at Skel.

"Mike! Stay down!"

Without hesitation she fired four shots.

They hit Skel squarely in the chest.

Mike pushed on Skel as Skel struggled to hold himself up.

Skel looked at Nicky. His face registered both an ugly sneer and a hideous smile. Then he looked to his chest at the gaping holes that were spurting blood. His head spasmed from side to side and his eyes rolled back.

Slowly, he fell over.

Dead.

Directly onto the plunger.

Neither Mike nor Nicky breathed or moved as a full second went by. A moment later, all hell broke loose.

69

The rumbling began deep within the earth, inside the highwall. It was more a feeling, than a noise. The charge had been timed and set so that the columns of ANFO would detonate sequentially, one tenth of a second between each blast. The boreholes, holding the ANFO, were fifty feet deep. The licensed blaster designed the shot so the highwall would peel away from the side of the hill. Thus, the outermost line of boreholes detonated first, with the second, third and fourth lines of boreholes detonating sequentially afterwards. If all worked according to plan, the rock face would fall away and the overburden would break into small-sized rocks that were manageable by front-end loaders and track-hoes as they loaded out the overburden from the muck pile at the bottom of the lift.

Licensed blasters are, by nature, cautious and hard-working men, heavily regulated by DEP, who avoid the kinds of blasts one sees in Westerns and war movies. When a mining blast is perfectly controlled, the blast area should break off from the hillside and no rock should missile across the sky. Many factors go into the loading of the ANFO or other explosives, using special packing to avoid faults and fractures that could cause the blast to blow out in a cataclysmic explosion. It's not unknown for faulty blasts to project rocks thousands of feet from the mine site, but the only thing that *should* rise from the site is the dust from the rocks in the muck pile on the ground below.

Rhino's blasters were paid to be fast more than careful. Their blasts were conducted during times when neither the miners nor

DEP inspectors were expected to be present, such as weekends, lunch breaks, or early in the morning, to minimize the chance that anyone would be hurt from fly-rock hurtling from the blast. Rhino's blasters took more than a few shortcuts and ignored the ordinary precautions. Small bits of fly-rock began to rain onto Mike and Nicky almost immediately.

As the blast began to detonate, Mike immediately recognized what was happening and leapt onto Nicky pushing her backwards into the snow. He covered her body with his, not knowing if the blast would eject tons of fly-rock which could kill anyone in the line of fire instantaneously. They heard Rinati and Wolfie yelling and cursing. Butch barked furiously. After a second or two, the sound of the explosions drowned out the sound of the men and the dog. The noise grew louder and louder, both the explosions and the sound of the side of the rock face peeling into the mine below. The ground spasmed. This close, the sound was like standing next to railroad tracks as a freight train barreled by at ninety miles an hour in a category five hurricane. The charges kept detonating in rapid fire and the hillside kept exploding into the pit.

Mike had no way of knowing whether the charges had been properly placed or whether the ANFO was properly loaded. He expected the work lights were supposed to remain at the top of the highwall, but if the blaster made a mistake, then they, and even the area on which Mike and Nicky lay, could be swallowed up by the blast.

The first piece of fly-rock to hit Mike was the size of a pea and buzzed Mike's head hitting him in the back. A moment later, handfuls of smaller and larger stones hurled their way. He tried to cover Nicky arm for arm, leg for leg, and head for head. It was the first time he'd ever laid on top of her.

"Stay down! It's fly-rock. Even a small piece could maim you. A large piece will kill you," he yelled over the noise into her ear.

Nicky pulled her hands loose and used them to cover Mike's head. A moment later, a marble-sized stone hit her in the hand, near Mike's eye. Reflexively she pulled her hand away and they both could see in the flash of the explosions the blood that streamed from the giant pock in the back of her hand. She covered him again, and Mike pressed down on her, wishing he could push her into the earth.

The milliseconds stretched on like hours until the rock stopped flying. Stones tumbled off the wall, and continued falling into the pit for many minutes. Neither Mike nor Nicky moved.

Finally, the detonations were over. No more hurtling fly-rock. The only sound was some rocks falling off the highwall and ricocheting into the muck pile below. Mike did a quick evaluation and realized he was more or less in one piece. He was bruised in the back from some of the rock, but nothing fatal. Nicky's hand had saved his eyeball.

"Nicky, are you okay?"

She didn't move or respond.

Mike pulled his head out of the shallow snow pit and said, "Nicky. Nicky? Answer me."

Silence.

70

The light bank had been blown out by the explosion. The only illumination came from the stars, reflected off the snow, which was obscured by the dust rising from the mine.

"Nicky!"

She didn't answer.

Mike lifted his head through the snow and rocks. Nicky's eyes were closed, then they fluttered open. They looked at one another in the dim light. No words were necessary. They didn't utter a word. Then, she pulled him close and wrapped her arms tightly around him.

Nicky whispered, "Let's get the hell out of here."

Mike got up first, shaky from the hypothermia and the beating and the raking from the fly-rock. He helped Nicky to her feet and the two of them stood in the snowy wasteland, the wind whipping around them. They stepped over Skel's body which was quickly freezing in the snow. In the starlight, they could only make out his shape and the growing black pool of his blood in the snow.

As they stumbled in the snow and searched for the trail back to the car, holding each other's hands for warmth and support, Nicky stopped and squeezed Mike's hand.

"What's that?" Nicky asked.

They listened intently. The loudest noise was the continuous howling of the wind as it whipped across the mine and hilltop. Rocks were still falling into the muck pile and Mike could hear them as they bounced against the highwall and landed at the bottom of the pit. Then they heard a noise, a bark, more of a howl, but it was unmistakable.

"Butch. He's down in the pit. I don't know how he survived but he's alive. Christ, do you think Rinati or Wolfie made it too?" Mike asked.

"I hope not," Nicky said coldly. "I hope they're dead."

They continued walking, taking small steps in the dark woods and snow. They searched for the trail that would take them back to the road where Nicky had left the car. Finally, they found a tire rut and followed it through the woods. Behind them they could hear Butch barking and howling from deep within the mine.

They quickened their pace as they climbed the trail back to the township road. The wind wasn't as intense in the woods but it blew the snow from the tree branches overhead creating near whiteout conditions.

They tightly held onto each other.

"What's that?" Nicky breathed, stopping abruptly.

Mike listened. "It's just the wind blowing the trees, hon. I think I hear tree limbs rubbing together."

They took several more steps and Nicky stopped, squeezing Mike's hand hard.

A flashlight immediately in front of them beamed into their eyes and a familiar voice deep and gravely, said, "Don't move."

Wolfie.

71

"Did you miss me, sweet pea?" Although he could barely see him behind the bright flashlight, Mike heard the smile in Wolfie's voice.

The light was directly in their eyes. Nicky squeezed Mike's arm. His arm was around her and he felt her tremble.

In one hand Wolfie held a flashlight. In the other, a revolver. Pointed at them.

"Well, I missed you," he laughed hoarsely. "Give me the gun. If you don't, I'll put a bullet in your boyfriend's head." He pointed his gun at Mike.

Nicky pulled Skel's gun from inside her parka, her hand shaking, and gave it to him.

"Keys, car keys. Give them to me now. Seems as though my pickup has a few holes in it. Guess I'll have to drive your car back to town."

Nicky gave him the keys.

"Now you know the old saying, two's company, three's a dead man. It wouldn't be much of a party with Ol' Mike duck-taped to a chair and me playing naughty games with this fine piece a' ass here."

Wolfie moved to the side of Nicky to get a clear shot at Mike, holding the gun with one hand and the flashlight with the other. Nicky kept herself between the gun and Mike.

"Get out of the way bitch, or I'll shoot the both of you and be done with it." He raised his flashlight to smash Nicky across the face when they heard the close-by and unmistakable sound of a rifle pumping. A high-intensity light flashed onto Wolfie who shielded his eyes with his flashlight hand.

"Give the guns to Mike, now." It was Ben.

Wolfie smiled and pointed his gun at Ben. Then he laughed. "Well, if it isn't the rope-sucker himself. Do you want to come here and take it from me, or would you like me to give it to you?"

Without any further warning, two powerful blasts exploded from the rifle in quick succession and Wolfie was blown back into the woods.

Nicky wrapped her arms around Mike and she buried her face into his chest.

The sound reverberated through the woods and echoed in the nearby mine pit. Finally, Ben said, "Well there, partner, I couldn't exactly leave you out here alone with the mob, could I?" There was a smile in his voice.

Wolfie had been blown onto a tree stump. Blood streamed from the holes in his body. His eyes were half-open. He was motionless.

Ben reloaded, then covered Mike who felt for a pulse in Wolfie's neck. He was dead.

When that chore was done, Mike asked, "How did you find us?"

"Those work lights were a dead giveaway, you can see them in the next county. I knew there was a back-road in. I parked here near the trail, behind yours. Then I heard the blast and came looking for you."

"Did you call the cops?"

"Uh *yeah*, as soon as we hung up. Staties, they're probably still driving all around the county trying to find this place. Where's Skel?"

"Dead."

"Rinati?"

"I hope he's dead too, but we heard his dog barking at the bottom of the pit after the explosion. I don't know, but we'd better get out of here, just in case."

Ben put his arms around his friends and he held up both Mike and Nicky as the three of them trudged through the snow to Ben's car. They said nothing. Mike put one shaky foot in front of the other as he willed himself to get to the road. Far off in the distance, he heard the wail of police sirens converging on the mine.

And a dog barking.

72

Rinati slid down the highwall path, cursing and slipping in the ice and snow. His shoulder had been dislocated by a collision with a boulder and he had lost three fingers from his left hand. With his handkerchief, he managed to tie a tourniquet around his wrist to stop the bleeding. He had broken his pelvis, but ignored the pain, dragging his leg behind him as though it was a sack of stones.

Pain meant nothing to him.

About halfway down, Rinati slipped and slid fifty feet, yelling at the ice and snow. Threatening it. When he finally reached the bottom of the pit, he stopped and listened. He could hear his dog barking and dragged his bad leg behind him as he made his way to the muck pile.

When he reached the rocks that had cascaded from the highwall, he called out through his broken teeth, "Butchie, Butchie, come to Papa."

Rinati listened and heard the dog not far from him, close to the highwall. He dragged himself over the ice, snow, and frozen boulders that no front-end loader could hope to lift. Then he stopped again and listened for his dog.

Instead, he heard a strange whistling noise that he couldn't place or understand.

Like a missile in a war movie.

A rock, the size of a fist, hurtled down from the top of the highwall.

Smashed him on top of his head.

Shattered his skull.
He was dead before he hit the ground.

73

Mike arrived in Somerset early, well before the service, and drove to Miranda's house in town. The snow was gone, replaced by green grass and daffodils. He stopped in front of the familiar frame house with its San Francisco paint job, so out of place for the neighborhood, and noticed both the "For Sale" sign planted in the yard, next to the law office sign, and the small "SOLD" placard the agent had slid into place.

Mike sat in his car wondering if Miranda was home, then saw the front door open. Miranda wore tight jeans and a low-cut blue sweater, as she came out of the house, carrying a box. He walked to her and took the box from her hands.

"Michael, what a surprise," she said smiling. Her blues eyes sparkled as she leaned over and kissed his cheek. "Just put that on the curb."

Mike raised his eyebrows.

"It's just some old clothes and knick-knacks." She laughed. "No sex toys for the neighborhood children to get into, I promise."

"So what's going on?"

"You haven't heard? I got the general counsel job for a national trucking company headquartered in L.A. Today's my last day in this dumpy little town." She smiled broadly and caressed his chest. "You look nice, Michael."

He wore his blue suit, a white shirt, and red-and-blue striped tie. He had lost weight since the night of the incident and his clothes were a little large on his frame.

"Not exactly L.A. style, I suppose," Mike said. "I have a funeral up north later today. You were very mysterious on the phone when you called and asked me to visit. Something about a little gift?"

"Well, come inside. The movers are coming tomorrow. You can have a drink—water—if you like." She laughed. "Also, I have that surprise for you."

Mike had wondered about what she had in store for him since he received the call from her earlier in the week. She'd been vague, but said he'd appreciate her gift. He followed her inside.

She gave him a glass of water, then went into her office. He watched her as she walked away, noticing once again her shapely hips and how they swayed. He didn't try to block the memories.

"Here you go," she said a minute later. She handed him two flash drives. "Those are my only copies. I swear. You and me that night in January."

Mike was surprised, but gratefully took them from her and slid them into his pants pocket. "Uh, thanks."

"You know, Michael, I've watched us maybe a dozen times. I have a few other memories in my collection." She laughed. "Okay, more than a few. But this is one of my favorites. Honestly, you weren't nearly the most talented man I've had, but there was something special about you. You seemed so...sincere or something. You're such a nice guy. I *enjoyed* making you feel good. I watched this over and over when I needed to feel like the sex means something."

"Thanks, I think."

"Anyway, those flash drives are all I have of you. You can throw them in the incinerator if you want, but I suggest you watch it. We had fun."

Mike wasn't sure if 'fun' was the right word.

Miranda took his hand as they walked to the door.

Mike looked at her and said, "The neighbors, your clients, whatever happened with the criminal case against them?"

"Over. Mr. Ransom, dropped the charges and the DA decided it wasn't worth it to prosecute the citizens who were just trying to protect their homes. I wish I could say I was such a good lawyer that I made the charges go away, but it's an election year and I think that was what really convinced him."

Mike nodded.

"Do you think we would have won the case?" Mike asked. "I mean if Rinati hadn't tried to kill me and died in the mine, do you think we did a good enough job to win?"

She smiled at him. "You did fine, you're a great lawyer, you helped me immeasurably…but I did better."

Mike looked at her quizzically. She dug in her pocket and held up another flash drive. "I call this one, *The Judge*. We would have won, Michael, I'm certain of that."

He moved to kiss her goodbye on the cheek but she swiveled and kissed him full on, long and sensually, rubbing her fingers through his hair and against his ear.

"You know, Michael, Mike, I really appreciate that you didn't bring any charges against me. I mean, extortion, blackmail, or whatever. Disbarment, that kind of thing. Even in this day and age that could ruin a girl's career." She smiled at him.

Mike shrugged. "When this ended, I really wanted it over. I didn't agree with what you did, but in your own weird way, I think you had a good motive."

Miranda made a face at him.

"Okay, a twisted motive. Whatever."

She smiled at him again, a bit devilish. "I've never felt this way before. I feel like I owe you or something. You know, I have an hour or so to kill. We could…"

She rubbed her hand on his cheek, letting it come to rest on his chest.

"Sorry, Miranda, that's unbelievably tempting, but I'm going to be late. Thanks for the flash drives."

He left her leaning against the doorway. She watched him get into his car.

About an hour later, Mike parked along the road near the small country church. The parking lot was full and cars were parked up and down along the road, a mixture of pickups, SUVs and sedans. He got out and breathed in the fragrant spring air of the backwoods of Cambria County. Unlike Harrisburg, where the trees and flowers had been in bloom for weeks, spring had just arrived on the front ridge of the Allegheny Mountains. The redbud trees were just beginning to bloom. If you looked for it, you could find snow in the hollows.

The church was in a beautiful setting, surrounded by tall hemlock trees, its white steeple reaching just a few feet above the spires of the blue-green trees. He looked to the graveyard next to the church and saw the open grave.

Mike somberly greeted a number of other DEP employees he recognized. He got in line behind John Hicks who held out his hand. Mike awkwardly hugged him the way most men do, slapping each other excessively on the back.

"He was a good man. Too soon, too young," Hicks said.

"Why this church? I mean it's really remote."

"You didn't know? He grew up just over that hill," Hicks said. They looked at each other for a long moment and nodded.

A Volkswagen pulled in at the end of the line of cars. Mike craned his neck and saw a familiar woman get out of the passenger seat.

Angela St. Germain.

She'd lost weight and her dress fit her fine as she smoothed it out. Then the driver got out.

Nicky.

"John, there's someone I have to see. I'll be right back."

Mike hurried to the women and briefly hugged Angela, kissed her on the cheek and noticed her hair had been cut and styled. She wore a slight amount of makeup and a hint of perfume, more than she had before. They held hands and exchanged pleasantries for a moment.

"How's the new job?" he asked.

"Well, you were right, I'm so glad we talked about this. The best thing I ever did was leave Pell, Desrosiers and get out from under that bastard, Feldman."

"The new place? The law clinic for…"

"The *Center* for Justice and LGBTQ Equality," Angela said, smiling. She seemed to smile a lot more now. "Honestly, for the first time as a lawyer, I'm happy. I'm so busy with work, the discrimination is awful. I have one or two new cases every day, but I love what I'm doing. The work is really rewarding."

Angela looked from Mike to Nicky then said, "I'll go get us seats." She leaned over and kissed Nicky on the cheek and briefly squeezed her hand.

Nicky wore a spring dress and was every bit as beautiful as the day Mike met her and the day she moved out of his apartment. They wrapped their arms around each other and hugged for many seconds. Mike felt a familiar stirring in his body.

"Are you still enjoying Philly?" Mike asked.

"Great, just fantastic." Nicky smiled her widest smile, holding both of his hands.

He noticed the bruises were gone and all he saw were a few light scars on her hands.

"And Angela?"

"Oh Mike, we're so in love. It's just ridiculous. She's everything I always wanted in another person, and more."

Mike tried not to allow his expression to change.

"Anything new since I talked with you the other day?"

"That promotion came through Friday. I waited to tell you the good news in person," she said. "The state's been good to me."

Nicky moved closer to Mike and said, "How about you, my nearest, dearest, handsomest, best friend?" She smiled warmly, reached out and hugged him again.

"Oh, pretty much the same. Still working at DEP. Roger had to forgive me, again, after Rinati tried to kill us, so I'm still trying cases for the department."

She pulled him closer until their hips touched and wrapped her arms around him, "That's not what I meant, Mikey. Any lady friends in your life?" She raised her eyebrows hopefully.

Mike paused for a long moment, "Like I've told you on the phone since you moved to Philly, just dates here and there, nothing serious."

No one remotely like you.

An organ played somber music from inside the church. Nicky glanced at her watch. "We should go in, they're going to start the service. Did you see Ben before he died?"

"I talked to him on the phone. He told me very explicitly that he didn't want me or anyone else to visit. He hated the way he looked with the brain tumor, a glioblastoma, and didn't want anyone seeing him. I didn't listen to him so I came out here and spent several days with him, his mother and sister at the hospital a couple of weeks ago. He was really doped up and sleeping most of the time, but I think he was glad for the company."

Nicky was silent for a few moments, then said, "And when did you first know he was gay?"

"Somehow or another after I knew him for a while. It never came up. I guess I just knew. I knew and really didn't care."

Nicky half smiled. "And Ben?"

"Honestly? After we worked together for a year or so, one night after work over beers at a bar in Ebensburg I said something stupid like, 'we're just friends, right?' Ben laughed at me, that 'eh-eh-eh' laugh of his and said, 'Don't worry partner, you're not my type.' I felt like an idiot. We never discussed it again."

They stopped outside the church and signed the guest list.

"Why don't you go inside and I'll join you in a bit," Mike said.

Nicky stood on her toes, hugged him tightly again, and kissed him. Her soft lips lingered on his for just a moment. "I'll always love you," she said.

Mike hugged her and noticed that her eyes had watered. She turned and went inside as the service began.

Mike stood on the landing for a minute, then walked along the path back to the road. From inside the church, he could hear a hymn, he had no idea which one. The organ and voices escaped from the church and filled the evergreen woods. It was a fitting setting in which to bury his friend.

Mike stood next to his car to leave, but after a few minutes, he returned to the church and tugged open the door. Ben's family sat in the front row. He found the seat Angela and Nicky had saved for him and sat down as the last note from the organ soared through the rafters.

THE END

Author's Note

There is an agency of the Commonwealth of Pennsylvania government called the Department of Environmental Protection, DEP (often called *PaDEP*, if you're not from Pennsylvania). I have taken great liberties and made up a *fictional* version of DEP. When James Patterson writes about the District of Columbia Police Department, Thomas Harris writes about the FBI, or Robert Crais writes about the LAPD, no one should assume that they are writing about the *real* DCPD, FBI, or LAPD. The same with my version of DEP. While I have loosely modeled my version after the real DEP, mine is a fictional version.

Acknowledgments

This book is a work of fiction. Nothing in this story really occurred and none of the people really exist, except inside my head. The characters are all my imaginary friends, with whom I have spent considerable (some might say too much) time. Some of the places, like Ebensburg, Harrisburg, Philadelphia, and Somerset, do exist, but don't bother looking for any of the businesses, houses, or mines on a map. I made them up.

Thanks to a number of people who assisted in technical matters: Jason Oyler, Esq. (for an environmental law plot twist that he didn't realize he provided to me); Ron Frye (mining and blasting), Frank Chiappetta (blasting); and Joe McNally, P.G., Richard Morrison, Esq., and Lou Vittorio, P.G. (coal mining).

Thanks also to my beta readers, critiquers, and commentators—Amy Bockis, Robyn Katzman-Bowman, Karen DiPrima, Linda Freedenberg, Chris Markley, Beth Michlovitz, Steve Picco, Irwin Richman, Eva Siegal, and Carrie Tongarm. I cannot overstate how much I appreciate their efforts.

Also, I must thank the members of Harrisburg's Midtown Writers' Group, in particular Albert and Anniken Davenport for all of their advice and assistance. My editor Jason Liller helped to smooth out the wrinkles and eliminate a few warts. Thanks also to the folks at Headline Books, Inc., my publisher, particularly Cathy Teets, for all that they have done—especially for taking a chance with me.

I must thank the *New York Times* bestselling author Steve Berry who is one of my favorite writers. He was my teacher at a master class at the International Thriller Writers conference and then spent an hour with me going over the first chapter of this book. His suggestions were sustained through the rest of the novel. They really fine-tuned the entire book.

Thanks also to my sensitivity reader, Lisa Pegram, for her insights, advocacy, suggestions, and assistance.

This has been a long process and I apologize if I left anyone out.

Again, I must thank the men and women of the real Pennsylvania Department of Environmental Protection. We don't always see eye to eye, but they work long hours in all kinds of weather protecting the environment of the Commonwealth of Pennsylvania. Often, they find themselves in the middle of a dispute, never satisfying anyone and never satisfied with the refrain that if everyone is unhappy with an outcome then "it must be right." Sometimes it isn't.

I also need to thank several mentors, some of whom are no longer with us: Roger Adelman, Esq. (1941-2015), Richard O. Brooks, Esq., Donald A. Brown, Esq., Robert P. Ging, Esq. (1949 -2015), John P. Krill, Jr., Esq., Prof. Robert Larkin, and Steven J. Picco, Esq. Each of them taught me something different as a lawyer and a person and forced me to become a better environmental lawyer which ultimately contributed to this book.

Thanks especially to daughters Dina Burcat and Shira Sarfati and son-in-law David Sarfati for all of their enthusiasm, help, and encouragement.

Finally, thanks to my wife Gail, who has made it possible in so many different ways for me to write and create. I could not write without her daily love and support.

—JRB